Aliyyah Eniath is a director at Safari Publications, a magazine
publishing house based in Trinidad and Tobago. She writes from
the perspective of East Indians whose forefathers were brought to
Trinidad from India though the British colonial indentureship
scheme in 1845.

The Yard

Aliyyah Eniath

SPEAKING
TIGER

SPEAKING TIGER PUBLISHING PVT. LTD
4381/4, Ansari Road, Daryaganj
New Delhi 110002

First published by Speaking Tiger in paperback 2016

ISBN: 978-93-86050-42-7
eISBN: 978-93-86050-16-8

10 9 8 7 6 5 4 3 2 1

Typeset in Adobe Garamond Pro by SÜRYA, New Delhi
Printed at   n Pre   ndia   td

This work is for my mother, Shahnaz—without her I would not be here. And for my husband, Ronald, who's my anchor.

Contents

Part One

1

The Stranger

Maya rested her arm on the sill of a magnificent bay window in the living room of her family's suburban home, and gazed outside. The bone-dry road ahead proved more interesting than her playmates. How could anyone have sisters as boring as hers? And three to boot! The twins, Mona and Saba, five years old, and four years her junior, played mindless games all day. She almost berated them for being only five.

Mona, the plumper of the two, sat with her knees folded, examining a half-broken doll with its long dark hair and rose-coloured sari (whose neck she'd accidentally twisted by throwing her down the stairs), while the other whiled away her time playing with her homemade dolls house, with its lights that clicked on and off.

Maya's elder sister, Zia, the responsible one, was engrossed in accounting, or some equally dreary work that she usually brought home from their father's office. Her lips were pressed in reproachful concentration, no doubt as a deterrent to the ebullient Maya.

Maya was anxious for her father's return. She wanted to grab hold of his legs and interrogate him about his day. Where had he been all afternoon? He usually came home earlier on Fridays, shortly after the Juma prayer.

Her father, for one, would pay her notice. Father Khalid, as he was called by all who knew him, on account of his legendary kindness and generosity. All she had to do in return was remove his socks and massage his smelly feet when he got home and hear about his day.

Maya was born and raised on an island-nation. Her country,

Trinidad and Tobago in the Caribbean, comprised two main islands and several islets. Her island, Trinidad, was the larger—1,841 square miles, the more populated and industrialised of the two. It was shaped like a rectangle with three projecting peninsular corners, and was crisscrossed by mountain ranges.

The Northern Range loomed over the country's capital, Port of Spain, and ran parallel to the north coast, with its vast rain forests of giant silk cotton trees interspersed with mahogany, balata, palms and flowering trees that provided cool wet shade in the year-round heat. The low-lying Central Range, where swampy plains rose to rolling hills and forested slopes, ran diagonally across the island; and the Southern Range comprised a scattered group of hills along the south coast.

The Yard, their family compound, was located off the Central Range in the village of Freeport. Her family valued the comfortable isolation their central location allowed, connected to nearby towns by a major highway, but sufficiently removed from cities and boroughs and the country's two major ports on the west coast. Sandwiched between the burgeoning towns of Chaguanas and Couva, a ten-minute drive to either of these locations was all they needed to find any necessities or luxuries. Theirs was an undulating street, Siewdass Road, where houses stood roughly two hundred metres apart, peeking out from untamed greenery. Maya occasionally saw other children playing down their street, hiding in frangipani bushes and swinging on Julie mango, sapodilla and pomerac trees. She was fascinated with their kite-flying and bike-racing games, and was tempted to chase after them when they played tag. But she was warned never to leave the compound without a parent. She didn't need friends, only family. Their family. Those you could truly rely on. Nothing was more important. Or so Maya was told.

Their estate imposed on the surrounding rural landscape, with its high fence wall—the only one in the area—with post lights. It comprised six bleach-white houses arranged in a semicircle around a spacious courtyard where family gatherings were held; an orchard on the extreme left of the houses slanted towards a steep ravine. Maya's immediate family lived in one of the houses, with each of the others owned and occupied by one of her father's four siblings and their respective spouses and children.

Her paternal grandparents, Latif and Sakina Ali, had worked hard to build The Yard. Their parents—Maya's great grandparents—East Indian Muslims from the town of Ghazipur in Uttar Pradesh, had come to Trinidad in the 1900s, brought by the British to work as indentured labourers on sugar plantations. They had worked as willing slaves on Brechin Castle Estate for five years, and when their bondage was over, were 'gifted' ten acres of Crown land. Maya's grandfather reaped the rewards of his forbears' hard labour. He was able to attend primary school and learn tailoring. Self-employed, by World War II he'd scrambled together enough money to buy a car that he reupholstered himself. Other drivers, impressed with his craftsmanship, offered to pay him to refurbish theirs. Thus, Grandfather Latif became an upholsterer; he earned enough money to make his family comfortable. Before he died, he oversaw the construction of The Yard, contented that he had secured his children's futures, and more importantly, kept the family together. More so, his children had remained devout Muslims, observing the call to prayer, reciting the Quran and fasting in the month of Ramadan. He'd kept them together in more ways than one. After his death, Grandmother Sakina moved into a cottage at the back of the courtyard, leaving the main house to their elder son, Ansar, Maya's uncle.

*

'He's here.' Maya clapped her hands in delight. Her father was speeding, his Volvo disappearing and reemerging into view. He swerved into the compound and pulled up at his parking spot to the front. 'Father Khalid is here!' Her companions took no notice.

As Father Khalid alighted from the car, Maya's face registered confusion. An unfamiliar boy, on spindly legs, was trying to keep up with her father's long strides. It was quite odd to see an unannounced stranger in The Yard. The tall man grabbed the boy's shirt collar to tow him along; he pulled him up the stairs, finally depositing him on the landing.

Maya met them at the doorway. 'Dad!' She wore a sneer. 'Who's this dirty boy?' Their visitor was caked with mud. His gaunt face and hands were brown and splotchy, swollen from mosquito bites; his dark hair clung to the sides of his face and neck like overgrown sideburns. Maya instinctively retreated; she covered her nose with a giggle. He stank like dead fish from the ravine.

'He's scared, Maya,' Father Khalid warned. He pulled the boy inside. 'Watch him, and mind your manners, until I get back!' He walked past them straight into her parents' room, leaving the terrified stranger in her company.

Maya's three sisters finally took notice. Their dour faces searched the boy's for a few seconds. The twins, assessing that he wouldn't be a good candidate to play with their Ken doll, resumed their game; Zia politely averted her gaze and returned to her accounting, glancing casually, intermittently, at the stranger.

But Maya chucked civility. Her eyes focused on his. What had this boy done to earn her father's attention? His protection? She stood taller, hands on her hips, appearing bigger than she was. She stepped towards him as her lips flattened into a disapproving line.

The unnerved youngster slunk into a shadowed corner—wide-eyed, wary, panicked. He opened his mouth but no words ensued. Instead, he shook his head pleadingly. Maya stopped in her tracks. She stifled a burst of laughter, hands over her mouth. Never before had she seen such a thing. This silly creature was afraid of her. This charred, gaunt thing. She wanted to punch him there and then, and laugh until she cried. But her father was in the other room, and he'd probably scold her and force her to make up with the funny being afterwards; she could not bear the thought.

Before she could threaten the boy with drowning him in the ravine, her father reappeared, with her mother at his side. Her parents' eyes, though firm and kind, betrayed their unease.

'We have some important news,' said Father Khalid to his two elder daughters. 'My Aunt Livy passed away this morning, and evidently this boy was with her.'

'We think she was caring for him,' said Mother Dianne.

'Aunt Livy?' said Zia. 'The old lady who lived in the board house?' Zia seldom saw her father's aunt, a recluse who lived in the bushy plains further south.

Mother Dianne nodded. 'I know you didn't really know her too well. Your father and I didn't see much of her either. Thing is…there's no one else who can take responsibility for this boy right now.'

Maya's eyes bulged. 'We have to keep him?'

'Why haven't we heard of him before?' asked Zia.

Father Khalid shrugged. 'Not sure. Livy wasn't exactly in her right mind of late. She was insanely private, and paranoid about everything and everyone in the end.'

'Great,' said Maya. 'We've inherited a crazy woman's lamebrain.'

Father Khalid shot her a warning glare. 'Be nice!'

'Don't worry, Dad.' Zia looked at the boy with her usual compassion. 'He's weary. But he'll be in great shape after I fix him up.' She smiled. 'You'll see. He's a brave boy.'

'Who needs a bath,' said Maya. Before her father could grasp her by the ear and drag her away to do homework, she quickly added, 'Does he have a name?'

'We don't know his name.' Father Khalid looked from his wife to his daughters and bowed his head. 'He seems to be in shock; he was starved and dehydrated. Hasn't said a word.'

He purposely forgot to mention the few words the boy did say at the old, broken house; and grimaced as he recalled him in the shadows, curled into a ball, covered with flies.

'I'll fill the tub,' said Zia, uncharacteristically putting her work aside. She held the boy's arm, directed him to the bathroom and shut the door behind them.

*

The boy watched as Zia rolled up the sleeves of her long white housedress and filled the bathtub with water. She added liquid soap that formed tiny bubbles. She grabbed a towel and clean clothes from the cupboards and placed them on the vanity, and after instructing him to step into the bath, left the room.

There was so much water. Enough to drown him, he thought. He turned the knobs at the head, and jumped back when a splash of liquid flew forward. He toyed with the knobs again, turning them on and off, and then jumped in, instantly comforted by the scalding heat on his skin.

He looked around, taking in the newness of his surroundings. Everything was so clean, polished, foreign. He planned to spend a few nights only. Surely this family wouldn't want him around longer than that.

The boy stepped out of the bath just as his fingertips were starting to get wrinkly. He grabbed the towel Zia left and gently patted his skin; he pulled on the clean clothes—an oversized T-shirt, which he thought probably belonged to Father Khalid, and a girl's shorts.

He sat on the rim of the tub and pulled his feet up. He felt safe in this confined space. His mind wandered to the curly-haired girl behind the door; her face scornful, amused. She looked about nine going on ten, his age.

He felt a slither of cold down his spine, and wondered if he'd ever have the courage to go back out.

2
Aunt Livy's Tale

*A*unt Livy lay frozen in bed. She could hear, see and think but her body refused to move. The vagabond boy was there again, beside her bedding on the floor. Who was he? Where did he come from? This time, a white smile was splashed across his dark face. His hair was way too long, way too slick. His face, gaunt.

He was tormenting her, saying he was going to kill all her chickens. He would chop their heads off, blood would splatter everywhere, and when he was done he'd wring her neck and pluck her head off too.

She awoke suddenly. Her bones creaked painfully against the concrete floor as she pulled her body upwards. The thin white sheets crinkled beneath her. They were layered with scraps of cloth, some piled higher than others, pressed against her most sensitive areas.

The boy had invaded her dreams five nights in a row. Now, she feared sleep. The night before, he was a rascal looking in from the window. 'Shh,' he hissed. 'It's only a matter of time!' Only, in real life, there were no windows.

Despite her maladjusted sleep and subsequent distress, she set to work the following morning, selling bundles of red hot-peppers that, against all odds, had sprouted in the clayey squatting yard. Pain shot through her joints with every movement.

Osteoarthritis, the doctor had said, warning that she'd be completely bedridden before long. She scoffed at the idea. She would not be in a position to accept pity from anyone; she'd fend for herself like she always did.

A couple, meandering along the dirt road, hand in hand, on

their way to deeper, more isolated territory, stopped to buy two fresh bundles, which she sold for one dollar each. Hours later, a man and his young son stopped by. The boy watched her in alarm, while his father made a show of creating his own bundle, picking out the best ones, only to decide that he did not need any after all. At the end of the day she was only a couple of dollars richer.

*

The sky was red when Aunt Livy returned to the shack. She slid against the wall and eased herself onto her bedding; for once, her unruly bones cooperated. She patted the floor, reaching for a banana she had stored nearby. The fruit was from her nephew, the one they called Father Khalid, who dropped by every Friday after the Juma prayer. She did not encourage his visits. In fact, she was apt at showing her displeasure.

Each time he came around, she'd work herself into a frenzy. She'd bawl at him to leave her alone. Shriek at him to take his groceries, packaged with guilt, to someone else. But recently, she'd been so starved that she was secretly grateful he'd left the food by the door anyway.

She gobbled the banana, tossing the peel aside, and lay down on her side. Her body grew weaker with the blackening sky. Soon, she was immobile. Any attempt to sit up or roll over was met with sharp, jabbing pains across her torso and down her thighs. To rise seemed more painful than to die. She closed her eyes and drifted away.

And the nightmares resumed.

The boy was sitting cross-legged on the floor of her one-room board house eating fruit. Her fruit! Thief. Rascal. Just waiting for her to die so he could rob her of everything.

Angered by her tongue-lashing, he pried open her pliable mouth with rough fingers. He was stuffing something down her throat, her windpipe bulging in protest, making her gulp and gasp for air. 'Aiee,' she cried out. 'Get out! Get out my house!'

She heard his laughter ring out in response and covered her ears. Her body's failings incensed her. *How was she to fight this devil?*

She drifted in and out of sleep for what felt like days. And whatever the reason, the boy was always there when she woke. Her lids had fluttered open that once and she saw him holding a chicken upside down, blood spewing against the dark wood. His face serene in the blackness.

Was she dreaming? Seeing things? She'd goaded him, 'Get the hell out! You killing me! You murderer. You killing me!'

She awoke with dots of sunlight peering through the boards, and breathed a sigh of relief to find herself alone. She pulled her body up. Had she frightened off her tormentor? *Just let him come again*, she thought.

But release quickly turned into paranoia. She wondered if the creature, in hiding, was the angel of death who had come to collect her soul. For surely, she would die on the hard floor.

Soon, her nephew would come looking for her, she thought. He'd know from her silence that something was wrong. It wouldn't take much effort for him to push in the door. She would wait, more comfortably, now that her phantom had disappeared.

The boy emerged through the creaky doorway into the dank room that smelled of rot, that he had made his home. A green banana in his mouth stuck out like a pipe from the corner.

He needed to get the single dirt-stained sheet that was his bedding. He often slept on the grass outside, but it had rained earlier and the ground was damp. The grimy sheet was better than nothing.

His eyes grew wild when locked into the old woman's stare; he was surprised to find her awake. He catapulted to the opposite end of the room, fearful that she'd rise and whack him with her treacherous walking stick.

He'd assumed she was crazy. She'd hold her head and bawl that he'd slaughtered her chickens and that she knew he was going to pluck her neck off too. She'd call him a thief, a dirty rascal, a jinn. Then at night she'd pray, 'Oh God, oh God, let him take me. I ready to go.'

In truth, he didn't want the old lady to die. He depended on her for food. He would starve without her. He assuaged his guilt with the knowledge that she needed him too; he had found her dying on the floor, and had forced food and liquid down her throat.

He'd killed a yard fowl some days before. He'd boiled some water in an iron pot on the little gas stove, something he saw the old woman do, skinned and dunked the poultry. When the meat cooled, he bit into a leg, and gagged. It tasted awful.

The woman sat up against the wall and ate a little that day. Luckily for him, she had lost all sense of taste, or that meal would have come pelting after him. She was probably too starved to care.

She talked to him that evening, about why little boys should not light stoves, and about fires. He was grateful for the advice. But as the air cooled, she grew wary and her body collapsed once more. 'Where you have me? This is not my home. I want to go home.'

Oftentimes he'd try to remember where he was before he came to be with the old lady. He recalled nothing. He knew no family. Only her. This woman who blessed him by day and chastised him by night.

Just then, the woman's mouth twitched, but no words ensued. Her lids fluttered, then closed slowly once more. Noting that his sheet was caught under hers, he decided to do without. *Let her sleep*, he thought. *Everything is better when she sleeps.*

The next day, the boy sat outside on the clayey soil—his back resting against a guava tree overtaken by fungi. A weather-beaten road led from their shack, to and fro. Less than one mile, southbound, was a faded street sign that read 'Chickland'. This sign marked the southern edge of his world. He'd never ventured past it, and had never walked the same distance in any other direction.

Nonetheless, he was prepared to run if he saw the man with the blue Volvo approaching, the one who brought the groceries. He had a terrifying vision of this man hanging him upside down while he tried to explain why he was stealing from a crippled old woman.

The boy drifted off to sleep, exhausted from the lack of success in planning his escape route. Truth was, there was no escape. There was nowhere to go, nothing beyond the shack. He didn't belong anywhere.

The sky was dim when he awoke and went inside. He half expected the old lady to be waiting for him with her knotty walking stick—prepared to duck should she swing it at him.

Instead, he found her limp body unnaturally stretched along the floor, her lips parted with mucus settled around the corners. He glanced at her stomach; it did not rise and swell like normal. Her pupils no longer moved rapidly beneath her lids. She was strangely silent. Instinctively, he knew to feel for a pulse. There was none.

He slunk into the shadowed corner and curled up into a ball on the floor, rocking back and forth. He was certain; he had done it. He'd killed her. Just like she'd said. He'd stolen from her and driven her mad.

The man with the blue Volvo will come, he thought. *That man will make him pay.*

*

Father Khalid parked the blue Volvo away from the shack. The sound of his car would only panic his aunt. He rapped on the small wooden door, the usual bag of groceries in his hand. The woman did not answer, or complain, or yell. No one bellowed for him to leave. Was this a new tactic of hers? To ignore him? He pushed against the door until it gave way.

Immediately a foul stench, urine mixed with some kind of decay, filled his nose. He staggered backward as a swarm of flies came at him. He jammed the door shut again, and gasped for air. Then, he held in a deep breath, shoved the door back open, and gingerly looked inside. His aunt's stiff body lay bloated and motionless, stretched along the floor, on the grimy sheet she used for a bed. She was dead.

Then, something stirred. In the corner huddled a little boy, so dark, he was camouflaged amongst the shadows. A handful of flies buzzed around him.

Father Khalid grasped the child by his arm and guided him outside. 'Who are you?'

The boy's mouth twitched, but no words ensued.

Father Khalid shook the boy gently, and repeated the question.

The youngster pulled away. He closed his eyes as a teardrop settled upon his cheek. 'I live here. I kill her.'

'What?' Father Khalid was confounded.

Later, he chalked this confession up to delirium. The doctors had confirmed his aunt died of a stroke. There'd been no foul play. He had no choice: he had to take the boy to The Yard.

3

The Council

*T*he Yard was a hustle and bustle this day, when finally the Ali family would present its newest member to the rest of the clan. Behrooz preferred to remain a stranger and would sourly retreat to the solace of his room when company arrived, much to the disappointment of those who hoped to catch a glimpse of the creature rumoured to be as dark and hushed as night.

He'd absented himself from Aunt Livy's funeral, which was held in the courtyard with only close family members and friends present. The Imam had said a few words, which came through the upper window, words that sounded strange to him, before the designated men hoisted her body away.

But the others were becoming impatient. After all, it was argued, they had a right to know the stranger who lived in such close proximity, on the same compound even, with the rest of them. Plus, this was how it always was. Everyone usually had his or her say about everything and everybody.

Father Khalid grew apprehensive about the flurry of questions he knew would come once the boy was officially part of their family. He didn't have the answers himself.

Their general practitioner had ascertained that, despite being the victim of mild starvation, dehydration and endless mosquito bites, his new charge was in reasonable shape; Father Khalid could breathe easy knowing that the boy had neither contracted a fatal or contagious illness, nor was he a discernible victim of physical abuse.

Father Khalid mulled over the situation—the boy could be a criminal or a runaway. His parents could be looking for him.

He watched the news every night, but no story of a missing child ever came up. And when he looked at the boy, he did not see a criminal. He couldn't ignore the strangest sensation that this child was brought to him for a reason. That somehow their paths were supposed to cross. He already felt ultimately and hopelessly responsible for him.

It was Zia who thought of naming him. 'How exactly do you plan to introduce him, Dad? We must call him something.'

Father Khalid was hesitant. Zia's affection for the boy made him nervous. Was he theirs in the first place? 'Perhaps his memory will return soon. Then we'd know his real name.'

'But it would be more fun to name him, mould him.' Zia affectionately squeezed the top of the boy's head, as if he were something to be shaped from clay. 'He is our brother.'

Maya rolled her eyes. 'So this is Zia's new pet?'

'How about Adam...Imran...,' Zia pressed.

'How about Behrooz?' Maya offered.

Father Khalid and Zia shot her a surprised glance.

Did she just name the kid she so despised?

Maya flashed the boy a sinister look. 'Because he's going to need all the luck he can get when we introduce him to The Yard.'

'Behrooz, "lucky",' Zia consented. It was a new Arabic word Miss Grace had taught them in Maktub class. She was surprised that Maya had even paid attention enough to remember it.

The boy moved closer to Zia. He nodded his consent to the name, and seemed scared yet curious when he looked at Maya. She had named him 'the lucky one'.

The sky shone velvety purple. Majestic trees loomed skyward, flowered in canary yellow, blood red, and jade green, beneath twinkling stars. Regal couches were situated in the courtyard's periphery, whilst a long oak table with a succession of lantern candles stretched across its length was lined on either side with chairs crisscrossed in white silk.

The three-four beat of tassa drums thumped through the air, creating energy, making the night festive. It was tradition to mark a special occasion with the sound of drums, and Father Khalid had hired the Freeport Drummers from down the street for the evening.

A cool breeze wafted the scent of curry into the upper windows where Behrooz looked on with trepidation as nightfall approached. It was preposterous that all this fuss should be made over him. His nose turned up. He hated curry. But at least there would be paratha roti.

Downstairs, name tags that read 'Maab & family', 'Lulu & family', 'Heba & family', and 'Hala & family', were being distributed along the table. The toddlers would sit with their parents, whilst the older kids would all sit together at the table's end.

Aunt Maab, the wife of Uncle Ansar, the eldest of the Ali siblings, was the first to saunter in. She seemed to float around in full garb, her black one-slip dress reaching her ankles and wrists. Her two kurta-clad boys—Riaz, the younger, and Riyad, the elder—traipsed behind her.

She scanned the table for her name, her mouth immediately flattened with disbelief that she was placed smack in the middle. Didn't they know that she preferred end seats?

Riyad sat next to his mother, chattering, while his brother ran around the courtyard flying a paper plane. Riaz collided with the table and pulled on the tablecloth to right himself; a decorative lantern tipped precariously. Ignoring his mother's pleas to take his seat, the boy leapt onto the couches on the periphery, bounced off, and scampered into the trees; his mother chased after him.

Soon after, Uncle Ansar, long-bearded with deceptively kind eyes, the hem of his pants pulled above his ankles, joined the table and looked on as his wife scuttled back and forth. He felt anxious. He pondered any plausible reason his brother would have for bringing a stranger into their family, into The Yard. Had he considered that the other children might be at risk? Who knew who this boy was?

Uncle Ansar was startled when Riaz, who'd hoisted himself atop the table, casually toppled a lantern to the floor. Uncle Ansar restored the object and lifted his son onto a chair alongside his. He patted the boy's head reassuringly. No harm was done; there would be no rebukes or corrections for bad behaviour, only fruitless pacifications.

Aunt Lulu peered out her window with her new pup, Waggles,

nestled in her arms. Below, she observed Aunt Maab enticing her younger son with sweets to stay seated. She turned Waggles into his doghouse for the night, stuck her feet into a pair of beaded sandals, and made her debut. She greeted her sister-in-law with 'salaams', and sat across from her.

Her husband, Uncle Khidr, emerged shortly afterwards with their two little girls, who sat on his right side; she was seated on the left.

In her younger days, Aunt Lulu was renowned for her beauty; but now her angular face was pale, drawn. Her healthy body was slight after two difficult childbirths, and her draped headscarf made her eyes bulge just a little more.

Dogs, she knew. They were always happy to see you, wagged their tails all the time; all they required was food and a little loving. Most times, she wasn't sure what to do with her girls. They were so complex, calm in one moment, screaming the next, and constantly demanding.

She was not a natural mother. She didn't understand the nuances of her children's expressions. So, during their baby years, she wasn't inclined to feed them, cuddle them or put them to sleep. These tasks were entrusted to her husband.

And now there was that familiar bulge in her stomach again. Another mistake.

'Protection?' Aunt Maab had berated her. 'It's not allowed; the Prophet of Islam never condoned it. God will always provide for us.'

And she, none the wiser, accepted this admonition, her husband too timid to disagree.

Behrooz made a quiet entrance, just as he'd hoped, escorted by Father Khalid. Uncle Ansar observed with some dismay the way Father Khalid's hand was protectively placed on the boy's back.

Mother Dianne had gone ahead, and greeted her sisters-in-law with kisses on their cheeks, thanking them for coming to dinner. She motioned Behrooz to Aunt Maab, who greeted him with 'salaams'; but the woman could barely spare him a glance before her younger son stamped on his toes, and she moved to snatch him up. Then, Aunt Lulu tried to hug Behrooz, but was kept off as her bulging belly got in the way.

Father Khalid ushered his new charge to the end of the table where Maya and three other boys sat; Behrooz slunk less than comfortably into his seat. Zia often checked on his table and shot warning glances at Maya.

Aunt Heba, the latecomer, noticed her three boys—Zaki, Arif and Umar—sitting with Behrooz. She sat with the adults, the lone member of her family. She'd divorced her husband some seven years ago. On their honeymoon night she'd recoiled as he casually removed his full set of teeth, dropped it into a jar, and crawled into bed.

After she'd had their last son, he became so uncontrollably guarded and jealous of her that, one day, he hit her hard against the jaw, drawing blood. And she ran semi-clothed through The Yard, shrieking for her sisters. That was the end of him. Now, she marvelled at her sons in her usual way. She'd brought them up by herself, and weren't they decent boys!

Aunt Hala, the eldest sister, and her daughter, Alia, remained indoors to look after Grandmother Sakina—the matriarch of the family—who was terribly unwell, though she never tired of talking.

The old woman sat upright as her granddaughter ran a wide-toothed comb through her oily grey strands, which fell sparsely down her back. Her brown face was webbed with creases from her sleep. Her skin slack. Fingers knotty.

Like her mother, who had been brought to Trinidad as a child to serve the sugar lords after slavery was abolished, like others of that second generation who'd known hardship from their youth, she had aged quickly.

Despite her burning stomach and aching joints, she'd mandated that each of her children and grandchildren pay her at least one visit every night. But she did not look forward to meeting Behrooz.

'My son too kind for he own good,' she'd told Aunt Hala. 'That stray would take good 'vantage of him.'

Aunt Hala stroked the woman's back. 'Hush. That boy won't be here long.'

Grandmother Sakina had left school at the age of nine to attend to the household chores and ease the burden on her parents who were bone-weary when they returned from the sugar fields.

Resigned to her daily duties, she fetched water from the wells, cooked on the step outside their one-room mud hut and washed clothes in the river.

When she married Grandfather Latif, he was already a tailor, a self-made man. They sacrificed every comfort to save and make a better life for their children. In the early years of their marriage, they slept on hard benches parallel to each other in their mud hut. Tears streaming down his face, Grandfather Latif would rub her back promising her a brighter future. And he kept his promise. By the time Father Khalid was born most of their worries were over.

This family gathered tonight was their legacy. Each successive generation would be a little more successful. Her children had done well in school, and had taken over the family businesses—her two sons Khalid and Ansar ran two separate branches of the upholstery, and her daughters were primary school teachers (with the exception of Lulu who was a hardworking housewife).

She was proud of their accomplishments. They had families of their own; and there was a comfortable and enviable solidarity amongst them. Nothing and no one would hamper that.

'People out there not worth the trouble,' she'd said. 'I fed up tell my son that. I had a neighbour back in the day who adopted a boy. Did everything for the boy since he was young, treat him like she own, and when the boy was growing up, and keeping bad company and drinking and coming home late, know what he told her?' She spoke slowly, her words peppered with Trinidadian creole, 'He raise his hand and said, "you is not my mother".'

'And the Calypsonian, the one down the road, he adopted son did kill somebody. I know he must be do all he could've for the boy. But when is some other person genes in them, you never does know!'

Uncle Ansar, galled at the pleasantries around him, decided to take matters into his own hands. He was repulsed that the boy was named and would no doubt be treated as part of their lineage. This was a danger to all involved. What if a person looking for the child later on couldn't find him? Or the boy met or married a relative and didn't know? More so, he felt the boy was hiding something and resolved to question him.

He rose and clicked his glass commanding everyone's attention. 'Now, now. We have a newcomer in our midst. It's only befitting to make him a toast.'

His family looked on, surprised. After all, he wasn't the host for the evening.

He smirked at Behrooz. 'Stand up, boy.'

Behrooz stood up warily.

'To Behrooz, shrouded in mystery. The last to see our dear aunt alive, and the newest member of our family, welcome. Tell us. How did Aunt Livy pass her last hours?'

Behrooz squirmed. 'I don't know…'

'Don't be shy.' Uncle Ansar's long beard danced under his chin. 'You can say what happened.'

'I was asleep…'

'Why were you with her exactly?' Uncle Ansar demanded. 'Our aunt lived humbly. She wouldn't accept any charity. Wouldn't see us…or anyone. Yet, you. She kept you hidden? Did someone send you there to be found?'

Another 'click click'. Father Khalid stood up. 'I will do the introductions myself.' He shot his brother a cross look. 'We don't put innocents on trial.'

Uncle Ansar smiled icily and sat. 'Surely, everyone is curious; it was a fair line of questioning.'

Father Khalid addressed the gathering, 'As you know, when our dear Aunt Livy passed away, this boy was in her care. I found him in her wooden shack when I discovered her body.

'He has no recollection of who he is or where he came from. No one is looking for him; there have been no reports about him. I'm willing to care for him as if he were my own.'

He glanced at each of his siblings in turn; his brother wore a scowl, but the women's faces did not betray their thoughts. 'I feel this is my responsibility. One that I plan to live up to.

'My eldest daughter cares for the boy and believes strongly in the decision we've made.' Zia smiled encouragingly from across the table. 'It is this love, which I have nurtured in all our children, that leads me to believe I'm making the right decision.

'Therefore it gives me great pleasure to introduce Behrooz as our adopted son; the newest member of our family.' Father Khalid walked over to the boy who smiled up at him uncertainly. 'He'll live in The Yard from this day. It will be like he's lived with us all his life.'

*

After dessert was served and tummies were filled, the real talk began. Mother Dianne found herself accosted by Aunt Maab who decided to occupy a now vacant chair next to hers.

'You haven't considered the rest of us in this decision,' said Aunt Maab. 'But your daughters! Did you consider them?'

'My family wants this,' said Mother Dianne. 'That includes the girls. Father Khalid made that quite clear.'

'I mean, really…if he's adopted there's no stopping him from *wanting* one of them. And clearly you won't be able to stop them.

'He'd never be their mahram; it's allowable to marry an adopted brother or sister. Even the sheikh in Medina confirmed it on the BBC,' Aunt Maab concluded, lips pursed in disapproval.

Mother Dianne pulled her headscarf protectively about her. She had not entertained thoughts about that particular consequence. 'Legally, in this country, that kind of thing is *not* allowed.'

'But can you legally adopt him without knowing who his parents are? There would be countless investigations, and you may lose him in the end. Are you going to declare him to the authorities? I thought that was out of the question? I mean, I'm just warning you about the possibilities.'

What about protecting the needy and the downtrodden, Mother Dianne thought. Was that *allowed*? But she sealed her lips. She knew she'd get nowhere with her sister-in-law.

'My husband says he's not to mingle with our kids,' Aunt Maab added. 'Not ever.'

*

'Recite to me, dear,' Grandmother Sakina urged, and Alia began singing a tune in Arabic. It was this Behrooz interrupted when Zia, after a fruit cocktail dessert, took him by hand to visit the old woman, banished to the back of the complex, yet still queen of it all.

The scent of Limacol, intermingled with Vicks Vaporub and coconut oil, lashed at him. He gaped at the woman's sagging face. She looked like a ghost with white hair, raggedy and doll-like.

Alia continued her recitation. And no one seemed to notice Behrooz for some minutes.

Near the bed stood a walker. Behrooz could picture the woman pressing her weight on it as she stood. There was a ball in the palm of her hands, her muscles contracting and relaxing around it. He wondered if her bones hurt like Aunt Livy's, her deceased sister.

Suddenly, the singing paused.

'Mama, this is Behrooz,' Zia announced.

Grandmother Sakina tilted her head and eyed the boy. Her protective instinct to keep her own close and dismiss anyone else threatened to take over.

'Behrooz,' she repeated. She looked almost disappointed. 'But you not born black and ugly like Maya say.' She wrinkled her nose. 'But them toes could use some extra scrubbing!'

Behrooz knotted his fingers together, suddenly aware of the dark curry stains under his nails.

'They tell me you dunno where you from. You dunno your mother, or your father. That true, boy?'

'Yes, ma'am.'

'You know anyone in Chickland, where they found you?'

'No ma'am.'

'Hmm,' Grandmother Sakina muttered. She firmly believed you could only judge someone by their family's background. 'You have any schooling? Know any Arabic or mathematics?'

Behrooz shook his head.

'Come here, boy. Come dab some Limacol on my forehead.'

Behrooz approached the old woman's bedside, took a piece of cloth from the nightstand, and gingerly patted her face.

She spoke earnestly. 'You must remember how lucky you are today. My younger son was kind to you…he went against my wishes. You must remember that he take you as his son. And you must treat him like your father. Promise me you won't trouble him, won't go 'gainst him.'

He nodded.

'Well, boy?'

'Yes, ma'am.'

'Good, good. Kiss me.'

He planted a kiss on her cheek, as did Zia. The scent of Limacol lingered on his shirt as they both exited. Alia remained inside to prepare her grandmother's sponge bath.

Behrooz returned to his table in the courtyard where Maya was still seated. The adults had scattered; Aunt Maab was in the kitchen, still chatting with Mother Dianne, and Uncle Ansar had taken temporary control of the children.

Behrooz recalled Uncle Ansar's speech with sadness. That man certainly did not want him in The Yard. And could he blame him?

Maya interrupted his gloomy thoughts. 'Did she make you kiss her?'

'Maybe.'

'Kiss me. Kiss me,' she provoked. 'I can smell her on you.'

Behrooz grew noticeably agitated. 'So what if I kissed her?'

'So you smell like old people.'

'That's okay with me.'

Maya laughed scornfully. 'Really? If you like to smell bad, maybe you should sleep in the ravine!'

Behrooz put on his bravest face. 'You are glad I'm here.'

'I am?'

'I must've come just in time to be your only friend.' His stomach was sinking but he continued. 'Who'd want to play with an awful girl like you?'

Maya shrugged nonchalantly. 'You won't be here long. I give you one month, tops.' She leaned in towards him. 'You know what the grown ups saying?'

Behrooz shook his head. He did not want to know, but was certain he would be told anyway.

'They're saying, "Poor Father Khalid. Why he just didn't let the boy go? That boy going to be a burden upon him." And some others are thinking, "I know that boy going to cause trouble".'

Behrooz flinched. 'I'm not going to cause trouble!'

'Anyway, Zaki, Arif and Umar—Aunt Heba's sons—are waiting for you in the orchard. They want you to carry out a prank.'

'What?'

'Do it.' Maya shook his shoulders. 'You'll prove you can be friends with us. Earn our protection.' There was laughter in her eyes. 'You won't chicken out now, would you? Scaredy-cat!'

Behrooz gaped at the girl. He saw himself as she saw him. Dirty, pitiable, laughable. He wanted more than anything to see another image there. To be something different. He smiled his consent to conquer whatever dragons fate had in store for him.

That was the only invitation Maya needed to seize his hand, pulling him into the orchard. Behrooz easily met her pace. He stepped on the hem of her long dress, and she snapped at him, 'Watch your step, idiot.'

Uncle Ansar looked up from babysitting, startled at the both of them running off together.

In the greenery, camouflaged amongst the massive trunk of a samaan tree, three boys stood, each slightly taller than the next. They were eagerly awaiting Behrooz. The shortest seemed slightly scared.

Maya proudly handed over her victim.

'If you tell anyone 'bout this,' said Arif, the taller, 'come up 'gainst any of us, we'd have Uncle Ansar drag you out of here by the hem of your pants.'

Behrooz nodded.

'This is how it's going to go down,' said Zaki, the tallest. 'You are going to break into Aunt Lulu's house…'

*

Behrooz cautiously waited until The Yard was still.

Just a harmless prank, Maya had said. Harmless…

He grabbed the laminated school ID card that was his weapon and walked briskly towards Aunt Lulu's house. He jammed the card in the crease of the door until the bolt retracted. With one easy push he was inside. None of the houses in The Yard were tight on security, as no stranger could easily get into the compound itself.

He noiselessly climbed the teak staircase across from the door and entered the sage-green bathroom on the left. The door creaked slightly behind him. Sure enough, there, on the porcelain toilet stand, stood two aluminium spray cans—one red, one yellow.

He tiptoed back into the hall and entered the playroom through the opposite door on the right of the hallway. Inside, a trolley box jammed the window on the left, illuminated by the glow of the garden light outside. He anxiously riffled around in the box, until he felt something soft at the bottom. Sure enough, he found two small dolls decked in fluffy pink dresses. The girls' favourites.

He stuffed the dolls into his pocket and exited into the upper verandah where Aunt Lulu's three-month-old pot hound, Waggles, was asleep in his makeshift puppy house.

The puppy squinted curiously as Behrooz grabbed him up and crossed back over from the playroom to the bathroom. As silently as he could, Behrooz lowered the toilet lid and warily planted the pup on it. His hands trembled as he attempted to stuff the creature's mouth with the two dolls, nice and tight. When it was obvious that only one could fit, he absent-mindedly placed the other between his own chattering teeth.

Then, he grabbed one of the spray cans and began to colour the whimpering dog, striping him neatly in red, then switching cans and applying the yellow.

Something creaked outside. He had to hurry.

He threw the cans randomly on the ground. Now for the worst part.

'You have to leave a trail of pee behind,' Zaki had shouted as Behrooz had run off from the orchard. And here he was, conceding to their wicked prank.

He unzipped his fly, and started to pee from the shut toilet lid outward. The striped dog shivered in its place.

Concurrently, a whimper made him turn. A little girl stood in the doorway, a white feather pillow clutched in her tiny arms.

And there he was, zipper down, pee on the ground, frilly doll flopping out of his mouth.

And standing at the girl's side, was Aunt Lulu.

4

The Prisoner

Aunt Lulu let out a loud wail and ran through the hallway in a flurry, shouting, 'My baby…my baby!' only to remember that she'd forgotten her daughter at the bathroom entrance. She dashed back, grabbed the now confused girl, and ran straight out into The Yard, screaming, 'He in my house! He in my house!'

Uncle Khidr, clad in blue plaid boxers, emerged into the courtyard, his face clueless, his hair floppy from sleep. Waggles ran to him, prodding at his feet. He stared blankly at the striped dog. Then Behrooz emerged from the opening, startling Uncle Khidr.

The house lights clicked on. One, then the other, then the other.

Mother Dianne came out onto their landing. She was surprised to see Behrooz in the courtyard, faces peering down at him from all directions. 'What's going on here?'

Aunt Maab, whose abode was situated to the front right of the compound, at a straight angle to hers, looked on from her upstairs verandah. The woman's neighbours behind her and to the left, Aunt Heba and her three sons, also came out onto theirs. Aunt Hala, to their left, and closest to the back of The Yard, followed.

Behrooz looked desperately at Mother Dianne.

'This boy was in my house!' yelped Aunt Lulu, her white nightgown tapered around her.

'He was in my house, stealing my child dolls, and peeing all over the place! And look, look what he did to Waggles. My poor, poor Waggles.'

Waggles still prodded at Uncle Khidr's feet, red and yellow stripes blaring, pink doll stuffed in his mouth. His owner seemed confused as to whether he should pick him up or not.

'What in the world…,' muttered Aunt Maab.

Mother Dianne's face registered shock. 'Don't be silly, how would Behrooz…where would…'

Aunt Maab shook her head. Trouble, she'd warned. This child was trouble.

'It was him! I saw him! In my bathroom!' yelled Aunt Lulu.

Aunt Heba looked on pityingly at Behrooz, whilst her two elder sons shot giggly glances at each other.

'Shh, you all would wake Mama,' Aunt Hala warned. 'Then we won't have silence until dawn.' She retreated and shut the door to her porch.

'Behrooz, get to your room, now!' Mother Dianne commanded.

Behrooz bolted for the familiar steps. Father Khalid met him halfway up. He said to their audience, 'I'm handling this.' He grabbed the boy by his collar, pulled him the rest of the way, and toppled him inside.

'You better handle it.' Aunt Lulu retreated to her house. Waggles wagged his tail and padded along after her.

*

Behrooz spent the days that followed bolted in his tiny room, his single low, oak bed pushed against the door, facing a tiny window that was jammed shut. A solitary chest of drawers, sparsely filled, stood idly to the side. He'd been pacing the floor between the bed and the window like a prisoner, four steps backward then four steps forward, only stopping to count the bricks on the wall. Barely eating, barely sleeping.

'I'm sorry,' he'd told Father Khalid and Mother Dianne. All three were seated at the kitchen table in the aftermath of the prank. His embarrassment had given way to deep regret.

'But why, Behrooz?' Father Khalid questioned, his face earnest.

Behrooz remained shamefully silent.

'To embarrass yourself? To embarrass us?' Mother Dianne accused.

'These people don't know you, Behrooz,' said Father Khalid. 'They have no reason to trust you. And for sure they'll be locking their doors now.'

Behrooz reflected on when Father Khalid had found him in the shack. The man was patient at first, but then demanded answers.

'What were you thinking?'

Behrooz's veins boiled. He was unable to answer the man's questions or meet his intense gaze.

Mother Dianne, overcome by the need to protect her family, grew more and more suspicious. 'Don't make us regret bringing you here.'

There was nothing he could say to comfort her.

After all, it was his decision to carry out the wicked prank. No one had forced him; it hardly seemed fair to involve the rest of them.

That kitchen scene replayed in his head—his humiliation in the courtyard was nothing compared to the hurt he had caused the two people who took him in.

Intermittently, a knock on the door would interrupt his thoughts, and he'd remain as quiet as ever. At night he'd sneak into the kitchen to get his dinner—Zia always left it out. Though he'd never fasted a day in his life, he thought he knew how Muslims felt when they fasted in the month of Ramadan, only able to eat after sunset.

After the strained conversation in the kitchen that night, he'd heard a loud rap on the front door. He recognised Uncle Ansar's melodious greeting voice, and heard Mother Dianne welcome their visitor, commenting on the late hour; he heard Father Khalid cough dryly, and the loud drag of a chair.

After some hurried, hushed murmurs, voices grew louder.

Keep him away from the rest of The Yard.

He's your responsibility.

We don't want him amongst our children.

A door slammed.

*

Behrooz wondered if his new family would ask him to leave, if he didn't leave on his own. One night, he waited until lights were out, and packed what little clothing he had in a plastic bag. He pulled the handle to the door that led to the verandah. It was locked. He searched under the mat, on the space-saver and the kitchen table for the key. It was hidden. He felt relieved. Surely then, they meant for him to stay.

Otherwise, where would he go? Would he end up sleeping in the ravine, like Maya said? He shuddered at the thought. He reasoned that once he stayed, locked away in his room, he could cause no harm, and no harm could come to him.

It had been one week plus two days since he'd locked himself in, when Maya decided to make her fiendish presence felt. There was no denying her. She'd just come home from school, and still wore her green pleated skirt and white blouse. She made a huge pother outside his door, banging and shouting, her curly hair in a fury about her, until he moved his bed to an adjacent wall and opened the door, for fear of the neighbours hearing more commotion on his account.

She lounged on his bed, head propped on her palm.

'Poor you,' she teased. 'Can't even play a prank without getting catch.'

'You should be saying "I'm sorry" right now,' said Behrooz.

'Oh please,' said Maya. 'If you so upset, why don't you tell Mother Dianne the truth?'

'Because that won't make me feel better.'

'I'll tell her myself, then.' Maya sprung off the bed. 'Right now.'

'No!' Behrooz grabbed her dress.

'Telling her would solve your problem, stupid.'

'I'll deny it. So will your cousins.'

She settled next to him once more. 'Why don't you want her to know?'

So you could mock me for being a sell-out? 'None of your business.'

Maya's mouth twisted into a wry smile. 'Zia is spending holidays with our cousins in Couva. And the twins…I broke all their dolls already. So that's no fun anymore. You should've heard them screech when I pulled the stuffing out of Elmo.'

'So you and me,' she continued, 'we're going to be spending plenty time together.'

Behrooz was not amused. This wicked girl would just cause him trouble, when all he wanted was to stay out of trouble. 'I will ignore you.'

Maya observed him intently. 'You're not as dumb as you look,' she said. 'You went to school. Maybe a good school.'

'No, never did.'

'I heard you read the paper the mornin' of the dinner party. You read well. Better than some adults I've heard.'

Behrooz doubted it.

Maya turned sideways on the bed, and closed her eyes against his soft pillow. She was not tired, not asleep. But her mind wandered on, creating fantasies about where Behrooz came from.

Behrooz relaxed beside her, his chin propped on his knees.

Then the spectacle of him being dropped from a mango tree popped into her head and she burst out laughing. Behrooz was startled silly. There was no keeping up with Maya.

Father Khalid was happy that Behrooz was talking again. But it did not go unnoticed that Maya had only shown real interest in the boy after his behaviour had proven as foul as her own. She'd stood outside Behrooz's door, day by day, waiting for him to come out, furious that she had to be hauled off to school whilst he did not.

He recalled his daughter's amused expression when she'd purposely left her Cavendish banana skins on the concrete steps and Zia had come tumbling down sliding on her bottom and grazing her elbows.

Maya would often provoke the twins, ripping the arms off their Barbie collectible dolls, when they paid her no notice. One afternoon, when it was clear that each of the twins' nine dolls had already lost a limb, and the placated twins were still insistent on playing 'dolly house games', Maya showed her displeasure by lobbing their goldfish from the fish bowl down the rough-edged, concrete steps to the back; she watched the orange display as the fish catapulted upon each other from step to step.

Punishing Maya did more harm than good. Father Khalid recalled the spectacle of a vandalised bale of toilet paper, rolls wadded up, white tissue covering the entire floor of the twins' room. This was Maya's response to Mother Dianne's rebuke, for snipping off chunks of the twins' hair in a ziz-zag pattern while they slept. Mother Dianne was compelled to shave off the hair to restore it—two bald girls squawking in response.

Father Khalid remembered the turtles Maya had collected at the ravine; and how she'd poked their bottoms with a ball point pen until the poor creatures retreated into their shell for the hundredth time.

He had rescued those turtles from their captor; but Maya's tears spilled surprisingly, uncontrollably even, when morning came and she discovered they were missing. Mother Dianne tried to convince her they had walked away while she slept, but she didn't believe that. There was no way they could have crawled out of their three-foot tub.

Father Khalid often thought that Mother Dianne was too much of an innocent to deal with Maya. The girl had convinced her unsuspecting mother of many things. For days she'd had her mother believe she was drinking her glass of milk, whilst each serving was really being stored under their dining table, growing mold; the glasses were eventually discovered by an unsuspecting guest.

And though Maya was much smarter than kids her age, she had no discipline at school or any patience for conventional learning. She couldn't sit still in class, and her teachers always complained. Once she'd laughed so loudly at an already embarrassed girl who'd peed herself, and whose green uniform was drenched and dripping from the back, that her teacher ousted her from class.

And Maktub classes were a worse and more pervasive nightmare. She refused to memorise any surahs. She'd say her prayers without her scarf on, and giggle as she bowed in sujdah as if she and God were sharing a private joke.

Mother Dianne would ask each day, what she'd learnt—an inquiry that was always met with a disgruntled reply. This one day, Maya claimed that she'd rather be attacked by bees than go back to Maktub.

'Why?' Mother Dianne asked.

'They teach us stupid things, Mama,' said Maya. 'I mean, why would God care if I ate with my right hand or left? He made me a left-hander. But Ms Grace forces me to do everything with my right hand. She says, God says!'

Clearly Maya did not believe her teacher.

The child was one of a kind. And now that he'd seen her colluding with Behrooz—the boy being a permanent distraction for her—he wondered how much she had to do with what happened at Aunt Lulu's.

But he never voiced his suspicions to his wife. Mother Dianne didn't seem to recognise the shady parts of their daughter as well as he, or at least, never acknowledged them fully.

5

Three-man Cricket

*B*ehrooz vigilantly stayed out of eyesight and earshot of everyone in The Yard. Recently, there had been no dinner parties, funerals, trials, scenes of humiliation or any such event, and the illusion of theirs being just another house on the street brought him strange comfort.

Zia was still spending holidays with her maternal aunt Zara, Uncle Sham, and her cousin Sara, in the district of Arima. The town was situated in the foothills of the Northern Range, about twenty miles north-east of The Yard. She'd telephoned once and Mother Dianne put her on speakerphone. She'd regaled them with tales of horseback riding in Santa Rosa, and of how she'd met a Carib descendant on a ranch. She said they planned to drive south-east to Mayaro and spend two nights at the seaside where waves toppled high, one atop the other in the distance, and you could find sand dollars on the shore. Her jubilant tone made Behrooz anxious. He secretly wished for her to return, to comfort him.

Mother Dianne decided not to send Behrooz to primary school with her nephews; she would home-school him instead. The boy had demonstrated some outlandish behaviour in the short weeks he'd been theirs and she was afraid of his tendencies, unsure about how he'd interact with other children in a formal setting. There was also another rationale—it was too late to enroll him for the current term as there were only a few weeks left.

Home schooling seemed an ambitious objective at first, but she soon realised that Behrooz posed no challenge in the learning department. He was an 'A' student like Maya except that he sat like a statue at the kitchen table for hours at a time, focused intensely, requiring little instruction or supervision, and was uncannily interested in the working of things.

Mother Dianne ruled his mathematics times-table book in bright red and blue columns, and he learned by rote—or rather revised, as he seemed to know it all already. She taught him about decimals, percentages, fractions, mass and volume. She read to him from *Old Man and the Sea*, *Tom Sawyer* and *Miguel Street*. She taught him about Columbus, the Caribs and Arawaks, and then about slavery, emancipation and indentureship.

Behrooz revelled in learning as the weeks flew by, and Mother Dianne quizzed him on everything that he read; he'd answer effortlessly, slinging the pieces of a puzzle together in no time. Knees pulled up on the blue suede sofa on afternoons, he passed time reading Charlie Brown encyclopedias and learning about planes, planets, the human body, the animal kingdom, evolution, and the solar system. Soon it came to be that he knew things Father Khalid never knew.

He did not attend Maktub classes in Calcutta Masjid—East Indians in Trinidad randomly named places after those in their home country, and the Imam of the Freeport Masjid had decided to name it after the capital of Indian state of West Bengal—with Maya and her cousins, as Aunt Lulu was having a hard time forgiving his breaking and entering. But he asked Maya what she learnt, and she told him stories of Adam, Noah, Jesus, and Muhammad.

Then, one evening, he stopped. All the effort had been drained out of him. 'What's the point of learning about planes, if I never see them up close?' he told Mother Dianne.

He longed to leave the all too familiar, all too suffocating house—the kitchen with its rigid bar stools, the blue sofa, surrounded by taupe walls. He needed a complete change of scenery but he did not know how to communicate this to Mother Dianne.

*

'I don't want to go back,' Maya told her mother. The driver had dropped her home from school and her eyes were brimming with tears. 'I want to stay home like Behrooz.'

Maya and her sisters attended Montrose Vedic School in

Chaguanas, where their mother had studied, known for fostering academic excellence. Theirs was one of many faith-based primary schools on the island. Trinidad was a land of ethnic minorities; East Indians were roughly one in three, predominantly Hindu with a spattering of Muslims. Africans were in similar numbers and the remaining population was a callaloo of Chinese, Syrians, Lebanese, Europeans and those of mixed origins. However, schools were chosen on merit. It was important to pass the Common Entrance exam at the age of eleven to gain entry into a prestigious high school.

Earlier that morning, Maya stood as usual in her school's quadrangle, before the start of the school day. The sun's rays beat down on her head; the L-shaped two-storey building with classrooms to her front and right did little to shield her. She and her schoolmates were lined up according to their classes, from first year to standard five, from left to right. They recited the national pledge and anthem. '…Side by side we stand/Islands of the blue Caribbean sea/This our native land/We pledge our lives to thee/ Here every creed and race find an equal place/ And may God bless our nation…' Then, the principal shouted, 'Hands up, out, down' and the children's hand motions followed to suit, before they were dismissed class by class.

Maya sat on her wooden classroom bench and recited the Hindu prayer, the Gayatri Mantra, as it came across on the public address system. She could say her own if she wanted but didn't care either way. Once her first class began she felt sweaty and crabby. It didn't help that she sat at the front desk, in front of the teacher's table, sandwiched between two unpleasant boys, Jankie and Amit.

Behrooz, twiddling his thumbs on the blue sofa, appraised her curiously. Why on earth would she want to stay home? 'Trust me, that's a bad idea.'

Maya sat at his feet, pulled her knees up, and allowed her green uniform skirt to spread around her. There was a red gash on her right knee. 'It's not.' She covered the cut quickly, before Mother Dianne could see.

'What's wrong this time?' said Mother Dianne.

'Nothing, Mama.'

Mother Dianne removed herself to the downstairs laundry

room, carrying a basket of whites. Maya's antics often exasperated her.

Silent tears rolled down the girl's cheek.

'Does it hurt?' Behrooz didn't know much about treating wounds.

Maya shook her head. 'Not anymore.'

'What happened?' said Behrooz.

'Booby trap,' she said.

'Booby trap?'

'It's a game where you tie knots with grass and wait for someone to trip. I never trip. But lunch time, Amit and Jankie dare me to go in the bush behind the school and I did. When I was running back my shoe got caught in the knot.'

At the back of Maya's school was a tiny gate leading to a savannah where the children played. To the right along the perimeter were cotton trees they stayed clear of, believing ghosts inhabited them. Beyond the trees was an area where the savannah grass grew higher, and therein was a circular paved spot about five feet across where the outline of a human eye was painted.

It was rumoured that black magic was practiced there, that the eye saw all who came by, and cursed them. And it was there Maya's classmates dared her to go.

Maya wasn't afraid of the dreadful eye. If it cursed her, she'd curse it back; if it chased her she'd run faster. She'd tied her shoelaces and ambled towards the bushes. She walked under the cotton trees until the grass reached her waist. She'd made it. She ran to the eye, and dared it. Then, convinced it blinked at her, Maya shot out, running helter-skelter all the way back to school. But the boys had set a trap for her; she was almost to safety when she tripped and started to cry. Everyone laughed.

'Why did you do it…listen to them?' said Behrooz.

Maya turned to him with a sardonic smile. 'I don't back out of a dare.' She quickly added, 'Plus, they threatened to tell Miss I cheat. She wouldn't believe me over them, and I didn't want everyone to think I did.'

'I forgot my vocabulary textbook today,' she explained. 'Miss Pear gave us work to do and left the class for a while. So I had to share with Jankie. Then, I just glanced at his notebook and he started shouting, "she copying, she copying". Like I would copy from a dunce-head boy like him!'

Behrooz was only slightly sorry for her. For once, Maya was the butt of the prank.

'Hate sitting between gross boys,' she groaned. 'They run like wild horses in the savannah during lunch. Then they come back and take off their socks and put up their feet…it smells awful!'

Behrooz chuckled. 'Why don't you ask to be moved?'

'I did. Miss said I'm too wicked. I'm there to be straightened out.'

'Well…behave better then.'

Maya stood and threw herself onto his lap; the couch reclined with the impact, enabling her to wrap her arms around him, and curl into his torso. Behrooz was startled; he didn't know what had gotten into her. He tried to shove her off, but she wouldn't budge. Minutes later, Maya thanked him for listening to her and casually retreated to her room. He was stupefied.

*

The next day, Maya went back to school, and Behrooz agreed to accompany Mother Dianne to Chaguanas Main Road. The company driver was deputed to manoeuvre them through the dusty, jam-packed streets lined with stores, where jaywalking was the norm. Behrooz was elated to be away from The Yard, but when he learnt the itinerary for the day he felt wretched once more.

They went to the market, grocery, various school supply shops and household stores. He pushed and loaded trollies, held bags, read the backs of boxes and packages and attempted to answer niggling questions about cooking pots and dining items, things he had no interest in. Yet, Mother Dianne insisted they were having fun. Behrooz gave her credit for trying.

He realised, much to his dismay, that Mother Dianne had a penchant for discovering cloth stores in the most obscure places; and by his third visit to one, he found the smell of fabric made him instantly sleepy. He yawned and sat on the floor whilst she chose materials for curtains, school uniforms, and housedresses.

He yearned to be free. To venture out and do things on his own. Things that didn't involve running a household.

He was relieved to get home and store their purchases. He asked Mother Dianne's permission to take a walk down their street. He'd seen a pholourie vendor on the roadside and wanted to buy a snack. But she wouldn't hear of it. 'I can't let a ten-year-old just wander about.'

'How do you know for sure I'm ten? Suppose I'm not. Suppose I'm eleven, or twelve?'

He asked if she could take him to the beach or museum. But she told him that the driver was rarely available—there were a lot of work deliveries to be made—and the family car needed servicing. Thus, she'd have to wait on Father Khalid to take the car to the mechanic.

'Can't we take it?'

'That's a man's job,' she'd insisted.

Behrooz didn't think her reply made sense.

After persistent negotiation, Mother Dianne relented, and permitted him to go out into the courtyard, at least, on his own. He could play there, take walks in the orchard and pick mangoes from the trees, or sit by the ravine. Her concern that he would cause trouble with the other boys had abated due to his good behaviour of late.

*

It was a fine evening; a sliver of sunlight peeked through overhead clouds, but The Yard was cool with gentle breezes passing through. Aunt Heba's boys had taken the opportunity to play a game of three-man cricket in the courtyard.

Behrooz observed from the verandah that Umar was both wicket keeper and fielder, while Zaki and Arif took turns bowling each other. It seemed they could use an extra player.

He strode purposefully towards them, and was greeted with some level of awe. Zaki's arm froze mid throw and Arif's mouth formed into an O at the wicket stump. Umar appeared nervous.

The boys hadn't seen Behrooz since the night of the dinner party. Perhaps they feared retribution?

Behrooz waved and smiled politely. 'Could I play?'

The boys seemed more at ease.

'You want to play with us?' said Arif.

Behrooz shrugged. 'Why not?'

'Okay.' Zaki gave a half-smile. 'We should have teams then.'

'Well,' said Arif. 'It's me and Behrooz versus you and Umar.'

'Not so fast.' Zaki looked betrayed. 'We'll flip for it. Heads, you choose, tails, I choose.'

'Okay.' Arif pulled a silver twenty-five cent coin from his trousers and passed it to his brother.

Zaki tossed the coin into the air. He caught the glistening silver with both hands, and placed it on the back of his palm. 'Heads,' he announced.

'All right!' Arif high-fived Behrooz, who positioned himself to bat.

Though there were a limited number of players, the rules remained the same. Each team would try to bowl out the other for fewer runs.

Zaki was determined to bowl Behrooz out for 'duck'. He ran up, releasing the ball, following through. The ball pelted fast and furious down the pitch; Behrooz, palms clammy from clutching the bat handle, hit defensively and ran for two.

Umar scurried after the ball, throwing perfectly back to his partner; and it came at whooping speed again. Behrooz hit for a four; the ball sauntered to the boundary.

Zaki stepped up pace, and threw with a vengeance; the ball tumbled through the pitch faster than ever, spinning, changing direction.

Behrooz, taken by surprise, missed entirely.

And the ball came again, fast as lightning, and he hit hard. It flew straight into the air towards the boundary. Umar scurried after it; he stretched and reached, ready to capture the wicket. He missed. The ball smashed into his face, and he collided with the ground. When he sat up, a trickle of blood streamed from his nose.

'Mama, Mama!' Zaki screamed. Aunt Heba emerged seconds afterwards, shooting warning glances at Behrooz, who looked on in shock as she pulled her youngest son off the field. She held the end of her white T-shirt to the boy's nose. Behrooz's mind registered red.

Unintentionally he'd become a jinx in The Yard.

He went to the orchard after all the Heba boys had gone to

rehearse his apology; still feeling unprepared, he slunk over to their house. Voices came from the doorway.

'You should've picked me for your team!' Zaki roared.

He was greeted with silence.

'Why didn't you pick me!' he insisted. 'You know Umar can't bat or bowl. So why did you choose Behrooz and put me on the losing team?'

'Relax. He ain't no Clive Lloyd,' said Arif, irritated. 'We always play together. I wanted to try something different.'

'Well,' Zaki reprimanded, 'The difference was the nose being ripped from your brother!'

Behrooz flinched. Surely, Umar's nose was going to be just fine. He hadn't set out to injure the boy. Nor did he want to cause a rift between two brothers. He walked away, refusing to apologise to his surly playmates.

And before he knew it, Maya was back from Maktub, bouncing at his side. He recapped the day's events and the gloomy ending to windball cricket; and Maya laughed as wild as the devil.

As they went towards their house, they noticed a strange car parked alongside the gate, and approached for a better view. A girl's head of long, black hair was jammed against the closed window, twisting in different directions.

It was Zia. She'd returned at last! They were both awash with relief. She knew their spirits, and never reproved them.

Then, Zia's head seemed to be twisting from side to side again, and fingers appeared at the sides of her temples. Then they noticed him for the first time. His lips pecking her neck. And they were revolted.

6

The Wedding

*F*ather Khalid sat across the kitchen table from both Zia and the stranger. His daughter had been shamelessly making out with John Doe, in the man's car, in full view of The Yard. He had received phone calls from both Aunt Maab and Aunt Lulu. Just as he'd slipped on his shoes to head outside and handle the situation, the miscreants had come sauntering up the stairs.

'Explain!' Father Khalid was chagrined that Zia's gaze was fixated upon the muscular stranger, whose chair rested indecently close to hers. John Doe wore a blue batik shirt with khaki shorts that rode up to mid-thigh; three of his shirt buttons were opened to the front, revealing a pale-skinned torso, with two strands of curly chest hairs peeking from the top.

He seemed taken aback by Father Khalid's command, as though he wasn't used to being ordered around. Nevertheless, he flashed the old man a broad grin, revealing pearly white teeth, and extended his hand. 'The name's Ron Rupert, sir.'

Father Khalid glowered and the offending hand was immediately retracted. 'You can start with how you met my daughter.'

'We met at Uncle Sham's,' said Zia. 'He and cousin Sara went to law school together for two years in Barbados.' Zia rambled on, 'Ron's in Trinidad for a short while, visiting family…so Sara thought to invite him.'

'I didn't ask you,' said Father Khalid. Every nerve in his body reverberated with conflict. Zia was much too innocent to be taken in by this impish, cocky stranger in short pants.

'Zia has said a lot about you,' said Ron, 'which is why I was skeptical about meeting the family. I was still working up the nerve. But here we are, and it's a pleasure, sir.'

Mother Dianne emerged from the kitchen with a tray of Lipton tea and carrot cake slices. Her face was unusually flushed from the bits of conversation she'd heard. She sat the tray down. But the other three were too absorbed in their conversation to pay attention. 'Please, have some tea, Ron,' Mother Dianne said.

'So, Sara hosted a sort of class reunion with Ron and some of their friends.' Zia continued her earlier story, despite her father's chagrin. 'The whole thing was too funny. Ron was the only guy there, and all the girls were checking him out; but he didn't seem to notice.'

'They weren't!' said Ron.

Zia rolled her eyes. 'They were all talking about you behind your back.'

'Anyway,' Zia said to her father, 'this girl, Susan, she dressed up...all sequins and stuff...like she was going to a nightclub. Followed him *everywhere*. And when he ignored her she sat there like a spoiled child, sulking. Seriously, you'd think a hot-blooded male would pick up on all this?'

Father Khalid was mortified. Did she just call this man a hot-blooded male?

'But I only had eyes for Zia,' Ron clarified. 'I noticed her sitting there, quietly. Only now and then I'd see her smile at one of my jokes...until she burst out laughing for no apparent reason. I had to know what made her laugh.'

'Which is probably why you didn't notice your scorned girlfriends making faces at you in the end. Who would think grown women would act *so*?'

'I was incredulous when Zia told me what was going on.' Ron placed his hand on Zia's jean-clad thigh. 'Luckily for me I came out unscathed.'

Father Khalid's brows furrowed. He was taken aback by Ron's heady British accent, unique charm and self-assuredness. He despised how forward the young man was. 'Remove your hand from my daughter's leg!'

Ron seemed confused. 'I'm sorry, sir...?'

''Scuse me,' said Mother Dianne, in an attempt to ease the friction between the two men, with something trite. 'I think we need more sugar.' She scurried back into the kitchen. Thus far, no one had touched their tea.

'Where are you from?' said Father Khalid, drumming his fingers against the table in a three-four beat.

'I was born in Trinidad, but my dad is from London. My family moved back there with me when I was just a lad. I still have a grandmother here, though.'

'Listen…uh, Ron is it?' Father Khalid moved forward in his chair, and fixed his eyes squarely on his subject. 'We do things differently here from what you're used to in London. For one, our daughters don't go traipsing around with random blokes.' His fingers resumed their drumming. 'Now, tell me, what exactly are your intentions with my daughter?'

Ron laughed heartily. 'No…God no, it's nothing like that!'

Father Khalid's eyes burned quizzically into his.

Ron grinned from ear to ear. 'I don't want to defile her, sir. I want to marry her.'

Father Khalid's fingers halted. 'What?'

Mother Dianne stood stunned at the kitchen entrance, sugar jar in hand. This was not something she'd expected to deal with so soon.

'I love him, Dad,' said Zia. 'I've already answered "yes".'

Ron's hand found her upper thigh again.

'Leave my house, Ron,' said Father Khalid.

'Sir…'

'Leave now!'

*

Mother Dianne had a wedding to plan.

There was no negotiating with Zia.

Her father had gone through the arguments: Ron was not from around here; no one knew his family; he must have an entirely different lifestyle; he was not Muslim. It was too risky. He wouldn't condone it.

Uncle Sham and cousin Sara showed up the day after Ron's visit. Uncle Sham was just as surprised that Ron and Zia were dating. He'd never picked up on anything between them during Zia's stay-over at his home.

But Sara was in on the scheming all along. And she was not at all happy about how Zia and Ron's announcement played out. 'Give him a chance, Uncle. He's a good guy. I've known him for five years! He's never paid attention to any of the other girls, and he loves Zia for her heart…because she's so warm and gentle.'

Father Khalid dismissed her. 'Don't list my daughter's good qualities. I know them all.'

He said to Uncle Sham, 'How didn't you see this happening under your own roof?'

Uncle Sham shrugged uncertainly.

Days later, Father Khalid went to the Calcutta Masjid Imam to seek counsel. Should he allow his daughter to wed this foreigner? Could he prevent her? What was the Islamic thing to do? The *right* thing to do?

'If this man is Christian,' cautioned Imam Faiz, 'how would the children grow up? With the mother practicing one religion and the father practicing another? Suppose he asks Zia to change her faith? Her way of life? What then? Without knowing how he was raised, we can't say what values he has. How do we know for sure that he would be a good husband?'

Thus, Father Khalid left with more questions than answers. When he returned home, his normally obedient daughter was geared up and waiting. 'I'm going to marry him, Dad. If you forbid me from seeing him, it won't stop us.' She warned, 'If you don't give us your blessing, we'll leave the country together and get married without you. But surely,' she continued, 'you love me more than that. You, of all people, know that him being different from us, does not make him unworthy. He's one of the best people I know. And I know you, Dad. I know you.'

'If he really loves you, he won't encourage you to run off on your family,' said Father Khalid, bringing the conversation back to more manageable terrain.

'He won't want to,' said Zia. 'I'd have to convince him.'

'And would you really convince him of that?' asked Father Khalid.

Zia looked coy. Her father had called her bluff. 'Ron has promised to learn about our religion and our way of life. He'll get married according to Muslim rites. What more can you ask?'

'I'm not asking anything of him. I'm asking it of you. Take some time to consider the whole thing. I won't ban you from seeing him, but just don't be so rash!'

'Five years from now,' said Zia, 'I'll still want this. And you won't. This is it, Dad.' She retreated to her room. Her long, black hair whipped behind her like a slap in the face. 'This situation is not going to go away.'

Father Khalid pondered his next move. As a girl, Zia would yield to any of his wishes. Nothing was too laborious or too inconvenient for her. As a young woman she worked assiduously in the family business, rarely asking for any favours or preference. He had never seen her this determined, but once.

Zia was eight when Maya was born. The nurses warned to pay attention to her, for fear she might be jealous of the newborn. But their fears proved unfounded.

Maya developed a bad case of chicken pox when she turned two. The adults were advised to keep Zia away from her, as the virus was highly contagious. But when Zia saw the red rashes on her sister's skin there was no reasoning with or preventing her.

When Mother Dianne tried to restrain her, she, wise beyond her years, refused all food and drink, till her parents relented.

Zia, once at her little sister's bedside, played with her, fed her, administered liquids and applied calamine lotion, till every inch of red on the girl's body had crusted over and healed. Days later, she contracted the disease herself. But it was all worth it for her.

Father Khalid knew his daughter would do anything he asked. He also knew that on the rare occasion when she outright refused, there was nothing he could do about it.

His daughter's mind was made up.

And his was made up for him.

*

The Yard was festive again.

Tea-lit flowers hung from tall trees. Several round tables were evenly spaced in the courtyard, with white cushion-padded chairs around them. There was so much to do. And Aunt Hala was taking care of it all.

She assigned tasks accordingly. Aunt Heba was in charge of

pulling white covers over each chair, and placing the royal blue jewelled tie-backs in place. Her three sons traipsed behind her— Zaki holding sashes on his right arm, Arif carrying tie-backs and Umar sulking behind with no task at hand.

Aunt Hala had meticulously re-washed and re-ironed each royal blue table overlay. She never trusted rentals. In fact, she'd spotted some miniscule holes in one of the tablecloths and painstakingly mended them the night before. Aunt Lulu, whose job it was to place each overlay over its respective table, now carried the pieces haphazardly in her arms, obviously not knowing the immense effort that had gone into making them so perfect.

Aunt Hala sighed. Some of the chair sashes appeared uneven, the tablecloths were getting slightly crumpled, and the overlays weren't perfectly straight. But she could not focus on that now. She had to decide the broader vision, the overall impact to be made as guests walked in.

The water fountain had just come in and she'd instructed the delivery men to place it at the entranceway. The guestbook table would be placed there as well. For centerpieces she and Mother Dianne had chosen tall royal blue candleholders in a tree design. Each had five wiry branches; each branch bore one crystal-white candle.

Aunt Heba had been watching Aunt Lulu place the table overlays and decided to intervene. The tablecloths were clearly uneven, hanging curiously longer in some places than others; overlays were angled awkwardly above them. She started from the southernmost table, moving across, then northward, pulling and tugging at the linen, until they were perfectly positioned blue squares on white.

Just when Aunt Hala became aware of the warring glances between her sisters, Aunt Maab—her usual long, black, head-to-toe garb floating about her—decided to join the helpers. Riaz, her younger son, accompanied her.

'Why is everyone doing everything?' said Aunt Maab. 'Isn't there a system here?'

Aunt Hala felt uneasy. After all, it was her responsibility to ensure that everything ran smoothly. 'Why don't you just fall in Aunt Maab? We're all just doing what we can.'

The trellis had just arrived, which was just what Aunt Hala was hoping for. She would use this on the stage, under which she would place a comfortable couch for the bride and groom.

After Uncle Khidr and Father Khalid lifted the trellis into place and shoved the white couch beneath it, Aunt Hala started wrapping rows of twinkle lights and gossamer over the top of the structure.

Aunt Heba appreciated minimalist designs, so the stage scene unfolding before her was alarming. 'There are too many lights. I think we went from perfect to overdone.'

Aunt Hala disagreed. 'Lights, lights and more lights. That's what weddings are about.'

'Zia has more simple tastes, remember?'

Aunt Hala continued draping layers of lights and fabric. 'She left the decorating to me!'

Moments later, when Aunt Hala felt satisfied with the stage, she diverted her attention to the guestbook table, and when she decided that that area was perfect as well, she glanced once more at the stage to admire her creation.

Her brows furrowed, eyes hardened, and body shook with rage. Seven strands of twinkle lights were missing! Not missing, but purposely removed.

She spotted Aunt Heba at the opposite corner smugly sharing her latest manoeuvre with Aunt Lulu who was nodding her head in agreement.

Infuriated, Aunt Hala approached Mother Dianne with a mission. 'Please tell me who's in charge here. Am I in charge? I need to know, because I have my vision, and the others are going against it.'

'Zia prefers simplicity,' said Mother Dianne, obviously on edge to have said anything at all.

Aunt Hala swirled around and stomped out of the courtyard, whilst Aunt Heba, Aunt Lulu and Aunt Maab gaped at her retreating back.

Just then, Riaz, who had crawled upon a table unnoticed, toppled a centerpiece to the ground, shattering it. Sensing anger from his aunts, he pulled the tablecloth to cover his face.

Zia, who had chosen that inopportune time to check on her

relatives and ensure preparations were running smoothly, shook her head at the broken decoration. Perfect, she thought. Just perfect.

Without uttering a word, Aunt Maab grabbed her son by the hand, and pulled him from the courtyard.

Meanwhile, Maya and Behrooz, witnessing the commotion from the bay windows above, chuckled their amusement. If Zia wanted to abandon them, they were glad that the process was going to prove infuriating.

*

The wedding was perfect.

Zia walked down the aisle arm in arm with her father, preceded by her smiling twin sisters throwing white petals from velvet baskets.

She walked tall and graceful, in a white delicately embroidered gharara with a French lace veil draped over her head and gently touching her shoulders, holding a splendid bouquet of white roses and stargazer lilies.

She'd emerged from a booth at the back of the hall, concealed with fabric, where the nikkah was done. Her father and Uncle Khidr, acting as witnesses, had entered the booth to get her consent to the marriage. She gave it thrice; they departed to ask Ron for his and returned with it.

As she neared the stage she caught Maya's eyes and smiled. Maya was seated next to Behrooz on the children's table upfront. She knew how hard her leaving would be on them. They'd been sulking since they heard the news.

But when she saw Ron at the end of the aisle, her mind cleared. He was regal in a white embroidered sherwani that Mother Dianne gifted him. He took her hand and they sat on the couch under the trellis. Zia felt this was the proudest moment of her life.

Uncle Ansar joined them on stage to officiate. He called upon the Imam who came to the podium, recited surah Al-Fatiha, and began the marriage sermon.

All else seemed a blur to Zia until…

Behrooz coughed, and Maya giggled so loudly, that the Imam lost his train of thought.

'Shh,' warned Mother Dianne.

The Imam adjusted his tie and continued. 'Marriage is half

of one's faith. And the wife is meant to be a garment onto her husband.'

Maya snorted loudly, obviously still trying to contain the giggles, and quickly covered her mouth with both hands.

The Imam's eyes darted towards the irregular chortle. 'And whoever amongst you,' he continued, 'can afford a wife, should marry...And the worst amongst you are the ageing bachelors.'

Maya burst into laughter this time. Behrooz nudged her knee under the table. He was mortified. But he found that Maya's mood was infectious. His tummy started to quiver uncontrollably and his face shaped itself into strange contortions. Unable to control himself, he too erupted in laughter.

Guests at surrounding tables turned in his direction. Some glared. 'Sorry,' he squeaked. Both he and Maya put on a straight face and looked upfront. 'Stop laughing!' she chided, as guilty as Behrooz.

'He created mates from among you, so that you can dwell in love...' The Imam's voice was several octaves higher now.

'Why does Zia have to leave The Yard?' said Behrooz.

'Because Ron lives in London,' said Maya. 'I don't know what she sees in him. He's so pasty.'

'Yeah. He's horrible.'

'This marriage thing is horrible,' said Maya.

Behrooz nodded his agreement. 'What if Zia doesn't like it there? Wants to come back?'

Maya shrugged. 'Don't know. But promise me we'll never get married.'

'No matter what,' said Behrooz.

Maya was skeptical, 'What if when you're Zia's age you meet some stupid girl?'

'Never,' said Behrooz.

'Shake on it,' said Maya.

Behrooz grasped her bony fingers in his, and shook with conviction.

After the ceremonial wedding rings were exchanged and a glass of sharbat was shared between the bride and groom to celebrate their union, Zia humorously gulping more than her half, the marriage contract was signed and dinner announced.

The crowd scattered and mingled. But Aunt Heba understood that the photo session was priority. It took enormous effort to organise. She placed Zia and Ron towards the middle of the stage, shoulders back and torsos straight. Zia smiled brightly, white teeth gleaming; her aunties had put her through countless rehearsals for this moment. Each family was requested to stand with the bride and groom—girls on the bride's side, boys on the groom's.

Aunt Heba resorted to running around trying to round up Uncle Khidr, Aunt Lulu and their kids for photos. But when she managed to get two together, two always went missing. Meanwhile, Aunt Hala and Alia took their photos and other families were vying for their spot.

Hours later, Aunt Heba was very proud of herself. Every family at the wedding was photographed. Zia would always remember every face present on her special day.

When Zia looked at the photos, days after, they all looked the same. She and Ron stood in the same spot surrounded by whichever family was being photographed at the time. All stick figures, standing the same, smiling the same. But one picture brought a smile to her face; there was her grandmother, holding on to her walker, her body jammed into Ron's side, a big smile on her face. Zia was happy to have that photo.

On her wedding night, when the time came for her to depart, she looked for Behrooz and Maya, but they were nowhere in sight. No one quite knew where they were. But, knowing her sister as well as she did, Zia sauntered over to the side of their house, towards the orchard. And sure enough, she found them huddled under the lime tree.

'What are you guys doing here?' said Zia.

'Jinns live under lime trees,' Maya said, as though waiting for one to appear.

Behrooz went along with his partner in crime. 'We're calling them out.'

Maya had told him the stories about jinns that she'd learnt in her Islamic class. Miss Grace said that jinns did exist; there was no doubt. They were created from fire, invisible to human eyes, though they could see humans. They had families and responsibilities, and lived with humans in their houses. They knew things past and present, and could be called upon by humans for favours. But there were wicked ones amongst them who interfered with human life, and in rare cases, possessed a human entirely.

'I thought you were afraid of them?' said Zia, looking from one to the other.

'No,' said Maya. 'I want to be as wicked as they are.'

'You want to be an invisible creature from an alter-world?'

'Yes. When you go away, I going to make much more trouble than usual!'

'And Behrooz, you're in on this?' said Zia.

Behrooz shrugged. The thought of communing with jinns was terrifying to him, but he didn't let on. He half expected one to sneak up behind him and touch him on the shoulder.

'Behrooz won't 'bandon me, like you,' said Maya.

Zia raised an eyebrow. Until that moment she had not contemplated the effect her parting would have on her little sister. She assumed that Maya would be happy to be rid of her, and would go on laughing and chastising everyone in her path, like she always did.

She sat next to Maya, under the tree. Her heels dug into the soil, and her white skirt got soiled from behind, but she did not care. She hugged her little sister close. The girl's tears dripped endlessly unto her sleeve.

When she finally left, later that night, it was Behrooz who held Maya, as she sobbed.

'Never,' she said. 'I'll never get married.'

Part Two

7

Six Years Later

'*O*uch!' Saba screamed as Maya tugged at her hair.
'Can't you stay still?' Maya chastised, pulling her sister closer.
She grabbed a bunch of the girl's hair to the back of her head,
stretched it tight and rolled it onto a round salon brush. She then
applied heat from the blow dryer for a few seconds and loosened
the roll. Saba's usually straight hair fell into place with a lively
bounce, curled in at the ends.

'When is it going to be my turn?' asked Mona, suspicious of
the amount of time her twin's hair demanded.

Maya rolled her eyes. 'Just have patience, won't you? I can't
work magic.'

All three sat on stools at Maya's dressing table. Mona's eyes
roamed in wonder. Maya owned things she never had, things she
wanted. The dressing table was covered with make-up brushes
for cheeks, contours, eyes and lips. And compact eyeshadows in a
myriad colours. There were hairbrushes of different shapes, sizes
and textures. Bottles of magic potions were arranged in a neat row
to the back. Mona wished she knew what secrets they held.

After all, Maya was so grown-up, polished, beautiful—with
her long black hair, full lips and olive skin. She wanted to look
just like her.

Maya worked her way around Saba's head till every strand fell
sleekly into place. 'There we are,' she said. 'Now all your friends
are going to be so jealous.' Saba studied herself in the mirror and
smiled.

'Let's try a different look with you,' said Maya, pulling Mona's stool closer to hers. She heat-straightened bunches of the girl's hair to the front and twisted them into rolls. She then applied some extra-hold hair spray, and released the rolls. Perfect curls framed both sides of Mona's face. Maya was pleased.

It was late afternoon when she was finished teaching hair styling tricks to the twins. But there was no sign of Mother Dianne or Behrooz. They were both usually home by then.

Maya had graduated from Montrose Vedic, passing the Common Entrance exam with flying colours, and was now a sixth form student at Holy Faith Convent. Mother Dianne felt Behrooz had outgrown home schooling, and he had got into Couva Government Secondary after sitting for the exams privately. Both schools were located in Couva, a few miles south of The Yard, and walking distance from each other. Their company driver picked them up in the mornings, dropped them to school, and collected them in the evenings. But that day, after school, Behrooz hadn't shown up.

Maya had spotted him walking in the opposite direction; she quickened her pace after him and tugged at his backpack to slow him down. He said that he had an extra-curricular activity and wouldn't be coming home as planned. She wondered what that activity might be.

The twins were staring at her in awe, something Maya could not quite get used to. They begged her to teach them a few make-up tricks too, and she decided to indulge them.

She worked from one to the other, twisting their hair into buns to keep strands away from their faces. Then, she applied concealer around their eyes, on the bridges of their noses and upper cheeks; dabbed blush unto their cheekbones; and was applying berry red to their lips when she heard Mother Dianne come in.

She panicked. Mother Dianne would be livid if she saw the twins with their faces painted.

She grabbed the girls by their buns and pulled them into the bathroom. They both yelped in pain. She ripped the bobby pins from Saba's hair and the girl reactively stomped on her big sister's foot.

'What are you doing?' Saba demanded.

'Do you really want Mother Dianne to see you so?' Maya hissed. 'Wash your face, now!' Maya pushed Saba's face under the tap, whilst Mona looked on in shock.

'Don't go anywhere until your face is washed!' Maya warned, and Mona dared not move.

Meanwhile, Maya sauntered into the kitchen where Mother Dianne was setting down groceries from the car.

'Can you help me bring in the groceries?' Mother Dianne said. 'The driver is trying to repair a tyre.'

Perfect, Maya thought. She ran outside and returned with a carton of milk. The twins had come out from her room, faces freshly washed, and hair neatly tied into ponytails. Maya smiled as Mother Dianne embraced the girls. At least she was not in trouble this time.

When all the groceries were stacked on the counter, and Maya was gasping for breath, she inquired, 'What's with the extra indulgences? Are we having guests or something?' She'd noticed store-bought chocolate cake and buckets of ice cream.

'We're having a special guest for dinner.' Mother Dianne eyed the girl suspiciously. 'Don't you know? Your father is even coming home in time.'

'Who's coming?' asked Maya. And how would she know when no one mentioned anything?

'Don't you know?'

Maya was irritated by the repeated question. 'Would I ask if I already knew?'

'Behrooz is bringing his girlfriend,' said Mother Dianne. 'Said he really wants this girl to meet the family.'

'His girlfriend?' Maya scoffed. Clearly, there was some misunderstanding. 'Behrooz doesn't have a girlfriend. I think I'd know if he did.'

'Well, you two have some catching up to do. Because he does. And you're meeting her tonight.' Mother Dianne's brows furrowed. You spend practically every waking moment together. Why didn't he say?'

'And you're okay with this?' asked Maya, amazed. 'When Zia brought Ron home for the first time Dad practically threw him out…'

'I'd prefer he spend time with her at home, rather than out on the streets and have everyone gossip about it.'

Maya shook her head in disbelief. Did her mother think that Behrooz cared about some girl? When would he have time to meet one? They spent all their free time together skylarking in the orchard, telling tales, and pretending to be archeologists, excavating stones and pretend bones, and making up a whole world of their own.

Maya recalled the last week's escapades. They had returned from school and were lying on the grass, as usual, by the low orchard wall ten feet across in the middle of the greenery. This idyllic spot, their hideout, was hidden and shaded by an array of orange, mango, banana and guava and cashew trees all around. They were in the habit of bringing a picnic mat and snacks; their schoolbags lay nearby but they rarely opened them. They were too distracted usually. But Maya found she liked to sketch trees and Behrooz watched as her creations came to life on paper.

On Friday afternoon a toad decided to hang out on their mat. Maya went to the house for salt. They threw it on the creature for it to flee and giggled as it burned and hopped into the ravine. Maya found guppies in the ravine that day and decided to keep them. She scooped them up in a plastic container. But Behrooz felt sorry for the fish and threw them back in. He was such a do-gooder. Luckily for her, she could always catch more. They shared all their dreams and secrets; Behrooz wanted to be a historian, and always said that having a girlfriend would equate to a nightmare.

'Plus, you and Behrooz are always getting into trouble in the orchard,' Mother Dianne continued, '…sitting there each afternoon pretending to do homework. Don't think we don't know better. Some family or the other is always complaining about you screaming and laughing too loud, and about you two playing tricks on the children. Maybe this girlfriend can help improve things. You'll have less time together to make trouble.

'She comes from an excellent family. Her aunt went to school with me in Naparima. Business people, you know? Always in the mosque and giving to charity…'

Maya's ears burned. Though reluctant to participate in

her parents' scheming, she went along mechanically with the preparations. Soon, Behrooz would be home, and all explained. Sunset approached, and when her mother disappeared for the Magrib prayer, the doorbell sounded.

She yanked the door open, and there stood Behrooz, smiling an uncharacteristically broad smile, and linked arm in arm with a strange girl. Maya gazed at the couple. The girl was slightly taller than Behrooz, lean, with short-cropped hair, and a rosy complexion. Her eyes were like little slits slanted upwards and her whole face seemed to smile.

Maya shut the door. *Who's she?*

Behrooz banged from the outside.

If he wants to play games, I'll play along, Maya thought. I'll be as dandy and polite as anyone ever was.

She recalled when she and Behrooz were both fourth form students in Junior Achievement—a special after-school programme for high school students who formed themselves into groups to learn to manage small businesses. They were in the same group with sessions being held at his school. But they'd met students from different schools; one was Dena Radday. It was evident that Dena liked Behrooz. Maya had seen the girl staring at him on a number of occasions; Behrooz opted to ignore his admirer. On Valentine's Day, Dena decided to make her feelings known with a little postcard. She'd left it on her crush's desk and looked on to monitor his reaction from afar. Behrooz opened it and was aghast by three pop-up hearts. His face burned. Maya rocked with laughter, making a spectacle of it, banging her hands on the wooden desk. 'Is that the best you could do?' Dena's face turned crimson. She'd stomped out of the classroom, and never returned to Junior Achievement again.

Maya pulled the front door open once again, just as Mother Dianne was finished with her prayer. She was certain this new girl would prove just as silly as the last. 'I've got it, Mom.'

Mother Dianne had heard the commotion while she prayed and was dismayed at her daughter's behaviour. But mindful of a guest in their presence, she kept her composure. 'Salaam,' she said. 'Come in. Please come in.'

Maya was satisfied that the smile was gone from Behrooz's face. She moved aside to let the couple in. 'Right, whatever.'

Behrooz and the girl walked towards the dining table, and before formal introductions were made, Mother Dianne embraced the girl. 'Nice to meet you, Sara.' Sara returned the greeting.

Maya rolled her eyes. 'Lovely to meet you,' she said. 'Please, forgive my terrible behaviour at the door.' She sent Behrooz a scathing look. 'Just that I wasn't expecting company.'

'Come, take a seat,' said Mother Dianne, ushering the couple to their chairs. The smell of food was divine. Mother Dianne had made her famous chicken jalfrezi, red channa, and naan. The table was all set.

Maya sat directly across from Sara.

Mother Dianne felt uneasy. She had not expected Maya's reaction to the news. Truth be told, after all these years, she still found her daughter unpredictable. She could not keep up with the girl as well as her husband could.

The twins joined them at the table. Mona was already digging into a handful of crispy naan, whilst Saba seemed occupied, looking from Behrooz to Maya then to the new girl.

'Is Father Khalid making it for dinner, Mother?' said Behrooz.

'Yes, he's already on his way from the office,' said Mother Dianne. 'He's looking forward to meeting you, Sara.'

'How did you two meet?' said Maya, with a challenge in her eyes only Behrooz understood.

'Field trip,' said Behrooz. 'Geography teacher took us to an excavation site in Mayaro last month. A pre-Columbian Saladoid village.

'And...Sara was there too with her class. We were both interested in excavating the same spot. We didn't find anything, but it was fun.' He tipped his forehead towards Sara's. 'We were all muddy afterwards.'

'So we kept in touch,' said Sara. 'Behrooz called me every day since.'

'Every day, huh?' Maya was not impressed. This mousey girl was getting the better of Behrooz, just because she wasn't allergic to mud.

Father Khalid arrived just as Maya was about to vent her uncharitable thoughts, and she smartly decided to hold her tongue, for the time being.

Mother Dianne pulled a chair for her husband, and introduced him to Sara. He nodded and seemed pleased with their new guest. 'You should feel special,' he said. 'Mother Dianne rarely cooks authentic Indian. Maybe you should come around a lot more.'

Maya suspected that both her parents were gleeful about Behrooz's new arrangement only on her account. They'd observed that she was more volatile around Behrooz and thought this girl was the answer to their problem.

The twins were busy all through dinner, looking from one face to the other amidst the chitchat, listening intently, then secretly whispering to each other. Maya had begun to give them more credit recently for how perceptive they both were for eleven-year-olds. Though her parents appeared oblivious to what was really going on, the twins knew.

Sara kept up a stream of elaborate compliments on Mother Dianne's cooking whilst Mother Dianne, warmed by the praise, continued to serve her more and more food, until the girl flat out refused to eat even one more piece of naan.

Through it all, Mother Dianne repeated to Father Khalid every boring detail that they'd learned about Sara. And took to inquiring about the aunt she knew and the rest of the girl's family.

Sara obliged them with details about her family's ambitions in the masjid and the work they were doing to help the underprivileged, and how some day she hoped to wear the hijab as a way of dedicating herself to God.

Maya's stomach churned. How could Behrooz stand it? She ate as fast as she could and was glad when the plates were cleared and conversation wrapped up.

When Mother Dianne asked her assistance in serving cake and ice cream, Maya rose to the occasion, happy to be away from the puzzling scene before her.

But to her dismay, sweet, mousey Sara offered to join her.

'Whatever,' Maya muttered, as Sara followed close behind.

'Behrooz said that you two are very close,' said Sara. 'He talks about you a lot. He told me about Aunt Livy and his first memories in the shack. How he fought to keep her and himself alive. And how he had completely given up hope when your father found him and brought him here. Says that you two have been best friends since.'

'That's right,' said Maya. 'We've been best friends since Behrooz remembers himself. And what type of person entices someone to keep a secret from their best friend?'

'A secret?' said Sara.

'Do I need to spell it out for you?' said Maya. 'Behrooz and I spend all our free time together, yet he never mentioned you.'

'That wasn't my doing,' said Sara. 'Honestly, I didn't want it that way. But he acted like he was doing something wrong by dating me…like he couldn't be with me and keep your friendship too. But that's silly, right? Why would he feel that way?'

Maya concentrated fully on slicing the cake and placing pieces in saucers. She didn't plan to keep quiet. She had plenty to say. But not with Mother Dianne and Father Khalid in the next room.

'Behrooz is really great,' said Sara, in an attempt to change the subject. Oblivious to Maya's animus, she was actually sorry that she'd offended the girl.

'We had so much fun together at the excavation,' she continued. 'Though, truth is, and don't tell him this, I hate archaeology. I'm much of a home bug. I'm even allergic to insects, swell up all over with just an ant bite. I'd much rather curl up and enjoy a good book indoors, know what I mean?'

Maya feigned surprise. 'I see.' She smiled. 'You know what? You really don't have to worry about him finding out about all that.'

'What do you mean?'

'You're not going to be around long enough for him to care.'

''Scuse me?' Sara squeaked.

'You're just passing through,' Maya continued. 'When you get to know him better…you'll see that on your own. Surprisingly, I'm not being mean. Just trying to spare you the pain of realisation.'

'No, you're not!' cried Sara. 'You're trying to spare yourself the realisation that Behrooz may be capable of having someone in his life! Someone that's not you.'

'Right. I'm not gonna fight with you,' said Maya. 'It's quite boring.'

'You don't decide anything for Behrooz,' said Sara. 'He's a free agent.'

'I don't,' said Maya. 'But there are just some things that aren't normal. Not everything fits into a neat little packet, like in your world.'

'What the hell does that mean?' said Sara. She marvelled that her legs hadn't yet propelled her out of the kitchen door.

'It means…you wouldn't understand,' said Maya.

'Try me!' Sara insisted, unnerved at Maya's audacity.

'Behrooz and I…we don't come pre-packaged. Apart, we're damaged. But together, he and I, we know every tree, rock and blade in that orchard. We remember every blackbird that nested there. We've chased the frogs and the crickets, and grabbed lizards by their tails…You should see their faces when we disrupt the daily prayer or steal the children's shoes as they congregate.'

Maya backed Sara against the grey granite countertop. The slicing knife, still in her hand, contained at her side. 'So you see, Behrooz is not of your "holier than thou" world. He's different. Half of a whole of something bigger; that, you'd never understand.

'And he and I have a pact,' Maya continued, a mere inch from the girl. 'Don't kid yourself. He's never going to settle down, or worse, have a wife or a screaming baby. He's not that sort. Just ask him.'

'You're wrong,' said Sara, regaining her composure. 'What if there's a part of Behrooz that you don't know? What if this *half of something bigger* that he supposedly is has matured into something different?'

Sara moved forward now, ignoring the knife at Maya's side. 'You see…he was afraid to be a coward in your eyes, the pitiful thing you first saw him as. But with me, he's his true self. A gentle lamb. Not something against his nature!'

With that Sara pried herself from Maya's trap and ran to safety. She resumed her seat at the table and snuggled against Behrooz.

Maya was speechless, maybe for the first time in her life.

In one instance, she recalled Behrooz's alarmed face as she'd chopped off a lizard's tail. It would grow back, she'd insisted. But Behrooz wore a morose expression as the tail danced across the lawn. *Grow up, Maya*, he'd said.

In most ways, Maya considered, Behrooz was the 'gentle lamb'. So how did she make a devil out of him?

Behrooz noticed a change in Sara that night, and he suspected that it had something to do with Maya. But Sara insisted that nothing unusual happened in the kitchen, and Maya was acting the polite hostess. Instinctively Behrooz knew better than to believe either of them.

8

Zia Returns

*M*aya was still sullen over the dinner party the night before when Mother Dianne revealed some exciting news over a breakfast of toast and tea. 'Zia's coming home the day after tomorrow,' she told her daughter, a trifle apprehensively. Maya had been so sulky of late that Mother Dianne was not certain if the news would matter to her at all.

'What!' Maya shoved her breakfast aside. 'I can't believe it!' She beamed. 'How long have you known?'

'She called this morning,' said Mother Dianne. 'But before you get all excited you should know the circumstances.'

'What's wrong?' Maya tensed. 'Is the baby okay?'

'Yes. Nothing like that,' said Mother Dianne. 'It's just the usual third trimester stuff. She's suffering from back pains, and pain in her hips and pelvis. Her doctor wants her to get as much bed rest as possible. She really needs to stay off her feet, and since Ron is at work most of the day, they thought it better for her to come home until the baby is born. At least while she's here we can look after her night and day.'

'Yes, I will take complete care of her!' said Maya.

Mother Dianne was surprised.

Things were certainly changing.

In the days that followed Maya occupied herself with preparing for Zia. She worked tirelessly at fixing up her sister's old room. She vacuumed the carpet, washed the linens, scrubbed the bathroom tiles and sent the curtains to be laundered.

She even made a list of grocery and pharmaceutical items that they needed and dispatched the driver to get them.

Zia was going to be perfectly accommodated and rested until the baby was ready to be born.

Behrooz was rarely at home. And Maya refused to stare out of the bay window hoping to see him walking home in the evenings. Of late, he stayed out until night time and by then she was too unhappy to speak with him. It wasn't like him to spend so much time away from her. And she knew that it was because of Sara.

Zia and the new baby would be the perfect distraction. One she was determined to enjoy. She waited outside the airport's arrivals terminal for her elder sister, a bouquet of orchids clutched in her hands.

Zia emerged through the double doors in perfect time, her belly bulging before her, and Maya was taken aback. Zia looked huge! She hurried towards her sister and presented her with the flowers. Zia was taken aback—this was not the Maya she remembered. They had not seen each other in over two years. She pulled her close as they walked outside.

Maya pulled Zia's luggage behind her with her free hand, and the driver helped her arrange it into the trunk of the car. Both girls chatted non-stop all the way home. Zia inquired about Mother Dianne, Father Khalid, the twins and Behrooz. And Maya was happy to fill in the blanks, but made no mention of Behrooz's new girlfriend. She didn't confess to her sister how troubled she was, and tried to convince herself that she was not troubled at all. Behrooz was perfectly free and definitely capable of having a life that didn't involve her.

From the moment they arrived home, Zia was fussed over constantly. Mother Dianne stroked her daughter's bump whenever she got the chance, feeling for any movement. Zia was put to bed, and only sat up, propped against her pillows, for meals, which came in small portions frequently throughout the day. Mother Dianne preferred if Zia did not stand up at all, except when she needed to go to the bathroom, which was very often.

The day after Zia's arrival, Maya positioned herself next to her sister's bed for the entire time. They chatted about Ron, and his law practice in London, and Maya confessed to Zia that she'd often thought about studying law. Zia was delighted. She thought that Maya would be a great lawyer. The girl certainly knew how to argue a point.

Zia was grateful that her sister was taking such good care of her. For the first time, she saw Maya as a grown up, and was pleased to see this serious and nurturing side. But what confused her was that Behrooz was hardly around. He'd been out on the day she arrived, and he came in late, when she was asleep. That morning, he'd said a quick hello, given her a hug, and left for school. Usually he was more conversational with her. There was no sign of him after school, and not even Maya knew where he was.

*

It was sunset when Behrooz finally returned home. Maya was reading Zia excerpts from *A House for Mr Biswas* and they were both laughing wildly when he came in.

Initially, Zia saw only him. He'd changed so much. He looked clean and sophisticated, wearing a white-collared shirt, sleeves pushed to his elbows. His hands were bigger, more masculine. And there was a hint of muscle under his shirt. He was smiling at her, an impish glow on his face. Then, she was startled to see a tall lean girl peeking from behind him.

Zia had no idea who the girl was. She looked quizzically at Behrooz who hurriedly motioned the stranger forward. Behrooz introduced Sara as his girlfriend, and though Zia was taken aback by the revelation, she felt that things were finally starting to make sense.

'Glad to meet you,' Sara offered. 'Behrooz talks about you all the time. Maybe the most out of everyone.'

'Really?' Zia looked sheepishly at Behrooz. 'I wish he had mentioned you.'

Sara skittishly interlocked her fingers. 'Sorry, Zia.' She bowed her head. 'Behrooz didn't want to introduce us at all. But I insisted. I wanted to meet you while you were here.' Sara smiled, 'After all, we're like sisters already, aren't we?'

'Sisters?' Maya snickered. 'Don't you think you're taking this girlfriend thing a little too far?'

Sara flushed.

She'd almost deluded herself into believing that Maya was not in the room, and that the girl simply did not exist. She remembered what Maya had said at the dinner party and a wave of anxiety swept over her.

Her mind wavered.

Why did Behrooz try so hard to keep their relationship a secret? She questioned his sincerity. Was she as disposable as Maya posited? Was there a side to Behrooz that she did not know? Would not like?

No, she cautioned herself. Behrooz was himself with her. She felt certain of that. Why else would this incorrigible girl feel so threatened?

Maya enjoyed the transparent play of emotions on her adversary's face. 'After all, girlfriends soon become ex-girlfriends. Faster than you can bat an eyelid. And don't worry, I'm still here, and not going away.'

Behrooz seemed ready to pounce. 'Maya!'

'Easy, brother,' Maya cooed. 'After all, we're all family here.'

Behrooz showed his palm as a signal to pause the conversation. He and Maya were never siblings. Their connection was much stronger, stronger than blood. She was his best friend; his only necessary companion. And though their relationship was wild and erratic, he could always turn to her, for anything. Except now.

It hurt him that she hated Sara. He'd tried to reason with her when he came home at night, and apologised for keeping Sara a secret, but she was too ill-humoured to hear him out. Was she willing to give him up because of a girl? That made no sense to him.

In an attempt to distract herself and ease the tension in the room, Sara pulled a chair next to Zia's bed, and reached out to touch her tummy. 'So round. They say round tummies are girls, and pointy ones are boys. Do you know?'

'We believe it's a girl,' said Zia. 'She does not move much anymore…she's gotten quite big and fills all the space. The doctor says that that's when you know she's almost ready to come out.'

Sara patted Zia's bump. 'Hear that? You're going to be a big girl. Soon you'll be playing with Aunt Sara and Uncle Behrooz.'

Behrooz squatted next to the bed. 'Can I get you anything, Zia?' He touched his sister's cheek.

'I'm okay.' Zia smiled. 'Maya has been taking good care of me.'

Behrooz beamed at Maya. 'I know I haven't been around much. But I plan to be here a lot more until the baby comes.'

'I doubt the ladies want you intruding on their conversation all day,' Sara cautioned. The less time Behrooz spent with Maya, the better.

'Really?' scoffed Maya. 'Zia hasn't seen her brother in two years.'

'We don't mind Behrooz being here at all. You're welcome, too,' Zia assured Sara.

'Of course. I'll be here, then.' Sara moved her chair to the foot of the bed, and started massaging Zia's feet.

'You don't have to do that.' Zia quickly explained, 'Mother Dianne smothers me all day, so it's good to lie here with no one fussing.' She didn't want anyone exerting themselves for her.

'Plus, she's in my care!' said Maya. She wouldn't have mousey Sara laying claim to her sister, too. 'If Zia needs anything, I will provide it for her. Got it?'

Behrooz glowered. 'She's just being nice, Maya.'

'It's okay,' said Sara. 'Maya is just afraid that she'd have to get some new hobbies.'

Behrooz looked confused.

'After all…she and you know every tree, rock and blade in the orchard…sitting outside every day doing who knows what? What would she ever do if you two were separated?'

'Separated?' said Behrooz.

'Yes, separated,' said Maya. 'It's what your girlfriend wants.'

'It's not what she wants,' Behrooz corrected. 'She wouldn't be this way if you were civil!'

Zia looked back and forth between them helplessly. 'Guys, please. I know this is awkward, but you don't have to be mean to each other.'

Maya pulled open the room door. 'You two lovebirds are aggravating my patient. Time for you to leave.'

Behrooz looked dumbfounded. 'It's okay.' He pulled Sara to her feet, and wrapped his arm around her. 'It's going to be okay.'

Sara knew better than to believe him.

Three weeks later, baby Aara was born. She was delivered at the very hour she was due. She weighed seven pounds. And she was perfect.

Mother Dianne was the only one allowed in the delivery room to witness the birth, though Maya and Behrooz heard Zia's screams from outside. They had never seen Father Khalid so agitated. He stood straight-backed, pacing the waiting room, hands in his pants pockets.

He'd dialled Ron the instant the contractions began. Ron was ecstatic and desperate to be with his wife and baby. He was due to arrive the following morning, and stay on for one week until the baby's Aquiqah, the Islamic tradition of celebrating a child's birth. He expressed deep gratitude to Mother Dianne and the family for looking after Zia.

After the birth, Zia, still gasping for breath, asked to hold her baby, and Father Khalid, Behrooz, Maya and the twins were allowed to pile into the delivery room for a brief minute. Mother Dianne had asked the rest of the family to hold off until Zia returned home. She wanted Zia to have enough privacy and time to recover.

Upon Zia's request Father Khalid recited a beautiful sing-song rendition of the Athaan, the call to prayer, in the baby's ear. The children bowed their heads respectfully. Even Maya held her giggles. They were all besotted by the angel before them, and before they could avert their admiring eyes, the nurse took the newborn out of Zia's arms and into the paediatrics ward.

Maya and Behrooz stood where the baby was housed, looking at her, in awe, through the glass doors. At first Maya could not tell which was Zia's, but then Behrooz pointed her out. He was certain of it from a tiny mole he'd noticed on the baby's left wrist. They wondered what Zia would name her; neither of them had asked. But they were sure it would be something beautiful.

They sat within perfect view of the baby, and barely noticed as the hours passed. It seemed for a moment that they were completely in sync, at peace. Behrooz tenderly draped his arm around Maya and pulled her closer, treasuring the moment. Maya sank closer into him. He felt warm and smelled sweet, with a tiny hint of fruit. He rested his chin on her head, and inhaled deeply. He seemed to hold his breath.

Maya wondered where Sara was, but after the latest incident, she dared not ask. She had no doubt the girl had decided not to be anywhere she was. But those thoughts left her head, as she focused on the feel of Behrooz's arms wrapped around her, and Zia's miracle before them.

And just when Maya felt completely tranquil, a continuous wail of babies fired up across the ward.

She and Behrooz, jolted from their reverie, laughed at the irony. And they laughed and laughed until they finally got home. They adored the baby, but what on earth would they do with one if they had one to keep?

They were still laughing when they landed in Behrooz's room. Maya romped beside him in his bed. He hugged her close, her wild, curly hair, in his face. And they both drifted asleep.

9

Baby Aara

One week later, the Ali family prepared to introduce baby Aara to The Yard. The Aquiqah was a much anticipated affair; a day of celebration and thanksgiving for the blessing that had come into all their lives.

The women had gathered in the courtyard, one hour earlier, chatting eagerly, and brimming with anticipation. It had been over a week since the baby was born, and it was just like the Ali family to exclude them for so long.

They wore heavily embroidered shalwars in reds and greens and golds, with sequinned dupattas bouncing haphazardly over their heads.

Aunt Maab was the only exception. She floated about in her usual black garb, covered from wrist to ankle. Her two sons, adorned in black kurtas, flanked her. Aunt Maab was particularly perturbed that she had been prevented from seeing the baby until now.

When she had given birth, the entire family was present in the waiting room. They saw the film of sweat on her body right after the delivery. She'd managed to throw her head scarf on, pull on a nightgown and was ready. They'd seen both Riyad and Riaz minutes after they were born. On both occasions they'd stayed until nightfall when the nurses advised that visiting hours were long over.

That was the way she'd wanted it. She loved giving birth and having the entire family there to support her, and would not have been happy had any of them been missing. In fact, only Maya and Behrooz were absent, but she did not mind as she and her husband had remained skeptical about Behrooz through the years.

She did not understand Mother Dianne's insistence that Zia not be visited until she had recovered. Yet, here she was, indignantly waiting her turn to see the much anticipated and elusive baby.

The grounds were covered in soft mattresses concealed by Indian silks in emerald green and sunflower yellow bordered with rich gold. Plush, sequined, tasseled silk bolsters in reds and oranges lined the edges. They served as decadent back rests.

A rhythm section was drumming a festive three-four beat. A light breeze carried the tunes around them and into the crisp evening air. Aunt Maab joined the other women who now sat cross-legged on the mattresses, knees touching, and shoulders swaying to the music.

The uncles sat on the opposite end with the Imam and a few men from Calcutta Masjid. They were a serious bunch, talking about wars and politics, and how violent Muslims were giving the good Muslims a bad name abroad. Behrooz and Aunt Heba's boys—Arif, Umar and Zaki—were seated close to them. All four were clad simply in white cotton kurtas and white topees.

Maya was the last of her immediate family to arrive. She stood at the side of the gathering, debating where she should sit. She was unused to this consideration. Usually she and Behrooz would be together at such events. They never made it through an entire one without evoking someone's wrath, and they'd take to the orchard when things became unbearable, making fun of everyone, and everything. It seemed odd to not have him at her side.

Behrooz was busy chatting with the Heba boys, and she wondered if he was telling them about Sara. Clearly, they were having a good time. All four were roaring with laughter.

Eventually, she approached cousin Alia, who was closest to her in age, and was sitting with Saba and Mona and Aunt Lulu's two daughters, Fauzia and Fiza.

Alia and Maya were an odd combination, practically opposites.

Alia was tall, poised, graceful and elegant. She had long, straight hair cascading delicately down her back. She was well loved and respected by everyone in The Yard. As a little girl she was Grandmother Sakina's favourite, as even then she looked after the old lady with enviable dignity.

She knew much of the scriptures by heart and had a beautiful voice for rendition. She spent hours reciting to Grandmother Sakina, whilst combing the elderly woman's hair, preparing her baths, changing her clothes, serving her meals with the appropriate prescription tablets and looking after her every need. She was a pure, sacrificial soul.

Maya could not be more antithetical. She could barely be described as graceful or elegant. Her hair was contrastingly wild and untamed, and she lacked patience with her entire being. She was prone to extreme feeling and to fits of rage and laughter. She rebelled against every convention, and only occasionally would one glimpse her softer side.

Her cousins and sisters seemed surprised when she joined their company. But thankfully they continued talking as usual. Surprisingly to Maya, the topic at hand was Behrooz. Aunt Lulu's eldest daughter, Fauzia, was regaling them with her first memory. It was the time Behrooz broke into their home, striped their dog, and was making his exit when Aunt Lulu walked in on him. Until now she has not been able to look him in the eye without giggling. Saba and Mona were laughing at the tale, and comforting her by saying how wonderful Behrooz had been to them since.

And Behrooz was terrific. He was less temperamental than Maya and humoured the girls by joining their storytelling escapades, telling funny stories and playing silly make-believe games. They weren't ambivalent about him like they were about Maya.

Behrooz noticed Maya's entrance; but feigned not to. They had bonded the night baby Aara was born, but when morning came Maya was missing from his bed. He wondered if he had crossed the line with her.

Since then, they had not been alone together. He was spending time with Sara as usual and Maya went back to avoiding him altogether.

She looked beautiful to him. She was wearing an embroidered sari in stunning shades of gold and yellow. He'd never seen her in a sari before. Nor had he ever seen her in those colours. Fussy and intricate clothing repelled her, and he wondered about the change. Her hair was swept up from her neck and pinned to the top of her head. Snaking tendrils cascaded around her face. One floated across to her red mouth and sat close to her lips.

What remained the same was her strained expression when with her family. Finding something in common with the rest was her affliction. Her smile seemed empty to him; her lids fluttered, and her feet shook of their own accord. He was tempted to go to her. But he remained where he was. She might choose then to unleash her fury. He could not risk that. She was jealous of him and Sara. That was wrong, and nonsensical. He had to put an end to it. And he hoped that she'd come around soon.

*

Mother Dianne, baby in hand, Zia at her side, made a welcomed yet noisy entrance to rhythmic drums. But when the baby started crying the music was stopped and a hush fell over The Yard. The newborn, calmed by silence, quieted down.

Mother Dianne toted her about in a hand-woven, maize basket lined with mulberry silk. The tiny creature was dressed in a comfortable white, sleeveless, cotton dress and wrapped in cozy yellow blankets.

Aunt Heba and Aunt Hala were the first to rush to her. Aunt Heba held the baby's delicate weight against her chest and swung gently from left to right. The baby's gaze wandered to Aunt Hala who reached out and touched her cheek. Aunt Hala was captivated by the newborn's stunningly wide, bonny brown eyes, and cooed to her until her face seemed alight with an enchanting smile.

Aunt Heba placed the precious bundle in her official spot for the night—a bassinet accented with a large yellow bow on a raised platform in the middle of the floor.

The Imam raised his hands in supplication for the well-being of the child. He recited a string of surahs and the men chanted along with him as loud as they could.

Zia nodded a non-verbal cue to the Imam that it was time to announce the baby's name. She stood near the bassinet flanked by Ron and her mother. Ron had returned one week earlier, the day after the baby was born; at the moment, merriment was etched on his face.

He proudly clung to his wife's left elbow. 'We will call her Aara,' he said. The laughter lines on his face sunk a little deeper.

'Aara, the adored,' said Zia. 'She'll know how her parents adore her.' She lifted the baby and spun her around so all could see her face. Everyone clapped and cheered. The chosen name seemed very appropriate for such a bewitching creature. At that moment baby Aara's legs abruptly shot out from below her. It was as if she knew that something remarkable had happened.

The Imam instructed guests to line up on both sides of Zia, who passed through the resulting human passageway. Ron picked up a pair of short scissors from a side table next to the bassinet and a coconut shell and followed through with his wife. Each guest snipped a piece of Aara's hair and placed it in the shell. It was recommended to pay, in charity, the weight of the baby's hair in gold. The hair was taken indoors for safekeeping.

Then the Aquiqah feast was served. The savoury scent of Indian spices—clove, cardamom and zeera—wafted through the air, unfurled by the night breeze, as the covers were removed from the serving dishes.

A piping hot feast of traditional curried goat, basmati rice, pumpkin, mango talkari, roti and cool cucumbers was waiting to be served. It was mandatory to serve a goat or sheep to family and community members. Father Khalid ensured that some of the best pieces were saved to send to the poor.

He looked on with pleasure as his family, served by efficient caterers, took their cushioned floor seats once more. They sat cross-legged, enjoying the camaraderie.

And when he was satisfied that everyone had had something to eat, he took his food and sat across from Mother Dianne, who barely noticed his presence. She was engrossed in conversation with Zia, determined to teach her daughter everything she needed to know, in one night, about caring for the baby.

Uncle Ansar, who had thus far stayed out of Father Khalid's radar, as he usually did at family gatherings, connived this moment, to start the conversation he'd wanted to have for some time. He sat next to his brother. 'When will you stop pretending?'

'Excuse me?' said Father Khalid.

'That you don't see what's going on. It's embarrassing. Everyone knows but you. Or, at least you pretend not to.'

'I'm not interested in your theories about some supposed goings on,' said Father Khalid. He was sure that his brother was ready to launch some new complaint about Behrooz.

'Not a theory. You just choose to turn a blind eye.'

'I'm almost tempted to ask what you're talking about,' said Father Khalid. 'But I won't. In fact, we wouldn't even be having this conversation if not for the whole family being here; it would upset a lot of people if I got up and walked out.'

'Then hear me out,' said Uncle Ansar.

'Don't seem like I have a choice,' said Father Khalid.

'That boy you adore so much, he's not your son! I'm sorry for this, but you will live to regret your decision.'

'Seriously? It's been six years! When is this ever going to stop!'

'When you get the courage to see what's happening!' said Uncle Ansar. 'In your own house.'

'What has Behrooz done in the last six years to deserve this? He has painstakingly stayed out of your way. He stays away from your children. During his first year here he was practically imprisoned in our house because of you. The younger kids are still afraid of him. And for what?'

'Maybe your own children would be more prudent to exercise some caution!' said Uncle Ansar. 'Don't you see what's going on with Maya, for Christ sake? The way she's been acting?'

'You don't know anything about my children. You barely see my children, or interact with them. How could you possibly know what's bothering my daughter?'

'There is talk,' said Uncle Ansar. 'Ever since Behrooz got a girlfriend, she's been walking around with a broken heart.'

'A broken heart, ha!' Father Khalid gestured towards Maya. 'That does not look like a girl with a broken heart to me!'

Maya, sitting alongside Alia, directly across from the two men, was laughing heartily with a newcomer. Father Khalid was taken aback. He had never seen this boy before, who at that moment leaned forward to move a tendril of hair from his daughter's face. Perhaps he was a friend of Alia's or one of the Heba boys?

'She looks like a girl with the world at her feet,' he continued.

'Because she has the attention of some strange boy?' said Uncle

Ansar, unconvinced. 'Don't fool yourself. She will soon forget him, and be crying over Behrooz again.

'You have a responsibility to this family. People respect you. Look up to you. Trust you. Come to you for advice. How can you betray us, by keeping this boy in your house, pretending he's your son, when he is fixated on your daughter? What is your plan? Do you intend to marry them off? You've had them living in sin this long. Romping together! Sleeping together! Who knows what they've done.'

'Sleeping together...?'

'Saba and Mona saw them sleeping in Behrooz's bed the night the baby was born. They mentioned it to Fauzia.'

'I see...'

'You've let us down. You've tainted your own daughter. She could barely face herself in the mirror. And who knows what he has in store for your *other* daughters!'

'Enough! You've crossed the line,' warned Father Khalid.

'You've tainted this family's good name! You went against what is acceptable!' said Uncle Ansar.

'I did what my conscience dictated,' said Father Khalid. 'Perhaps you can turn away a homeless boy. But I can't. I won't. I didn't want to!' He pointed at his brother. 'Your self-imposed rules aren't infallible!'

'Self-imposed? It's not up to us,' said Uncle Ansar.

'You need a sheikh in Saudi Arabia to make decisions for you?' said Father Khalid. 'To tell you that taking in a homeless boy as your own is unadvisable because he's allowed to marry your "real" children? Where's the humanity in that?'

'You could have fed him, clothed him, found him somewhere to live. But you were not supposed to call him your own.' Uncle Ansar stroked his beard meditatively. 'There are consequences to that. And what's happening with Maya, you're paying the price.'

'It would not have been enough to just find him food and shelter and step out of his life. Children need love. A definite sense of belonging. He deserved that.'

'So, you're perfectly content to ruin your daughter?'

'She is not ruined,' Father Khalid shot back.

'You're condoning this blasphemy?'

'Blasphemy? I thought it was allowed.' Father Khalid smirked. 'First you're upset because in your head Behrooz is fixated on my daughter, and vice versa. Then, you tell me that it's allowed between them. Then, you say that it should be stopped. Your argument runs in circles.'

'Don't play smart.' Uncle Ansar steeled his gaze. 'You cannot allow them to continue this way unless you marry them off. In shame. Are you willing to do that?'

'I chose the boy regardless of the consequences,' said Father Khalid. 'I don't regret my decision. I've opted for the lesser of two evils.'

Uncle Ansar clenched his fists. There was no reasoning with his brother.

Father Khalid, unable to entertain the conversation further, shoved his dinner aside and sauntered into the orchard.

Behrooz was close at his heels. He was paying attention to the conversation between the two and was confounded that they were speaking at all. And from the look of things he could tell that Uncle Ansar was once again berating Father Khalid on his account. He hated that. Hated that since the day he came until now, he'd managed to stir such hostility between them.

'I'm sorry,' said Behrooz. He quickened his pace behind Father Khalid.

'For?' said Father Khalid.

'For causing a rift between you two. By now I thought…'

'It's not your fault.' Father Khalid strode along a stone path comprising a series of rocks surrounded by dried leaves. He went further into the foliage, shoes crunching against gravel, and reached the end of the plot on the eastern side. He rested his palm against a laden pommerac tree, gazing down into the flowing ravine ahead. Rainbow fish scurried by in a blur.

'I wonder if I hadn't come,' said Behrooz, 'if you never found me…if things would be better here for you.'

'Nonsense.' Father Khalid turned to the boy behind him and touched his shoulder. 'Listen, Uncle Ansar seems to think that something undesirable is going on between you and Maya.'

'Undesirable?' Behrooz paused. 'It's just that she's upset. Jealous of Sara. So she's giving me the cold shoulder.'

'Jealous?' Father Khalid resisted the urge to light a cigarette, a habit he'd given up long ago. But even if he'd wanted to give in, he had no tobacco roll-ups on his person.

'You know how she is,' said Behrooz. 'She's used to having me around all the time. She was never one to share. It's in her nature to throw a tantrum. She'll get over it soon.'

'Do you love this girl?' said Father Khalid. 'Want to marry her some day?'

'Sara?' said Behrooz.

Father Khalid nodded.

'Maybe.' Behrooz looked concerned. 'Do you want me to…?'

'I would never force a girl upon you, Behrooz. Plus, you have college to think about. You're too young to be in love.'

'College?' said Behrooz.

'What did you think was going to happen after graduation?'

'I didn't think of it. Think I would have the money…' said Behrooz.

'Money was never an issue.' Father Khalid smiled. 'You know that.'

Behrooz nodded.

'Now, what are you going to do about Maya?' said Father Khalid. He was more than a little concerned about his daughter.

'I'm not going to give in to her demands,' said Behrooz. 'She'll come around, eventually.'

'She's not known for reason,' said Father Khalid.

'Still, you can never tell with Maya,' said Behrooz.

And Father Khalid knew he was right.

*

Father Khalid rejoined his family in the courtyard. His mind wavered.

Had he done the right thing by his daughter? Would she be able to let go of Behrooz? Would she suffer?

There were no right answers. Only assumptions. Only questions.

And his heart weighed heavy with the knowledge that there was no win-win situation.

Zia and Mother Dianne were sitting and whispering together, not where Father Khalid had left them, but now to the edge of the cushioned flooring, with feet housed in kitten-heeled sequined shoes, dangling off the edge.

Zia had gone to see Grandmother Sakina at the back of The Yard, and was expressing her worry over how frail and wary the old lady had seemed. Grandmother Sakina had lost her hearing in one ear, and Zia had to talk much louder than normal and repeat her sentences several times. What bothered her most was that her grandmother was struck with a certain paranoia that someone was spying on her, though she had no reasonable explanation for any of her theories, and there were no strangers in The Yard. Zia worried that the elderly woman was worrying herself into despair when there was no need, and regretted this state of events, though she was uncertain how she could help. After all, she was only in The Yard for a few short weeks.

Mother Dianne dispatched Maya and Behrooz to visit the old woman, and say goodnight on behalf of the family. She was familiar with the paranoia that had consumed her mother-in-law of late, and knew exactly the state of mind to which Zia referred. It was better that the children went to see her before she read more into their absence than was necessary.

Grandmother Sakina had grown used to Behrooz over the years. In fact, she was quite fond of the boy, though Behrooz avoided her at all costs. He was conflicted about how the old woman regarded him—sometimes with deep affection, other times with pure snobbery, suspicion and downright scorn—and other times with an air of importance as if she knew something about him that he did not.

Meanwhile, Aunt Lulu, in her embroidered green shalwar and plain red shawl that draped across her shoulders and hung down her back with one side longer than the other, and contrary plaid flats which seemed ready to fly off her feet at any moment, was running helter-skelter in the yard, apparently searching for Fiza, the younger of her two daughters. Many a time, feeling like her mother was from some bizarre planet, the girl would go into hiding, until rescued by her father. Fiza was feeling particularly like this now.

Her mother, wracked with guilt, and constantly unsure about her parenting, had been parleying with Aunt Maab, who had a terrific rapport with her sons, about how much time she and her daughters spent together. She proclaimed that they did everything together and could barely be apart.

This, Fiza knew to be untrue, but lacking the maturity to see the circumstances as they were, she was convinced that her mother was a blatant liar.

To make matters worse, her mother insisted on serving her plate this night, a task usually left to her father. Enough food for a grown man was lumped onto her plate, and she was mandated to eat it all.

When Fiza flat out refused, her mother resorted to the ancient method of flying food on a spoon into her mouth, imitating the landing of a plane. As though she was two years old. She was forced to eat the entire plate, and her tummy felt hard, stiff and unnatural. Frustrated and desperate, she'd decided to hide from her mother, until her father could rescue her.

But Uncle Khidr had left the celebration earlier on, with his elder daughter, who was tired from their day's play. He'd left without saying goodbyes or playing with baby Aara, and his wife had no idea when or why.

Unluckily for Fiza, Father Khalid spotted her little foot sticking out from under some floor cushions at the margin where the brick met the orchard. 'I found her!' he said. Fiza was mortified. Her mother flew to the spot and yanked her from her hiding place.

'Khidr! Why do you disappear all the time!' Aunt Lulu bellowed into the air at her husband, who was nowhere in sight, while pulling the terrified girl by her upper arm, towards their house.

Moments after, The Yard was quiet. Everyone had left, besides Aunt Heba, who remained to help Mother Dianne stack the floor cushions. Just as their task was complete, and the women were retreating to their houses, Maya and Behrooz came running from the back of The Yard where they'd gone to visit their grandmother. Both were wide-eyed, panting, exhilarated.

'We're not going back, Mother. We're not going back!' said Maya. 'She's crazy. Crazy!'

Behrooz looked sullen.

It had not been a typical encounter with Grandmother Sakina. This time, affection gave way to panic and terror, instead of the usual suspicion and scorn. And neither Behrooz nor Maya would speak of it, or confess a word of it. Not then anyway.

10

The Newcomer

Sara, affronted by her absence in Behrooz's life and in The Yard of late, and certain that this dry spell was due to Maya and suspiciously sweet Zia, insisted that she meet Behrooz in The Yard this day.

She needed her presence felt, to claim him as her own. And though her conscious mind would never accede, she hoped that Maya would spot them together, and finally realise that Behrooz had charted a new path.

Behrooz had asked her to wait for him by Aunt Hala's house at the back of the compound. She sat on a low brick wall that separated Aunt Hala's herb garden from the rest of The Yard, revelling in the fragrance of fresh basil, rosemary, shaddon beni and freshly cut grass intermingled in the cool afternoon.

Sara was grateful for the open air, and the clouds that protected her from glancing shafts of sun.

But the solitary wait brought on her nerves. And when Behrooz finally showed up, she looked wan.

Behrooz smiled comfortably. 'What's the matter? Seen a ghost? I mean…I know The Yard is strange, but try as I might, I've never seen one.'

His humour put Sara at ease. 'Just happy to see you.'

She looked beautiful. She'd changed out of her school uniform into a red cotton dress that draped down over her knees, and sported a looped band tied comfortably around her waist.

Her face was flushed. The length of her body seemed stretched towards the sky; only, her gaze was fixed upon Behrooz.

'How was the party last night?'

'It had its moments,' said Behrooz. 'Never a dull moment in this family.' He pulled himself onto the wall. Sara wrapped her arms around him; he thought she smelt like soapy lavender.

'Yeah? What were the highlights?'

Behrooz remembered what Grandmother Sakina had told him and tensed. 'I won't bore you with the details.'

Sara's hands fell to her sides. 'I'm still banned from family gatherings then?'

'You aren't banned.'

'You said I couldn't attend. Remember?'

Behrooz locked his fingers together. 'It's not a good idea for you and Maya to be in the same place…'

'Forget Maya,' said Sara. 'Why should we do what she wants? Nothing about her…about this…is normal. The way she looks at you…the way she behaves…she's like a filly defending her colt!'

When Sara was eight years old, her father took her to Santa Rosa Park. She'd never liked the outdoors, yet he'd insisted that she'd love horseback riding. In the field were a beautiful stallion and mare, grazing side by side. Sara enjoyed the sight of them. Then, the stable boy introduced another mare, who got the attention of the stallion. The slighted female kicked, squealed and charged at the other two, scaring Sara.

'She thinks that you're hers. And now that you're with me, she'll kick and scream until she gets her way.'

Behrooz could not totally dismiss the girl's concerns. 'Listen. This is just an adjustment period.' Surely, Maya could not perpetuate her current behaviour. 'I've found someone. And it's just a matter of time before she does too. Okay?'

'I want to believe that.'

'Believe me. She's not as irrational as she seems. She will calm down; and find someone of her own. And soon there would be four people in this picture. Perfectly complementary.'

'Provided that she actually grows up some time soon.'

'You'll just have to trust me. I know it's asking a lot. But I'll make it up to you. I promise.'

Sara planted a kiss on his ear lobe. 'Then you have a lot of making up to do.'

Behrooz touched his forehead to hers. 'I know, and I'm good at it.' His mouth lightly grazed her lower lip. He was grateful that she was willing to stick it out with him, regardless of how strange his life was.

'My father wants to meet you,' said Sara.

'You told him about us? I thought you weren't ready?'

Sara had had her doubts about introducing Behrooz to her father. But once he'd assured her that he would not allow Maya to make trouble for them, she felt more settled. 'It's better this way. He should hear it from me, than someone else. You know how people talk.'

Sara placed her hands on her lap. She bent her fingers against each other. 'He wants you to come over for dinner tomorrow. So you can meet him and my mom. So they can give us their blessing.' Her heart banged like a drum in her chest. 'So, we can make it official?'

'Tomorrow? Sara…I don't know…' Behrooz's confusion even took him by surprise. Things were moving so quickly.

'I had dinner with your family.'

'And look how that turned out.'

Sara's face reddened. 'It turned out fine. Your parents like me. Unless you have some other reason?'

Behrooz did not want to disappoint her again. She didn't deserve that. 'All right. Dinner it is.'

She hugged him closer. 'But even now. I still don't know…'

Behrooz nodded at her to continue.

Sara looked towards the floor, her body instantly shorter. 'I still don't know if you love me.'

'Love,' he echoed.

'Love,' she said, looking up. Her fingers caressed his jaw line.

'I…think…I don't know what love should feel like.'

'It feels like this,' she said. She placed his palm on her upper chest and slid it over her heart. Behrooz felt the flesh at the top of her bra, soft and thick.

His breathing grew shallow. 'Does it?'

Sara moved to kiss him, and before he could react, there was a rustle in the trees, and Arif burst into view.

*

Arif's interruption could not have come at a better time.

Despite Behrooz's temporary distraction, beyond the heat he felt when he touched Sara's flesh and the immediate distraction of Arif's sudden fortuitous appearance, he was flustered at the idea of meeting Sara's parents.

He had never met any girl's father, and took that occasion quite seriously. He would have a lot of responsibility to live up to afterwards and he wasn't sure he was ready for it. But he did promise Sara to make their relationship official. And to bail on this would show insincerity on his part.

He wasn't certain of the exact cause of his doubts, only that he had them.

Sara was not pleased by the interruption. Arif came with an invitation for Behrooz and Maya to hang out at his house that night. It was Zaki's birthday and some of the older cousins were invited and a couple of the birthday boy's friends.

Sara was also extended an invitation, but much to her dismay, Behrooz insisted she could not attend.

She was disturbed by how much Behrooz relied on Maya, envious of how tangled his identity was with the girl's, and chagrined about how determined he was that she stay away.

And though she tried not to show it, she was cursed with the affliction of her true feelings being present on her face.

Sara remained sulky for the rest of the evening, and decided to go home earlier than planned, horrified that once again Maya and Behrooz would be having a grand time without her.

As Behrooz approached Aunt Heba's house, the party seemed in full swing. His aunt's Volvo was missing from The Yard, and Behrooz gathered she was not at home. Perhaps she wanted to give the boys some privacy?

He did spot another car, a Honda Odyssey mini-van, unfamiliar to him, in the parking space she usually occupied.

Music blared from the house. He was not a big music fan, but island tunes he recognised. A Bob Marley classic, 'One Love', was playing.

He turned the brass doorknob and entered. No one was in sight. He walked through the foyer in the direction from which the music pulsed, and slid the partition door to the adjoining living room.

He was startled.

Maya was locked mouth to mouth with a stranger. Then, something clicked. He recognised the boy. He'd seen him at baby Aara's Aqiqah. But why on earth was he kissing Maya?

Moments after, the rest of the room came into focus.

The kiss broke, and Zaki high-fived the stranger. 'Yeah! Who are the winners now?'

'Behrooz!' said Arif. 'You're late. Come sit here and get yourself a party slave.'

'What's going on?' Behrooz said to Maya.

Arif laughed. 'It's just a game bro. Relax.'

Strewn on a low coffee table, in the middle of them all, was the cardboard box cover of a game, Disorderly Conduct.

Arif had spotted the game at a toy store when Aunt Heba had taken the boys to New York city the year prior. He'd immediately seen the potential, and bought the game without his mother knowing.

Behrooz was surprised to see Alia sitting with the others around the table. She seemed quite uncomfortable, and he wondered why the boys would invite her to such a party.

Maya had ignored Behrooz's question, and was staring at the stranger with ardour. She usually had that fiery look when she was being particularly rebellious.

Behrooz reminded himself that he didn't need to protect her. She was a big girl. Plus, she probably wouldn't listen to anything he had to say.

Zaki shifted and Behrooz took his spot at the table, between Zaki and Arif, directly across from Maya.

'Girls against guys,' Arif explained, rolling a die and moving the token etched with the male symbol three spaces forward. 'Our dare!' He grabbed a card from their stack and slapped it down on the table.

'Have the girl who displays the best manners say one complimentary thing to each of the guys,' he read. The guys, besides Behrooz, roared their approval.

Maya was in no danger of being selected.

Alia it was.

'I'll start with Arif,' she said. Her usually dead-straight hair was

slightly dishevelled. 'I've always admired the way you never allow
Zaki to boss you around, no matter how hard he tries!'

Zaki laughed. 'What the hell? I thought you were supposed to
be complimenting us?'

'Behrooz,' she continued. Her eyebrows arched. 'I wonder at
your ability to deal with these morons.'

'Zaki…'

'Careful now,' Zaki sneered, 'or you may just be stamped a party
slave!' The boys erupted into laughter again.

'You always know how to make things interesting,' she said,
with an innocent curl of the lip.

She immediately rolled the die, and moved the girls' token five
spaces forward.

'Wait!' said Zaki. 'You forgot Dean!'

Dean? Was that his name? thought Behrooz. He glared at the
mysterious intruder who at that moment caused a rage to swell
in his chest.

Alia looked down at her toes. 'I don't know what to say about
Dean.'

Zaki teased, 'Are you forfeiting?'

'No,' Alia stumbled. 'Dean, I think you're the most handsome
guy I've ever met.'

Arif laughed, 'Seriously? You need to get out of The Yard more.'

That explains it, thought Behrooz. That's why Alia had come.
She has a crush on the idiot.

'Hold your horses,' said Maya, 'don't you see that Dean only
has eyes for me?'

Dean buried his nose into Maya's hair, and the girl solemnly held
his head in place, almost as though she were a witch casting a spell.

Behrooz's chest hardened. Did Maya actually like this jerk?

He tried to put the visual of them locked mouth to mouth out
of his head, and ignore the only slightly less inappropriate scene
before him.

Even if it was just a stupid game, it was wrong of her to be so
familiar with a stranger who was clearly up to no good.

Maya rolled the die and moved their token five spaces forward.
'Have all the guys do a split, as far as they can go, and hold it for
twenty-five seconds!'

'All right!' Arif high-fived his brother, then Dean. He must have seen the morose expression on Behrooz's face and ignored him altogether.

The three boys each stretched out their hamstrings and dropped side by side in a split. Behrooz, attempting to keep the peace for the occasion, grudgingly followed.

Zaki toppled over twenty seconds later, and the girls, roaring with laughter, stamped him as their party slave.

'Fetch me a coke, slave!' said Maya, wasting no time in placing her first order. Zaki, grumbling under his breath, obliged.

Arif rolled the die, and moved their token to the end spot on the board, which transferred him to an unadventurous square.

'Darn!' he said, slamming his fist on the table. 'The girls are ahead.'

Maya cast the die, and pulled her card.

'Have the guy with the best judge of character tell each girl what her favorite flavour of ice cream should be and why,' she said, disappointed by the lack of challenge in the dare.

Neither Zaki, nor Arif, considered himself to be a good judge of character, so Dean owned up to the task.

Behrooz wondered what the girls found so fascinating about Dean. There seemed in his features nothing special. He had an ordinary oval face, with a slightly pointy nose, and eyebrows like a line across his forehead. There was a hardness about his body, though. More than likely he spent time training at the gym.

But this asset was negated by a smirk permanently etched across his face. And his laughter roared a few octaves higher than the rest. He was too loud. Too confident. Obnoxious. Behrooz did not like him.

'Alia…umm…you remind me of a good chocolate mint,' said Dean. 'Rejuvenating, curing, sweet and calming.'

Alia was uncomfortable with praises, and could not ascribe any other meaning to the words than the literal. She was even bewildered by them.

Behrooz did not care whether this was simply a game. He'd lost all sense of humour from the moment he'd walked in. He did not like the way this bloke summed up Alia, as if she could be defined with just a few adjectives. Nor did he like the double meaning intended.

Alia, he felt, was one of those rare people who were totally content in the service of others. Everyone present should be in awe of her and respect her.

'Maya…you are a delight, my favourite, my double chocolate-chunk!' said Dean, completing his part of the challenge. 'Yummy!'

Maya's face lit up devilishly. Behrooz caught her expression and wondered for a moment who was in worse trouble, Maya or the irritating boy. He couldn't, not for the first time, read her signals.

Zaki and Dean roared with laughter at the subtly demeaning descriptor.

Arif was silent. Like Behrooz, he took offence to some stranger calling his cousin a 'double chocolate-chunk'.

Behrooz's patience was wearing thin.

Alia looked like she wanted to leave but did not know how. And Behrooz knew that if Maya wanted the attentions of this new boy, Alia was not going to compete for it. She was selfless that way.

It seemed to Behrooz that Arif rolled the die, just to ease the tension.

'Blindfold the girl of your choice,' he read. 'One guy must kiss her. She must identify the owner of the lips in two guesses.'

'No way!' said Maya, 'And risk one of my cousins kissing me? Not a chance!'

But she was okay with Dean kissing her, thought Behrooz.

Dean looked seriously disappointed. Didn't she realise that it was going to be him? He was thinking of having his double chocolate chunk dessert a bit earlier.

Just like that, the horrid game was over, and Behrooz was relieved. The only thing that would be better was if the bloke left altogether.

But Dean seemed to have no intentions of leaving. And Behrooz was not about to leave Maya in his company unsupervised.

As Maya and Alia went into the kitchen to scoop ice cream and indulge in some girl talk, Dean confessed to Zaki that kissing Maya made his heart pound. He found her crazy ways endearing. She tasted delicious to him. Appetising!

Behrooz swallowed so hard, he thought the two boys could hear it. His chest raged again.

And when Maya returned to the room, Dean, taking her by surprise, grabbed her in a forced embrace and kissed her harshly on the lips, then tenderly. She responded just a little, out of shock. And when the kiss broke she looked at him with an incredulous expression.

Dean, obviously thinking that he had conquered, winked to Zaki, and signalled a hand gun sign of victory.

Behrooz slammed his fist on the table.

Everyone looked at him, startled. Only Zaki had an amused smile on his face.

Maya's eyes stormed. 'You have no right,' she said to Behrooz. 'You have no rights over me any more!'

Dean had the distinct impression that he had missed something very important.

As Behrooz looked on in helpless rage, Maya grabbed Dean by the elbow, and led him out into the orchard. She needed him, an anonymous face in an all too familiar crowd, to give her comfort.

Behrooz would just have to live with that. She would not allow him to control her, not while she felt so out of control.

He had his life, she had hers. And as it was, she could not see how they would be intertwined. Not while she suffered.

11

The Grandmother

The moon was closest to earth this night, more luminous than Behrooz had ever seen. White light danced off the pale sand beneath his toes, reflecting his image.

He turned his gaze towards the ocean. Waves rose high in the salty air, pounding, thundering one upon the other. They made him nervous. He thought of how they would cover him, topple him, if he swam out.

He shivered as the coldness reached his toes. The tide was rising, and soon water would cover where he stood, taking everything with it.

The wind rushed and howled. The coconut palms above bent towards the ground, their leaves like fingers in the shadows. Some welcoming, comforting; others, threatening.

But no one was there. No one was coming. It was time to go home. He turned and walked in the direction from whence he came. The trees rustled in protest. They didn't want him to give up. Drizzle pelted at his back. She was coming, they warned. And she belonged with him.

He felt his heart swell with the far off waves. There was hope yet. If he'd walked just a little further, perhaps she would have found him. His path would have joined with hers, and they would walk their own path, away from the icy waters, away from the shadows.

He turned back, determined to continue his journey. He'd barely walked five feet, before he saw her, luminous in the moonlight, stepping towards him. Her mouth red. Her hair brazen about her face.

The waves died.

She quickened her pace, and finally, stood shivering in front of him. She was drenched. He had no jacket to comfort her, but grabbed her hands in his, squeezing the blood from her fingers.

Her eyes touched his and softened; they leaped to his mouth, then chin. He gently pulled her closer, and she contoured her body into his, nestling her head into his neck. He pressed his lips to her hair, to the delicate shell of her ear.

He'd fallen.

The crab holes opened like a wide trap beneath his feet. He was falling through sand…falling backwards through time…

They were back at Grandmother Sakina's house.

'You rascal! I know what you do. The first day you come I tell you to be good to the people who take you as they own.

'Now I hear my granddaughter have a spell cast on she. Walking around with a broken heart! And my two sons not talking.'

Behrooz remained quiet. The old woman was right to berate him. She knew his heart; all the things he was guilty of.

'And you never even come to see me. I tell you to come every day. And you never come.

'I know you have people watching me, waiting for me to die. You want to kill me like you kill my sister.

'I tell my son to put you back in the road where you belong boy. You doh belong here with good people. And you leave my granddaughter alone, you hear? Leave her alone!'

And in that second, before Behrooz could decide whether to attempt to calm the irate woman, or defend himself, the old lady's four-legged walker came flying at him. She'd used every ounce of her strength to throw it.

And though he tried to duck out of the way, one leg hit him in the stomach. He doubled over in pain, choking back the scream that rose in this throat.

He ran from the room. A baby was wailing in the distance. He hastened towards the sound. Zia would be where the baby was. He would find her. He needed to talk.

*

Behrooz awoke suddenly. His clammy hands clutched at his bedspread. He wondered whether he was truly awake, or was in a dream within a dream, but quickly discerned the accuracy of the former. He raised his T-shirt, and rubbed his index finger over the bruise on his stomach. Ouch.

He'd hidden this bruise from Maya the night of the Aquiqah—the night Grandmother Sakina threw her walker at him. Though the girl had witnessed the incident, he'd told her that he had barely gotten a graze and was perfectly fine.

A baby wailed, as it had in his dream state. Behrooz pulled his tee over his torso, wiped the drops of perspiration off his forehead and walked into the hallway.

Zia was awake, attempting to soothe baby Aara. More than anyone, he needed to be with her just then. She was the only one he trusted with his secrets.

Zia held baby Aara to her chest, rocking her to sleep on the wooden chair Father Khalid built them when the baby was born.

She wasn't having much luck. The child, angered at her mother's attempts to shush her, bawled defiantly.

'Gosh. I'm sorry about all this,' said Zia.

'It's not Aara's fault that I'm up,' said Behrooz. 'I had a bad dream. A good dream actually, until it turned into a nightmare.'

'What about?' said Zia.

Behrooz sat in the chair next to her. 'It was terrible.'

'What's bothering you?' said Zia. She placed her hand on his. 'I'm leaving tomorrow. I don't know when next I'll see you. Tell me?'

Behrooz sighed. 'You're the only one I can tell.'

Baby Aara, comforted by the conversation around her, finally closed her eyes. 'Wait one sec,' said Zia. She went into her room, transferred the baby to Ron, and returned with her undivided attention.

'I dreamt about Maya,' he said. 'She's been so crazy lately. I mean, more than usual. She's so jealous of the time I spend with Sara.'

'So that's what it is? That she's vexed with you?'

'Yes. And no,' he said. 'When I went across by Aunt Heba tonight, I saw her there, with this strange boy, Dean. They were kissing.'

'Kissing?'

'Yeah.' Behrooz bowed his head. 'And I felt…I don't know…'

Zia squeezed his hand. 'Protective of her?'

'Yeah. She told me to mind my own business.'

'She's not going to listen to you. You're in her bad books now.'

He looked at Zia. 'I guess so…'

'Is that it? 'Cause Maya has gotten herself into lots of trouble before, and I didn't hear you having nightmares or freaking out.'

'Remember when I first came to The Yard?' he said. 'I was so alone. But you cared for me; you were so kind, I would never forget.'

Zia smiled. 'You were always my brother.'

'Maya, she despised me. She and her cousins laughed at me all the time. She saw me as I was. Pitiful.'

'She loved you too, in her own way.'

'Love. Hate. I don't know,' Behrooz glanced away. 'It turned into something else.'

Zia's brows crinkled together. 'I see.'

'I really hate that Dean. You know…?' Behrooz struggled with the words. 'Can't stand the thought of him.'

Zia's face registered understanding. 'Oh.'

'You hate me now?' Behrooz looked at her chin. 'I mean…I know what I'm sayin' here is shocking. Repulsive even.'

'I don't hate you. I am grateful you told me the truth.' Zia knew how difficult talking about personal feelings was for him. 'It's just that, there'd be a lot of consequences.'

Behrooz's eyes beseeched hers. 'Just tell me what to do. And I'll listen.'

'About Dean?' said Zia. 'Well for one, don't try to punch him or anything. 'Cause I'm sure he could take you.'

Behrooz was stony-faced. 'Is he that buff?'

'My, you're really reeling here,' said Zia, trying to make light of a tense situation. 'Don't worry partner, you're just as good-looking.'

'I mean, tell me what to do about Maya,' said Behrooz. 'Should I tell her?'

'Should you? I don't know.' Zia exhaled slowly. 'Look, I've known this day would come since the night of my wedding, when I left The Yard, and you two were huddled together under that lime tree. But I could never figure out how to deal with it.

'There are those among us who would hate you if you choose to act on these feelings. The only thing I can tell you is to be brave, 'cause it won't be easy either way.'

'Grandmother Sakina has already warned me off.' Behrooz raised his shirt so Zia could see his scar. 'She threw her walker at me.'

'I can't believe she hit you!' she said. 'Behrooz, Grandmother Sakina hasn't been herself for a long time. She has become so paranoid, and quarrelsome…she sees and hears things that aren't there…she's really losing her mind…'

'I know. I'm not taking it personally.'

'That aside, tongues would definitely be wagging. You and Maya would be the talk of The Yard, and I don't know how comfortable you'd be here after. How comfortable she'd be.'

Behrooz hugged Zia. 'I think I should find her.'

'What are you going to do?'

Behrooz shrugged. 'I don't know.' He was sad that Zia would be flying out the following morning, but tried to appear brave. 'Pray for me.'

*

Behrooz unlatched the door to Maya's room. He was anxious to see her. He hadn't decided his course of action, but he knew the moment he sought her out, the moment he saw her next, would determine everything. That his mind would be made up on its own accord.

The hair on his arms and the back of his neck rose in anticipation. He knew he could deny whatever he felt, if he so desired. He was used to suffering in silence. Only now, he wasn't sure he wanted to.

Maya had been talking with Dean in the orchard that night; she'd come in late, momentarily played with baby Aara and retired to her room for a late night shower. She'd already towelled herself dry and slipped into a long, white robe. She stood by the window at the opposite end of the room, looking out into the greenery, towel-drying her wet hair, scrunching it from the bottom up. Her curls pulled to one side of her neck.

Her bedroom door opened soundlessly, and Behrooz had barely made a rustle when she looked over her shoulder and saw him standing there. 'You here to lecture me? I have nothing to say to you.'

They were often together in his room, had slept side by side even, but this was the first time he'd come into hers. It was one of the barriers he had created between them. But now, he'd ventured in without knocking.

Behrooz glanced at her bed, that divided the room, and divided their space, then to her dressing table, and back where she stood.

She stopped massaging her hair with the towel and turned to face him. 'I mean you have absolutely no manners. To just barge in here.'

He strode past the canopy, making no apologies, and stood an inch away from her. 'You lecturing me on manners? When was the last time you showed any?' She felt his breath play on her skin. 'How did you treat Alia tonight?' he continued. 'You humiliated her.'

Maya swallowed, and pulled her robe closer. His closeness made her conscious of each pore, on every inch of her body.

She hardened her eyes. 'I know this is about Dean. About why I came home late. You're not my caretaker okay!'

'I know.' Behrooz touched her earlobe, and quickly retracted his fingers. She stared at his hands.

'You know…I don't care if you ever came home,' he said. 'You can do what you want, who you want…don't give a crap.'

'Don't give a crap.' Maya turned away. 'Don't!'

'Okay, then. In that case, you'd never find out why I came here.' Behrooz turned towards the doorway. Took two steps in that direction, then turned back.

'I mean…you tried to ruin my chances with every girl who ever liked me.' His tone grew demanding. 'Why is that, huh?'

'Because I want you to be miserable!' she said.

'I am. Happy?' he sneered.

Silence.

'Dean, you did that to get me mad, didn't you? That was your childish way of making me jealous?'

More silence.

He spun her around.

Maya's eyes remained downcast. A teardrop rested on her cheek. 'I'm sorry. I won't ruin your chances with the girls any more.'

Behrooz was immediately disheartened. 'No...please don't cry.' He wiped off the offending tear and pulled her into a soft embrace. 'I'm sorry...'

'Me too...,' she whispered. 'For everything.' He felt the wetness of her face on his neck. He pressed against her robe.

Maya closed her eyes, enjoying the feel of him. Then discretion crept in. 'What's going on?' She cautiously pulled away, and looked at his face.

Behrooz's hands fell to his sides. He deliberated on an explanation. 'Have no idea...I've been thinking...I've just been thinking.' He grinned. 'I didn't want any of those girls anyway.'

'You didn't?'

'No. I don't.' Behrooz's eyes remained soft upon hers, in an attempt to say all the things he couldn't. Somehow he hoped she'd spy all the answers there. 'I feel...differently...about you.'

'Different how?' Maya's heart throbbed anxiously. She leaned into him once more.

Behrooz's mouth pressed against her forehead. The words came out without warning. 'Enough to know that I can't be with anyone else.'

Maya felt the wind knocked out of her. Her mouth found his, and her lips lingered there for a second. 'Good,' she said. Her knees wobbled, and he held her straight. 'I feel differently about you, too.'

'Crap,' said Behrooz. Every sound was suddenly magnified; her breathing; the sound of the wind in the shutters; the crickets chirping outside. He lifted her onto her bed and sat next to her. 'You're going to get me into so much trouble.'

'Yah?' Maya sneered. 'So run.'

'That makes so much sense.' Behrooz knew that his behaviour would disappoint the people who'd brought him up. They didn't deserve that. 'What if I don't want to?' He would prove all their naysayers right.

'Run anyway.'

Behrooz caressed the sides of Maya's face; he kissed her forehead, her nose, her lips. 'In the morning, we tell everyone. I owe that to your family...to Father Khalid.'

'Can't we wait a while before we tell them?' Maya took his hand and traced the lines on his palm.

'No waiting.'

'Are you sure?' She dropped the hand.

Behrooz cupped her chin. 'Hiding this from them is only going to make things worse when they find out.'

'Right.'

He plopped onto a pillow and pulled her onto his hard torso. 'I do love you. You don't know what it is, until you feel it.' Maya buried herself into him. 'I love you, too.'

12

The Betrayal

*B*ehrooz awoke in Maya's bed. Morning smiled at him through the windows, innocent and calming. The sun full on his face. It was a newborn day, and he was at peace. They'd drifted off to sleep the night before, the crickets chirping their lullaby.

He turned around feeling for Maya, but she was not there. She'd risen before him, which was unusual. He smiled knowing how anxious she must be to confront the day. Though, he found all his anxieties had vanished during the night.

He straightened the bedsheets, which were pulled to her side of the bed. His heart gave a delicious squeeze as he recalled the night—her tangled into him; all legs, and arms, and torso. He walked towards the window. The three Heba boys were playing their customary, rambunctious game of cricket.

Usually, of late, they thought to invite him. But Behrooz figured that they were probably still getting over the Dean incident. Did Arif just look up at him? Or did he imagine that? No. That was his guilty conscience talking. No one knew that he was in Maya's room. And if they did, he would have known about it already.

He went to the bed again and slid under the covers. He was anxious to see Maya in the morning light. To know that everything that happened, everything they decided, was as real as he remembered.

She must have gotten dressed and gone somewhere. Her make-up was disarrayed on the dressing table. Compacts, lipsticks and various bottles that he hadn't seen the night before were scattered about; and some clothes were strewn at the bottom of the bed.

Several minutes ticked by, before the door creaked open. He looked up expectantly; his mind registered the unexpected.

Behrooz slid the covers off, and sprung off the bed, as Father Khalid walked in. He was alarmed, not only because he'd been discovered, but also because Father Khalid looked completely devastated.

'Maya is gone,' said Father Khalid.

His pulse raced. 'Gone where?'

Father Khalid passed his hands through his hair. 'To London, with Zia. She says she's not coming back.'

'What? That's not possible.' This was some kind of trick right?

Father Khalid was somber. 'I'm afraid it's true.'

Behrooz walked to the closet and yanked open its doors. Inside was an empty space towards the middle, as if a bunch of clothes had been grabbed from that spot. He glanced at the dressing table once more. He should have known that something was wrong.

'You sent her away?' His chest was raging. Maya wouldn't leave just like that.

'I didn't.' Father Khalid sat on his daughter's bed.

Behrooz shook his head in disbelief. 'No. You knew what happened. And you wanted her to leave.'

Father Khalid looked weary. 'No. I didn't want her to leave just yet. Not like this. And not before she was ready for college.'

'So why would she leave?' They had made a plan. They were going to tell everyone today, that they wanted to be together, forever.

'There is something else you should know,' said Father Khalid.

'Zia and I tried to reason with her,' Father Khalid continued. 'But she wouldn't listen. Then I tried to physically restrain her.' He looked remorseful. 'So…she ran out into The Yard shouting… awful things. Everyone came out to hear.'

Behrooz swallowed. 'What things?'

'Let's just say, everyone knows that you slept here last night,' said Father Khalid. 'Stuff she said, wasn't nice.'

'She wouldn't do that.' The gentle hands that caressed his heart earlier, now squeezed the life out of it.

Why would Maya give ammo to the people who hated him from the start? Wanted him thrown out?

'I won't lie to you about this. I'm sorry.'

Did she loathe him that much?

'I need to know what happened here last night,' said Father Khalid. 'Everything that happened.'

Behrooz defied the knot at the base of his throat. 'I love her,' he said. 'That's all that happened.'

Father Khalid sighed. 'She left you a note. I found it in your room this morning when I went to find you.'

'You read it?' Behrooz accused.

Father Khalid shook his head. He could not muster the strength to read that letter. He did not even tell Mother Dianne about it. He was terrified to learn what news it held and the consequences they'd all face.

Behrooz unfolded the note. The words were scrappily and hastily written in red, as though even the letter was decided on a whim. He read slowly, word by word, line by line. Each moment filling him with grief and dread.

Dear Behrooz,

Just as suddenly as you came into The Yard, I've decided to leave it. I know Father Khalid and Mother Dianne will be upset, but do not blame yourself. This is my decision. I simply have to go.

There is so much of the world that I have not seen, too much left to discover. When you first came, you were my escape from the sameness around me. I often thought of The Yard as a cult. They had all these bizarre rules to follow, and if you didn't follow them, you were something 'other'.

But I'm a big girl now. I no longer need your protection. Truly, you were just a childish, piteous thing that I used as an escape. Now your role has expired.

Whatever you thought happened between us, well that was funny to me, simply for my amusement. Did you seriously think I wanted to be with you? That I would jeopardise my future for you? I don't think so.

You were hilarious last night. All worried about telling Father, and what everyone would think. Thanks to the courtyard scene this morning, they all know how badly you wanted me and how I've rejected you.

I'm sure you're even more amusing to them now than you were before. Don't expect my return.

Maya

Behrooz felt everything he'd ever known, or believed in, wash away with that letter. He sat on the ground by the windows, and hugged his knees tightly to his chest.

Father Khalid, disturbed at the boy's expression, snatched the note, and read quickly, trying to get a glimpse into his daughter's mind. What he found there bothered him no end.

He felt betrayed by both his children. Behrooz should have known better. Yet, he felt a deep regret that Maya was unforgivably manipulative and hostile towards the boy.

Outside, Mother Dianne was beside herself, sobbing loudly as she scrambled around the kitchen deciding on the menu for the day. The twins had just gotten out of bed and weren't aware yet of what had transpired, so they were looking at their mother in confusion. Saba became particularly upset and started crying on account of her mother's tears.

Father Khalid knew that Mother Dianne regretted his bringing Behrooz home. Though she loved the boy, she considered it a grave mistake. A distinct error in judgement.

He could not confide in his wife that his main regret was not bringing Behrooz into The Yard, but rather not quelling his daughter's diabolical ways. He could not confess to her or anyone else how he longed to protect the boy from all his suffering in The Yard, and how he had failed at doing so, and how he had suffered as a result.

On more than one occasion he'd considered keeping Behrooz away from Maya. But intuitively he feared that a separation would have made them closer. Nor could he keep Behrooz from the only friend he'd known. He couldn't yield to treating him like a criminal, or ever regret having him. These thoughts he kept to himself.

Now, having read the note, he found he had no answers for the boy. No words to comfort him. For he himself needed direction. Continue like all was well...normal even? Berate his daughter on Behrooz's account or vice versa? He felt that each foreseeable option would make things worse. For the first time in his life, he decided to do nothing.

He crumpled the letter and threw it in the wastebasket in Maya's bathroom. Saba, having been informed of what happened, barged in, and glared at Behrooz, 'I hate you!' she said, her face streaked with tears. Father Khalid wrestled her away, warning her to watch her mouth.

*

Hours later, Sara arrived at the house, and asked for Behrooz. They had a date with her father that evening, and Behrooz was supposed to be dressed. Father Khalid welcomed the distraction as the boy had not left Maya's room the entire day. He pushed the door open, and was startled at what he found.

Behrooz had curled into a ball on the floor, by the window, rocking back and forth. He didn't respond to Father Khalid's entrance or entreaties. He blocked his ears. The crickets were chirping again outside, and it was too loud. Too loud.

PART THREE

13

The Newborn

'Daddy, can we go in now?' asked Asim, expectantly. He was sitting on a spongy sofa which was jammed against the louvered wall of the hospital waiting room. His hands were wrapped around his knees, which were pulled to his chest.

'We have to wait on the doctor,' said Behrooz. He sat across from Asim, on the edge of his chair. 'Daddy can't go in unless the doctor says it's okay.'

'Mr Ali?' Dr Mormon Stanley hobbled into the waiting room. The doctor's spectacles were perched on the tip of his nose, making his long sideburns and round face stand out uncertainly.

'Yes?' Behrooz stood anxiously. 'What news, doctor?'

'Congratulations. It's a girl!'

Behrooz and Asim locked eyes for an instant and bolted towards the delivery room. It was about time someone told them what was going on! They heard the baby's screams as they approached and intense relief washed over father and son.

When they arrived, Sara was holding the pink, crinkled newborn close to her chest, blue sheets scrunched up below her. Asim stood in awe at his mother's side whilst Behrooz kissed her forehead and proudly examined his new daughter.

Though Asim had been waiting for the baby for months on end, he could not help but feel a twinge of jealousy as his father took the newborn in his arms. He turned up his nose as he caught a whiff of wet earth. He wondered if his sister would always smell so funny, and thought she looked gross, all wrinkly and bald.

Nurse Terry insisted that Sara be allowed to rest, and took the wrapped bundle away. The delivery was not an easy one; the baby could not be born naturally and her patient had eventually delivered via Caesarean section. She wanted Sara to wash up and have lots of time to recuperate from her ordeal.

Behrooz did not take his eyes off the baby until she was carried away. He was so proud of Sara, and impressed by her braveness. He could not imagine what she must have gone through in the past hours. She did not want him present for any of it, so the doctors had already checked the baby's vitals, delivered the placenta and stitched her up, before he was invited in. He squeezed her hand tenderly, knowing that she'd be in pain for the next three weeks at least.

Sara's pregnancy had gone well until the ninth month. They'd expected smooth sailing, as it had been with Asim, but that did not happen. She became very uncomfortable two weeks before she was due. She could barely sleep or eat. They tried natural labour-inducing methods but nothing worked.

Behrooz took her for walks in the recreational ground near their home in Lange Park, a nice residential area very different from The Yard, and gave her castor oil mixed with orange juice as recommended by her doctor. But the baby seemed willful.

It was laughter that finally did the trick.

Behrooz had indulged Asim in a Nerf gun battle right after breakfast, the morning Sara went into labour. The boy had had a love relationship with these guns since he'd turned four, and practiced shooting lessons every day. The two were hiding from each other, swiftly turning corners, pointing their guns forward, until Asim outdid his father, catching him in the leg. Behrooz refused to admit defeat and threw a big round ball with rainbow stripes (a present from Father Khalid, which the boy loved) at Asim, who pelted it right back. But the distraction was enough for Behrooz to send an underhand blow.

'No fair,' said Asim, rolling over with laughter. 'You tricked me, Daddy!' Behrooz motioned the boy to his lap. 'That's what daddies do. How else would I win you, huh?'

Sara shook her head at them from the kitchen corridor. 'I can understand Asim,' she said to Behrooz, 'but what's your excuse?'

Father and son registered the same thought. No one dared interrupt their shenanigans. They bulldozed the unsuspecting Sara, tiny foam bullets falling off her arms and legs. Asim doubled over with laughter, 'We got you, Mummy!'

And though Sara was usually reserved, she found the foolery of her two men contagious, and started laughing too. She ran up the staircase to find a Nerf gun. She needed to show them how dead on she was, and put an end to their teasing. She'd gotten to the top of the stairs when a gush of water rushed out from beneath her.

She yelled for Behrooz as she maneuvered her way to the bathroom and turned on the shower. Behrooz followed the thumping sound of water and was astonished to find his wife standing inside the tub, her skirt pulled to one side, and a pinkish liquid seeping down her legs.

'My water broke!'

'It's pink!' said Behrooz. The laughter had drained from his face.

'Get me to a hospital!' Sara stepped decidedly out of the tub, one leg deliberately in front of the other, and marched passed her husband. 'Now!'

'Asim, get your mom's hospital bag,' said Behrooz. 'We're leaving now.'

'Got ya!' said Asim, shooting a dart at his father's chest.

'Get your mother's bag, now!'

Asim, suddenly convinced of the seriousness of the event, grabbed the bag and followed his parents out the door and into the car. He wondered at his mom's mouth which was puffed out like a goldfish; his father was driving faster than he'd ever seen, screaming at other drivers though his window was up.

'Go, Dad!' said Asim. He shot red foam bullets against the window pane. Recouped them, and fired again.

At the hospital Behrooz was told that Sara was going to have an impromptu Caesarean. She'd requested that he and Asim wait outside until the baby was delivered. The last thing she wanted was for Behrooz to see her all bloody and screaming.

In the waiting room Behrooz had explained to Asim what was going on and the child was instantly worried for his mother.

Behrooz was now grateful that the delivery went well, and

thankful that his wife was no longer in pain. He and Sara had waited so long for the baby. He had been there for every doctor's visit, poking Sara's belly to see the baby's heartbeat skyrocket on the monitor screen. He had read to the baby every night and rejoiced in her every movement.

When Sara cleaned up and got comfortable again, he and Asim snuggled up with the new mummy until she fell asleep.

*

Father Khalid, Mother Dianne and the twins, were anxious to see the newborn, who had been taken to the nursery by the time they arrived. They ran helter-skelter though the maternity ward corridors until they found the very room in which she was housed. Nurse Terry was at hand to point out their baby, who had a tiny mole on her nose bridge and wore a wrist band that read 'Nisa'.

'My precious granddaughter…so beautiful,' said Mother Dianne, cooing at the newborn behind the glass pane. Father Khalid beamed with pride. He'd been waiting a long time for his second granddaughter. And wasn't she adorable!

Father Khalid loved his family above all else, and felt a powerful sense of hope that this little angel was going to bring everyone together once more. It had been a long time since he'd seen Zia and even longer since he'd seen Maya. His heart was bruised with the knowledge that he had not seen Maya since the day she left The Yard, seven years ago.

Mother Dianne still suffered from that emptiness; a void they shared together. He knew that she missed their family terribly, and that she would give anything to have everyone together under one roof, even for one day.

She had suggested that Behrooz and Sara return to The Yard. She'd presented the case that Sara would need all the help she could get with the newborn during the summer, while Asim was at home for the school holidays, and that the doctors warned that Sara's body was weak and would require a lot of rest.

'It doesn't bother me,' said Mona, when Mother Dianne asked her input. The teenager smacked her red lips together and peered into her compact mirror. 'I'm not staying here for much longer, remember? I'm starting college in the fall.'

Saba rolled her eyes. She knew that her twin was not yet accepted into any college in the United States, and could not understand why the girl chose that country when her two sisters were in London.

'Don't you want to be with Zia?' she'd asked.

'I want to be where I can be free for once without someone looking over me,' Mona said. 'Could you imagine Zia? Mona this... Mona that...I can't think of it.'

Saba herself had not yet decided her near future; but she knew that it wasn't in The Yard; and that her mother was bracing for an empty nest. She was sensitive to her mother's misgivings, and hoped to make things as easy as possible for her.

Mother Dianne pressed her forehead against the nursery glass. 'She's so pinkie and cutie.' She traced the contours of the baby on the pane. 'I love her already.'

'I think she has Sara's eyes,' said Mona. 'See how they're turned upwards?'

'You can never tell with children,' said Mother Dianne. 'They change so much in the younger years.' She recalled how round and plump the twins were when they were born, though for some reason she'd expected each to be half a baby.

'No, she definitely has Sara's eyes. That's no mistake.' Mona hugged her mom around her waist. 'Just like I have yours.'

Father Khalid smiled. 'I think she's right.' He felt certain. This baby was just what they needed to bring his family together once more; some of them, at least.

*

Sara and Behrooz arrived at The Yard one week later with both children and red Wilson luggage in tow. Mother Dianne had outdone herself preparing for them. She'd outfitted Behrooz's old room with new drapes and linens, and even changed the mattress. She wanted the room to feel different from his childhood space and more like a fresh start.

She'd already decided to expand the room to include a nursery should the couple wish to stay on. And she hoped they would.

Sara's tummy was still very sore and tender after the Caesarean, so Mother Dianne confined her to bed immediately after her arrival, with the exception of approved and scheduled afternoon walks which were recommended by her doctor.

She helped Sara pack away her bags, ironed her clothes, designated drawers to each set of items, and attended to towels and extra linens. More importantly, she kept her grandson out of trouble, whilst the new mummy took care of the newborn.

Although the boy was particularly active, she learnt to keep up. She played Nerf gun battles with him, made him eat when he wasn't hungry, read him books to get him to stay still, and comforted him when he was missing his daddy.

He clung to her legs as she attended to the housework or any other business, and asked a myriad of questions while he was at it, like, 'Grandma, how do planes fly without flapping their wings?' He had his father's inquisitive mind.

Sara, too, came to rely more and more on her mother-in-law, as Behrooz's job kept him away for even longer hours. She didn't feel guilty as she knew that the woman needed her and Asim just as much.

Behrooz worked at the Archeological Centre in the capital, the Port of Spain, about thirty minutes north-west of The Yard; he rose before sunrise to beat the morning traffic and returned late in the evening. He loved his job, which required him to excavate old artefacts and re-map the nation's history, as well as teach that history to the new breed of high school teachers.

'The Caribs and the Arawaks weren't the first ones here,' he'd say. 'That's just another high school myth.' He'd even won a certificate award that Mother Dianne framed and kept in the entranceway of their home.

Sara herself had been a housewife since she and Behrooz eloped six years earlier in a secret ceremony with only themselves, and the Calcutta Masjid Imam. 'This Imam does those type of weddings,' said Nura, her sister. Sara had heeded this advice and managed to convince Behrooz of this recourse.

Both their parents believed that it was too soon for them to wed; they were mistrustful that Sara was the rebound girlfriend. So the couple managed to keep their marriage a secret for one month before they told their families, and it was months after that before they secured their parents' blessings.

*

Sara awoke crabby and exhausted. It was a rainy Tuesday morning, and four days since her family had moved back into The Yard. But in that second, she could not remember where she was. Then, she realised that she was missing her daughter.

She strolled into the living room. 'Where's Nisa?' Her mind refocused.

Mother Dianne had just come up from the laundry area, Asim in tow. 'Is something wrong, darling?'

Sara rubbed her eyes. 'Didn't sleep much. Where's she?'

'She's in her crib, in your room. Didn't you see her?' said Mother Dianne. 'I didn't hear the baby crying last night. I thought for sure you would have gotten some rest.'

Sara headed back into her room, and there was her little bundle in her pink sleeper, sound asleep on her tummy. She felt relieved. How had she not seen her there before?

She climbed back into her bed and fell asleep. Twenty minutes later she awoke again, to the baby's wails. She took the newborn onto the bed and plopped a nipple into the child's mouth. The crying stopped. Ha! she thought. Silence at last.

Mother Dianne entered and sat on the bed next to her. 'I heard her crying.' She reached out to rub the baby's back.

'She's just hungry.' Didn't her mother-in-law know she could handle it?

Mother Dianne continued to massage the baby. 'Maybe I can give her her bath today?' She was worried that Sara hadn't eaten any breakfast. She'd prepared tomato choka, which had gotten cold and remained on the kitchen table. 'So you'd get the chance to eat something.' Mother Dianne firmly believed in breakfast.

'No. I'll do it,' said Sara. She wanted to feel like the capable person she was. Hadn't she done all this before? 'I just feel a little exhausted.'

'You do look tired.' That was an understatement. Aside from the obvious dark-grey bags under the girl's eyes, she seemed barely coherent. 'Give her to me a bit, and get some rest?'

Sara was tempted to be rid of the baby altogether, so she could relax and do all the things she pleased. This thought seemed so unnatural to her that she clung even more strongly to the newborn. 'I am fine!' she said. The corners of her eyes raised defiantly. 'I mean, I can handle it.'

'Okay.' Mother Dianne had the feeling that Sara was not fine at all. The girl was too reluctant to leave the baby even for a minute, seemed completely exhausted, unusually crabby, and anxious even.

But when she mentioned her concerns to her husband he did not take it too seriously. He reasoned that Mother Dianne herself took a few weeks to recuperate from her last pregnancy with the twins. She'd been just as irascible and he'd borne the brunt of it.

So Sara spent the days isolated in her room. The new baby felt different from Asim at that age. She would spit up often, cry constantly, and would not sit well for feedings and even sometimes rejected milk altogether. Sara was constantly trying to figure out how to soothe her.

Behrooz became concerned in good measure when he arrived home on a Friday evening, a little later than usual (he had a department meeting with some colleagues), and discovered that Sara had fallen asleep so deeply that she did not hear the baby crying. He picked up his daughter and tried to comfort her. There was nothing he could do; she needed to be fed, and she was not able to drink from a bottle just yet. He asked Mother Dianne's advice.

'Try squeezing some cucumber juice,' she said. 'And put some drops in her mouth. That should do it.' But the drops of juice did not satisfy the child. He had to wake his wife.

Behrooz felt guilty. He knew that he should be home more often, but his boss was always on his case. He considered whether he should join the family business. He'd never shown any interest in that direction, and hated the thought of leaving his job, but he had to put family first. More than anything, he needed that flexibility with his wife and children. He resolved to talk it over with Father Khalid the next day.

14

Father Khalid

*B*ehrooz stood at the kitchen counter whipping six raw eggs into a froth. The non-stick frying pan was already heated. 'Where's the butter?' He made scrambled eggs and French toast for Asim every Saturday morning. His son thought that he was the best chef in the whole Yard, and had no idea that breakfast-making was the aggregate of his father's culinary skills.

'Supposed to be in the dairy compartment.' Sara peered into the double door refrigerator. 'Oh, here it is. It was under the pizza box. Why is an empty pizza box in the fridge?'

'The garbage doesn't go out until Monday.'

'So?' said Sara.

'So there's still one slice left. Why would I leave it to fester in the trash two whole days?'

'So it won't take up space in the fridge, maybe.' Sara stared at him, bewildered. 'You're disrupting my system.'

Behrooz sighed. He knew her systems all too well. The juices, bottles, eggs and cereals were placed on the very top shelf, with condiments on the door. Breads were always on the middle shelf. And you dared not leave pasta or rice in the cupboards. 'Don't you know they'd get weevils?' she'd say.

Sara set out placemats by the bar stools and three glasses of freshly squeezed orange juice. Once her husband was finished with the first batch of eggs, she loaded a plate and shoved it towards Asim. 'Eat up. Maktub class starts in twenty minutes.'

The boy ripped his toast into bite-sized pieces. 'I'm not going.' He'd used all his arguments in the past not to attend Maktub.

He didn't like learning to read strange letters that weren't in the alphabet even.

'Seriously? We have to go through this again?'

One ripened tear dripped into the boy's whole wheat bread. He stopped eating altogether.

'You want Grandma to see you crying?'

'Why is he crying?' said Mother Dianne. The delicious smell from the kitchen had beckoned her.

Mona followed right behind and sat across from her nephew. 'Lots of butter on my toast!'

Sara pulled some extra plates from the cupboards and set them out. 'It's the usual Maktub drama.'

Asim looked to his grandmother for sympathy.

'Can't help you there, sonny boy.'

'Don't want to pray,' said Asim.

'Hah! He's turning out just like Maya,' said Mona.

Silence.

'She used to say that Miss Grace came from the devil, remember?'

More silence.

'Okay, then! You people are so touchy!'

Behrooz scraped eggs into the newcomers' plates. 'Honestly, I don't see why he has to go. He's only four.'

'Honey, it's important to start at this age,' said Sara. She passed the toast and a stick of butter to her in-laws. 'Kids can be influenced the moment they start school. This would give him proper grounding.'

'I never went,' said Behrooz. 'I have grounding.' He sat next to Mother Dianne and poured orange juice down his throat.

'I'd back Sara on this one,' said Mother Dianne. 'The Yard is too small. He'd be exposed to more kids, and learn to get along better with others. He needs the exposure.'

Mona had already devoured her breakfast. 'Yes, Mother. It's good for kids to stand on their own two feet.'

Her mother eyed her warily.

'Asim, go wash up!' said Sara.

'I got in,' Mona continued. 'Vancouver. University of British Columbia. I got a partial schol.'

'I thought we'd decided you'd stay with Zia?' said Mother Dianne.

Mona looked at her mother. 'Dad told me...he promised that if I got this schol, he'd let me go.'

'Mona, that's great news!' said Sara.

'I didn't tell my twin,' Mona confided to both women. 'I want to be the one, okay?'

Mother Dianne could not think of a way to bend Mona to her will. She could not argue with a scholarship. She'd have to deal with the girls being gone, and in different directions at that.

'Asim, I said go wash up,' said Sara. She was losing her touch. The boy, no matter how unwillingly, always listened to her.

Asim zoomed around the rectangular dining area. 'Catch me, Daddy!'

'Asim, now!' said Behrooz.

He charged past his father's legs. 'Can I stay home, Daddy? Pleeeaaase?'

'No you can't!' said Sara, sending her husband a scathing look.

Then, the baby started wailing as though she sensed she was being excluded. Sara was familiar with this particular cry. She hastened to their room and grabbed up her bundle. 'You're hungry aren't you? Don't worry, Mummy's here...' She shut the door.

Sara forgot all about Asim attending Maktub.

And neither Asim nor Behrooz reminded her.

*

'No, Mom, we're just having something small,' said Sara. She'd finally gotten a moment to invite her parents to the baby's Aquiqah.

'No, I didn't invite the whole Jamaat. It's just family, Mom, that's how they do it here.'

She wrung a straight lock of hair around her index finger. 'Yes, just this family, and you and Dad.' She paused, listening. 'I know we have certain people...I know it's always twenty-two extras, but things change, Mom.' She listened a few more seconds. 'We just want something small. I don't want to inconvenience Mother Dianne.'

'Okay,' she said once more, and hung up.

'How did they take it?' asked Behrooz.

'I don't like to disappoint them. I mean just like this family has its ways, so does mine.'

'Well invite them all.'

'I can't invite them all. Do you have any idea how many people that would be? I would have to double the catering, and the chairs, order more chairs, and the desserts are already frozen...don't you know?'

'Okay, it was just a suggestion. I mean, so we'll have less desserts, so what?'

'So what? What do we say to people who did not get any? That they are less important in our daughter's lives? And the gifts, what if a person with a really expensive gift ends up getting no food? No, we can't just invite them all!'

'I'm just trying to keep everyone happy,' said Behrooz. 'They are her grandparents, too.'

'It's too late. Just two days before? Not possible.'

'There's two whole days.'

'No,' said Sara, sending her husband a withering glance. 'I hate last minute.' She walked towards the baby's crib. The newborn opened her squinty dark-brown eyes; her little pink face was crinkled, and her fingers were in a bunch. 'Yes, you agree with Mummy, don't you?'

'All right,' said Behrooz wearily.

Sara didn't hear him. 'You know, I think I forgot to burp her earlier. She could get gas!'

'She seems fine, don't worry.'

Sara patted the baby's back with the base of her palm in an attempt to burp her; the infant began a high-pitched wail. Sara sat on the side of the bed and held the baby to her chest. The child would neither drink nor be comforted. Instead, her cries reached an octave higher each time.

'Her tummy is so hard!' The baby had suckled countless times for the day; she'd slept, and had been cuddled. What could be wrong?

'Let me feel.'

Sara turned away. 'Go through the guestlist. The ones I've already invited are ticked.'

'Let me feel her tummy.'

Sara was resolute. 'You can help me by calling up Aunt Heba and Aunt Lulu.'

Behrooz reluctantly picked up the phone and dialled Aunt Heba. He was forced to talk above the baby's screams. 'Sara and I are having the baby's Aquiqah this weekend. Can you and the boys make it?'

'Things good over there?' asked Aunt Heba. 'Why the baby crying so?'

'She's okay,' said Behrooz. 'Her tummy is a bit hard. We don't know why.'

'She might have colic,' offered Aunt Heba. 'Zaki had that when he was little.'

'Colic?' said Behrooz. He didn't remember Asim having colic.

'The baby does not have colic!' said Sara.

But she was later forced to consider that Aunt Heba might be right. Baby Nisa didn't let up on the screaming. She'd pull her knees towards her chest, and arch her back as if in pain; her fist remained clenched. She refused sleep; not even the comforting touch of her mother could soothe her.

Mother Dianne dispatched the driver to get gripe water. 'It's the same bottle I used for my children,' she said. She comforted her daughter-in-law. 'It will go away soon. Colic goes away completely after the first few months.'

Behrooz became more certain that he needed to be closer to home. His daughter was proving to a handful, Asim was becoming more distant and irritable due to the amount of attention the women bestowed on the baby; and though Sara would not readily admit it, she needed his help.

*

Behrooz waited on Father Khalid to arrive home. Father Khalid worked every day, including weekends. On a Sunday he'd work for half the day, and could usually be relied upon to attend Sunday lunch. But he'd missed lunch this time. And Mother Dianne had learnt not to delay meals on his account. The rest of her family was fed; and she busied herself with her grandson.

Behrooz thought that Father Khalid seemed wearier of late.

The man's eyes were more wrinkled, and his features creased and drawn. He pondered what Father Khalid would say about his inquiry, and mentally rehearsed his proposition. He would not ask for a big salary or anything like that. The important thing was that he'd be close to home.

Father Khalid seemed surprised that Behrooz was waiting for him. Usually guilt and shame lingered between them like a stench.

Father Khalid felt contrite. He knew that time could not mend all hurts; and it did not mend Behrooz's. It just made them more livable. He had not been able to shield his son from harm, or bring their family together. He was a man of action. Yet, seven years had passed, and he had accomplished nothing.

He was grateful to Sara. She had found Behrooz abandoned and broken, and patched him up again. She had done what none of them could. She'd stepped in when he'd failed.

Behrooz detected the helplessness in Father Khalid's stares; and instinctively stayed away. He did not want to cut any deeper into the old man's wounds. Or feel his own. But time had slipped by. And he now had more pressing concerns—a family of his own, who needed him.

Father Khalid would give him a chance. He felt certain.

'I was hoping we could talk,' said Behrooz.

Father Khalid dished his lunch from containers laid out on the kitchen countertop. 'I've got all evening.' The place smelt like 'Trini' stew.

Behrooz put the leftovers in the refrigerator and sat across from Father Khalid at the dining table. 'Mother Dianne mentioned that you might need some help over at the shop...?'

'Yes. Someone applied today.' Father Khalid popped a baby carrot into his mouth. 'Seems like he can do the job.'

Behrooz wondered if he was too late. 'What does the job entail exactly?'

'To help me manage purchasing, inventory, work flow...' Father Khalid looked confused. 'Why?'

''Cause, I think I know someone who can do it better.'

'A friend of yours? Because I pretty much offered this person the job already.'

Behrooz placed his hands on the table and interlocked his fingers. 'I was hoping it could be me.'

An intrigued smile formed across Father Khalid's face. 'You know it would call for a lot of long hours with your old man, right?'

Behrooz grinned. 'I was counting on that.'

'Yeah?'

'I wanted to be closer to Sara and the children.' His eyes touched Father Khalid's. 'It's a bonus to be closer to you, too.'

Father Khalid was pleased. 'Good. Tomorrow, 8 a.m.' He felt an ease in his shoulders that he had not felt for a long time.

'I have to give two weeks' notice,' said Behrooz. 'Unfortunately.'

He was finally making things right with his son. 'What's two weeks, then?'

*

In the evening Asim searched for Father Khalid, turning corners carefully with his Nerf gun. The old man was hiding, he was sure. He turned sharply into the living room and spotted his grandfather stretched out on the grey recliner.

'Got ya!' said Asim, firing a string of neon darts, hitting his target on the chest and shoulders.

Father Khalid did not respond.

Asim moved closer, sure that Father Khalid was playing pretend.

Then he saw tiny bubbles rising out of his grandfather's mouth, and when he looked at the man's face he was panic-stricken. Father Khalid's eyes were open and colourless beneath drooped lids.

Asim catapulted to his parents' room. 'Daddy, it's Grandpa!'

'What's wrong?' asked Behrooz.

'Grandpa's not playing!' said Asim.

'Maybe Grandpa is tired,' said Behrooz.

'No, Grandpa is blowing bubbles with his mouth.'

Behrooz followed Asim's lead into the living room, and was staggered by what he found.

Father Khalid's face was still warm. There was colour in his skin, but his body was twisted unnaturally upon the chair; his legs were flopped to the sides. There was no heave of his chest, or raise of the brow. The man wasn't alive.

'Call for an ambulance!' Behrooz yelled. Sara came out on

hearing the commotion. 'Now!' He was frantically feeling for a pulse. There was none.

Behrooz blocked the man's nose and blew breath into his mouth. He compressed his chest for any shred of life left.

His mind wavered to the little wooden shack where Father Khalid found him, bundled and lifeless. The scene replayed in his head like a bad dream. Father Khalid pulling him from the shack. Father Khalid's kind eyes. Father Khalid, without whom he would not be alive.

He was on four hundred compressions when the ambulance arrived. The medic explained that there was nothing to be done. Father Khalid was too long gone.

That night, Sara cancelled the Aquiqah, and planned a funeral.

15

The Facade

*B*ehrooz looked on at the funeral scene below. It reminded him of his very first moments in The Yard; he'd peered out the same window, when Aunt Livy's body had lain beneath. But now, it was Father Khalid in the coffin, frosty and hard.

That day he'd felt sadness, slightly abated by the possibility of a new life. Today, there was only sadness. Asim and Sara emerged from their room, both elegant in a dazzling shade of black. Asim, wearing a suit for the first time, Sara, in a kaftan that he'd never seen before. But not even Sara's smile could melt the cold in his stomach.

The Yard had been a hustle and bustle all morning. Chairs were set out, theatre style, under white tents, and Aunt Heba attempted to usher guests to seats. Aunt Lulu ran around offering a tea plate and drinks. The gathering was the largest he'd seen in the courtyard and seemed under-catered. Persons he did not recognise, perhaps Father Khalid's clients as well as associates from mosques, temples and churches, wore somber faces. No doubt, they grieved for the man whose kindness knew no bounds.

The latecomers lingered about, hoping to find a vacant spot. Some topee-clad men preferred to stand in the gateway and line the streets. They seemed a conversational bunch, while Behrooz found it hard to utter a word.

The twins emerged, and the family was ready to descend the steps to the forlorn ceremony that would take their father away forever. Only Mother Dianne was missing.

Sara went to find her. Mother Dianne had been silent and remote since she heard the news. She'd curled up on the sofa that

stood at the bottom of her bed, tangled up in her clothes, and his.
She barely spoke or ate and even seemed to have forgotten Asim
and the baby. She preferred to grieve alone. She kept whispering
to those who came around, 'It's going to be so hard now, so hard.'

Sara took her by the arm and led her towards the others. 'It's
going to be okay,' she said to her mother-in-law. 'Let's just deal
with all this and get it over with. People have come from all over
the country.'

All six descended the stairs in procession, as if Mother
Dianne were the Bride of Death, the others her bridesmaids
and groomsmen. Mother Dianne's face registered contempt. It
felt ridiculous to be seen, to publicly demonstrate her grief. Her
husband would not have wanted that. He would have wanted her
to appear strong and give courage to others. She tried to muster
some, holding her head high and absently nodding at those who
whispered condolences.

'Zia and Maya made it on a flight,' said Saba, to no one in
particular. 'They were on standby all night, they should be here
soon.' It was customary to bury the dead as early as possible; the
process waited on no one.

They all took their seats in the front row. And Mother Dianne
felt even more ludicrous, as though she had a VIP seat to her
husband's funeral.

The Imam had already begun his sermon. 'And each soul shall
have a taste of death,' he said. 'Then shall ye be brought back to
your lord…'

Mother Dianne drifted off.

'He alone is the one who gives life, and it is he who takes off
life…'

She turned her face towards the sky. She did not want to think
of death, or beyond; she wanted the light on her face, the breeze
in her hair.

'The angel of death will come, and on that day, you will recall
your deeds…'

To be alone on a sandy beach. Yes, that was it. Streaming
sunlight and endless sand. In her peripheral vision she saw Zia.
Zia? Mother Dianne looked sideways towards the shuffle.

Zia had arrived; she was maneuvering past everyone; they were clearing a path for her. Her face was red and splotchy. Maya was following behind; her nose was so red, it looked about to fall off. Mother Dianne felt Zia's arms around her in a familiar, comforting way. But she could not focus on that right now. Could not bear to think of how long Zia had not seen her father. She did not want to think of Maya, and the regret she must feel. No, she could not think of them.

Father Khalid's body was rolled out in front of her, cleaned and shrouded in white linen. Did his brothers bathe him in sweet water? He would have wanted that. But his eyes were closed now. He was asleep, she thought. Peacefully asleep.

Alia wheeled Grandmother Sakina to the coffin. Her grandmother was the only one sobbing loudly. 'A mother should never have to bury her son...should never have to...' Alia patted the old woman's long, grey streaks to comfort her.

People stood in a neat line viewing the body in turn and saying their final goodbyes. Soon after, another line formed. Men in spotless white kurtas and round topees stood for prayer in throngs. The Imam stood to the front of the congregation.

They will sing him to heaven, thought Mother Dianne.

Right after the prayer, Behrooz hoisted one end of the coffin, whilst Uncle Ansar and Zaki held the other. The men would witness the burial; the women weren't allowed. 'Mark the spot,' Mother Dianne had said to Behrooz. 'I want to be buried next to him, when my turn comes.'

*

It was Asim who found Behrooz, later that night, sitting atop the familiar low wall in the orchard. 'You all right, Daddy?'

Still, after all those years, it was this place, this melancholy space, laced with memories, that comforted Behrooz; and it was just like his son to intuit that.

'I am now.' Behrooz hoisted Asim unto the wall. 'Why don't you sit here a while with Daddy?'

'Is Grandpa going to be all right?'

'Grandpa is in heaven, my boy.'

'I hope heaven is a nice place. Maybe one day I can go there too.'

'You,' said Behrooz, 'must always be where your daddy is.'

There was something wondrous about the boy, who was bound to his father in an inexplicable way. 'Okay, Daddy.'

Behrooz held his son tightly to his body.

Father Khalid had loved him as his own son, without having reason to. Loved him as much as he loved the little boy in his arms. Just as much.

*

Zia rose just after sunrise and started preparing breakfast for the family. She and Mother Dianne preferred the traditional sada roti; the rest of them opted for scrambled eggs and toast.

Maya woke just in time to brew tea and pour the drinks. She'd learnt to make a good cup of tea over the years. The hot beverage had kept her warm through many winters.

She gave a cup to everyone, except Sara, who didn't understand hot drinks in warm climates, and opted for cold orange juice instead.

Maya's eyes were still red. She felt groggy and listless. It had been a long time since she'd slept in her old room. The days seemed like an alternate reality. She was back in The Yard, and Father Khalid was gone, forever.

Never in all her imaginings did she picture home as she saw it now. The colours on the walls had changed. The soft pastels in the kitchen were replaced by rose red. The whole setting was remade with modern bar stools and stainless steel appliances.

And Mother Dianne had a full house.

She'd pictured two parents and two beautiful, grown girls getting ready to leave for college. She had forgotten, or perhaps completely erased the rest. There was Behrooz, married with children. The reality of it was a lot to absorb.

She'd never met Asim before, and felt odd when he called her 'Aunt Maya'. Really odd. But she could not allow her mind to linger on the reasons why; it was all in the past.

They were all getting to know each other again. And Maya felt hope. And regret. Overwhelming regret. The kind you couldn't shake.

She pulled plates and cutlery from the cupboard and drawers, in an effort to distract herself. She helped Zia set the table for eight.

The letter was still in her purse. The one addressed to Father Khalid, that she'd delayed mailing. She had contemplated dropping it in the post on countless occasions. Was it fear that paralysed her? She didn't want to face what she was coming home to, to see the consequences of her actions.

The letter read:

Dear Father,

I'm coming home in just two short months.

My flight is booked and this time I guarantee I'll make it.

I've completed my final exams and for the first time in years I have nothing to do with myself. Do you believe?

But that's not why I'm coming.

I've really missed you, more than you know. Every day I think of you and Mother and imagine what you might be doing. I think of the twins and long to see how they've changed. I imagine you all sitting around the kitchen table talking about what a character I am.

I don't blame you for being angry. I of all people know how you feel. Ironic isn't it? See, we both feel the same way. It was all my fault.

Rest assured that I'm paying the price for my actions. Call it karmic retribution?

Don't worry, I won't cause you any trouble when I'm there.

I love you so much, more than you know.

See you soon,

Maya

Would she have gotten on that plane? How many times before did she try? She didn't know. And now Father Khalid was gone. She yearned for another small chance to make things right, to say goodbye.

She could not have imagined the look on Mother Dianne's face at the funeral. The sad eyes with irises that stayed centred and focused, and lips that remained parted and seemingly impossible to close.

Her mother for once was quiet at the breakfast table. She did not obsess over who ate and who didn't or who needed refills.

There was something, someone missing from the home, and it weighed heavy in the air. Memories haunted every spot, and the chill of the wind coming through the kitchen window seemed to carry them around.

'More toast?' Zia asked Saba. The girl had been eating non-stop lately. She was the only one who had developed an increase in appetite, some type of coping mechanism that was lost on the others.

Saba took that as an invitation to ignore the stillness around her and start on her breakfast. 'I don't mind,' she said, biting into a slice of bread, and heaping a little more of everything unto her plate. They all followed her lead and started picking from their plates.

'Sugar?' Saba asked her twin, as she gulped her drink. Mona shook her head. Her stomach quivered at the thought of food. Even the thought of sweetened tea repulsed her.

'Mother, I know this is a bad time,' Sara said. All heads turned in her direction. Any distraction was welcome at this point.

'Behrooz and I have decided that we will leave The Yard,' she continued. 'It's crowded here now. You can't be bothered with helping us out at a time like this, and Asim misses home.'

'No,' said Mother Dianne. Her eyes were large and frightened, her face creased with sleep marks.

'No more changes,' she said. 'Not now. Stay a while.'

Sara nodded, dismayed that she had even dared to burden her mother-in-law with such news.

'For a little while longer,' said Behrooz.

'I'm going to have an empty nest soon,' said Mother Dianne. 'Stay as long as you like.'

Maya was yet to acknowledge Sara or Behrooz; she was still trapped in that barrel of guilt. She'd spotted Sara looking her way once, and the girl nodded in her direction. But Behrooz avoided her gaze completely. It was clear that he had much on his plate, but she wondered how long it would be before he spoke to her again.

He had barely even spoken to Zia since they arrived, yet she knew that they had kept in touch.

Zia was happy that Behrooz consented to stay on a while longer. She wanted to tell him how much she needed him there, how Mother Dianne needed him too; but Asim was a constant reminder that Behrooz had bigger priorities. And wasn't he adorable? Zia was instantly taken with him, and while he seemed scared of Maya, his eyes were fixed on her face. He wanted to sit right next to her, and allowed her to pat his back and break his toast into bite-sized pieces.

Zia passed around refills, but no one took up her offer. She collected plates and placed them in the sink.

'Mother, why don't you rest today?' she said. 'Maya and I have everything under control for later.'

'Later? They're coming? Seriously?' Mother Dianne had forgotten about the three-day tradition. For three nights after a person passed away, the bereaved family usually held a prayer session, open to well-wishers.

'Everyone will be expecting it,' said Zia. 'They're grieving too.'

Mother Dianne recalled that. Yes, Zia was right. There was a whole family in The Yard that would miss her husband, and they'd want to be together tonight. She was too weary though, to think of it. The twins took her back to her room, and spent most of the day there, to ensure that their mother got her rest, and forgot for a while that someone was missing beside her in her bed.

Behrooz and Sara retreated to their room, and spent the rest of the day there, looking after Asim and the baby. The baby cried constantly. And when Sara emerged occasionally into the kitchen she looked exhausted.

'Can I help?' asked Maya. Sara seemed taken aback by the offer.

'I mean, I heard the baby crying,' said Maya. 'I know…I don't have any experience with babies, but I thought…maybe I could help out.'

'Uh…sure. Actually, if I could just get these sterilised.' Sara dropped a baby bottle and pacifier onto the countertop.

Zia, who had more experience with these things, and witnessed the scene with slight amusement, took over the task. Eventually the baby stopped crying. The silence was welcome.

*

The night took on a strange force. Everyone from The Yard was there in the open courtyard, except Grandmother Sakina who was not feeling well enough to leave her room. There were also a few people from Calcutta Masjid as well as some of Father Khalid's friends and employees.

The men sat by a long rectangular table with bowls of burning incense; fragrant smoke wafted throughout creating an almost mystical atmosphere. They opened their Arabic prayer books and each read aloud from a different part at once, making their recitation unintelligible. The women sat in scattered chairs facing them, fingers moving along tasbihs glorifying God. The Imam, after speaking about the punishment in the grave for wrongdoers, made a long closing duah, mentioning a plethora of saints and prophets known throughout history. Mother Dianne was relieved when it ended and retired then. Nonsensical questions about her well-being could wait.

After tucking her mother into bed, Zia went to visit Grandmother Sakina and took a reluctant Maya with her. The girl's memories of the old woman were harrowingly peculiar. Even after all these years Maya still recalled that spectre of grey hair, the outlandish and unending conversations, and curious objects that took on a life of their own in the woman's possession. Grandmother Sakina's room was bare and unchanged. Maya recognised the same old walker, its aluminum tubular frame jammed against the bottom of the bed; the blue, albeit slightly more dingy, plastic bowl next to the woman's nightstand; the layers of cloth in different shapes and textures that covered her mattress; and the round ball that she clasped in her hand and habitually squeezed.

Zia had heard that her grandmother could only walk with the aid of the walker now, and stayed in bed more and more. Alia visited the hapless woman on mornings; she'd fill the blue bowl and take it to her so that she could brush her teeth; she'd sponge her off in the bathroom; and return on evenings to ensure that she took all her prescription tablets.

'Salaam, Grandmother,' said Zia, gingerly greeting the old woman, and anxious that they were intruding on her rest.

'Salaam, salaam,' Grandmother Sakina replied, making a considerable effort to turn on her creaky bed and face them.

'Maya, that you girl?' Grandmother Sakina's dark-grey eyes were wide with surprise. 'How long now your Grandmother ain't laid eyes on you?'

'It's me, Grandmother,' said Maya.

'Come here, come closer.'

Maya stepped closer to the bed and patted her grandmother's oily strands of hair. 'I'm staying a while.'

'How long is a while girl?' said Grandmother Sakina. 'You come back to torment the boy after you left him?'

Maya was shocked at the question. It had not occurred to her that her grandmother still held that grudge. 'I came for my father's funeral.' She pulled her hand away. They were now as greasy and slippery as her mind.

I didn't come for Behrooz, she thought.

'Your father ain't see you in seven years. Seven years that man pine for you. And you never come to see him while he was alive. Now you come?

'You must have hear that the boy have a daughter now? And now you want to come to make trouble!'

Maya's eyes shifted. She blinked rapidly so that threatening tears would stay where they welled.

'Grandmother, that's enough, you hear?' said Zia. 'Rest now.'

'I disappointed in you,' Grandmother Sakina said pointedly to Zia.

Then her voice changed to a hushed whisper. 'You encouraging this? You encourage she with the boy, and then keep she away. Now you bring she back here again, when it was best she just stay where she was.'

The tears now freely glided down Maya's cheeks. Was it best she stayed where she was?

'Maya should be here,' said Zia. 'Father Khalid would have wanted her here.'

The old lady coughed. 'She didn't care he wanted her here the last seven years.' The cough soon turned into a racket.

Zia rubbed the woman's back rapidly, trying to soothe her. 'Rest now.'

'He gone,' the old woman choked. 'My son gone before me, and leave he old mother here, could barely walk. Why he had to go b'fore me? Why it couldn't be me? And this ungrateful girl. He give she life and she left him, and she left she grandmother. Why she come back here for?' Grandmother Sakina turned up her nose, and looked away. 'Go, yuh hear? I want nothing with you, yuh hear.'

Zia held her sister by the elbow, eager to guide her out of the room. She'd had enough. Maya had followed and stumbled out the doorway, when a disturbing thought occurred to her. 'Wait,' she said. 'Grandmother is right.'

Maya returned to the old lady's bedside and knelt so that they were face to face. She had left her family in pain. She could not expect instant forgiveness. Not even from her grandmother. She was an ingrate after all; her father deserved better.

Moreover, she knew about regret; the way it ate you up inside. Her grandmother was consumed by something equally destructive. Guilt.

The old woman felt guilty that she was alive, and her son wasn't. Maya was sure that her grandmother would have traded her life for her son's.

'It's okay,' she said. 'There was nothing you could do.'

The old woman's tears came soft and slow, then all at once. 'Wasn't his time.'

Zia looked on in surprise. For once, her sister and grandmother understood each other.

Later that night, Mother Dianne and her four daughters huddled together in Mother Dianne's king-sized bed. It had been a long day; fatigue descended hard and strong; no one stirred.

16

Father Khalid's Legacy

The alarm clock went off at 7 a.m. Behrooz had to get to the shop early. Father Khalid was always there on time. Not a minute later. He had to maintain the order of things.

Uncle Ansar was livid when Mother Dianne told him over the phone that Behrooz was taking over their branch of the upholstery. He had called to find out just that.

'He's not even family,' Uncle Ansar cautioned.

'Who did you think your brother would leave it to? The girls aren't interested. I can't run the place on my own right now. You and Khidr are consumed with your shop. The Heba boys? Yes, they are family. But Behrooz was his son!'

Uncle Ansar scoffed. 'You're just as stubborn as my brother was.' Mother Dianne, much to his surprise and hers, dropped the receiver, before he had a chance to say anything further.

Father Khalid saw Behrooz as his son; he wanted Behrooz to follow in his footsteps. He did not have to say it in his will. Mother Dianne knew his heart, and she dared any one of them to contest it.

Behrooz's chest tightened as he recalled Mother Dianne's end of the conversation, as well as the parts she'd filled in for him. After all these years, nothing had changed with Uncle Ansar, and probably never would.

He purposely grabbed a blue pin-striped shirt that reminded him of Father Khalid, and khaki pants, and carried them to the ironing board. Great, no starch, he thought. Perfectly ironed clothes would at least make him feel more in control of things.

He got into the shower early enough, but when he came back out he realised that he'd spent way too much time bathing.

'You're going to be late,' said Sara. She turned on the bed.

'I'm doing fine.' He kissed her forehead. 'Go back to sleep.' He vaguely remembered the baby crying during the night, so he knew she must be lacking rest.

'You should have ironed yesterday,' said Sara. 'I already put out your clothes.' She pointed to a crumpled heap on the chair next to their bed.

'Darn. I didn't see them.'

'You never see.' Wouldn't he have known that she couldn't sleep all these nights? That she had bad dreams…terrible dreams?

'What?'

'You don't observe.' In the dream, she'd given Nisa away. She couldn't produce milk for the child. Another couple came to claim her, and she gave her away; Sara felt happy because she didn't have to worry anymore.

'Sara, what are you talking about?' Why doesn't she say what she means? he thought. Then he scolded himself for thinking such things, when she was obviously exhausted and having a hard time as well.

The baby was sleeping for longer hours as the colic had more or less disappeared. So at least that was one less thing to worry about.

Sara slumped out of bed. 'Where is that tie, where is it?' She ruffled though his drawer. 'The blue one that goes with that shirt; it's your first day.'

'It's okay, I've already grabbed one,' said Behrooz. He had the feeling that this wasn't just about the tie. He knew that Sara was used to steering, and that now she was feeling a bit off course.

'But I had it here just yesterday.' She was pulling everything out of his tie drawer. 'I usually have everything colour-coded…'

'I know. And it's okay if you can't find it. The world is not going to fall apart. I will be fine today.'

Sara exhaled sharply and crawled into bed again. She lowered the temperature of the air conditioning, pulled up the covers and lay on her back.

Behrooz kissed her lightly on the forehead. He brushed the straight strands from her face and touched her cheek. 'See you later.'

Sara turned on her side and closed her eyes. She needed rest, but she wouldn't allow herself to fall asleep again.

*

Behrooz had asked Father Khalid if he could join the family business so he could spend more time at home. Little did he know that he'd end up running the place. Luckily, Father Khalid had employees who had been there for over fifteen years, from whose experience Behrooz could benefit.

He had never taken an interest in the shop, and was almost clueless about upholstering methods. There was a steep learning curve and a very short time to learn.

Kayo Mohammed was the longest standing employee. Behrooz knew this from a few award functions he'd attended with Father Khalid. So he was the obvious choice to give Behrooz his first tour in years.

Behrooz examined everything and everyone with a meticulous eye. It was what he was trained to do at his previous job. He inspected rolls of material, the sewing room, the carpentry building, and the tool room.

He was introduced to Seema, his secretary. Apparently she was new and had worked for Father Khalid a mere few days before his passing. Apart from answering the phone and running personal errands, she was responsible for logging all ongoing and pending jobs, and he went over them with her in great detail. He knew that he asked the staff a lot of obvious questions but he had to understand the running of the business in its totality.

After inspecting Seema's log he'd questioned her on an overdue job. He'd heard reports that the customer was not very pleased with their service. The problem, he discovered, was that they were out of stock on the particular fabrics and part components needed to complete the work.

He spoke to 'Ash' in purchasing—he soon discovered that most of the men had a nickname, and even Father Khalid did not recall their real names—for a budgetary report, and a list of all purchases made in the last year.

His update by the accounts department was not encouraging. The cost of supplies had increased in the last few years, making reupholstering furniture more expensive than it used to be, which meant that the customer would simply prefer to purchase something new for the same price.

Behrooz would have to convince them that they in fact would be getting a better deal, as a lot of the low-priced furniture manufacturers create their products using inferior materials that would last two years as opposed to well over ten. Further, each item produced at the shop would be unique, as opposed to being constructed on an assembly line.

Behrooz spent the rest of the week going through reports, making purchasing decisions, supervising production and seeking counsel on ongoing business matters. The days didn't seem long enough; he immediately forgave Father Khalid for all the family dinners he'd missed.

It was Saturday evening, and he was still at his desk, eyeing the paper work he couldn't get done during the week. All of his staff were gone, except for Kayo who seemed to remain with him out of concern. He found it hard to concentrate with the man keeping watch, and decided to wrap up. He did not want to keep any employee that late on the weekend, as he knew they had a 'no overtime' policy.

In reality, he yearned to see his wife and children. He pulled into the driveway under the dark sky and bolted upstairs. Sara was not in the common area. He found her in their bedroom. She looked like she did when he left that morning. She was in the same T-shirt, curled up on the bed, only she had a paperback in her hands. Behrooz gathered from the illustration on the cover that it was romance fiction.

The baby was sound asleep in the crib next to her. Behrooz could tell by the way her little tummy rose and fell. 'Sara, honey?'

Sara bookmarked her page and put the paperback down on the nightstand. She usually read before bed, but it wasn't an evening habit. 'You're late.'

'I'm sorry I'm late,' said Behrooz. He took off his shoes and loosened his tie. 'Thought you'd know that the first couple of weeks would be like this.'

Sara sighed. 'Thought you were supposed to be home more often.'

Behrooz kissed his wife on her cheek. 'I wish.'

'Kiss the edges.'

'Huh?'

'Kiss the edges of my face,' said Sara. 'Don't like kisses on my cheek. Makes my face feel wet.'

'I never knew that.'

'Now you do.' She rubbed her face against his sleeve.

'Where's Asim?'

'Haven't seen him since lunch. He must be with Mother Dianne.'

'You haven't seen him?'

'I said he's with Mother Dianne.'

'You said you think he's with Mother Dianne.'

'You know how hard it is, looking after the both of them?' Sara confessed. 'I have to rely on others to see to Asim because I can't give him the attention he needs. I never thought it would be this way, but it is. And I hate it.'

Behrooz was saddened that he'd troubled his wife. 'Mother Dianne is here for you; she'll take care of Asim. You just need to focus on yourself and the baby.'

Sara's eyes were downcast. 'But you come in here blazing guns because I don't know where our boy is. I feel bad enough already. Guilty enough.' She looked at him. 'I'm not Superwoman, okay? I may seem like Superwoman but I'm not.'

'I know you're not. And I feel bad, too.' Behrooz sat towards the edge of the bed. 'I would love to be here all day, but I can't. I have a job. I am responsible for Father Khalid's legacy now. And that's rough.'

They both knew how Father Khalid struggled each day to keep the business afloat and make it profitable; and that he wanted his children to keep it in the family, always.

'But you're also responsible for us!' Sara knew that Behrooz had to fulfil his obligations, but her need was also great.

It wasn't just about dealing with the kids. She had gotten close to her mother-in-law over the years, but when Mother Dianne was with her daughters in this time of grief, she felt the odd one out. She didn't want them to see her weaknesses.

'And I'm trying my best. Sara, ever since we had the baby… you've not been yourself. I mean, what do you want me to do?'

Asim had come in from the living room and held out a paper plane. 'Mummy! Look what Aunty Zia made me.' He glided the plane across the room. It fell at his father's feet.

Behrooz was about to comment on how wonderful the paper object was when Sara snapped, 'Mummy is having a time out, Asim. It's Daddy's turn.' Sara turned on her side and closed her eyes.

'Go tell aunty "thank you",' said Behrooz. Asim left the room, less than thrilled about his parents' reaction. He looked for his aunt to make him a boat next.

Behrooz crawled into bed with his wife, and hugged her around the waist. 'If we're going to take turns with Asim you'd better give me the schedule.'

Sara traced her finger along the Caesarean scar that was hidden under her T-shirt. Didn't her husband understand her at all? That she needed him. Not Mother Dianne, not anyone, only him. She shoved his hand away. 'Don't want to be touched.'

Behrooz knew that the Caesarean had left both physical and emotional scars on his wife. He also knew that life was throwing them lemons at the moment and that she was having a hard time dealing with them. Didn't she realise that he was too?

He ignored her request and continued to run his fingers lightly across her tummy. 'It's going to get better. But you need to start taking care of yourself, okay?'

'You need me to be stronger.' Sara's tone was resentful. 'But I am chained here. I can't breathe without worrying.'

Why would Sara worry so much? She'd raised a child before. 'It's not like I take all the freedom in the world, Sara. I don't leave you to go lime or drink somewhere. I'm providing for us!'

'You're not getting it.'

Behrooz did not wait for an explanation. 'You know what? You're starting to sound like a broken record. Going on and on and on about all the things I'm doing wrong.' He walked out the room and slammed the door.

Only then did he realise that Asim had witnessed his exit. Maya stood with the boy across the living room, looking directly at him. She held a paper plane that looked a lot more floppy than Zia's.

Behrooz stooped to his son's eye level. 'Go give your Mummy a hug for me, okay? Daddy is going for a walk. I'll be back soon.'

Asim nodded. 'Are you mad with Mummy?'

'Not mad. Grown ups have little arguments sometimes, that's all.'

'Okay Daddy.' Asim obliged his father and went into their bedroom.

'Behrooz…' said Maya. It was the first time she'd said his name since she arrived. He ignored the familiar stab that accompanied it.

Why does she always have to witness my low moments? he thought. He walked past her and closed the door behind.

17

Ghost

*M*aya placed her horizontal canvas on the verandah where she had a peaceful view of The Yard in the early morning light; her paint and brushes were scattered on the ground around her. She recalled her first art lesson in college. Her professor went to great lengths to explain the importance of vantage point in order to capture the ideal foreground.

Maya had often thought of The Yard while in London, but could never bring herself to paint it. It all seemed so obscure in her memory, though she had lived it for so many years. Being removed gave her the opportunity to see what she'd missed, and now she felt like she'd never really seen her home.

She noted subtle changes. The grass that led away from the courtyard now grew scraggly and uneven. The courtyard itself was the same, only the tiling was different, a grey colour with shades of white; and there were chairs still stacked to the sides, which had remained after the funeral service.

She was not interested in that. From where she stood, there was an opening between two large poui trees, providing a view of the orchard beyond, with its calming foliage and overgrown trees. It was her favourite spot as a child.

As she painted the scene, she could hear the crickets chirping, the lizards running, and the turtles pulling in under their shells. She gave herself one week to finish, as she worked on the backdrop.

Her cellphone buzzed. She grabbed the phone from the banister. 'Hello, Jules?' Maya had met Juliana in art school, and they had been best friends ever since.

'Hi, stranger.' Juliana teased, 'This is your long-lost friend from Camden Town.'

'It's great to hear your voice, Jules.'

'Really? Because I've been calling constantly. You haven't returned any of my calls since the funeral.'

'Sorry about that. It's been strange here the last few days.' Maya resumed her seat and continued making haphazard strokes in acrylic.

'How's it going? You all right?'

'Fine. Back in the twilight zone. How's Edward?'

Edward was Juliana's annoying yet adorable brother. He was one year younger than Maya and completely smitten with her.

'He's great. He misses you.'

Maya blushed. 'Looks like I'm going to be here a while again, Jules.'

'Darn. They're keeping you?'

'I'm keeping myself. Can't leave my family again so soon.'

'You know, if you need me I'll fly in...say the word.'

'Still looking for an excuse to turn down that job offer, huh?' Juliana had just been offered a position as an auctioneer at an art museum in New York.

'It's bloody crazy,' Juliana sighed. 'I still have to pack. Don't even know where I'm going to stay yet.'

Maya was less than enthused that her best friend wouldn't be there when she returned, but was happy that Juliana's career was on track. 'How will I get by without you?'

'Don't worry. You're cute enough to get into the clubs solo.'

Maya laughed. 'It was my unruly strands that did it last time.'

'And Edward is still here. Just in case you decide to come back.'

Maya frowned. 'I am coming back.'

'It's my last week in London. Zia's not here to monitor us. Ah, we're so missing out.'

'I know, right?'

'All right, pretty lady. I've got to run. Let's catch up soon, 'kay?'

'I can't just leave!' said Zia into her handset. She'd walked unto the verandah.

'Okay, Jules, later.' Maya clicked off her phone.

'Ron, Mother Dianne needs me here,' Zia continued. 'Okay, well you were used to managing on your own before, and you have Aara…it's just a little while longer…no, she does not eat avocados… you know this…Ron!'

Zia hung up. 'He needs me to come home.'

'But we just got here,' said Maya, resting her paint brush in the palette tray.

'He's moved into our new flat in West Hampstead and he hates it. Says the floor gets all wet when it rains; gross. And the landlord is proving to be difficult.'

'We were supposed to help him move,' Maya recalled. Her elder sister had insisted she stay with her all these years. Zia would have never felt comfortable otherwise.

'Aara is not making things easy either. She's not getting along with the sitter. We should've just brought her.'

'She's too young to deal with death,' said Maya. Aara didn't remember Father Khalid. She didn't need to witness their mourning.

'Think Mother Dianne would be okay without us?'

'It's different for me,' said Maya. 'If she needs me, how could I leave her again?'

Zia sighed. 'You're right.'

'You go,' said Maya. 'I'll stay a while.'

Zia knew her sister was pretending to be brave. She knew the girl felt strange in her bones to be back, and was trying to find out where she fit in, in this new version of their cosy home.

She hated leaving Maya in the firing line. It was obvious that her sister's presence was less than warmly received by some. But she knew that Ron also felt Father Khalid's loss, and needed her comfort. She would have to talk to Mother Dianne.

Maya sat in the verandah in the afternoon light painting the scene before her. Somehow the lighting made everything different; she felt like she was painting a completely different picture from earlier, but didn't care. She wasn't going to be graded on this project.

She didn't like people in the sceneries she painted, so she distractedly erased Sara and Asim from her vision. They were both walking in the orchard.

Erasure required more focus as Asim, being a regular boy, was making a game of jumping from one big boulder to the next, which reminded her of herself and Behrooz when they were younger. The sight also brought back the smell of the green, the growing trees and scattering creatures. It was this she pondered as the scene progressed before her.

She thought that she'd take this painting back to London. She might even give it to Edward as a gift. He'd never been to Trinidad, and could not imagine the year-round summer and endless green foliage as wild as she knew. But then she reasoned she might not be able to part with the picture once she returned.

How removed The Yard seemed when she was abroad. She felt so distant from the hearts of the people then. This expression on canvas was the perfect tool to help her reconnect.

Maya was so engrossed in her art and what it represented that she didn't notice Asim had tripped and fallen over a tree stump, until the boy cried out, 'Mummy, my arm!'

Sara ignored the child's cries. Maya grew alarmed. It seemed like something was very wrong. The boy's body weight was resting on his forearm. Did his mother think he was crying wolf?

The boy cried out again and finally got Sara's attention. Maya looked on as Sara lifted him off the ground and hauled him up the stairs. She met them halfway and yanked one of the boy's arms over her shoulder to help carry him. The women plopped him onto the sofa, and examined his forearm and bruised knee.

Tears streamed down Asim's face. 'It hurts.'

'I think he must have broken it,' said Maya. 'We need to immobilise his arm.' She grabbed a clean towel from the kitchen counter, and created a sling, placing his lower arm in a hammock-like structure, tying it over his arm.

Sara emerged from the kitchen with ice cubes wrapped in cloth that she pressed to the bruised areas. 'I think that's fine now.'

Maya was pleased with their team effort. 'We should take him to the hospital though.'

Sara was amused. 'Looks like just a sprain. Not a fracture.'

'It's better to be sure,' said Maya. 'I don't know how sturdy this sling is.' Why didn't Sara want to consult a doctor?

Sara was firm. 'We can treat him at home.' Who did Maya think she was? She knew all about children. How to care for them, and tend their bruises. She'd raised a rambunctious boy. 'I can handle it from here.'

*

Maya rapped on Sara's door. She was concerned that Sara had locked herself, Asim and the baby in their room. Behrooz was at work and both Zia and Mother Dianne had gone to visit relatives. The baby was wailing intermittently.

Sara opened the door.

'Heard the baby crying,' said Maya. 'Was just checking if there was anything I could do.'

Sara made a stern face. 'Hardly likely.'

'Sara, I know you don't care for me.' Maya paused. 'But the past is the past. I only want to help.'

'We're doing just fine. Thank you.'

Maya shoved her foot in the doorway before Sara could lock her out again. 'I don't think you're doing just fine. You look really tired. With two kids. And I'm here…with all this free time.'

Sara wore a smug expression. 'I'm not buying it.'

'What?'

'You don't want to help me,' said Sara. 'You're just the same old troublemaker you were when you left.'

'Right.' Maya sensed there was nothing she could say to convince the woman otherwise.

'You're lucky that your mother and father have been good to me. Or, I would have taken Behrooz and our children so far away from here, you'd never lay eyes on him again.'

Maya gaped at her.

She understood then that the one thing that would hurt her most was not being able to make things right with Behrooz. Sara could smell her regret; and it was within the woman's power to keep Behrooz away. Could she blame her for considering it?

'Now let the door go!' said Sara.

'No,' said Maya. Not until Sara gave her a chance.

'This is my room! Or do you think that since your father is gone you own the whole damn house?' Sara shoved the door again, but Maya's foot was still in the way.

Asim, who'd witnessed the entire conflict from the start, sided with his aunt. 'Mummy, I want Aunt Maya to take me to the doctor.'

'Shut up!'

Asim whimpered at his mother's rebuke. Baby Nisa, as though sensing her brother's distress, began a high-pitched wail at once.

The two women, locked in their mental battle, ignored the screams of both children. Years had passed, yet here they were, like teenagers again. Both vying to prove their point.

Maya's voice was firm and even. 'I'm just here to help.' Her eyes, fixed on Sara's, were serene. 'We don't have to be friends. Don't have to be anything at all.'

Sara was astonished. It was the first time she'd seen anything calm in the girl's features. 'Okay.' She left the door ajar.

*

The sky was orange when Maya plopped into the sofa in front of the television, exhausted from the day's events. Sara had taken her advice and she, Mother Dianne and Zia had gone with Asim to the hospital. Once it was confirmed that the boy's arm was merely sprained and would be back to new in a few days, the women took him out for celebratory ice cream.

'I heard what you did for Asim earlier.' Behrooz stood beside the couch.

Maya was nonplussed.

She felt as though a ghost had punctured the air; not only had she not realised that Behrooz was home earlier than usual, but she had nearly forgotten the living, breathing, talking reality of him. He had been dead to her for so long. They'd completely avoided each other since her return.

'Thank you,' he continued, and then turned away. He was obviously heading out to join his family; he held *Tom Sawyer* in his hands, which was Asim's favourite book.

'Wait.' Her voice stuck in her throat. 'It's only us here.' Maya struggled with her thoughts. 'What I mean to say is…it's weird that we don't talk. We're friends. Always friends.' The painting in the verandah was about him, she thought. Not The Yard, just him.

Behrooz chuckled dismissively.

'I know what I did in the past was…' Maya dared herself to continue but nothing she could say could describe what she had done. 'It was heartless, soul-less, and unpardonable.'

'Don't sweat it,' he said, walking towards the door.

'Wait,' she managed again.

'I wanted you to know that I didn't come here to cause trouble, for you or anyone. Or to make you feel uncomfortable. I came because…I had to come home. I've wanted to see my family, for a long time.'

'Sure,' he said, taking another step towards the door.

'I'm here for my family. But for you too.'

Behrooz stood still.

'Well…not for you…,' she clarified. 'But for the you that I grew up with, who saw beyond the pranks and the laughter…to the tears…you, who understood me more than anyone…' She was aware of how rehearsed her speech sounded.

'That person is long gone.' Behrooz's eyes captured hers. 'I don't even know who that person is anymore. And I must have been a serious whack job to understand anything about you.

'The day I met the rest of The Yard, when you talked me into that prank, I knew you were trouble. Even then. But, I always saw what was best in you. Never allowed myself to see your true nature. Now, after all these years, I see you.'

Maya compelled herself to straighten up on the couch. 'You don't know how the last few years…'

'You know,' he continued, 'I don't know…but I hope you've actually started to see beyond yourself…for your sake.'

'I didn't leave because I was selfish,' she said.

'Now you want to tell me why you left? Guess what? I don't want to know. I honestly don't care. I've been free from you for a long time. I want to keep it that way.'

'I've learnt some things since I've been away,' she said. 'I've made new friends. I never had friends before.' Her words glided on. 'Jules…Jules gets me. I mean, she's my opposite. We've known each other for six years. And her brother Edward, they're my best friends, really. But I have other friends that are more like acquaintances, like Amanda and Suzy.' She rambled on, 'And I've told them, told them all about how we grew up, and how we loved the orchard and the sunshine and we'd just want to be by ourselves, you know… and how we were opposites…but I never told them…'

'Maya!' said Behrooz, his voice hard and even. 'I meant to say thank you for what you did for my son. I'm not interested in your friends, your carrying on, or anything else.' His face registered no emotion. 'I'm not your friend.'

Behrooz marched out the door.

Maya's tears stilled at the corners of her eyes. They were too stunned to roll down her cheeks.

*

Mother Dianne called a family meeting. Zia, Maya, Sara and Behrooz were all sitting around the dining table twiddling their thumbs, awaiting her arrival.

The twins were sleeping over at a friend's house, and Asim and the baby were asleep. Mother Dianne was smart enough to seize this opportunity.

Zia wore a worried frown. She had just gotten off the phone with Ron and Aara. Ron was still crabby. He'd had to shampoo and dry the carpet, reupholster some furniture, and haul all their possessions and Maya's in by himself.

His voice sounded tired, and accusing.

And Aara had asked her when she was coming home.

She had to tell Mother Dianne tonight that she was leaving in the morning. 'I need you too!' Ron had said.

Maya held herself statuesque at the table to keep from crumbling. She was unstrung by Behrooz's earlier dismissal of her. He was not angry, or hurt, or strange as she'd expected. He was calm and perfectly clear. He wanted nothing to do with her. Her brightest memories were his darkest recollections.

Sara kept an eye on the tiny crib in the hallway where the baby slept. It was the same crib that Father Khalid had built for baby Aara. Behrooz placed his hand firmly over his wife's, and she seemed to relax a little. He played with her long fingers, one by one. Her slanted eyes smiled up at him.

He, unlike Maya, was completely at ease. And it was this that brought nausea to the girl's throat. Maya realised that somewhere at the back of her mind, she had thought that one day she would return and they would be friends again. She knew now that that was easier said than done. But her mind was erratic in its affection and reasoning; she believed that the pieces of their lives would magically fall into place like they did in her head. Behrooz was right. She was whack.

Mother Dianne joined the solemn group. She wore a stern expression. Though she was engrossed in her own grief over the last few days, she'd guessed at some of the inner feelings of her daughters, son and daughter-in-law. She felt a heightened and uncharacteristic sensitivity to everything that was happening, and was too weak to deal with it. She decided that she'd just have to let them know she could not.

'Mother, Sara and I have to leave,' said Behrooz.

'No!' said Zia. She quickly explained. 'I'm leaving. My husband is a mess without me. He can barely get himself ready in the morning.' She looked at her mother. Her eyes shone with affection. 'But it won't be like before, I will be here more often...I promise.'

Mother Dianne smiled at her eldest daughter. 'It's okay,' she said. 'You go.' She looked at the rest of them. 'You three, I need you here.'

'Why would you need me?' said Maya. 'I'm the reason Sara and Behrooz are leaving. I should go back with Zia and then everything would be back to normal. And you need normal, Mother.'

'You think you're the reason we're leaving?' said Sara. 'You give yourself too much credit.'

Mother Dianne ignored their sniping. 'Alia is getting married in a month's time,' she said. This was news to her audience. 'Will you at least stay for that?' She looked at Maya. 'I need my daughter, whom my husband loved more than himself. Now that you're back, I can't let you go just yet.'

'Mother, Father Khalid never knew...I never got a chance...' said Maya. She had never addressed this topic openly; the pressure was on.

'I need you and Behrooz to get along,' Mother Dianne looked from one to the other. 'Your father wanted that.' She peered at Maya. 'Just because we didn't grant him this wish while he was alive, doesn't mean we shouldn't now.'

Sara looked down at her fingers in her lap. This was exactly what she wanted to avoid. She remembered the scars Maya had left on her husband, how deep the bruises were, and how tough to sand away. Not that she thought those wounds could ever be reopened. She just didn't like the reminder, the source of them right before her. She hated that Maya was family.

'Can you do this?' asked Mother Dianne. The question was meant for Behrooz. 'Maya returns to London after the August holidays, and you and Sara can make this your home.'

'Okay.'

Sara nodded her consent. She understood the conflict of interest, but her affection for Mother Dianne made it hard for her to deny her the thing she needed most. She would have to be bigger than that.

She would not allow Mother Dianne to live alone after Maya left, and she knew Maya would leave.

She would stay on.

Behrooz squeezed her hand under the table, and she held on to his fingers.

'I can do it,' said Maya, as if trying to convince herself.

She glanced at Behrooz and Sara stared back with a half smile. Maybe she and Sara could become friends, Maya thought.

Later that night, when the phone rang, Zia was happy to tell Ron that she was coming home. Aara screamed in delight. And Maya surprised herself by calling Alia to congratulate her on her engagement, and offer her two cents on ideas for the party. She smiled as she thought of Alia leaving her honeymoon bed to clean Grandmother Sakina's bedpan.

And a bizarre thought occurred to her. Maybe she could help out.

18

Dry Season

*I*t had been a rough dry-season so Mother Dianne was happy when the rains finally kicked in. She rose early in the morning and drew her curtains, breathing in the scent of wet grass and growing trees. She glanced at the Julie mango tree across from their house and felt pleased at the new growth of leaves. There was hope that the plant would survive after all.

She opened the door to the living room and an unusual wetness reached her toes. Did the rain come in? she wondered. There were watermarks on the ceiling and the corners of the wall. Obviously water had found its way in and her roof was in need of some repair.

Perfect, she thought. She dialled Aunt Heba who knew a guy who did roof construction. The man promised to send a crew the following day. She placed a yellow plastic bowl on the floor to collect dripping water in the meantime.

Behrooz examined the ceiling; it was certainly aged, and he was convinced it should be replaced altogether to avoid worsening problems. Since he and Sara would eventually settle in The Yard, he assumed responsibility for the project.

His wife barely noticed something was amiss. She was holding the telephone receiver and attempting to burp the baby at the same time. 'Calm down, Mother, it's not like this hasn't happened before. Okay, he took three days to come back last time...at least give him a week this time.'

Behrooz intuited that she was talking about her father.

'He can't take criticism like you can,' Sara continued. 'The jamaat is talking? Mother, father has left; who cares that the jamaat is talking?…I didn't say you made him leave…I can't come over…I can't…well why don't you go find him then?' Sara hung up.

'I think you need to go over there,' said Behrooz.

'No. This has happened before. He gets fed up, he leaves, he comes back, and everything is peachy again.' Sara had her own issues to contend with.

'It's just that last time he left, I wasn't so sure he was coming back,' said Behrooz. 'Your mom asked me to find him, and I did, sitting at a street corner with a bunch of teenagers drumming barrels. I'm just saying that it took some convincing.'

'I can't go there with Asim and the baby. Not when she's like that.'

'Leave Asim with me, and spend the weekend over there. I'll help Mother Dianne with the construction here during the day, and I'll join you in the evenings.'

'You'll bring him to me to spend the night?' she asked.

'Of course. He'll never go to sleep without his mummy.' Behrooz kissed Sara lightly on her forehead.

'Only for the weekend then,' she said. 'Oh, and please apologise to Alia for me; looks like I'll be missing her bridal shower.'

'Alia is the last person to hold a grudge, so you're good.' The boys were also getting together while the girls had their party.

'Hmm…we never had any wedding party,' Sara recalled.

'Somehow I never missed it,' said Behrooz.

*

The women assembled at Aunt Heba's split-level home at noon. Arrangements were made on the upper floor for the party; sequinned silk cushions in lemon green and orange and some folding chairs with tie-backs were scattered for seating. Though the venue was a bit crammed, and the younger ones wore silly expressions, anticipation was high as it was the first event of its kind in The Yard. Alia was the first cousin to have a bridal shower.

Maya had assured the girl that she would take care of Grandmother Sakina during the wedding preparations, and even afterwards, and though the gesture was appreciated, both Alia and Aunt Hala had some reservations. They remembered too well Maya's unpredictable ways and knew how changeable Grandmother

Sakina was towards the girl. But Mother Dianne smiled proudly when Aunt Hala related the proposition. She, for one, was certain that her daughter was up to the task.

Guests sat according to the unspoken rule; the aunts took the chairs and their daughters sat on the floor. The party was supposedly meant for girls only, but Maya noticed the boys could peek at them from the lower level. And it was for that reason Aunt Maab refused to remove her hair covering.

Privacy was no big concern for the others, because no one would feel right playing naughty games and making lewd jokes in Alia's presence. But Aunt Maab had other ideas.

She opened the evening by collecting gifts and piling them up next to a throne-like seat where Alia sat. The game was decided; the bride-to-be would be asked a set of personal questions about her fiancé, and would receive a present for each correct answer. Fauzia and Fiza were delighted at the possibility of their older cousin's secrets being revealed.

Alia was mortified at the end of the game. It turned out that she barely knew anything about her betrothed. She didn't know his favourite colour, or movie, or song. In fact, she was sure that he rarely listened to music or looked at television. 'It's not recommended,' he'd say. He belonged to that recent movement where young Muslims considered everything outside of their religion to be a corrupting influence. Alia herself was much more carefree than that.

The only questions she aced were related to his hobbies and favourite foods; and though she was suppose to collect two gifts only, Aunt Maab gave her all the presents at the end. She blushed bright pink as sneaky bags revealed neon-red and see-through items. Her cousins troubled her to model the lingerie for them, but stopped when they thought she was going to bolt from the party.

The second round of games involved making bridal dresses from toilet paper and penises from plasticine; it resulted in bouts of laughter. Aunt Maab even caught a couple of the boys looking up at the commotion and reprimanded them.

Fiza and Fauzia were experts at moulding penises, and engaged in a one-on-one competition to see who could make the best one.

Aunt Lulu was mortified. She'd assumed that her girls were too dignified to engage in such behaviour and scolded their effort. The girls gave each other a knowing look, and Aunt Lulu had the strangest notion that whatever she said was nonsensical to her daughters.

Alia shunned the plasticine creations but Aunt Maab did not buy her innocent act. She thought that the girl must have been thinking about penises all along and feigned not to.

Then came the advice from the older folk.

'A wife should always be obedient to her husband…' Aunt Maab said.

Maya shuddered at the thought.

'Yes, remember for you, your husband comes first, but for him, his mother comes first,' said Aunt Hala.

'And men love food, you must always make sure there's food,' said Aunt Lulu.

'And never deny them in bed,' Aunt Heba interjected. 'It's frowned upon, lest they find someone else.'

Maya's uneasiness was palpable. She was truly sorry for her cousin; moreover, she knew she could never be this dutiful wife. The thought was just as repulsive to her as it was twelve years ago.

Maya was relieved when the bridal shower ended. She'd started to feel stifled and all the reasons she left The Yard came flooding back. She found the boys a merrier bunch.

The girls joined them downstairs, and Maya sat with Aunt Heba's three sons, who were having a raucous chat with Amir, the bridegroom. The boys and Amir attended university locally. It was through this alliance that Alia met her beau.

'You remember when he first saw her?' asked Arif.

'Yah. He said she was okay.' Zaki laughed. 'Didn't think she was all that.' He picked from a bowl of mango chow. 'Then the next day he begged all of us to go on a date with them!'

'Like we all needed to date her,' said Arif.

Amir, a statelier companion with a perfectly round face, hooded dark-brown eyes, and a beard that reached the base of his neck, was mildly amused; but he wore a silly ear-to-ear grin for his audience.

'Said he didn't like local girls,' teased Zaki. He punched his adversary on the shoulder. 'Where is Miss Arabia now?'

Maya sniggered at the thought of all three boys and Amir going on a date with Alia; the unsullied girl must have been petrified. 'So what happened on this date?'

'Let's just say we didn't even get to first base,' said Arif. The boys laughed and Maya shot Arif a drop-dead look.

The party was growing in size. Behrooz had arrived and was greeted with high fives from Maya's boy cousins. He sat across from her but avoided her altogether.

'You up for the challenge, brother?' Arif grinned.

Behrooz eyed him quizzically.

'My boy here,' said Arif, gesturing to Amir, 'is a pretty good batsman. I claim him for my team.'

'I still have Behrooz,' said Zaki. 'He kicks butt!'

Uncle Ansar, together with his two sons, joined his wife at an adjacent table. Despite his disapproval of loud music, slacking off, or anything that could be deemed fun, he was curious as to how the bridal shower went, and the girls shot Aunt Maab a warning look lest she gave them away.

Arif turned on his chair. 'Up for a game of cricket, Uncle?'

'I hear there's plenty time for games,' said Uncle Ansar. He looked at Amir. 'You gonna be living in The Yard, boy?'

'Yes, sir. It's Alia's wish.'

Uncle Ansar seemed speculative. 'Hmm…seems like in this compound some people marry into a home, some never own one.' He glanced at Behrooz. 'For others, house and property just falls into their lap.'

The boys laughed awkwardly. They had nothing against Behrooz, and had in fact grown fond of him. They were also smart enough to know that the comment was directed at him.

Behrooz left the group and walked into the orchard. Maya wondered if she should follow. Before she realised that she was battling her nerves, her legs propelled her forward. She was risking rejection, and her heart thumped wildly, but she had to face her demons.

*

Maya sat next to Behrooz on the orchard wall. 'He still gets under your skin, huh? Uncle Ansar?'

'Sure.' Behrooz decided to be polite, but not bare his soul.

Maya was grateful for his response. 'For me…being back here… reminds me of why I left.' She continued, 'I know you don't want to hear…but I want to tell you…for my sake.'

Behrooz remained silent.

'I remember what it was like now,' she said. 'All this while in London, it seemed to me like I'd imagined some of the things, the way they made me feel. But I see now that things here were always strange to me, as if I'd never been born here at all.'

'Get to the point.' Behrooz had no intention of being the girl's therapist.

'The point is, it wasn't about leaving you, or Father, or Mother, or the twins. It was more about learning to be on my own, you know?'

'Right.' Behrooz smirked. 'Poor little jailbird.'

'I didn't know this exactly back then, but I felt that Sara was right. I wasn't wife material.' Maya searched for words. 'Not that I didn't want to be…I did. But I wasn't.'

You didn't have to be my wife or do anything you didn't want to, thought Behrooz. 'I never asked you to marry me.'

'I wanted to marry you. And Father would have seen to it once he found out. I had to do something…'

'Well, I must say, you hatched a very mature plan.' Behrooz smiled derisively, 'Your got out of jail free. I hope now you have all the freedom you want.'

'You know I don't. There's nothing freeing about what I've done and the pain I've caused.' Maya paused. 'I regret…I want to regret all of it, but how can I? I look at you and Sara, and I know I did the right thing. I mean if not for…Asim and baby Nisa wouldn't be here. None of us can imagine the house without them. So how can we wish it didn't happen?'

'I don't wish. I'm glad it did. I was never going to be the one to keep you here. No matter how cushy that would have been.'

'I'm sorry, Behrooz. I hope that one day you, and Mother, and everyone can forgive me.' Maya rested her hand on his. 'Please say you can forgive me.'

Behrooz pulled away. 'Don't sweat it.'

Maya decided to let the topic rest. 'Tell me what happened after I left. No one said anything about you to me afterwards.'

'I'm sure you'd find that story boring.'

She understood the implication. 'You're right. I don't have a right to know.'

'When you left? I didn't curl up and die.' He didn't think he could survive her departure. 'I got by.'

'I'm glad you did.' Maya moved to rest her head on his shoulder but changed her mind. That seemed too familiar, too wrong.

Behrooz looked impatient. 'Are we done here?' But he remained exactly where he was. And so did she.

They sat there until the crickets chirped high in the night. When it was time to take Asim to his mother's Behrooz walked off towards the house. 'Hey,' Maya called behind him. 'Never mind Uncle Ansar. Father Khalid always knew how to deal with him.' Behrooz didn't look back.

Maya remained in the orchard until her eyelids drooped. Not wishing to fall asleep outdoors, she returned to the house, and plopped on Mother Dianne's bed. She felt her mother's boney lower arm drift around her.

*

...They were buckled in on the airplane, she and Zia. She was dressed in denim jeans and a simple tee. Zia was all dressed up. She had not seen Ron in a few weeks. She held baby Aara in her arms.

'Why are you doing this?'

'I can't stay there anymore,' said Maya. 'It's humiliating what happened. It's good that I told everyone. What must they think?'

'Cut the crap. Since when did you care what people say? You're not making sense. What about Father Khalid and Mother? You're going to leave them just like that?'

Maya snuggled into her blanket. 'Is this how it's going to be with you?'

'I want you to know that you're going to regret this,' said Zia. 'If not today, or tomorrow, you will the next day, and for the rest of your life.'

'The only thing I'm going to regret is being stuck.'

'You can't start and stop feelings,' Zia warned.

Maya took a pillow from the stewardess, curled into a sleeping position, and closed her eyes.

She'd felt so content the night before, next to Behrooz, as if an angel had held her heart and massaged it. But whilst he slept harrowing thoughts crept in. She'd pondered that Behrooz was bound to Father Khalid in an inexplicable way; he was never going to leave The Yard, especially if she stayed. When the sunlight came in strong on her face she'd bolted from the bed. She had to get away.

'Can I get you a drink, madam?' asked the flight attendant.

'Drink?...No...thank you.'

'We'll soon be landing at Heathrow....' The pilot was mumbling something unimportant.

'Landing soon,' Maya repeated. 'Is this a return flight? When will we be going back?'

Zia shook her head in confusion.

Maya was not happy with that response. Instantly, she remembered the ache she'd felt as she ran from that bed, like wiry strings forcing her back, as she yanked free.

'No, turn this plane around!' She unbuckled her seatbelt and ran towards the cockpit. She banged on the door. 'Sir, Mr Pilot, please turn this plane around. I have to go back!'

Zia was at her side, baby Aara still in her arms. 'Maya, what are you doing?' Her voice was hushed. 'You know they can't do that. Come back to your seat. Please.'

'Madam, the seatbelt sign is on,' the stewardess warned.

'No.' Maya gasped. She bent over, feeling nauseated.

'Ma'am, compose yourself. We'll be landing soon.'

Maya released her anxiety on the cabin floor.

'We need some help!' said Zia.

*

Maya awoke with a jolt, her breath heavy in her chest. Her mother's hand was still around her waist. Mother Dianne was so deeply asleep that she didn't realise her daughter was having a nightmare.

Maya felt dazed, her head muddled. Did it happen in real life? She searched her waking memory.

Yes, it did. It was the same dream she'd had for a year, after she arrived in London.

She curled into Mother Dianne, and tried to relax once more, but she shivered, even when covered with the warm blankets, and was not able to return to sleep that night.

19

Forgiveness

'How's Sara doing?' asked Mother Dianne. 'Did her dad come home?' She set out a plate of pancakes for Behrooz, who was sitting on a kitchen barstool flipping through the daily newspaper.

'Not yet. But Sara is working on him.' Behrooz shoved the paper aside. 'She expects him back any day now.'

'Will she be staying there much longer?' said Mother Dianne.

'For a few days again. Asim too. He's worried about his grandmother.'

'Poor thing. Why don't you bring him by today? Or, wait, not today. I have too many errands today. But tomorrow for sure?'

Maya was helping Mother Dianne pack away clean dishes. 'You're out today?' She realised that she and Behrooz might be spending more time alone, and the nausea rose again.

Mother Dianne heard the pleading in her voice. 'The contractors will be here any minute, and Behrooz has a lot of work to do.'

'I won't be in your way,' said Behrooz. 'You could paint, or do whatever it is you do.'

'I have a dental appointment at nine,' said Mother Dianne, putting her frying utensils into the sink. 'After that, the twins want to go to the embassy to get their school visas.' They were already waiting for her outside.

'Help me wash up the rest of the dishes, would you?' she said to Maya. 'And don't forget to defrost lunch for you both.'

'Sure.'

Mother Dianne grabbed her purse and keys, shot them a warning glance, and headed out to the car. The contractors arrived just as she was pulling out.

Behrooz led them to the living room. The furniture had been removed and the entire floor was covered with plastic. He pulled on his goggles, to observe them at work as they screwed the new drywall into the ceiling studs. When the last piece was placed, the contractors left, and promised to return the next day for a final inspection.

Maya followed Mother Dianne's mealtime instructions and carried out a plate with food to Behrooz when she saw the men depart. She secretly hoped the gesture would lead to another polite conversation. She found him sitting on the dusty floor looking up at the ceiling.

'Admiring your work?'

'Actually, I'm only just learning how this stuff is done. It makes Mother Dianne feel better to have me involved.' He stood to accept the plate, and a big chunk of plaster fell and hit him on his head.

'I don't believe it!' he said. He took the ceiling ladder, and climbed to investigate. 'I think they screwed them too close to the edges. The whole thing is going to crumble!'

This prognosis proved correct. Another chunk fell into the plate Maya still held; and the centre, which Behrooz hoped would hold, fractured. Maya gasped.

Before the larger pieces broke and came crumbling, Behrooz dove off the ladder and pushed her out of the way. The plate in her hands fell and shattered. His fingers were still resting on her shoulders, both breathing heavily, when they heard someone come in.

'Anyone there?' Aunt Maab called.

They fruitlessly attempted to dust themselves off. White particles floated around them and into the kitchen and foyer.

'We're here,' said Maya, emerging from the catastrophe. Her skin still burned from Behrooz's touch.

Aunt Maab gave a disapproving nod. 'What on earth is going on?' She glanced at their dust-covered clothing. It didn't surprise her that these two were up to no good.

'We're fine,' said Behrooz. He sounded slightly out of breath. 'The drywall fell.'

'Oh!' Aunt Maab walked into the living room and scrutinised

the mess. She made a show of fanning her nose delicately with one hand, whilst she rested the other on the base of her throat. 'Looks like a lot of cleaning up to do.'

That was an understatement, thought Behrooz.

'Well, I'd heard you were home all alone,' said Aunt Maab. 'Thought you might be needing lunch.'

'We have lunch,' said Maya.

'Surely, seeing the mess in here, you could do with a fresh plate.'

Aunt Maab returned moments later with two plates of stewed chicken, white rice, red beans and broccoli. Behrooz thanked her politely; but the absence of conversation indicated that no one was up for a soiree. With another glance around, the older woman exited.

'Is it just me, or did she come to spy on us?' said Maya. She sat at the dining table and dug into her meal. 'I mean, when was the last time she came here?'

'You're right.' Behrooz sat with her, but didn't feel hungry. 'She's always hated me. Didn't make things better when you left.'

Maya felt the broccoli stick in her throat.

'When we got on that plane,' she said, 'before we took off, Zia told me that I'd regret it, maybe not that day, or the next, but certainly for the rest of my life.'

'The statement didn't warrant another explanation, Maya…'

'The moment we took off I was certain she was right. I wanted to turn back and come home.' She looked at him, 'You probably won't believe me now, but nothing was worth leaving you behind.'

He stared back. You're right. I don't believe you.

'I called Dad when we landed and told him my decision. But he said he didn't want me back right away. That I couldn't just change my mind on a whim. Said I should give myself a few days to clear my head and then we'd talk. So I stayed.'

Behrooz remained silent. Father Khalid never told him about that conversation.

'After a while, I started to like the cold air. I was feeling better. Breathing easier.

'Why didn't I cool off and come home? I pictured your face clearly the night you came into my room. You had made up your mind…you wanted me just as much…you were putting your life and future in jeopardy for us. I couldn't picture your face when I left. Didn't want to.'

Behrooz lowered his head. He'd thought of that night every day since. He'd been determined to be with Maya. Nothing would have deterred him. Not Father, not the family, not banishment or poverty. Nothing but her betrayal.

'I heard they found you curled up on the floor,' she continued. 'I knew that I'd broken your trust and there was no going back.'

'I can see how inconvenient trying would have been for you.'

'You couldn't risk everything again for someone like me.' Maya stood abruptly and walked out into the verandah. She was saying too much too soon. Behrooz followed her as she bounded down the stairs and went into the orchard. He sat two inches away from her on the familiar low wall.

'I'd heard soon after that you were feeling better,' said Maya. 'Sara was coming by every day and things were looking serious. You were over me.'

Silence.

'Still, I'd be looking over my shoulder thinking you were miraculously going to show up. Whenever I talked to Jules about you, I was careful, thinking that somehow you were going to overhear me.'

'Did they tell you when I got married?'

'No. Zia stopped telling me anything. She was upset with me, and I was too proud to ask. I just pieced together the bits I overheard.' Maya paused. 'Did you want me to know?'

'It didn't matter.'

Of course it didn't, she thought. 'Can I tell you about Jules?'

Behrooz nodded. He was glad that the conversation had been redirected.

'She and I met in art school. After our first few lessons, our class was sent to Hyde Park every day for one week to capture the beautiful scenery. We all sat on benches; we had the most beautiful weather with gentle breezes and clear skies. My classmates were enamoured with shady trees and babies in strollers. The only thing I painted was the weeping beech, until I started to weep myself.

'Jules sat on my bench and rested her hand on my shoulder. She wanted to know why I painted that tree, and pretended not to see the tears in my eyes. She was the first person who spoke to me at school. After a while, I confided in her. Told her why I left here. She helped me figure it all out…to piece my thoughts together. Though, sometimes I regress. I feel like I haven't figured anything out.

'Through her, I met her brother, Edward. He's one year younger than me, but very sweet. He became very attached to me. The three of us used to go out partying all the time. One evening I went to visit Jules at her apartment in Camden Town, which was close to where we lived, but she wasn't at home. Edward was there, so we took a stroll down the street and ended up at an Irish pub. He had a few drinks. And well, tried to kiss me. I wanted to give it a chance, honestly. But I didn't.'

Why is she saying all this? thought Behrooz.

'Because…when you love someone, when you're holding out for someone, there's nothing or no one that can take their place. It's either them or nothing. That's how it is for me. That's how it is with you.'

Silence.

'I thought of sending you an apology. Of getting on that plane, and making nice with you and everyone. Each school break I'd go to the travel agent and buy another ticket I'd never use. I'd write another note to Father, making promises I'd never keep. I never imagined Father would leave me. Never thought of it. But that's why I'm telling you now. Even though it's the worst time. I don't want to take this to my grave.'

'You're wrong,' said Behrooz.

Maya eyed him questioningly.

'You said you didn't come home because you'd broken my trust and there was no going back. That you weren't worth the trouble anymore.' Behrooz looked at her intently. 'You were wrong.'

Maya swallowed. 'You would have taken me back?'

'I would have forgiven you, then.'

Silence.

'That said, I'm sorry for what I said before, about you being self-absorbed and selfish. I judged you. I'm thinking that maybe I was out of line.'

'You have every right to judge me.'

'No. I felt abandoned by you, but it wasn't all about you. It was about being found in that shack. Left by whoever gave me up. And then by Aunt Livy. But I blamed it all on you. It never occurred to me how much you suffered too. I never called or tried to find you. I gave up on you.'

'You were never good with conflict. We both knew that it was up to me.'

A chill, which was unusual in the tropical clime, blew straight through the orchard. The shiver brought Maya back to an evening when she and Behrooz had trekked to Aunt Hala's with disturbing news, and the circumstances that lead them there.

They had been walking home from school when they spotted Zaki and his brothers in the shortcut that connected their street to another running parallel to it. The boys had decided upon that track which was actually forbidden to members of their family, as it attracted petty thieves and other criminal elements.

Behrooz decided to stop and investigate out of concern, but like most things back then, the spying was pure sport for Maya. What they found amused her to no end. Zaki was harassing a pale-skinned girl whom Behrooz recognised as one of Alia's school friends. The girl had her scarf properly pulled across her head, and, unlike some of the other girls who wore scarves, had no snaky tendrils or frontal display of hair.

'Take it off,' Zaki said. 'You don't expect any guy to marry you with that thing on your head, do you?' The girl's eyes were wide and wary. Removing her scarf was the equivalent to standing naked.

'My brother wants to marry you,' said Arif. 'Who are you kidding? Do you want to remain a spinster? Come on, one peek so we can approve.'

Behrooz was about to intervene on the girl's behalf when Maya held him back. 'Leave them,' she said, 'they'd make your life hell in The Yard if you meddle.' He reluctantly walked away.

The following morning Maya informed him that Zaki had performed 'nikkah' with the girl in secret. She'd explained that 'nikkah' was a Muslim marriage with no legal rights, but a marriage nonetheless. Behrooz was outraged.

'How is that possible? Why would she marry a guy who was ridiculing her just a few hours before?'

'Apparently, Zaki fell in love with what he found under the scarf and talked the girl into marrying him,' said Maya. 'The only other man who has ever seen her hair was her father. She probably thought she had to. Silly girl.'

Behrooz vowed that the Heba boys would not get away with their latest indiscretion. He marched to Aunt Heba's house, ready to tell her everything. But it wasn't the first time he heard something completely unexpected upon his arrival there. He'd stepped into the foyer and found the living room door ajar.

Zaki was sitting on the sofa. 'I'm a bastard. She hates me.'

'What do you expect?' said Arif. 'They tell us we can't have anything to do with the girls till we marry them, then we can't marry them less we know them! So it's better to marry them then get to know them and decide.'

Behrooz understood the argument, yet did not agree with its conclusion. However, after seeing the plight of the newly wedded Zaki he decided to abort his mission and keep the boy's secret. He knocked on the door and announced his presence. 'Married men don't sulk.' The Heba boys were dumbfounded. Till then, they had no idea that Behrooz knew anything.

'Want to know how she'd stop hating you?'

Zaki nodded.

'Stop being a wimp, and man up to her parents.'

Zaki did work things out with his bride; he confessed his sins to their families, and formally requested her hand in marriage. Of course, his wife's parents were so infuriated when they first heard the news, that they refused him. It wasn't so much that their daughter was only seventeen, but more on account of Zaki's violation of her.

Aunt Heba was so disappointed herself that she would not intercede on her son's behalf and avoided the marriage topic altogether. In the years that followed, Zaki worked at regaining the trust of his mother, in-laws, and that of his bride. He'd gotten a job as a teacher's assistant to support the girl, and both families had recently consented that the girl could live with him.

Behrooz had been intent on avenging an innocent girl's honour, yet was merciful to, and came to the rescue of, her transgressors. Yes, Maya thought. Behrooz would have traded his executioner's role had she returned all those years ago. It would have taken no less than the drop of a tear. She was certain.

Behrooz's touch on her shoulder brought her out of her reverie; and the chiming of his mobile brought her back to earth. He grabbed his phone from his pocket. 'It's Sara,' he said, glancing at the caller ID. 'I should take this inside.' Maya heard his car start soon after. He drove out of The Yard in a hurry.

20

Changes

'He was coughing non-stop, then it looked like he was choking, like he couldn't breathe,' said Sara, sitting in the sterile waiting room of the hospital. She'd felt scared and clueless. She had no idea what was wrong with Asim until the doctor suggested asthma.

'Why didn't you call me earlier?' Behrooz sat beside her on the edge of the sofa.

'I needed to get him here as fast as possible. Plus, I didn't want to bother you if it turned out to be nothing.'

'You didn't want to bother me?' said Behrooz. 'Asim means the world to me.'

'I know that,' she said, flatly. 'Aunt Maab came by.'

'To the hospital?'

'She called my mobile when I was on my way here. She came right away. And told me you were in a bit of a plaster covered mess.'

'She came to tell you that?' said Behrooz. Why would Aunt Maab deliver such news while Sara was already upset?

'The drywall ceiling came crumbling down,' he explained. 'Maya was the only one at home, so she helped me clean up. We also had a little talk in the orchard.'

'Oh?'

'Understandably, she needed to clear her conscience about why she left.'

'And has it been cleared?'

'I think so.'

'Right.' Sara seemed incredulous. 'I have no qualms with the girl besides the fact that she has always found a way to hurt you, and you've always let her.'

'So really, you're just concerned for my sake?'

'Aunt Maab, who has known her much longer than you and I, thinks it's best we both stay away from her till she leaves.'

Just like the woman to meddle in our affairs, thought Behrooz.

'She's looking out for me, you know?'

'She's not looking out for you, Sara. She and Uncle Ansar have always hated me. They've never wanted me in The Yard. You know that.'

'They've been nothing but nice to me since the day I came.'

'They're nice to you because they want to make sure that we stay together so that...'

'So that?'

'They were always opposed to me and Maya. It was Uncle Ansar's best argument for Father...that she was not forbidden to me under Islamic rights and that I'd use her up.'

'Use her up?' laughed Sara. 'Seriously?'

'I imagine they were happy when she left, proving their point exactly. They were the source of all my nightmares growing up.'

'If their agenda is to keep you and Maya apart forever, then what's so bad about that?' Sara prayed that the next few weeks would fly by, so things could go back to normal.

Doctor Ramjattan entered the room. 'Are you Asim's parents?' he inquired. They were in fact the only parents in the waiting room; the other occupants seemed either younger or much older in age.

Behrooz stood. 'Yes, doctor. How is he?'

'He's going to be fine. It was an asthma attack like we thought. Just had to give him oxygen.'

'Oxygen?'

'I had no idea it was so serious.' Sara glanced apologetically at her husband.

'It's not,' said Dr Ramjattan. 'Patients with asthma experience a blockage of air to the lungs, so we administered a bronchodilator through an inhaler to open up the passageways so that he could breathe properly. It's a mild case. More than likely, with the proper treatment, you won't have to visit the hospital for this again.'

'Can we tell if his condition will improve or worsen in the coming years, doctor?' asked Sara.

'Most children grow out of asthma in their teen years. Hopefully, he would be so lucky. Meanwhile, he must be carefully monitored. Come, come, I will show you the prescribed treatment.'

Moments later, Asim rejoined his parents, smiling an angelic smile that proved infectious; it lightened everyone's mood. 'I'm sorry I scared you, Daddy.'

Behrooz stooped to the boy's eye level. 'It's only because I love you so much.'

'Let's go home,' said Sara.

Asim held both his parents' hands as they exited.

*

Behrooz drove to his mother-in-law's house. He and Sara intended to sleep at Annie's that night.

'Just one night,' said Sara. Dad only came in this morning. He seems happy. I just want to make sure that he settles in nicely. Then we'll go back to Mother Dianne's.'

Annie was waiting for them at the curb when they pulled in. She was wearing a cream silk knee-length nightgown; her hands were folded across her chest, her back slightly bent.

'Mom, what is it?' said Sara. She'd gotten out of the car before it came to a complete stop.

'He's left, baby,' said Annie. 'This time it's for good.'

Sara placed her hands on the woman's shoulders and rubbed up and down. 'You shouldn't stand out here like this, come inside.'

They sat on a floral sofa in the living room. Sara brewed two cups of Lipton tea and set them on the table. 'Mom, tell me what happened. He was here only this morning, promising you the world. Why did he leave?'

'He's allergic to peanuts,' said Annie. 'I put peanuts in our lunch salad earlier. But he's allergic. His mouth started itching. Oh, it was terrible.'

'Dad was never allergic to peanuts!'

'Well he is now,' said Annie. She glanced away. 'Says his body has changed.'

'Mom, this does not make any sense.'

'He'd been to a spiritual teacher in Preysal,' said Annie. Preysal was a village a few minutes south-east of Freeport. She continued, 'Told her he's unhappy with his life and where he's at. She's been teaching him all about his destiny, and about how he's not living up to it, or something so. He thinks he's meant to be a healer.'

'A healer? Does one have to leave his family…to be a healer?'

'He wants to give up his retirement. To move east to be a teacher. She's found him a post there, so he can help children find their way.' Annie was sarcastic. 'Bless her.'

'He can teach here.'

'He's changed, mind and body, Sara,' said Annie. Her hands shook as she made a pretence at sipping her tea. 'He's readjusted his heart and I'm not in it.'

'How did he seem when he left today?'

'Happy. He says he feels like twenty-one again. He's got himself a chance to make up for all the things he missed out on, and I sure as hell am not going to stop him.'

'Oh, Mom. I'm so sorry.'

'I'm sorry too, dear girl.'

'He shouldn't blame you, you know, for not living up to his own potential. You've never done anything but support him.'

'Sometimes that's what holds them back. Having that anchor. Someone to be there for them all the time, to fill that space, for a while.'

Sara rested her head on her mother's shoulder. She wondered at the woman's strength, that she was not out screaming on the streets. It had been twenty-five years of marriage, and she was brave to let it go.

But Sara's heart felt lumpy and cold. Her father had left her too. And she did not know how to forgive him. There was no reason he could not have both worlds, to fulfil his destiny and his obligation to his family. Did he not know she needed him?

She was only eleven when she knew he was unhappy. He'd returned home from a fishing trip in Grand Riviere on the north coast. Sara had never been there.

'It was the most bewitching Flamboyant in bloom,' he said, 'like nothing I've seen before. Its trunk like a brave man in armour, its branches like strong hands with long, twisted fingers, its flowers like blood-red triumph, the whole thing tipping towards the ground, bowing to the old fishing village. I felt like bowing too, as if I'd come home.

'Ah! The freedom! If only I could spend the rest of my days in that quietness.'

'Away from me and Mom?' Sara asked, peeved that her father hadn't taken her along.

He'd slumped on the couch and removed his boots, an astonished look still on his face. Either he did not hear the question, or he did not bother to reply.

Sara came back to the present and held her mother close. They both fell asleep on the couch, till morning, when she finally saw a trace of dried tears on the woman's face.

*

Behrooz drove through wild and rugged terrain spanning an array of farming and fishing communities along the northeast coast about three hours away from The Yard. He would pass Matura Village and Salybia Bay before getting to his final destination at Galera Point. Asim was buckled into the passenger's seat.

'Did this Grandpa go to heaven too?'

'No. This Grandpa is still with us, just in a different place for now.'

'Is he an angel?'

'He's going to help kids like you be the best they can be. Isn't that great?'

'Will he come back to see me?'

'Of course he will, some day.'

Asim opened his window halfway and sea breezes gusted around them. They passed flat wooden houses with colourful clothing flapping on outside lines. The road went winding to Sally Bay, and Asim gaped at the calmest waters he'd ever seen. He caught the tiniest glimpse of a river that flowed into the ocean where a sky-blue canoe idled by. He wondered if they would be allowed to take the canoe out to sea, and at the little waves he saw splashing in the distance.

'Where are we going?'

'You'll see. Somewhere neither of us has ever been.'

'You've never been too?'

'Never. Since your Mummy is taking time out with Grandma, and baby Nisa is with Mother Dianne, I thought you and I could do something extra special together.'

The winding road led further uphill to a place surrounded by trees. Palms stood tall and majestic, their strong trunks bearing history's own secrets. Ferns and silver blades of grass sprung sporadically from damp earth, with rocks and stones thrown asunder.

Behrooz turned off the engine and met his son on bare earth. He pulled the boy onto his back and trekked upward walking into the sky until they reached the Galera Point Lighthouse that stood seventy feet tall on a rocky promontory surrounded by a white picket fence.

Asim read the sign at the opening, 'Take nothing but pictures, leave nothing but footprints, kill nothing but time.' Behrooz planted him on his feet. 'But what does it mean, Daddy?'

'It means here will always be pristine. Nothing can touch it.'

Asim pulled his father closer to the lighthouse hoping to ascend its staircase but the entranceway was closed. 'What's it used for?'

'To guide seafarers safely back to land,' said Behrooz. 'It was opened in 1897 in honour of Queen Victoria of the United Kingdom of Great Britain.' He tossed Asim onto his back again and walked through a narrow pathway of sea grape shrubs sculpted into tight windswept hedges.

They stood on an outcrop, the northeastern tip of the island, a point so tiny that the ocean below surrounded them on three sides. Out in the sea were scattered rock masses, brown and brick-like; waves thundered upon them in sequence and from the fissure below came the bellowing sound of a blowhole.

Thankfully it was a clear day. 'Here's exactly where the Caribbean Sea meets the Atlantic Ocean. See how the waters are deep blue on one side and turquoise on the other?'

'Wow! I can't believe it, Daddy. How did you find here?'

'I was at the parlour down the street yesterday and I heard two men talking about this farting blowhole. I thought I must see it for myself.'

'Can Mom come when Grandma gets better?' asked Asim.

'Sure she can, but for now, this adventure is our little secret, okay?'

Asim sat on his bottom and skidded down the cliff, moving closer to the ocean. 'Can we swim out?'

Behrooz grabbed him and lifted him back to the top. 'No, my boy. It's not safe.'

They peered outward. 'See that land mass up ahead?'

Asim squinted. 'Where?'

Behrooz placed the boy on his shoulders. 'Look carefully. You'll see a faint line.'

'I see it!'

'That's the sister isle, Tobago.'

Asim frowned. 'How come I've never been?'

'I plan to take you everywhere from now on,' said Behrooz. He set the boy down once more. 'You, me, and many adventures.'

They walked back from whence they came and found a picnic bench on the side of the lighthouse near a towering almond tree. They sat enjoying the shade.

'Daddy, I miss home,' said Asim.

'Home by Mother Dianne?'

'No, home. Where we were before Mother Dianne and Grandma. When it was just me and you and Mummy.'

'What about baby Nisa?'

'Baby Nisa too.'

'But won't you miss your grandmothers?'

'Yes. But I don't think Mummy likes them.'

Behrooz rested a hand on the boy's shoulder. 'What makes you say that?'

'I think Mummy has been sad a while.'

'Hear what. You and I, we're always straight up with each other, right?'

'Right.'

'And I would always tell you the whole truth, right?'

'Right.'

'Mummy and I know each other better than anyone, don't we?'

'Uh huh.'

'So if there was anything wrong with Mummy, I would know. She'd tell me, right?'

'I guess.'

'So would you believe me when I tell you, that your Mummy is okay, and that she loves you so much? She's just getting used to the baby, and Grandpa passing away and her own dad leaving. So she's going to be different for a while. But she, and us, we'll be okay!'

'I believe you, Daddy.'

'Good.' Behrooz put Asim on his back once again. 'Ready for a real beach?'

'Yay!'

They savoured the view from the flat of the cliff once more, then headed towards the car. Behrooz drove in a westerly direction to a quaint, untarnished beach. He spotted a lifeguard and made a mental note to stick to the shallow.

The sandy seashore gave way to coral as they stepped into the ocean. 'It's coral beneath your feet, from the reef,' said Behrooz. But Asim was too happy to be in the sea to notice the lack of smooth sand.

His eyes were transfixed on the splashing waves in the distance, which never reached the shore.

21

Turning Point

*T*he ceremony was simple, as Alia was simple. She did not require pomp and festivity, only the purest union. Chairs cinched with white bows were placed around tables set in rows and columns. A splash of green from illuminated foliage encased the scene. Clever love seats were placed all through the orchard, where couples strolled for romantic walks, whilst cracker-barrel lights twinkled from treetops like tiny fireflies all around.

Aunt Hala was exceptionally proud. She had reared the most accomplished and revered granddaughter in The Yard. Alia was kind, pure and astute. She could not recall any circumstance in which the girl had displeased her. She was happy that Alia had found her own path and no longer offered up her life as a sacrifice for others.

Grandmother Sakina, for the first time in years, would make her presence felt in the courtyard. Everyone was aware that she would rather face instant death than miss this occasion, the wedding of her most adored granddaughter. For this reason, all her daughters were on their toes. The day had to be perfect.

Aunt Lulu ushered guests in an orderly fashion; Aunt Heba ensured that vendors were properly handling both decor and catering; and Uncle Khidr and Uncle Ansar saw that all other elements were in place. Aunt Maab assumed her usual supervisory role, and took it upon herself to remind Aunt Lulu and Aunt Heba that Amir was a religious boy, and that no frivolous music, singing and dancing would be allowed.

When Aunt Heba rolled Grandmother Sakina into the

courtyard in her wheelchair, there was a greater urgency about everything. The caterers rushed to serve virgin coladas in crystal glasses, the photographers were instructed to take more photos of the old lady than the bride, and the videographer took his cue from that. Guests were beckoned to greet Grandmother Sakina, in turn, before they took their seats.

Amir arrived one hour earlier than planned and seemed an anxious bridegroom. Alia's cousins took turns greeting him, and sitting at his side, for fear he might feel silly sitting upfront all alone. There was a formality about the occasion that stripped their usual joviality; everyone in The Yard took marriage seriously; the union was professed to be half of one's faith.

Aunt Hala was absorbed in the most fitting task. She had to ensure that her daughter was the most beautiful bride. And she was. Alia's dress was the palest pink, with a scoop neck, long laced sleeves and pink satin border. It sat daintily on her hips and flared outwards, draping over her delicate figure. A white hijab covered her hair and draped over her chest. She looked like a priceless figurine.

And Aunt Hala was pleased that her mission was fulfilled. She peeked outside and saw splendid white tables filled with the people who mattered most; and instead of sadness she felt perfectly at ease. Nothing mattered but her daughter's happiness.

Mother Dianne and her three daughters were seated next to Grandmother Sakina. They were to look after the feeble woman and ensure that she remained hearty all through the ceremony. All that was required was a listening ear and an ability to take instant commands. Grandmother was sure to articulate her needs and instruct appropriately. Whilst they could fend for themselves, she could not. She relied on all her children, and what she lacked in the ability to move and navigate, she made up for with speech.

Maya felt odd seated where she was. Usually she was placed with Alia who was regarded as her peer, and the strangeness intensified as guests in attendance assumed she would be wed next on account of her age.

She was subjected to frivolous comments from almost every guest who greeted Grandmother Sakina and Mother Dianne; and was chagrined at their petty clichés: 'It's time Maya; before all those eggs dry up. You only have half of them left by age thirty, you know?' or 'I know someone from the masjid who's looking for a wife,' or 'Poor Maya, it's a pity you'll turn out a spinster.'

Maya remained composed and responded politely to each person. She was aware of Behrooz's intermittent gaze upon her and mandated herself to refrain from any outbursts or self-righteous indignation. He was seated with Sara, Asim and Aunt Heba's boys on an adjacent table. Whenever she looked at him full on he shifted his eyes and pretended not to notice.

A quiet descended as the Imam sat next to Amir on stage. There was a scuttle as the bridal party readied to begin the ceremony. A melodic song in Arabic (the only piece of music allowed for the occasion) rippled through the courtyard as Alia descended. None of the guests stood to welcome the bride; it was not what she wanted. But each person's gaze was fixed upon her.

Amir did not take her hand as she reached his side. They had to be married first.

Alia paid no attention to the Imam's khutbah and it was evident that her reserve had taken a back seat as her eyes constantly sought the man she was marrying, and her face flamed each time he looked her way. He, however, maintained his poise through it all. When it was time to share the symbolic drink he carefully drank one-half, leaving the rest to her. And when they were pronounced husband and wife, and their witnesses had signed as such, he greeted his bride with a brief hug. His passion would wait for later.

After the ceremony, Alia first sought the company of Grandmother Sakina. Her new husband greeted the woman warily. Grandmother Sakina noted something pitying in the boy's eyes, and disapproved of the way he rushed her granddaughter away. They had a lot of people to meet, he said. And the girl would only be one house away. But Grandmother Sakina could not shake the feeling that something had changed forever; something bigger than they imagined.

The happy couple was to leave that night for an extended honeymoon that would take them from London to Paris. It would be the first time that Alia would leave the country, as previously the girl could not bring herself to leave Grandmother Sakina for more than a few days at a time.

Mona announced that Alia was ready to throw her bouquet. The bride's younger cousins found themselves ahead of the throng; each was anxious about the possibility of her own marriage, though none was really superstitious. It was Fauzia who turned out the winner; the girl gleamed whilst her mother sent her a wary glance.

Aunt Hala maintained her composure as she bade the newlyweds goodbye and gave her daughter a quick kiss on the cheek when the car arrived. No one had shed tears that day, and she wanted to keep it that way. There was no sense in that, as the girl would return in a few weeks to stay on in The Yard, hopefully till her mother passed on.

The younger girls, elegant as they were, passed around wicker baskets, filled with thousands of white petals, which they scattered as the newlyweds walked towards the 'Just Married' Cadillac. Alia looked up as hundreds of petals descended on her porcelain face, and her beaming bridegroom locked her arm in his and ushered her into the waiting vehicle.

It was Sara who observed him first. She too was joyously throwing white petals at the retreating Cadillac when she saw Asim shrinking amidst the crowd. She blinked for clarification just as he fell to his knees and forward.

'Asim!' A barrier of well-wishers shifted under the twinkling lights to accommodate a narrow passageway to the boy.

Behrooz, Mother Dianne and Mona rushed towards her; someone from Amir's party went to find a doctor. 'We have a cousin who's a doctor. He's looking after Grandmother Sakina; he's coming now.'

Sara shivered at the look of her boy. He was making grotesque wheezing sounds and struggling for breath. White petals were stuck to his palms and the asthmatic inhaler was thrown to his side.

'Breathe slowly.' Behrooz grabbed the boy into his arms. 'Take your time, and breathe slowly.'

'He can't breathe. My God, he can't breathe,' said Sara.

'Come away,' said Mother Dianne, taking her daughter-in-law by the elbow. 'The doctor is coming; you don't want to panic the boy.' Sara relented and stood a few feet away with her head buried in the base of Mother Dianne's neck.

Dr Furlonge, a burly man with trimmed beard, emerged from the south apartment. He was apprehensive about the situation and felt he could not do much. It was evident that the boy needed a hospital. Mona had already dialled and an ambulance was on its way.

Dr Furlonge stooped to the ground and raised Asim upwards to loosen the boy's bow tie and unbutton his shirt. 'I need a chair, quickly!'

Mona responded to his call; Behrooz helped to hoist Asim onto the chair. The doctor tilted the boy's head, pinched his nose and breathed into his mouth, repeatedly.

'We need an air tube inserted,' he told Behrooz. 'I don't have the equipment. His air passage is sealed.'

'Sealed? Completely?'

'Better hope the ambulance gets here soon.'

Behrooz grasped Asim's hand. He hoped the boy would feel his desperate need for him to breathe and be all right. 'Daddy's here. I promise you, it's going to be all right.'

He looked on in dismay as Asim's lips changed from mild pink to grey then blue; and held on tighter as the boy's body turned a sickening grey. 'Just stay with me,' he repeated, like a mantra. But Asim was no longer conscious; he no longer clung to his father's words, or struggled for breath.

'It's in God's hands now.' Sara was at her husband's side. She took Asim's free hand in hers and turned her face away.

'No!' said Behrooz. 'Stay positive. Help is on the way.'

But when the ambulance arrived, and the paramedics could not get that air tube down Asim's throat, due to the boy's clenched jaw, Sara knew it was over.

'There's nothing we can do,' said the medical officer in charge. 'He has passed.'

'No! He can't leave me!' He pictured Asim sitting on the orchard wall comforting him, Asim looking over the cliff at the point where the Caribbean Sea met the Atlantic, and Sara smiling up at him when Asim was born.

The boy's parents clung to opposite sides of his chair, locked in solitary grief. Behrooz murmured into the blankness, 'Adios, my love.'

His sorrow resounded, whilst Sara, composed and steady, dried her silent tears, and said a prayer. She stood carefully, not wanting to look at the dead body before her, and walked decidedly into the house.

It was all written, she believed. When life is going to be breathed into you, and when it's going to be taken away. Each person's mission on earth is pre-planned. There was nothing they could have done to prevent death.

Maya emerged from the main house, stirred by the commotion, passing a grief-stricken Sara on the way. 'What's going on?'

No one answered. She spotted Behrooz curled into a ball on the floor, jammed against a chair; and it took only a second longer to register that Asim's lifeless body lay upon that chair. 'No! This can't be.'

22

The Departure

*I*t had been one month since Asim's death. Behrooz spent his days alone, besides the days that he and Sara saw their therapist, who he hoped would bring them out of their solitary melancholia.

When he was not losing himself in the daily humdrum of work, he was sitting still in the orchard. Nonetheless, Maya dared not go to him. No one dared. Her going to him would be a slap in the face, like professing that another human being could replace the one he'd lost, or was capable of giving him comfort when there was none.

Thus, Maya was surprised that morning when a buoyant Behrooz invited her on a road trip to nowhere in particular. She cautiously consented. There was something desperate about the request that scared her, but she was more afraid for him to venture out on his own. Behrooz was, after all, the worst navigator she knew.

He sped along the Valencia stretch and the car shook and shuddered as it dipped into potholes. The roads led to Salybia Bay en route to Galera Point, the place he took Asim that had so fascinated the boy. He ignored Maya's protests that he was going way over the speed limit, and her pleas about where they were going, why they were going there, and what madness had gotten into him. And he pretended not to hear the questions about whether Sara knew where he was and what he was doing.

He stopped by the Galera Point Lighthouse. 'Get out,' said Behrooz. 'Take in the view.'

Maya obeyed and stepped out into the salty air. Warm breezes caressed her face and steadied her nerves. She followed Behrooz to the rocky outcrop overlooking the endless ocean. Her breath stilled at the splendour. She had only heard of this place, but had never been, and could not have imagined something that beautiful was only three hours away.

They descended along the rocks, stepping from one jagged point to the next, moving closer to the sea. The waves surrounding them made a haunting sound as they splashed up against giant rocks, which were little islands in the ocean, blasting sea spray. Currents swirled in the deep and a blowhole squawked below.

Maya held on to her hat. 'Why are we here?'

'To celebrate.' Behrooz tossed a stone into roaring waters.

'What occasion?'

'Sara and I,' said Behrooz. 'We're dealing differently with grief. She's content that it's all a test for us, one that we can pass to meet up with Asim in heaven. She has all these reasons and theories why things happen. Me? I haven't got any. They're all a waste.'

'You don't believe in anything?'

'How should I know? I don't know why this happened to us. Is it a test? I asked Sara...how can one pass a test that is unfairly written?' His hands formed fists. 'I don't come with a manual or set of beliefs to be studied. And I don't have answers.'

'You have more answers than you think. Do you remember what Father Khalid taught us? He said never to worry about heaven and hell or anything. He was good and strong. He showed us how to live.'

Behrooz was grateful for the memories. 'I hope Sara is right about one thing. That Asim is with his grandfather.' He paused. 'Is it really true, Maya? That I had this little angel for a while? And now...feels like a dream.'

'God sent you his angel, then it was time to take him back.'

'I don't need another theory.'

'You're right.' Maya pushed her dishevelled hair back from her face. 'A good theory won't help us. Only time and acceptance.'

'You sound like our therapist.' Behrooz peered at her. 'You even believe the things you say?'

'I believe it's what you need to hear. Is the therapist helping?'

'She says there are things about us, that were there before Asim's death, that influence how we cope with tragedy and each other. Yet, I think that she's more flummoxed than we are when it comes to me.'

'Yours is a different situation,' she reminded him. 'You don't have a childhood, things she can draw on; nor do you want to recover it.'

'I don't want to recover it,' he said, looking at her intently. 'How can she draw on something that never was, and more importantly, how is that going to help me?' He softened, 'Besides, what I have is much better.'

'Better?'

'My first memories.' He stood closer and whispered into her ear. 'I wouldn't change them for anything.'

Maya turned her face feeling his stubble on her cheek. He pulled back and gazed at her, and for a few seconds she saw in his eyes everything she'd hoped to find. 'All this time I thought you'd regret...'

'Regret you?'

She nodded.

'No. Never you. Never us.' Behrooz wrapped his arms around her and rested his head on her shoulder. She planted the tiniest kiss on the tip of his earlobe and closed her eyes as he exhaled.

Tender seconds lingered in their gratification before he spoke again. 'There is so much I wish to say.'

Maya smiled. 'You can tell me.'

'There really isn't time.' The sky was suddenly grey with thickening clouds and there was a slight drizzle. Soon the sea would rise higher and they'd be soaked.

'Are we heading back now?' A corbeau fanned its wings, swooped into the waters, and emerged with a fish in its hooked bill. Maya saw dead fish washed up, slammed against the rocks. 'You'll tell me in the car.'

'We're leaving The Yard. Sara and I.'

His words pounded in her ear like smouldering waves crashing and dying. 'Leaving?'

'Yes, today. For good.'

Maya felt her soul collapse. 'You're leaving with her?' Raindrops stung her skin where they landed.

Behrooz looked stricken. 'I need your help. I can't face Mother Dianne, or Zia. I need you to tell them for me. To explain everything.'

The blood drained from her face, and bile rose to her throat. 'How can I explain to them what I don't understand?'

'I will make you understand.'

No, if he wanted to abandon them, he'd better be forthright about it. She held on to his shirt collar. 'Don't do this. Please.' The winds growled, whipped, and warned; egrets wailed and flew to safety.

He held her shoulders lightly and peered into her eyes. Please don't go, they screamed. If you go you'd break my heart.

'You'll do this for me, Maya.' His voice was soft. 'So Sara and I could have a chance of happiness. A real future.'

Maya stumbled away from him.

He held on to her wrist and commanded her chin upwards. 'You've taken happiness from me once,' he said. 'If I stay here, you'd do the same again. Sara and I would never make it here.'

She silenced her pain this time and listened to his. His future was with Sara, the mother of his children. That's what he was trying so hard to tell her. Hadn't she known?

'I need you to do this for me. 'Cause all I want is to save my marriage. I need to save my marriage.'

'Okay,' she said. If that was what Behrooz wanted, truly wanted, she would offer it like a present, a sacrifice. She wouldn't interfere.

They drove home in silence, drenched and exhausted. Maya turned away and hid her silent tears. The rains subsided once they returned to Valencia; and Behrooz sped on, breaking the speed limit, and violating several traffic laws. Maya almost wished that they were stopped or arrested to delay the inevitable.

She watched him hastily ascend the familiar steps to their home for the last time; watched as he disappeared into his room and emerged with four oversized red Wilson suitcases. She was his only witness. He hauled the luggage into his car on his own.

When it was all done, and he was ready to go, he did not come to her again. He stood, boyish in the courtyard, looking up at her standing in the verandah and waved goodbye. She watched him get into his car and dissolve.

She stood there, upon shaky legs, long after he'd left. Her heart fractured into a thousand pieces.

Part Four

23

Uncle Ansar

When Uncle Ansar was a young boy, he and Father Khalid were the best of friends. Father Khalid looked up to his older brother, seeking his advice and judgment on every aspect of his life, from books and girls to debate on sport and religion. For, to Father Khalid, there could not have been a more just or wise arbiter, counsellor or mentor.

Uncle Ansar was a contemplative soul. When he was younger he observed much about his parents that made him so. Grandfather Latif, for instance, was a different person then from the person the younger children knew. He worked hard all day, and at night released his frustrations in bars 'liming' with friends. Grandmother Sakina was left to raise their children on her own.

Uncle Ansar, seeing how tired and overworked his mother was, would sweetly volunteer to sweep the house and clean dishes. One day his father came home to find him standing at the sink scrubbing an old iron pot. In anger, he picked up a ladle and whacked him on the behind, 'Woman worker! No son of mine should be doing woman work!' This was Uncle Ansar's most lucid childhood memory.

By the time Father Khalid had enough sense to understand and recall, Grandfather Latif was a changed man. His business was booming, and he was released from the immense pressure to provide for his family. He had painstakingly earned the reputation as the best upholsterer in central; and become charitable and involved with the community and mosque.

By the time Aunt Hala was born, he was reformed. He was

practicing Islam with fervour, and had been to Hajj. He wore a topee everywhere, and had prayer marks on his forehead. He embodied the type of religious zeal common to folks of that era, in the spirit of community, freedom, justice and union with God. So it was in this new environment that the other children were raised.

Aunt Hala was doted upon the most. She was the first girl, and he'd wanted a girl. Not to say that having boys disappointed him. He was grateful for the two boys who would carry on his legacy. But he was captivated by Aunt Hala's soft smile and calm nature. He was so besotted with her, that when Aunt Heba and Aunt Lulu were born his heart soared; he could not imagine anything lovelier than having three daughters.

Uncle Ansar remained the dedicated son. Regardless of his father's preference, he helped his mother in the kitchen and garden and with all the other children, who demanded time and constant attention. Father Khalid in particular grew up under Uncle Ansar's care.

The family was poor in those days and without the comforts they enjoyed as the girls became toddlers. At a young age, Uncle Ansar was responsible for taking Father Khalid to the toilet, situated behind their then tiny house in Freeport. He would even clean up after Father Khalid; so well had he loved the boy.

Father Khalid took all this for granted, and in fact, was so young at the time, that he did not remember it happening at all, unless he was reminded by the older folk.

One external factor that bonded both boys during their pre-adolescent years was love of music. Father Khalid loved music, and Uncle Ansar had the biggest collection of any boy in Freeport. He had all the popular blues and rock n' roll songs of the '40s and '50s and listened to them throughout the day. In fact, neither boy could fall asleep without a track jamming peacefully in their ear.

Uncle Ansar also loved animals, and would keep hamsters, turtles, ducks and fish; his younger brother admired how well he looked after them all. Father Khalid loved looking at girls on the street, and would take advantage of Uncle Ansar to appear chivalrous. He would send a duck scuttling down the road, chasing after it, in order to catch the attention of a pretty girl. Uncle Ansar had no time for such trivialities. His life was his music and his animals. He was pervasively calm, peaceful and quiet. Only his eyes vaguely expressed what he felt or thought; and so sensitive was he to others, that if he had a bad thought, he kept it to himself.

There came a time however, during their adolescence, when a set of circumstances so strong, polarised their beliefs and attitudes to the point where they could no longer relate to or understand each other. Father Khalid was studying by night for the London exams that would determine his subject choices for the Cambridge A Levels. During this period of separation, Uncle Ansar, who had already graduated from high school and decided not to pursue his academic studies, joined a Muslim brotherhood in the mosque. Classes were held every weekend and participants were welcome to spend the night.

During the week it was business as usual. Uncle Ansar, with his father's help, opened the second branch of the upholstery business in St James, a district of Port of Spain. He already had an influx of customers, and Grandfather Latif was proud of how industrious he proved.

But it was on the weekend, when he opted to spend nights in the Chaguanas mosque, that he felt like part of a community staggeringly different from the one into which he was born. There was a Muslim brother from the United States, for whom his affection grew. This brother regarded him as a younger sibling, a feeling he liked, as he'd never been anyone's younger brother and had never had a real caretaker.

This friend had studied Islam in the United States under an esteemed sheikh from Saudi Arabia, who had a 'superior' interpretation of the religion from what the forebears understood. The sheikh taught this student so well that he came back to the Muslims on the island nation to teach them the right way, bring light to darkness.

The faith he practiced took one back to the times of the Prophet in a literal sense, encouraging the Muslim student to practice everything the Prophet did in the seventh century. The Prophet did not look at television, hence television was an evil force; the Prophet never listened to music, so music was the devil's influence.

Almost every single element of the modern day world was attacked, in particular, how Westerners lived their lives. For instance, ladies with their heads uncovered in public were deemed the future inhabitants of hell. Furthermore, he believed that it was his duty as a Muslim to point out these transgressions whenever he got the chance, and embarrass those who did not follow the rules. No action was sanctioned unless there was proof that the Prophet or his closest followers condoned it.

To Uncle Ansar, this new interpretation of the old religion was the modern, improved version that was better than what his father practiced. It placed him and all Muslims on the same level, but those who refused to follow were lower.

However, Uncle Ansar wasn't consciously aware that his new faith was a form of rebellion against his father—a way of feeling better, prouder and mightier about himself, knowing that he was amongst God's chosen. He decided to live his days in honour of God and the true religion, and guide everyone to that path lest they burn in hell eternally. Consciously, Uncle Ansar was doing what was good for all.

So he rebuked Father Khalid for being overly compassionate. We are not meant to show compassion, we are meant to follow the rules and follow them exactly, he'd say. But for Father Khalid, religious rules were purely contextual; their literal implications were often insignificant compared to the bigger meanings behind them, and religion on the whole was void without compassion, love, respect and intrinsic tolerance towards every human being. He valued the Golden Rule and found himself relying on it when in doubt. His faith was not practiced like his brother's. It wasn't overt; but innate, intuited.

Thus, when Maya first left home, Uncle Ansar felt incredible release. He was no longer obligated to speak out on the unsavoury relationship between her and Behrooz thrust upon them all. Though he still objected to Father Khalid calling the boy his own. But after his brother's death, when Maya moved back to her childhood home, where Behrooz and Sara resided, old animosities flared.

His wife was convinced that Behrooz would disregard the sanctity of marriage and betray his spouse. Everyone knew in their bones that Behrooz and Maya loved each other, despite the choices they'd made for themselves; so it followed that poor, unsuspecting Sara would need a friend in The Yard, and Aunt Maab opted to be that guiding force.

How exactly did Aunt Maab justify her meddling?

She and Uncle Ansar had met at one of the 'revamp' meetings where Uncle Ansar had changed forever. He married her a few days after, firmly believing that courtship was the work of the devil. He taught her everything he knew about the true religion, and she was the most willing student.

However, information is not always construed or internalised the same way by each student, so Aunt Maab combined Uncle Ansar's teachings with the value she held dear: superiority in meddling. Hence, Aunt Maab acquired religious justification to say what she saw was wrong, to hate it in her heart, and speak out against it.

So when she became convinced that Behrooz and Maya were sinful souls, it was her duty to inform The Yard. 'You'll see,' she told Aunt Hala, 'that girl going to destroy their marriage. She'll never get him out of her soul.'

Aunt Maab also saw Sara as a potential ally in Father Khalid's household. After all, Mother Dianne and her daughters seemed intolerant of her, suspicious even, on account of her family's feelings towards Behrooz. She figured that her friendship with Sara could change that.

At first, Mother Dianne seemed reluctant to have her meet Sara. 'She's busy with the baby,' Mother Dianne told her. So she waited until her sister-in-law left the house to pay an impromptu visit. On the first occasion she baked a macaroni pie and pretended to drop it off. On the following visit she suggested that Sara come over to her place for tea; and Sara did, bringing the baby with her. It was convenient that Asim spent most evenings running errands with Mother Dianne. And though Sara's interludes with Aunt Maab were short, she was happy for the brief escapes; there came a time when the two had tea together almost every afternoon.

It was during these visits that she confided in Aunt Maab. 'When I had this baby, I felt different,' she said. 'Like the happiness drained out of me. I feel like I'm going through some depression, and I just hope it goes away soon. Did you experience that with your second boy?'

Aunt Maab said she did not. She told Sara that she felt pure joy at the birth of her children and how she and her husband had tried for more but weren't lucky enough to get pregnant again. She was in fact envious of pregnant women. She suggested that Sara must not be doing something right, and from then on began instructing Sara on the correct way to feed the baby, clothe the baby, burp the baby.

When Sara's depression persisted despite Aunt Maab's advice, her aunt-in-law suggested that she must still be recovering from Father Khalid's passing, and its consequences. One consequence in particular being Maya's return.

'It's perfectly natural if her presence makes you feel worse,' she said. 'After all, they do have history. Unresolved history. And that's the worst kind.'

Sara dismissed the idea at once, but the thought, like a hangnail, stuck with her. The following day was Behrooz's first day at work in the upholstery business and Sara had been crabbier than usual. She'd rebuked him for not noticing that she'd already put his clothes out.

After all, didn't he know that living in the same house with Maya, given their history, would make her uncomfortable? Then she scolded herself for thinking such things. How could Behrooz have faith in their marriage if she did not?

On a subsequent evening, Sara confided that it was Mother Dianne's wish that they got along with Maya. Aunt Maab scoffed, 'It's not fair for her to put you in such an impossible situation.' Only when that was said, did Sara feel brave enough to agree, but by then she'd already given her word to Behrooz, and there was no concrete reason to go back on it.

Perturbed by his wife's indignation about Behrooz's unethical behaviour and her sentiment that something must be done, Uncle Ansar, caught in nostalgic unease about what Father Khalid would say, rebuked his wife's suspicions and stated emphatically that the situation was now beyond their control, that Behrooz and Sara were married, and that married people could sort out their own affairs.

Aunt Maab reminded her husband of the right way; that they had a responsibility to speak out, to bring things to the open. 'He was with her in the orchard the night of the bridal shower,' she said. 'They sat there all cosy till sunset. That counts for something.' But Uncle Ansar insisted that there was no proof.

So, Aunt Maab, learning that Mother Dianne had left The Yard earlier than usual that day, and that Behrooz and Maya were at home alone, decided to investigate. She was content to find them colluding together beneath a fallen ceiling, and spied on them as they spoke in the garden, appalled by Behrooz's arm around the girl's shoulder.

She'd resolved that she would be doing Sara an injustice if she kept that information to herself. After all, the poor girl seemed so wretched.

So this was the information she imparted to Sara that afternoon at the hospital when Asim had first fallen ill. Aunt Maab noticed the girl's cheekbones had sunk in. Look at what he's done to the poor girl, she thought. 'I'm here for you, whenever you need me,' she said. And Sara seemed grateful. Aunt Maab was content that she had done her duty.

'You need to convince him to leave The Yard,' Aunt Maab told Sara, three weeks after Asim's death. 'With the boy gone, and her to give him comfort, well, you're walking a fine line.'

'They haven't even spoken since,' said Sara. 'He's dealing with his grief on his own. We both are.'

'What happens after?' said Aunt Maab, 'Do you want to stay here to find out?'

'She's leaving soon,' said Sara, nonchalantly.

'It's been one month since Alia's wedding. She's still here. That girl is not going anywhere.'

'Her nephew just died,' said Sara.

'Do I need to remind you? He's not her nephew.'

Sara shrugged.

She didn't need a reminder; she'd just lost her son so there was no room for any other concern.

That evening, when Sara and Behrooz left Dr De Casa's office, Sara was crying uncontrollably. The rain pelted on her face as they walked to the car. The doctor initially liked Sara. She saw that Sara was well adjusted and a good mother with a cool temperament and kind heart. But after a few visits, Dr De Casa kept her opinions to herself. This day, she leaned back in her chair, looked at Sara with immense concern, and declared, 'I don't think you actually feel emotions any more.'

Sara started to laugh and cry at once in release. The thought seemed so ridiculous, yet so real. She was so debilitated by fear and uncertainty that her only defense was her endless preoccupation with Nisa and the monotony of everyday life.

She did not want to experience anything new, to feel anything different, or anything at all. For to feel would be to confront all the things she feared.

The following day Behrooz and Sara left The Yard. Aunt Maab observed Maya on the verandah, looking on as Behrooz's car exited. She was pleased. At least she had helped Sara to save her marriage.

24

No Regrets

Sara loved their new house. It was a one-storey with a beautiful backyard halfway up a winding hill, Mountain View Terrace, one hour south of The Yard. The houses on their street were loosely strung amidst dense foliage. The altitude made the location cooler, the air soft and sweet.

She was not bothered that The Yard would come to intrude on their sanctuary, for Behrooz insisted they leave without a trace. They didn't leave a phone number or forwarding address. Furthermore, their house was in the middle of nowhere, serviced by small shops nearby; and since the Ali family usually stuck to their locality while working, shopping and such, she and Behrooz were not likely to run into any of them.

Nisa was perched on Behrooz's jeans-clad lap. Her father held her perfectly, balanced upon both knees, and made a show of touching her feet to her elfin chin. She was rarely as pleased anywhere else, and in fact was so comforted and undisturbed in this spot that it was on these occasions she'd poop quietly in her pampers. Behrooz wasn't clear on the poop signs, so it was Sara who grabbed her up for a smell-check, changed her diapers, and set her again on her father's lap, so that her puny dimples alighted once more upon her face.

Sara felt content. The days of therapy were behind them and she credited Dr De Casa for that. She fancied marriage counselling was the most fulfilling job someone could have, equating it with harnessing the joy of living. She could find no reason to be displeased with Behrooz. His conduct towards her was honourable, and all the fears she'd harboured were subdued.

Once Dr De Casa helped her to accept loss, to be grateful for the time she had with Asim, and to choose to feel positive about their future, Sara found herself on the road to recovery. The move to Mountain View certainly helped; she felt the depression lift off ever so gently. The place was infectious and invigorating.

She sat next to Behrooz and propped her feet against a low centre table. The table held her fascination from the day they acquired it. Below the glass surface was an engraved map of the world, and on many occasions she was tempted to remove the glass altogether and press her fingers against the engraving.

She'd purchased the piece at a garage sale when they'd gotten married. It had moved with them from their first home in Chaguanas, to Mother Dianne's, and had finally followed them to this sanctuary.

They sat in the same spot for the entire morning; Behrooz was reading the daily newspaper and Sara was absorbed in another paperback. On the wall across the room hung a photo of Asim embedded in a stone frame. He sat, smiling from ear to ear, on the sand, with a sand dollar in his hands. The image was captured on their first visit to Mayaro beach when he was two years old. His happiness seemed to jump out of the picture and infect anyone who looked at it.

Next to the photo frame, a back door opened to a beautiful view of a small, glittering pond. In Sara's imagination there were little white ducks all around the water, and she kept the door open to absorb the vision.

She felt content that there was no one around mandating activities, telling them what should and should not be done, imposing their will, whispering doubt, bringing up the past or laying on guilt. It was just the three of them now. In this cocoon, they were finally free.

She closed her eyes and reclined in her chair. 'I could do this forever.'

'I know,' said Behrooz. 'But it's time for me to start looking for a job.'

'But I was just starting to enjoy this. Can't we just be for a little while longer?'

Behrooz propped his feet against hers, tickling her toes. 'I saw something in the paper.' He held the newspaper above the objecting bundle in his lap.

Sara snatched it. 'History teacher? It's perfect for you!'

Sara climbed into the couch with Behrooz and Nisa and it reclined upon impact. She loved that all three could fit, perfectly.

Her mind was transported to the two-seater swing next to the pond. The previous owners had two little boys and they'd left the swing behind. She felt nostalgic each time she looked at it, wondering if Asim would have enjoyed playing there. She pondered if she and Behrooz would have another baby. A boy, perhaps.

Later that day, Sara's mother paid them a visit. They were always happy to see her; she was their only visitor. She'd brought them a barbecue pit as a housewarming present, and Behrooz had it fired up for some jerk-seasoned steak. Baby Nisa watched him from her high chair.

'Your father called,' said Annie. The women sat on a bench in the greenery.

'How is he?' said Sara, surprised. Her parents had not spoken in months.

'He's doing okay. Living in a fishing village.'

'Thought he didn't want to keep in contact?'

'It's just like your father to have everything on his own terms. Didn't even leave a call-back number. But, know what? Even if he wanted to come back, to talk, I wouldn't have him. Just won't feel the same.'

'You have us. You're welcome here any time.'

'I second that,' said Behrooz. He set a plate in front of his mother-in-law.

Later that evening, Behrooz and Sara found themselves alone together for the first time in a long time. Sara's mother had taken Nisa for the night, much to the child's delight.

Behrooz felt like he needed a tutorial before he took his wife in his arms once more. But as he touched her face and his fingers cascaded down her arm, he found that he remembered quite well. In bed, later that night, he told her what he was thinking since they'd left The Yard.

'I don't regret it. Leaving.'

'You don't?' Sara was surprised that he'd broached the topic at all. He was never one to talk when it really mattered. He tended to avoid arguments or any issue that was potentially aggravating. 'I know what they mean to you.'

'I'm grateful to them.'

'Grateful? You love them.'

'Yes.'

'So why did you leave them?'

'Why did you stop feeling?'

'We ran away,' said Sara. 'You know I love it here, I do. But we have to believe we can survive anything.'

'We can,' said Behrooz. 'By whatever means.'

Sara disagreed with Behrooz's approach, but the joy she felt from their new-found freedom and renewed relationship negated any attempt to argue. She snuggled closer to him and tried to think other thoughts. Everything else could wait.

Behrooz himself was untroubled. He permitted his mind to see things in a very literal sense. Sara was happy, and he was fulfilling the promise he made to her. It was his life's mission to do so till death took him.

For the first time he enjoyed doing the little things, like cooking, changing the light bulbs, polishing her favourite centre table, buying magazines for their bathroom stand. He'd never been this involved in their daily life, and marvelled at how appreciative it made his wife.

Maya he saw as he left her, standing on the verandah, her hair soft about her face. In his mind she'd remained that way, beautiful and accepting of him, finally. He never wondered or guessed at the pain she'd felt, because there were no tears in her eyes as he left, none he could discern. So from what he saw, there was no concrete reason to expect that she would be in pain. She would remain in his memory exactly as he saw her last. She was his anchor, out somewhere in the world; but the ties no longer bound that tight. She had loosened the bonds to allow him freedom.

25

Moving on

Maya informed Mother Dianne and Zia about Behrooz's departure on the very evening he left. Mother Dianne had returned home a little later than usual, holding a brown grocery bag. Maya was still on the verandah peering at the retreating road and the dust that flew behind speeding cars. She knew that the news would bring pain to those she loved, and resolved not to let them see hers; there was no need to trouble them further. Thus, when Mother Dianne reached her side at the top of the staircase, she turned bravely. 'Mother, Behrooz has gone.'

'Okay, did they go to Annie's? I heard she's not feeling well.'

'He's gone for good. They aren't coming back.'

Mother Dianne rested the bag of groceries on the porch bannister. 'I see. Did they go back to their old place?'

'No. I don't know.'

'Well…why didn't they say? I'm going to call him.'

'He left his phone behind.' Maya's voice was even. 'He doesn't want to be found.'

Mother Dianne held her daughter's eyes. 'What happened?'

'He said he and Sara needed to leave…wouldn't make it here.' Maya looked away. 'That's all I know.' How was it that despite all her efforts she was once more the cause and bearer of bad news?

Mother Dianne, who had learned to read her daughter better, the way her husband did, felt wretched for the girl. She hugged Maya who, unused to being the recipient of physical displays of affection, stumbled backwards. Maya wondered how much her mother guessed about her.

Zia was in fact less surprised at the news than Maya thought she'd be. 'He wasn't ours,' she said. 'I always had this feeling he had another life to live.'

Maya was not happy with that response. But what could she say? Insist that Behrooz belonged with them when he had chosen otherwise? Throw an adolescent fit? Truth was, she was faced with real responsibility now.

She dialled Jules that day to tell her she'd be staying in The Yard longer than planned. With Saba and Mona leaving for college, there would be no one there for Mother Dianne, or to help with the family business. Without her intending it, it seemed like The Yard determined she'd stay.

When Jules pressed her about what happened with Behrooz she gave the basic information and changed the topic quickly. There was nothing to discuss. This time, there was no hope, no chance of being with him. She needed to pick up the pieces as best she could and move on.

*

It became customary for Maya to look after Grandmother Sakina in the days that followed. Alia's extended honeymoon was over, but she and Amir were staying in Melborne, a village two hours south of The Yard, with Amir's parents and were not due till the following month.

Alia wrote to Grandmother Sakina frequently, constantly disturbed by their separation, to enquire about her health. Aunt Hala collected her letters, read them for Grandmother Sakina, and replied to assure her daughter that all was well at home.

Had it been up to Grandmother Sakina though, the daily letters would have been much different. They would detail the old woman's struggles, her urgent need to see her granddaughter, and her indignation that the less than pure Maya was ordained her caretaker.

Maya paid no heed to the woman's complaints about her. She was now used to them and chalked them up to the follies of old age. There were more pressing matters to contend with.

'You missin' the boy?' Grandmother Sakina asked one evening.

'Yes,' she said. She was decidedly honest about that; it took more energy to deny the truth. Also, her honesty usually surprised the lady into silence. But that was not the case this time.

'Yet, you have courage. You not fallin' over yourself, ready to die.'

The imagery in the comment was morbid but Maya smiled at the intention. No, she would not fall over herself in tears. She kept herself filled with purpose that did not involve herself. So much so, that whenever she spoke with Jules, she felt like she was a different person and her friend felt it too.

'You, looking after sick people?' Jules laughed. 'Incredible.'

Grandmother Sakina rarely consented to outside visitors, but on one afternoon a man walking with a cane and a lively woman at his side called on her and she acceded. Maya received them at the gate. The man's face was marred with sallow wells around his eyes and furrows across his forehead; nonetheless Maya could discern a bygone charm in his bright eyes and symmetrical features. The woman's sprightliness alongside his feebleness jarred at her. She wondered who these people were. Surely, they were important to her grandmother.

The mystery was soon solved. Grandmother Sakina introduced the couple as Bandhu and Vishma, Grandfather Latif's friends from the 'old days'. Maya was quite aware of who Grandfather Latif was in those days and the type of friends he kept. They comprised mostly of drinking buddies. But this couple did not fit the stories in her head. The old man, in particular, seemed quite concerned about her grandmother's health, though Maya feared more for him. What her grandmother lacked in body she made up with speech, but this man was bereft of both.

Maya brought in two plastic chairs from the courtyard. Bandhu sat across from her grandmother, but his wife preferred to stand. He lowered his head and pressed his palms together. 'Salaam, namaste. Is long time I ain't see you.' His chest rattled with cold.

Grandmother Sakina gazed at him. 'Namaste. Salaam.'

He reached out and touched her cheek. 'I tell Vishma I have to see you today.'

Maya intuited that there was more to her grandmother's

relationship with this man than what was apparent on the surface. Due to respect for them both, she didn't run forward to stop him from touching the woman with his germy fingers. Later, she was convinced it was from him that Grandmother Sakina contracted a flu that stayed with her for weeks afterwards.

'I doh know why you hurting your head,' said Grandmother Sakina. 'I good.'

'You see? I tell you so,' said Vishma. 'They say you could hear she mouth from the road.'

'Yes,' said Grandmother Sakina. 'Who need leg? I could run a whole country from me bed.'

Vishma pulled her husband by the elbow. 'You see she. Now, let we go.' She exited and the old man reluctantly hopped behind.

Grandmother Sakina turned her head and did not bid them farewell.

Maya gave her grandmother a head-to-toe sponge bath once her visitors departed; she noticed that the old woman was especially sad. 'Who was that man, Grandma?'

'That's a story to take to my grave, girl.'

'Did you love him?'

'Yes,' she said. 'But I love your grandfather more.'

This reminded Maya of her own situation. 'Why did you love this man less?'

''Cause I was already married to your grandpa, and we had a good life.'

This made sense to her, for once.

Maya was aware of how marriages were contracted two generations prior. They were mostly arranged by parents who placed emphasis on the upbringing and religious dispositions of the parties involved.

She'd heard tales of how Grandmother Sakina, at fourteen years old, had admired her teenaged grandfather from afar, as he rode his Boys Commuter bike in Freeport. He was thin, fair-skinned and handsome, with a voluminous head of hair; the bicycle rattled beneath him and Grandmother Sakina watched in awe and fright as he maneuvered through speed bumps.

Grandmother Sakina's mother, Nanna, also noticed the

ambitious tailor who held her daughter's attention and immediately made marriage inquiries. Grandfather Latif's parents were pleased with the match, and a few months after Grandfather Latif gave his earnest approval. Thus, the date was set and Grandmother Sakina married the most eligible bachelor in the community; and became pregnant one month later.

Her grandparents built a good life. But Maya had noticed they were more formal than jovial with each other. It was the old way, she was told. But she had wonderful and lucid memories of them sitting under the mango tree in the orchard till the sky grew dark, looking at their grandchildren play. She understood that after forty-two years of marriage her grandparents were happy.

The following day Bandhu returned to The Yard alone. Maya announced his presence and ushered him in. This time he carried the air of someone on a specially important mission. Maya was apprehensive about him and pretended to refill the water jar at her grandmother's bedside. Then, eavesdropped at the doorway.

'They say I won't be able to walk soon,' he said.

'Why you come back?' said Grandmother Sakina.

The man put his head down in shame. 'You remember the first time I saw you by the bus?'

Grandmother Sakina nodded. 'I was going nursing class. We was poor then…wanted to do something too.'

'You were crying 'cause you had to leave your baby home.'

'I leave Ansar with a sitter. It wasn't done those days.'

'Remember how I wait there with you every day since that?'

Grandmother Sakina coughed involuntarily in response.

'I vowed to wait there every day with you, to make you feel better.'

'Look, I too old to remember them thing.'

'It was that day I wrote you a letter I've been writing ever since. I never sent it 'cause I never finish it till yesterday. A schoolgirl living next door help me.'

Bandhu pulled a yellow stack of pages from his pocket. Maya was sure that if she could see the date on the letter it would be the very one on which her grandmother was crying by that bus stop. The old man held the paper far from his face and squinted. He could barely see; yet, he was so familiar with the written content that he was able to read it.

'I don't want to hear what you write!' said Grandmother Sakina.

'You stop me then, but now I on me deathbed, so not again.'

Grandmother Sakina sucked her teeth and turned her head.

'You sat on the bench in tears,' he began, reading in an earnest voice. 'And I wonder why a pretty girl like you was so upset. I didn't need transport, but I waited there with you. The next day I waited, and the next. Some days you ignored me, and on others you smiled.'

Bandhu pressed his hand to his chest, willing the mucus to dissipate. Nothing would stop him from telling his story. 'On the sixth day the bus was one hour late. It was Divali day…wasn't a holiday then.' He cleared his throat. 'Do you remember how I offered to hold your bag? And you let me?'

'The bag was heavy. And I was pregnant.'

'I didn't know you were pregnant with Khalid, but your face look exhausted. I fed you prasad to lift your spirits.' Bandhu continued, 'The next week my old friend, Latif, invite me for dinner. I didn't expect to see you. Everyone know he had a pretty wife, but I never know it was you. You greet me by the door and pretend not to know me. I just smile and said "hello" and told my friend how glad I was to see him. I remember you made barfi that night. I wasn't a big fan in those days, but that dry and semi-sweet taste stay with me long afterwards. I always buy sweet barfi now. It remind me of you.

'When I saw you at the bus stop the next day, you were laughing. You said Latif didn't suspect a thing. You brought leftovers from dinner and we made a picnic. We laid in the grass and I touched your fingers; I wondered what you saw in me. It was my poetic soul, you said. But I didn't know any poems. And neither did you. When you kiss my mouth I knew it was for the first and last time.

'My life change that day. When the library opened in town I learn many sonnets; there was a clerk willing to read to me and I learn by rote. And when my parents bring Vishma home for me, I propose to she with verse. I love thee, as I love the calm of sweet, star-lighted hours! But you I never forget. You were the poem written just for me.' The old man leaned forward. 'So now in my final days, my final hours, I come here to say goodbye.' He kissed Grandmother Sakina on her mouth. Maya caught the woman's expression, one of a lover on fire.

After all these years, here was her grandmother's love, at her side, barely alive, and saying goodbye. She was unsure what to make of it.

Bhandu grabbed his walking stick and hopped into the courtyard. Maya didn't even pretend that she wasn't eavesdropping. She guided the man to the gate, and returned to find the old woman turned on her side, sobbing.

She understood that her grandmother had just lost a dear friend, once again. Gently, she closed the door and left the woman to her thoughts.

*

The Yard celebrated the day Alia arrived; everyone came to greet her. Even Uncle Ansar's sons, who barely spoke with any of their cousins, made themselves present. They, in fact, came to greet Amir of whom they were quite fond. The newlywed couple brought only the luggage they left with and when Aunt Hala questioned Amir on when he'd be bringing the rest of his belongings, he seemed evasive.

Aunt Hala had moved in with Grandmother Sakina, and left her house vacant for Alia and Amir in the hope that they would settle there and bring forth many grandchildren. She wanted them to have a sanctuary, a place of their own where they would not have to worry about her interference. This suited everyone just fine as Grandmother Sakina also needed a constant nurse and Aunt Hala was more than happy to fill this role.

Shortly after their arrival, Alia and Amir called a family meeting with Aunt Hala, and revealed some surprising news. They informed her that they'd decided to sell their property in The Yard. After all, Aunt Hala had transferred the property to them as a wedding present and it was theirs to do as they pleased. Aunt Hala was dumbfounded. Why would they want to sell her property? And to whom? The Yard was not for sale. It was meant as a family community.

She glared at her daughter who winced under her stare. Alia explained to her mother that Amir thought it was best that they sell. They would ensure that the new owners were good people and would use the sale money to start their new life together. But Alia knew the value placed on The Yard as family property and was aware that their decision would infuriate her mother, so she let her husband explain further.

Amir explained that he was happy to accept the house as a present, but he'd recently found out that the home was renovated with a loan which Aunt Hala paid every month. He was aware that Aunt Hala had only recently paid off this loan, but was loath to live in the space because under Islamic law any purchase involving usury was frowned upon. In fact, he denounced the whole system as being haram.

Aunt Hala could barely believe her ears. Usury? Then why bother to sell the house at all? Why not return it? This stranger, who'd married her daughter, had taken her kindness for folly. There was no recourse as the property was already transferred in their names.

She asked to speak with Alia privately, and as soon as the girl was alone with her mother, she began to sob. She was indeed sorry about her husband's methods. Aunt Hala hugged her daughter and decided that her only concern was this person's happiness; to that end she would let the youngsters do as they desired without brewing trouble in their young marriage. She'd heard many young men talk like Amir of late, and the religious beliefs they described seemed alien to her own. She felt helpless.

Alia, whether out of shame or guilt, did not visit Grandmother Sakina. She'd peeped at the woman and found her lying on her side facing the opposite direction. She'd heard her cough and clear her throat. She knew that her grandmother had contracted a terrible flu. The last thing she desired was to grieve her.

She asked her mother to keep her relocation a secret from Grandmother Sakina for as long as possible. She and Amir would be staying with his parents until they got a home of their own elsewhere.

When Alia departed later that day, she promised that she and Amir would visit soon and often enough; but Aunt Hala didn't count on that.

*

The following week, Grandmother Sakina was moved to the hospital as her sickness worsened. The prognosis was not good. The doctors explained that her sugar levels had skyrocketed and once they had that under control, her lungs started to fail. They suspected that the virus had morphed into pneumonia. Aunt Hala, Aunt Heba and Uncle Ansar converged at the hospital during visiting hours. On day three Grandmother Sakina was having much difficulty breathing and the doctors told them they would have to move her to the intensive care unit.

Merely minutes after she was moved the doctors summoned Aunt Hala inside the unit. Only one family member was allowed; the doctors feared that despite their efforts the old woman was slipping away. Grandmother Sakina smiled a weak smile, whispered Alia's name, and implored Aunt Hala with her eyes to see the girl one last time; the love of a husband, lover or child could not compare with that of the girl who, from the day she could walk and talk, became her grandmother's selfless caretaker. In that moment every other image faded but the one of her dearest Alia, and though the girl never came the old woman passed away with her granddaughter's name on her lips.

Alia was in fact unreachable till the following day, which was the day Grandmother Sakina was buried. She attended the funeral, eyes behind dark sunglasses. She sat next to her mother and held her hand. Though she loved her mother, her grandmother was her strongest link to The Yard. Now, there was no house in The Yard and no grandmother. Her expression did not reveal guilt or grief. It displayed nothing outwardly, so it was anyone's guess what she felt.

Mother Dianne was under the weather so Maya took it upon herself to look after her mother, Aunt Heba and Aunt Hala. The women converged at Mother Dianne's house in the evening to comfort each other with memories of Grandmother Sakina. Though Maya found her grandmother ominous she had grown fond of her of late and took a peculiar comfort in the woman's frankness. There were no guessing games or pleasantries to contend with. It was this easy feeling that she chose to remember. And it was in fulfilling the needs of the mourners that she found comfort.

26

Edward

*E*dward slung a brown duffle bag over his shoulder and gazed up at the bleach-white houses before him. He knew the one to the furthest right was Maya's. Bordering the houses to the left was the greenest orchard he'd ever seen; he fancied it greener than all the ones in London.

He knew for certain that he was in the right place; the reputed 'yard' where so much happened, yet did not. Two round-faced boys wearing white topees eyed him suspiciously; he waved zestfully and made his way to the verandah. Jules was his reliable informant. He'd learned that Maya was at home taking care of her mother and decided to surprise her.

He came in from the upper porch. 'Something smells here.'

Maya was caught offguard in her morning pyjamas. She was sitting in the living room reading the daily newspaper.

'Edward! What are you doing here?'

Edward grinned, 'If I'd warned you I was coming, would you have done something about that smell?'

'It's just the ravine on a bad day,' said Maya. She was so used to the scent that she'd forgotten how visitors reacted to it.

'Oh. For a moment there I thought you'd stopped bathing since you arrived on this island,' Edward teased. 'Please tell me you have showers.'

Maya hugged him lightly around the waist. 'I'm sure that could be arranged.' There was something in his familiarity and newness that took her mind off funerals, illnesses and restless loneliness.

She beckoned him inside. 'What are you doing here? What

happened with the new job?' Edward had recently completed his business degree and attained an entry-level position at a paint manufacturing company.

Edward shrugged. 'I left. My boss couldn't handle that I was smarter than him.'

'What a doofus! No, seriously, what happened?'

'I decided I couldn't live without you.'

'Silly boy.' Maya shoved her hands through his mass of blonde hair. 'I missed you so.' She hoped he hadn't left his job to come after her. But she soon dismissed that notion. Edward's interest in her had been a mere flirtation.

'I missed you too, sweetpea.'

'Does Jules know you're here?'

'Just because she's older doesn't mean she must know my every move.'

'You're in big trouble, mister. She's going to kill you when she finds out you came without her!'

'You're worth the trouble for me.'

Maya flushed. 'I was just about to make breakfast for Mother Dianne. Want some?'

'You don't rear animals here do you? If so, order me up a slab of cow.'

'You're intolerable!' Maya pulled on a short green apron. Her pyjamas billowed out outlandishly beneath.

Edward sat at the kitchen island. 'When are you coming back to London?'

'Why? To cramp your style with all your women?'

'Can't blame a guy for loving women.'

'Who's the new bimbo?'

'Left her in my flat. You know what they say about different time zones?'

'You're trouble, mister.'

'Hey, can't help it if I want women globally. One over there, one out here…'

Maya rolled her eyes as she pulled out a large frying pan.

'Okay, the last time we sampled your eggs,' he said, 'we were able to pull them apart like pieces of rubber.'

'I'm terrible at scrambled eggs, I admit, but I did learn to boil eggs when I was eight. Grandmother Sakina always wanted boiled eggs, not too soft, not too hard, and I was always...'

'You miss her...'

'In my own way.'

Edward sighed. 'I know you're resigned to hanging around here. But I miss you too. And your lips, those soft beautiful lips...'

'Edward!'

'You never take me seriously when I'm trying to woo you.'

'No. I don't.'

'That's a shame,' said Edward. He fixed a cheeky gaze at her. 'Especially here in this beautiful weather.'

'Behave yourself,' Maya warned. 'Mother Dianne will be up any minute. I always get in trouble for something or another around here.'

'What did you do this time?' asked Mother Dianne. She glanced cautiously at the handsome stranger. She took in his perfectly angular face above muscular torso, the golden mop of hair, and the lightest brown eyes that reflected her image, and turned up her nose in derision. No one that handsome could come to see her daughter without there being some consequence.

Edward stood. 'Blimey. You're gorgeous.' He planted a gentle kiss on Mother Dianne's hand.

'Edward?' Mother Dianne guessed. She glanced at her daughter. 'I had no idea you were coming.'

'Maya didn't know,' he said. 'I surprised her. And I'm glad I did. I've never been in a house with such beautiful women.'

Mother Dianne was impervious to his charm. 'No earrings or tattoos. That's a plus. Do you drink? Smoke? Influence my daughter to do any of those things?'

Maya was gratified to hear her mother joking again. Or was she joking? 'Mom! You'd swear I was still twelve.'

'Once you're under my roof...'

Edward hugged Maya from behind. 'I assure you Mrs Ali, she is perfectly safe with me.'

Maya rolled her eyes. What her mother didn't know couldn't hurt her.

Mother Dianne instinctively felt to reprimand the boy for touching her daughter. Public displays of affection in The Yard between unmarried folk were practically unheard of. What would be next? Would they want to go out on their own? What would the 'others' think? Then, she felt silly for worrying. After all, these two were friends for all those years in London and surely Zia did not accompany them everywhere.

'We're just friends, Mom. Don't worry.'

'Friends with benefits,' said Edward. Mother Dianne looked aghast.

'Mother, what you'd realise about Edward is that he says the opposite of what he means!'

'Mrs Ali, can I ask your permission for Maya to take me to Maracas beach? I can't remember the last time I've been…'

'I don't know,' said Mother Dianne.

'You're welcome to come with us,' he said. 'In fact, you must.'

'Mom's not feeling well.'

'I'll grab my linen pants and tote,' said Mother Dianne. She'd decided to harness any opportunity to be away from The Yard, even for a little while.

*

Edward had ventured into deeper waters, a spot right before the waves broke in the distance. Maya stood closer to shore where Mother Dianne laid out her beach mat and umbrella. Edward could see her, and squinted at her outline; he'd marked her by her sunshine yellow shorts.

She beckoned him back but he was defiant. She was worried. He'd never taken swimming lessons. She'd tried to teach him to float on his back at the campus pool but his middle region would never stay above water. A few more lessons would have done the trick but he was not disciplined in this environment. He was having too much fun.

She ascended the lifeguard hut and asked the burly man on duty to keep an extra eye on the foreigner. 'Lady, boys will be boys,' he told her. Dismayed by the man's apparent lack of concern, Maya decided to take matters into her own hands; she got back into the water and swam to Edward.

'Red flag means strong current,' she said. 'You need to come back in.'

'Don't get your knickers in a bunch,' said Edward.

'I'm not kidding, Edward.'

Edward's eyes gleamed mischievously. 'Would you save me if I got caught in the tide?'

He secretly enjoyed seeing Maya all riled up.

'No. You're too heavy.'

'So you'd just let me die?' said Edward. An incredulous smile threatened to break from his face.

'No!'

'So you'd save me?'

'Fine,' said Maya. 'I'd leave you to drown since you're making fun.'

'And if I drown, what would you do?'

Edward submerged himself into the water. Maya grabbed his tee and held on. 'What's the matter with you?'

'Just having fun, sweetheart.'

'Okay,' said Maya, 'well I'm done with fun.' She waded away from him.

'I knew it,' said Edward.

'Knew what?' said Maya, exasperated. She turned to face him once more.

'Let me ask you something.' Edward wiped water off his face. 'What was all that about in London?'

Maya hated when he became all philosophical. 'I don't follow.'

'The "I don't care" attitude. Partying and drinking until you passed out in my arms.'

'Here is here. London is London,' said Maya.

Edward looked smug. 'A different personality for each country of residence. That's healthy.'

'This coming from the person who claims to have bimbos in each time zone.'

Edward ignored her jibe. 'And what am I to you here? Your acquaintance or friend?' He sounded hopeful. 'More than a friend?'

'Don't try to blur the lines,' Maya warned. 'I need to keep things in order.'

'Who are you kidding? You're perfectly messed up.'

Maya bowed her head. 'Don't mention any of this to Jules, okay? You'll only make her worry.'

'Is this why you told her not to come?'

'I didn't tell her not to,' said Maya.

'You didn't invite her,' said Edward.

'I didn't invite you either. Yet, here you are.'

'You seemed happy to see me earlier.'

Maya glared. 'That was earlier.'

*

The following day, Edward made a spectacle in The Yard, in true Edward-like style. Aunt Lulu's daughters, Fiza and Fauzia, had their gaze fixed upon the courtyard, their tiny noses pressed against the overarching windows, their breath fogging the glass, for beneath, was the most beautiful creature they'd ever seen.

His golden hair was coiled upon his head. They'd never seen that colour on anyone, not in person at least; Fauzia longed to touch it; she traced its pattern on the window pane. His stride was cool and confident. His build slight under his clothes; but when he sat on the orchard wall and removed his tee, both sisters were awed.

Fauzia felt certain that when the time came for her to wed, it would be one just like him, for now that she'd seen him, she could not imagine anyone better.

'What are you doing there?' said Aunt Lulu. As was their custom, the girls ignored their mother.

'Who is that?' Aunt Lulu demanded.

'Maya gets to date all the hot boys,' said Fauzia.

'And they all get to live with her,' said Fiza.

'Shameless girls!' said Aunt Lulu. 'Move from the window.'

Aunt Lulu was repulsed that once again a stranger was living under the same roof with Maya. Would Mother Dianne really encourage that? Didn't she learn her lesson with Behrooz? Did she even think of how this example would affect her nieces?

She plucked both girls by their arms. 'I said, move it!' But they pulled from her grasp. They were no longer intimidated by her; they merely tolerated her on account of her giving birth to them.

'They're adults, Lulu,' said Uncle Khidr, from his rocking chair.

He too found the boy in the orchard delightful and intended to introduce himself at the first opportunity. 'You can't treat them like children.'

'They're not children. They're hormonal teenagers,' retorted Aunt Lulu. 'And it's our job to protect them.'

'Don't you see that we're immature because you never let us grow up?' said Fiza. 'We've never lived twelve miles away from home. And you expect us to act like adults.'

'Mother, I'm getting married,' said Fauzia.

'To whom?' gulped Aunt Lulu. 'You've never been interested in anyone in your life.'

'Married?' said Uncle Khidr. He'd never truly considered the idea that any of his daughters would get married, and wasn't quite sure what to do with the thought.

'I don't know who yet,' said Fauzia. 'The important thing is that I'm getting married as soon as possible.'

Fiza delighted at this revelation. She glanced coyly towards the orchard. If her sister wanted to get married, she knew just the creature. She herself could not entertain such notions for real. She was too attached to her father who, in her mind, raised her, all on his own. Truth was, she could never part from him.

In that moment both girls peered downward once more towards Edward who, in artistic contemplation, looked up at their window; they blushed red at the possibility that he'd found them out. But Edward just pulled his tee over his chest and walked back towards the main house without another glance in their direction. And they both sighed with relief.

In the late afternoon, just before the third daily prayer, Edward found reason again to be in the courtyard. Intent on solitary pursuit, he took his canvas, paint and paint brushes. His time indoors was spent being cold-shouldered by Maya who insisted on avoiding him and kept herself constantly distracted by looking after Mother Dianne and fulfilling all the woman's needs, whims and fancies.

Uncle Ansar's sons and the Heba boys were congregated outside as the melodic call-to-prayer reverberated from a nearby mosque. But they were caught up in an argument, which to them was of utmost importance, signifying the superiority of one ideology over another on such an elementary level, that they did not notice when Edward waved at them en route to the orchard.

'I should lead the prayer,' said Riyad, ousting Zaki from the head congregational position. 'I have more knowledge.' He took his assumed spot to the front.

'Anyone who knows the surahs should have a chance,' said Arif, sticking up for his brother.

'No, in the Prophet's days the one with most knowledge led…'

'Then how are the others suppose to learn?' interjected Arif.

'We're not praying behind someone with less knowledge or less beard,' said Riyad. 'By the way, who's the blond?' He knew that he'd win any argument with his cousins, and so found himself transfixed by this new and more important arrival.

'I saw him yesterday,' said Arif. 'He's staying with Mother Dianne.'

'He must be Maya's friend from London,' said Riyad. The paint brushes gave it away.

Zaki assumed the leadership position again, in an attempt to divert Riyad's attention. He knew how his cousin felt about art. It was not allowed. According to the Prophet's sunnah, nothing could be created the way God created it, thus images of anything in nature were not to be recreated.

Worse yet, he knew that another stranger living with Maya would be taboo in The Yard. 'It's none of our business,' he said. 'Let's pray.'

'Who the hell are you?' asked Riyad, making his way towards the orchard.

Edward, who'd settled in front of his canvas, paint thrown helter-skelter about the grass, and who, thank heavens, still wore his tee, was unperturbed by the interruption.

'Edward.'

'Edward?' said Riyad. 'Just Edward?'

'I'm staying with Maya.'

'Ha,' said Riyad. 'I'd have you know, you're not the first stranger she's shacked up with.'

'Okay,' said Edward. 'I'll leave you to your prayer then.' He methodically gathered his equipment and headed back into the house.

'I'm still talking to you!'

Edward continued walking towards Mother Dianne's.

Riyad, barely satisfied with his bullying, and still annoyed at his cousins, left the customary prayer queue, and spread his mat in a distant yet parallel position. And just when prayer among the boys became divided, the strangest thing happened.

Maya, who had witnessed Edward's encounter with her cousins with much trepidation from the verandah (she could see the boys but could not tell what they were saying), and who'd just promised herself that she would take her visitor out the next day to prevent him from once again disrupting the afternoon prayer, now saw Fauzia, dressed in a fitting yellow silk dress, make her way towards their dwelling, stopping Edward in his tracks.

'Hello!' she waved.

Her five boy cousins were aghast. They'd never seen that much make-up on her face, nor her in such a slim-fitting dress. Worse, her waist had never, ever moved that way before. It was purely obscene.

And, it caught Edward's attention.

27

Aunt Lulu

*A*unt Lulu packed two large suitcases and one piece of hand luggage and waited in the balcony to be discovered; she rested her elbows against the railing and breathed in the dewy foliage. She'd risen just before sunrise, made herself a steaming cup of tea—Lipton of course, because that was her favourite—then settled in front of the computer. She'd sent out a few pertinent emails and all was set.

It was only recently that she'd become tech savvy; she'd seen the girls chatting with their friends online and decided to see what all the fuss was about.

Before long she'd made her own friend, a widow from Peru who was a retired schoolteacher in one of the old villages, whose husband had drowned in a boating accident and whose children were all married and away from home. This friend had invited Aunt Lulu to stay with her for a few weeks and Aunt Lulu had agreed; in fact, she was thrilled. More so, she wasn't certain if she was returning to The Yard anytime soon. It was entirely possible that this opportunity would open a new door, which would lead to somewhere lovingly unfamiliar; a place where no one knew her, judged her, relied on her, or was disappointed by her.

Her resolution was unsullied by her acknowledgement that her girls were just fine without her. It was their father that they'd always needed, and it was them that he needed. She felt that she'd served her purpose; and knew from the first bulge in her belly that she would never have a maternal bond with the ones she bore.

The girls woke and stood hesitantly in the doorway spying the curious luggage. Aunt Lulu grabbed her children into a tight, disconcerting hug. It was the first she'd hugged them since they were toddlers—and she felt that slither of sentiment crawl through her spine till it rested on a void.

'I'm going away girls,' she started. 'Mummy's going to Peru, and I don't know where else after. Not sure when I'll be back.' Aunt Lulu appeared unaware of the implications of her words. 'Now, I would take you girls with me, but I know you can't bear to part from your father; and well, he can't just leave, with his job and everything, you know?'

Fiza instinctively retreated. 'Peru? What's in Peru?'

Aunt Lulu shrugged, 'I just need to get away a little...you know?'

'A little? You said you may not come back,' said Fiza.

'Yeah, why did you say that?' said Fauzia.

'Because who knows? Suppose I love it there?'

Fauzia placed her hands on her hips. 'You mean...more than you love it here!'

'Don't take that tone with me!'

Fauzia was decidedly calm. 'I hope you have fun, Mom. Wherever you end up.'

'Yes, yes. I believe I will.'

'Does Dad know you're going?' said Fauzia.

'Won't you girls tell him for me?'

'You're kidding, right?' said Fauzia.

Aunt Lulu glanced nervously at her watch. 'Here comes my ride.'

A rickety PH car in gleaming silver drove straight through the open gate towards their dwelling. A dark-skinned, pot-bellied Indian man, with a halo of hair around his otherwise bald head, got out and called for Aunt Lulu who beckoned to him. He grabbed the two large suitcases and hauled them into the trunk.

Aunt Lulu gestured to her hand luggage. 'Can you two take that down for me?'

Her daughters glared.

'Fine.' Aunt Lulu pulled the bag down the stairs and hauled it into the back seat of the taxi. She settled into the passenger seat, just as Uncle Khidr, stirred by the sound of the unfamiliar engine, roused himself and came into the porch.

Aunt Lulu looked up at her house one more time, past her girls and Uncle Khidr, and sighed. She'd spent her whole life in The Yard. If anything, she would miss the trees, the foliage, the sky, the hubbub and noise and racket.

She knew the others in The Yard would be quite upset at her departure, but she had her own life to consider, and could not find any justifiable reason to stay put. She smiled as she thought of her brother and sisters, all worried and dismayed that she would leave her younglings; and decided it served them right. They were always a meddlesome bunch, taking on other people's problems.

Uncle Khidr's confusion was palpable. There was his wife, sitting in the passenger seat of a taxi, wearing her going-out face. 'Where are you going?' he shouted.

She seemed surprised to see him, and blew a kiss, resting her fingers delicately against the window. She turned backwards ever so slightly as the taxi pulled off. And, as the car exited The Yard, she leaned back and let the fresh air in.

Uncle Khidr remained standing there open-mouthed, first with curiosity, then confusion, then hurt. Finally, his mouth closed slowly and his features registered acceptance.

'She's going to Peru, Dad,' said Fauzia.

'Peru? She never said anything about Peru!'

'She says she may stay there a while.'

Uncle Khidr could not imagine his wife in another county on her own doing who knows what; but somewhere, in that deep, truthful place, he knew that despite the anxiety of needing her, there was a sudden and consistent ease, flowing like a gentle stream, through his body.

*

Edward was not certain why, but he figured the reason Maya decided to accommodate his wishes was that she wanted him to spend less time in The Yard. Granted, the altercation between him and her cousins was not the reception he'd imagined, but he believed she was making a bigger deal of it than necessary. There was much that could be better with the boys' approach, but all men were flawed, and Edward didn't see any reason to hold a grudge.

He'd long stopped expecting people to be logical, rational

creatures, which they weren't; and that fact seemed to him to apply to the whole human race. He thought: Okay, Maya had a bad experience with an orphan who grew up in the same house with her. Does that mean just because he, Edward, was there that history was going to repeat itself? Were the two situations so identical, driven by the same motivations? No. So why then did everyone have their knickers in a bunch?

And since the answer to that question was not forthcoming, he was resigned to being all right with everything. No one there meant harm, and he was willing to put up with some tomfoolery while he enjoyed his time in The Yard. Truth be told, he was having a good time, regardless of how cold Maya was towards him.

They were en route to the Botanical Gardens in Port of Spain. He drove around the Queen's Park Savannah, and Maya pointed out that the former sugar plantation was now the capital's largest green space and arguably the biggest roundabout in the world. Framed by the lush Northern Range mountains, it was lined on one side with colonial mansions, with a mishmash of Victorian, Edwardian and French baroque styles, in various stages of disrepair.

Maya opened the window taking in the sights, her mood instantly lighter. People were jogging, cycling and playing cricket on the recreational grounds.

Edward noticed that she seldom ventured out of her home as much as she did in London. In a way, The Yard was an all-encompassing fortress comprising everyone her family held dear; you stepped out mainly for necessities.

Some would dread the isolation, but Edward, who had lived his life in the complete opposite fashion, welcomed it.

Edward's father was a popular tour operator based in London who travelled across mainland Europe for days and weeks at a time. Edward spent most of his childhood accompanying his father on his travels and returning to a solemn mother who hated that her family was always apart. He would have given anything to stay at home with his family for long stretches…anything…and anything was preferable to being away from home.

Nonetheless, Edward was self-aware and aware of others enough to know that whilst he could survive The Yard, find a sense of comfort in it even, the place was the encapsulation of everything Maya feared most. She was too much of a free spirit. He was determined to ask her about this, to find out why she stayed. Was she truly so self-sacrificing as to stay on for her mother? Was she hoping that Behrooz would return? None of those reasons seemed plausible. She was not that much of a martyr. She knew Behrooz was not coming back. And there were places she could go.

Maya was now officially in charge of the family business, but whatever was mandated she did from home. He did not recall her going to work any day that week. These observations not only tickled his curiosity, but also created a sense of foreboding that dictated he get to the bottom of the matter.

The problem was that Edward lacked the means to find out what he needed to. His personality was such that he could never be entirely serious with anyone; he rarely showed on the outside what he was really thinking and feeling on the inside, and when he attempted to, it was done so clumsily, that every potentially serious conversation turned into a joke or argument as the case may be.

He parked on the western edge of the savannah where Maya bought Bake n' Shark and corn soup, stuffing it into a basket. He helped her spread the picnic mat underneath a pink poui tree and set down the food. When she sat down he lay across the mat, resting his head on her lap.

'I must say, I love the place...The Yard. I almost didn't smell the ravine today.'

'What's there to love?'

He grinned. 'The fact that your cousins might invent some kind of torture device just for me.'

'Okay, kidding,' he continued. 'It's family. The idea of them always being around.'

'Believe me, if you had them every day all year round, you probably wouldn't count that as a blessing.'

'Maybe, but that wasn't the case with me. I was always with my dad, away from my mom. When she died, my dad and I were away on tour.'

'I know you feel guilty about that,' said Maya. 'We're in the same boat. When Behrooz came to live with us, there were those in the family who were against it; and because we were close, everything I was and did was wronged and questioned.

'Then I just left, making my father question his kind deed towards Behrooz. I never got to say I was sorry; that no matter what, he did the right thing.'

'Is that why you stay here?' said Edward.

'You know that I only returned for Dad's funeral, right?'

Edward nodded.

'Something else happened that I didn't foresee,' she said. 'Behrooz left this time because of me. Sara was going through depression and he said his marriage couldn't survive if he stayed. Apparently, me being here, with all my baggage, made things worse for them. But see…Mother Dianne's the one who really got the raw end of the deal. There was no reason for him to leave her too. Now, she's so sad every day. She won't say it, but I know. He was her son.'

Edward hugged her waist to him. 'He made that decision. You hadn't even planned to stay here much longer.'

'Karmic retribution. Somehow my soul feels like it should pay the price for the trouble I caused before.'

'Whatever you say, I'm glad you left that first time. 'Cause if you didn't you'd never have met me. How would've that turned out?'

'True. Or Jules.'

'And how boring would life be without Jules, right?'

'Exactly. Maybe it's not the leaving as much as how I left.'

'Maybe nothing,' said Edward. 'What had to happen, happened. How do you know that you were even capable of doing things differently?'

'That's just the thing. I felt out of control from the day I left till the day I returned, and now that I'm doing some good here, I don't want to give that up. Don't want to be the selfish person I was.'

'I love that person so, and this one,' he said.

Maya could not help but smile.

'And…if you'd let go for a second,' said Edward, 'and take notice of how smouldering I look in this blessed heat, you might even see what a great guy I am too.'

'That, I already know.'

Maya switched positions with Edward. She lay on her back,

facing the sunlight, whilst he fed her the bake. He ran his fingers through her hair, touching her ear ever so lightly; and it felt soothing and heavenly. 'When you said earlier, that you love me,' she said, 'it sounded…'

'You're more than a friend to me, Maya. Much more.' Edward moved a soft, curly stray from her mouth and lowered his face to hers.

'Wait,' she said, sitting up. 'This is not why I was opening up to you.'

'I know, but this is how I'm going to show you that you can.' He paused. 'Plus, what have we been waiting for?'

'I just told you…'

''Cause you want to torture yourself for something you did years ago?'

'I have work left to do.'

'It's like you want to remain this pitiful thing that everyone needs to forgive.'

'You can't just swoop down and save the day, Edward.'

'You're absolutely right. You're not a princess,' he smirked. 'I can't rescue you.'

Maya tugged the picnic mat from beneath him. 'You know what, I don't care. Follow me here, prod me for answers and pretend to understand. I don't give a damn. You're no longer my guest, you're a free agent!'

'Nice,' said Edward. He grabbed the picnic basket and cooler and followed her to the car. 'I can see you've changed your wounding ways.'

'You, I've never hurt.'

'Right.' Edward looked like a truck rolled him over.

Maya held the door open. 'Edward, of course.' She looked at her toes. 'I'm really sorry.'

'It's okay.'

She sucked in her breath. 'You remember, don't you? The night we kissed?'

Edward nodded. 'I wasn't that drunk!'

'Maybe…maybe just give me some time,' said Maya.

'Sure, whatever.' He got into the passenger's seat and pulled his seatbelt on.

'Please,' she said, pushing her way onto his seat. He shifted to accommodate her. 'I don't want to do this. Fight with you. You're my best friend.'

'Friend?'

'Friend.'

Fauzia was wearing the yellow, slinky dress again; only this time she'd twirled and twisted her normally poker straight hair into a splendid display. She intuited that if Edward liked Maya that much, then he must have a thing for wild, curly tresses. Her mother's floral urni was pulled delicately over her head so that her ringlets framed her face.

She had the perfect excuse to go to Mother Dianne's. After all, someone had to inform the rest of the family that her mother had abandoned them and she was well-disposed to the task.

'She just stood there on the balcony, waiting for us to get up,' she told Maya and Edward over tea.

'Then she just left?' asked Maya.

'Yeah. She didn't even talk to Dad 'bout it, just took off.'

'How is your dad?'

'Well, that's the thing, we're not really sure...I mean...I can't tell. He didn't go to work, just sat around the house in his boxers reading the paper. Usually, he don't even go for the paper.'

'I think I'll leave you girls to chat...' said Edward, feeling suddenly intrusive.

'No!' both women replied in unison.

Somehow, Edward being there, a stranger to taper off the usual strangeness between them, made things better, made both girls feel a tad more open, like there was some semblance of balance in the madness that was the Ali family.

'The muffins...bring the muffins, would you?' said Maya.

'Sure,' said Edward. 'Anything you girls need. I'm at your service.'

'Do you think she'll come back?' said Fauzia to her cousin. 'Mom?'

'It's hard to say,' said Maya. 'She kind of left it open, right?'

'I really don't know if I want her back. She's my mother, but she's left us a long time now.'

'To have three children and not know what to do. That's tough.'

'So, you pity her?'

'In a way.'

'Okay, don't think I could ever get that. She abandoned her family!'

'Nothing makes that right. But look at me...I would be a horrible mother...so I can't judge her.'

'And thanks to her, me and Fiza are complete stress cases. And our younger sister who went away to boarding school, I don't think she even remembers home, or cares for it.'

'Here you go ladies,' said Edward, setting out the muffins on their place mats. 'And I would hardly call you a stress case. I don't think so at all.'

'That's the nicest thing any guy has ever said to me,' said Fauzia.

Maya rolled her eyes, 'It's the only thing any guy has ever said to you.'

Fauzia eyed Edward as she bit into her muffin. 'Umm... yumm...so English!'

Then she decided to milk the situation for all it was worth.

'Oh, what are we going to do?'

'Weren't you always closer to your father?' said Maya. She knew that Fauzia had never been dependent on her mother. She didn't even like her. In fact, she downright resented her.

'But how does a girl survive without her mother?' sobbed Fauzia.

Edward, not knowing what to do with the girl's emotions, and finding himself stripped of humour, wondered if it would be appropriate to give her a hug to comfort her. 'Oh, you poor thing.' He plopped into the chair next to hers.

Fauzia sobbed louder.

'It's going to be all right,' Edward cooed. He faced her squarely, passing strong, comforting hands over her hair. Fauzia snorted, and wiped her nose on his tee.

Edward recoiled. 'Excuse me, dears, I think I need to change my shirt.'

Fauzia nodded forlornly, and blew into his shirt once more.

*

Maya raced through the small wooden house with abandon, from one interconnecting room to the other. The walls were stained with slashes in deep red. Every step brought her closer to darkness, until she could no longer see. Hyperventilation kicked in; she was trapped without any foreseeable way out. Then, she spotted a trapdoor in the wall. Should she open it and crawl through? What if there was something equally horrific on the other side? How could she tell? She reasoned that staying put was not an option. In a vague movement she was out the hole and in the open air.

What she found surprised her. It was bright outside, and there was a group of old women with brown faces and sagging chins, sitting under a shed in the distance. They all wore gleaming white urnis and counted beads as they sang and prayed. They were praying for her.

She awoke suddenly with the breath knocked out of her, and a piercing crick in her neck to boot.

She propped her back on a pillow and rewound the dream in her mind.

She felt that the old women in her dream were trying to tell her something very important. They were so lucid in her memory; it was as if it were by intention. She could still hear them chanting but had no idea what they were saying. Were the old ladies praying that she'd leave the darkness and come into the sunshine? This would certainly be a fitting metaphor for how she felt in everyday life.

And why would she dream this now? Did Edward have something to do with the timing of the thing? Then she berated herself. Just because it seemed real and pointed didn't make it some kind of message or epiphany even. It just made it all her. One could always count on her to experience something bizarre. And for the millionth time in her life, she wished to be normal.

But the more the dream lingered in her mind, the more she felt she needed to see Edward. They were indeed having a tiff and she wondered if it were all her fault. Late nights and bad dreams never agreed with her, but somehow they always guided her to some knowledge. For instance, her constant nightmares about Behrooz after she'd left The Yard told her she hadn't let him go. She wasn't able to until he left with Sara; albeit, not so much in real life, but in her dreams at least.

She bounded out of bed flinching at the neck pain and went into the twins' old room looking for Edward. He wasn't there. She wondered where on earth he could be at that hour; it was almost eleven. Everyone in The Yard turned in early. She thought maybe he'd decided to go outside, but the outer gate was still locked and bolted. There was no way he could scale the fence. So she waited on the verandah, with only her gruelling thoughts for company.

She felt an inner sadness that he was not exactly where she thought. Had she really treated him that badly? He seemed to have taken it to heart. She knew that he was just trying to protect and comfort her.

Edward had said that Jules didn't know his whereabouts, but since he'd been on the island, Jules had not called. Maya intuited that they both must have set this up as Jules could not come herself. They must be very worried about her; and she could not blame them. She appreciated Edward's goodness; he'd been there for her since they'd met in London, in every way that mattered. He was a dear friend. But could he be more than that? Did she need more than that? And if she did, could she possibly let him in?

She nodded off again only to be woken intermittently by subtle changes in her surroundings—a bird on the roof's ledge, or a car on the street ahead. She restlessly scanned all the houses in their dwelling for any sign of light.

She decided to apologise to Edward when next she saw him. He was right about what he'd said at their picnic. She was self-pitying; she didn't want to dwell in darkness anymore. She didn't want to live the rest of her days broken and alone. Edward was sunshine. It wouldn't be hard loving him. After all, his dirty blonde hair and hazel eyes with their fleck of green were utterly adorable. Could she ask him to wait for her? It was selfish she knew, but those old women in her dream had promised her a sunnier tomorrow.

She woke up again at two minutes after twelve when a flicker of light caught her mind's eye. It came from Aunt Lulu's house. Surely, Edward could not have been at Aunt Lulu's. But sure enough he was. Fauzia, she thought. That girl had been working the whole sympathy factor on him all evening. She wondered how she'd managed to get him inside her house, especially with her father there. Edward slunk across the courtyard using all the dark spots to camouflage himself. He was surprised to find Maya waiting for him on the verandah.

He followed her inside. Neither of them wanted to discuss his whereabouts in full view of anyone, and Mother Dianne was not known for getting up these nights for any reason that wasn't life-threatening.

'I've been up for hours waiting for you,' said Maya.

Edward ran his fingers through his hair. 'Oh. I didn't mean to keep you up.'

'Why were you at Uncle Khidr's?'

'Fauzia invited me. You saw how distraught she was earlier.'

Maya frowned. 'She's still playing you for sympathy, then?'

'I don't mind. I enjoyed her company. You know I don't fall asleep early.'

'Right.' Maya's voice softened. 'Edward, I've been lousy company…and a very bad friend since you came…leaving you on your own…arguing with you.' She held his eyes. 'I was ungrateful. You're here for me. And I'm sorry.'

'It's okay, sweetie.' He smoothed her hair. 'I'm here to make you feel better, not worse. I don't expect you to be cheery all the time.'

'Listen, I've been thinking a lot about us tonight, and there's something important I have to tell you.'

Edward motioned for her to continue.

Maya took his hands in hers. 'I feel awful about the way I've treated you. I'm really sorry. I know you've just been trying to make things better for me. I'm going to do better. Try harder.'

'Try harder?'

Maya's eyes rested on his. 'To work on us.'

'I see.' Edward exhaled slowly. 'What does this "trying harder" involve exactly?'

'I don't know yet. You've been there for me this whole time. And when I couldn't find you earlier, I felt lost. I need you, somehow.'

Edward glanced away. 'You need me?'

'I said we're just friends. But when I couldn't find you earlier, I panicked. I needed you here.' Maya dared herself to continue. 'I don't want to be alone. So, I'm asking you…even though I'm being completely selfish…to wait for me…'

'That's what you want?' Edward swallowed. 'You think you can love me?'

Maya smiled in confirmation.

'Listen Maya.' Edward passed his hands over his hair. 'You're not alone, ever. If that's what you're worried about. I'm always going to be here for you.'

'This proposal is not perfect, I know. And I don't know how long it's going to take me to reach a better place.' Her voice was hopeful. 'But, will you take this chance?'

Edward lowered his gaze. 'I honestly don't know if I can fix everything for you.'

What did he mean? 'You're right. I'm sorry.' She lowered her head. If Edward didn't want to wait, she couldn't blame him. She'd given him the runaround for too long.

He lifted her chin. 'Maya, I'm not your last hope.'

Maya gaped at him. 'That's not why I asked you...to wait for me. I swear.'

'I know you're more fond of me when I make myself scarce. Would you have come to any of these realisations tonight if I wasn't missing?'

'I'm certain, I would,' she said.

'Don't worry about entertaining me tomorrow.' Edward glanced away. 'I've made plans with Fauzia. We're baking muffins.'

What? 'Edward, do not go across there.'

His eyes snapped to hers. 'Why not?'

'Because...Fauzia is five years younger than you, her mother has just left, and she's vulnerable. That makes you the stranger trying to take advantage.'

'Even if Fauzia is all grown-up,' she continued, 'this family does not see her like that...like she has the right to invite a man into her home.'

Edward smirked. 'I understand. And you're not jealous or anything like that?'

'Jealous? Of Fauzia?' Was she jealous?

Edward nodded.

'You feel sorry for her and want to make her feel better. That's just like you. But I know how you feel about me. Wait...should I be jealous?'

'Maybe I want to have a good time while I'm here, without worrying about crap.'

Where was this coming from? 'You'll get me in trouble if you go there again.'

'Get you in trouble?' Edward echoed.

'You're my friend,' Maya explained. 'This will fall on me.'

'Fall on you?' Edward looked incredulous. 'Maya, don't you see? Not everything is about you.'

Maya stared at him open-mouthed.

'Why don't you grow up?' Edward retreated to his room and slammed the door.

*

Those old ladies hadn't promised her peace after all. They were praying for her, perhaps because she needed praying for. It was also very possible that she was simply too exhausted to understand what they meant.

She left the house in a dewy drizzle and sat on the wet orchard wall. She doubled over as her neck twisted in pain all the way down her back. The still night and isolation made her feel a thousand times worse about the fight she'd had with Edward. He was right to despise her. She should not have shouted instructions at him. More so, what she asked of him before they argued wasn't fair; she'd messed up big time. She felt like she was back in that dream and the walls were closing in. Only there was no bright opening.

She dialled Zia, then pressed the end button. It was too late to call her sister. She dialled Jules. It was okay to wake her up; it was not like she had a husband or child. 'Hello?'

'Hi there, stranger. How are you?' Jules's voice was muffled. 'Yes, please tell Mr Jones I'll have his piece delivered on Saturday...'

'Jules?'

'Sorry honey, I'm at work here.'

'Where are you working at this hour?'

'Didn't I tell you? I got transferred to Singapore.'

'No, you didn't tell me. I haven't heard from you in weeks.'

'Is something wrong?'

Something, everything was wrong. But this wasn't the kind of conversation you could have with a friend who was halfway across the globe and busy at work. 'No, it's fine. Listen, I'll call you later, when you're not at work, okay?' Maya didn't know how she got the words out, or made them sound as cheery as they did, but she did.

'Okay…don't forget, okay?' said Jules. 'I really want to talk to you.'

'I won't.' She clicked off the phone and immediately regretted it. She desperately needed her friend but didn't know how to show it.

She reached into her pocket and pulled out the page she'd ripped from Mother Dianne's diary. Behrooz's telephone number was scribbled there. She found it as she was tidying her mother's room. The woman had certainly done her homework. Maya swore to herself not to use it or disclose it, but the information proved too tempting. Right then, it was the only silver lining she saw.

She dialled and after the second ring a female voice answered. At first she could not tell who it was, then she recognised the voice as Annie's. When she did not reply Behrooz took the phone.

'Hello?' he said.

The sounds of the crickets chirping in the orchard were magnified as if on microphone.

'Hello?' he repeated. This time softer. This time knowing who was on the other line.

They waited as minutes passed. Neither spoke.

Then Maya clicked off.

She ran up the staircase that ascended the verandah and pulled out a painting of Behrooz and her in the orchard; in it a lizard's tail pranced on wood. Behrooz never forgave her for that lizard. She hugged the image close to her chest, and sat in the porch till her eyes opened with the sun on the horizon.

28

Lewd Woman

*U*ncle Ansar and Uncle Khidr debated for quite a while before telling Mother Dianne their concerns about Edward. They knew how reserved she was about their opinions. Uncle Ansar had softened to her of late; he still thought of his brother with great affection and transferred that upon his widow. Her nonchalance about Behrooz's departure affected him more than expressed hurt; and despite rarely showing it, he respected her quality of self-restraint and candour, and didn't intend to upset her.

Nevertheless, Uncle Khidr had come to him for help; and as the eldest brother in The Yard, he resolved to do just that. Moreover, he could not recall another occasion when Uncle Khidr had come to him for something. Riyad, his elder son, much learned in religion and diplomacy, would accompany the men. Together, they went to Mother Dianne's house, and sat with her and Maya at the kitchen table.

'Edward was at my house last night, Dianne,' said Uncle Khidr. 'I saw him leaving a little after midnight.'

Mother Dianne set out saucers and three cups of tea for her brothers-in-law and nephew. 'That's not possible. How would he get in?'

Maya was disquieted that the issue warranted a family discussion. 'Fauzia invited him, Uncle. She was upset about Aunt Lulu leaving and Edward lent her an ear when she was here. Why don't you talk to her about it? Edward is a classic do-gooder. I'm sure he was only being nice.'

'There is something else you should know,' said Uncle Ansar. 'Something of delicate importance.'

Mother Dianne motioned him to continue.

'Edward and Fauzia were not just talking. They slept together.'

'Like in the same bed?' said Maya.

Uncle Khidr lowered his head. 'As in made love.'

'Right.' Maya laughed and shook her head in disbelief. 'That's impossible.'

'What proof is there?' said Mother Dianne.

'Since Lulu left,' said Uncle Khidr, 'things changed. I never had to question the girls or watch over them. She did all that. I didn't know how to ask Fauzia about Edward. So when I saw her diary on her bed this morning, I read a few pages...'

Riyad judiciously gulped his tea and set the cup down. 'Aunt Dianne, you know this is wrong. The Prophet warned...lewd women are to be confined to their houses. It's better to burn a house with a lewd woman in it.'

'Enough,' said Uncle Ansar. 'The Prophet was not a violent man. Don't turn him into one.'

'We're not here to argue that,' said Mother Dianne. 'Will you three get to the point? What do you want me to do about this?'

Uncle Ansar's voice was tense and serious. 'We think it's best you ask him to leave.'

'Leave?' Maya was incredulous. She turned to Uncle Khidr, 'This decision can't be based on some teen fantasy. You don't even know if what you read is real! I assure you, it's not.'

'He has to go,' Uncle Ansar commanded. 'If only to keep the peace.'

'Edward is my guest.' Maya's eyes hardened. 'And that's not how we treat guests. He is not going anywhere.'

'Let me handle this,' cautioned Mother Dianne.

'And if you men can't deal with that,' Maya continued, ignoring her mother's plea. 'If you can't deal with the real world, go bury yourselves somewhere.'

'This outburst is unwarranted.' Uncle Ansar shoved his cup aside.

Maya continued, 'When I was a girl, I used to look outside and wish as hard as I could that ours was just a regular house on the street where its members had jurisdiction over their affairs without fear and influence from others, where we didn't have to live our lives to suit this whole group dynamic.' She refocused her thoughts and eyed Uncle Ansar. 'You will not dictate what happens here. We'll make this decision. And I can tell you right now, Mother is not going to kick Edward out.'

'I respect you both, I do,' said Mother Dianne to her brothers-in-law. 'But I'm with my daughter on this. Edward will only be here for a few more days, after which he can leave without incident. I promise to keep a strict eye on him till then.'

'You will watch the boy like a hawk, Dianne?' Uncle Ansar conceded.

Mother Dianne nodded.

'Keep him away from Fauzia,' Uncle Khidr warned the women. 'I can't have any more harm come to my baby girl.'

'Very well,' said Uncle Ansar. 'It seems we have an understanding.'

*

Edward arrived with three boxes of Chinese food, and Maya left her unfinished depiction of him on her 'therapy' canvas and followed him inside. It was past noon but she wasn't hungry. She'd not spoken to Edward since their fight the night before, and needed to know for sure what happened at Fauzia's.

'What happened last night?' she said.

Edward placed the food on the counter. 'You know?' He lowered his gaze.

Maya's face paled. 'So, it's true?' Her voice was thin. 'My uncles came by earlier and informed us. I defended you to them!'

'How did they find out?' His voice was flat.

'Fauzia's diary,' she snapped.

'She keeps a diary?' Edward looked to his toes. 'I'm so sorry, Maya.'

'You're sorry?' She shook her head. 'No. I'm the fool.'

'I know how this reflects on you…'

'You think that's what I'm concerned about?' She tugged at the hem of his shirt. 'I told you last night…I wanted to try harder to make this work. To make us work.'

Edward rested his hands on her shoulders. 'I know what you said.'

'I begged you to wait for me, and you didn't have the decency to mention you slept with my cousin?' Edward's silence enraged her. 'Did you use her to get back at me?'

Edward looked horrified. 'Get back at you? For what?'

'For giving you the runaround all these years. I can think of several reasons...'

'Do you think I'm capable of that?'

Maya knew he wasn't. 'Then, what's going on?'

'I care for Fauzia. I'd never use her,' he clarified. 'But I didn't want to hurt you. I didn't expect you to want me...or rather, decide to want me. You surprised me last night.' He laced his fingers through hers. 'Maya, will you marry me?'

'What?' Her fury was temporarily replaced by shock. What was he doing?

'Will you still have me?' He kissed her forehead and pulled away to look at her. 'Even though I've been with Fauzia? Would that matter, if you truly love me?'

She shook her head. 'It wouldn't matter.'

Edward knelt on one knee before her. 'Leave this place with me? Because I would give up everything, and anything, to spend the rest of my life with you.'

'You would?' Maya's knees wobbled. 'That's even possible?' Edward scooped her up and set her down on the reclining sofa. He looked earnest. 'I'm making it very possible, darling. Just say "yes". I'll leave my errant ways behind and we'll start a new life together away from here.'

Maya's thoughts raced. She didn't ask for this. She asked for time. 'Get married?'

Edward nodded. 'We'll figure it out from there. You're sure you'd grow to love me, right? That's what you said...' He smiled broadly. 'And you find me attractive, right?'

Maya told herself to accept. Despite everything, she trusted Edward. He'd been there for her whenever she needed him. He was her balm, her solace. A reminder of what was possible. She'd decided to give love a chance. So, why couldn't she? 'You can't put this on me now,' she choked. She touched his face. 'I need you.'

'I need you too, baby. But maybe not in the way we thought.'

Edward stroked her hair. He was worried about her, now that he'd ripped off her bandaid. She needed him. It didn't mean she loved him, or ever could.

'You knew I couldn't?' A tear stilled on her cheek.

He wiped it off and held her face gently. 'I know you would never.'

'I want to,' she whispered.

He nodded, and said teasingly, 'I know. Who wouldn't want these abs?'

Maya shoved him playfully and refocused her thoughts. 'Wait... so, you really tricked me with a proposal and got away with it?' She was too drained to sound angry.

'Not at all. I pushed the issue of us being together to its inevitable conclusion, and saved our friendship in more ways than one.'

Maya wiped her nose with his sleeve. 'Ballsy move. But... suppose I had consented to marriage and this strategy backfired on you?'

'Marrying you wouldn't be the worst thing,' he teased.

Maya rolled her eyes.

'It wasn't likely to backfire,' he continued. 'I had much to gain and nothing to lose. I kept Fauzia a secret and argued with you when you questioned me...so I would have lost your friendship and supposedly broken your heart too. This way, at least I had a chance of preventing that. Desperate times, desperate measures.'

Maya was uncertain about Edward's strategy but accepted his explanation. By pushing her to refuse his proposal, he'd confronted her with a truth inside of her she couldn't acknowledge. That, she'd ponder later, when she mustered the courage. Edward had always been wiser than she and Jules gave him credit for. Clearly, he knew her inside out. The feeling unsettled her, made her more exposed. A change of topic was in order.

She wiped her hair from her face and composed herself.

'So, you and Fauzia? Explain!'

'It just happened.' Edward's face was relaxed. 'I think it started the first time I saw her in that yellow dress. I've never met a creature so innocent. The way she looks at me...all wide-eyed. It's bewitching.'

Maya snorted. 'She wanted to get your attention with that outfit.'

'I know,' Edward grinned. 'I loved the effort and the result.'

'So you really want to be with her?'

Edward nodded. 'It wasn't this way with us, love.'

Maya nodded. 'I know.' She smiled at him reassuringly. 'I could never ask you to forsake this for me. Not when you have something real already.' She berated herself once again for her actions the night before. It was unfair of her to offer him her broken heart and an uncertain future.

Edward looked relieved at her assurances and continued his explanation. 'I couldn't help myself with her.' He swallowed hard. 'I was her first. And I wasn't going to sleep with her unless I intended to see it through.'

'See it through...?' she asked.

Edward sighed. 'Would it be awful of me to ask your help?'

'You want me to go to Uncle Khidr's, don't you? To talk to him about Fauzia?'

'Would you go with me? Some tactful diplomacy might do the trick? And a dose of luck.'

'He's not going to listen to either of us,' Maya warned. 'Unlike me he's impervious to your charm.'

'Okay, maybe loads of luck then?' said Edward. 'We could at least try.'

Maya's eyes touched his. 'I don't know if I can give you up just yet.'

'You already have, baby.'

*

Uncle Khidr opened his front door and glowered at Maya and Edward. 'I told your mother to keep him away from here.'

'Uncle, we just want to talk, for a few minutes.'

Fauzia poked her head from behind her father. 'Edward?'

Uncle Khidr blocked her out. 'You're not coming in.' He pointed at Edward. 'And you're not talking to my daughter.'

'I am sorry, sir.' Edward looked downcast. 'For what I did.'

Uncle Khidr's reading glasses fell lopsidedly upon his nose. 'Leave, now. Before I have you thrown out.'

'It was wrong,' Edward continued. 'I did something under your roof that you forbade.' Maya had rehearsed the words with him and he hoped they sounded sincere. Not that he didn't mean them.

'I'm just as responsible, Dad.' Fauzia was still standing behind her father.

'Fauzia, please…' Uncle Khidr had no idea how to get his daughter to obey him. He stepped out and shut the door behind.

'I know what you expect of me,' said Edward to Uncle Khidr. 'I am sorry I disappointed you. It will never happen again.'

'You're right,' Uncle Khidr said. 'Because you're not to be left alone with my daughter again.'

'Unless, sir…' Edward cleared his throat and tried to sound brave. 'Unless you allow me to court her, under your supervision. I won't so much as look at her so long or so lovingly as to make you uncomfortable.'

'Court her for what? You're leaving in a few days. She'd be the laughing stock of The Yard.'

'I know she'd never leave with me. You mean too much to her, sir. Hence, I'm willing to stay.'

'You can't stay!'

'I know.' Edward placed his hands to the sides of his head. He hadn't prepared any speech for that response. 'I don't know what I was thinking.' He walked into the courtyard.

Maya followed. 'What was that about? Go back in there.'

'What does he want me to do?'

'The truth?' Maya took a deep breath. 'The only way you're ever going to be with Fauzia is if you marry her. Ask for an engagement at least.'

'I can't propose marriage to two women in one night.'

'Good. So forget her and move on because there isn't another option.'

'No option. You're right. I'm out of options.'

'I'll go away with you,' said Fauzia, from behind them. They were both surprised she was let out of the house.

'No, sweetie,' said Edward. 'What about your father? You'll break his heart.'

'You can court her,' said Uncle Khidr from the doorway.

'What?' said Edward. Was the old man drunk?

'You can court my baby girl.' Uncle Khidr explained, 'If Fauzia must marry, it should be to someone who's willing to stick around. I can't bear the thought of her leaving The Yard.' His voice turned tense. 'But, you dare not touch her again. Ever. Until the day I give you permission. Understood?'

'Understood.' Edward looked incredulous. 'It's more than I deserve. Thank you, sir.' A slight misgiving crept in that there was a price to pay for this generous concession.

Edward and Fauzia walked back towards the house. 'Dad…is it okay if Edward and I talked a while?'

'Sure.' Uncle Khidr sat on a single armchair facing the two-seater. 'You can sit right here and talk all night.'

'I love you, Daddy.'

*

Maya left Uncle Khidr's house and walked towards the courtyard. Had she done the right thing, helping Edward? She felt certain, she had. She'd taken his affections for granted and tried to give him hope where there was none; and he'd moved on from her. Edward had shown her, without a doubt, she'd never marry. Not him, not anyone.

Her house loomed across the courtyard, but she could not go there just yet. Instead, she walked to the orchard and sat on the wall. She pulled the piece of paper from her pocket again; the one with Behrooz's number. She knew the number by heart, and wondered why she kept the note. To remind herself that Behrooz existed somewhere else, besides in her memory? She felt her mobile in her shirt pocket but left it there. She crumpled the paper, threw it on the ground, and buried it in the earth with her foot. Calling him was futile, she decided. It would not fill the eternal void.

Those old women in her dream had promised her a better tomorrow, but they were wrong. There was no opening. There was only darkness. Only this darkness was worse, isolated. Even before Edward confessed his feelings for Fauzia, she'd somehow intuited that he belonged in The Yard, more than she did. She could not explain how; she just knew. She would move away on her own when Mother Dianne was okay without her, though she had no idea where she'd go.

Resigned to her fate, she walked towards the house, planning to snuggle in with Mother Dianne for the night, when something looked odd to her. Smelled odd, even. She rubbed her eyes to clear the haze. Then, she was sure. Her house was on fire.

She ran up the staircase, worried that her mother was trapped inside. She looked in from the verandah as righteous flames lapped at the pile of paintings on the floor. They were paintings of The Yard; paintings of Behrooz; paintings of Edward; of her plight and pain. Someone had composted them and set them on fire.

The fire had spread to the grey sofa, as flames rose higher in yellow, red and blue. She blocked her nose and mouth with both hands to protect against the smoke, stooped, and ran to Mother Dianne's room. She yanked the door open; no one was there. But it was white inside, so white. She could not breathe. She turned around to return the way she came, but there was too much smoke. Black now, and blinding.

She dropped to the floor and rolled into the furthest corner of the room. Heat scalded her skin; and her chest hurt from coughing. Above her head was the fire escape from the burglar proofing. The key. If she could find the key she could get out. She pulled herself up against the dressing table. Her hands searched the surface, then the top drawer, till she fell to the ground.

When she regained consciousness, Mother Dianne and Edward were with her in an ambulance. And somewhere between coherency and incoherency she told them, 'It was Riyad.'

'When a woman is shown to be lewd,' he'd said earlier, 'confine her to her house till death. It's better to burn a house with a lewd woman in it, than any other house.' Riyad had seen her take Edward to Uncle Khidr's. She'd broken their agreement.

It was him that she saw running off, only she hadn't registered it till then.

When she came to again, her eyes rested hazily on the verandah. Her thoughts moved away from the vindictiveness that befell her, to the place where it all made sense. She saw Behrooz, behind flames; then the flames cleared and he vanished. She blacked out.

PART FIVE

29

The Saint

*B*ehrooz had taken his love of history to the classroom. He taught Form Five students at a prestigious high school in San Fernando, and drove southward every morning against the traffic, and any imposing roads that would lead him to The Yard. His students were a meticulous handful—bright, energetic, and very curious about their teacher who never missed a day at school, could be counted on to show up despite unusual weather, low turn-outs, and stay-at-home advisories, and who was always impeccably dressed in tailored pants, crisp long-sleeved shirts and patterned ties, despite the humidity.

But Behrooz operated via a system of self-imposed rules. One law was that he was never to bring any student home. He wished to refrain from dual relationships; therefore he could not be friend and teacher in tandem.

However, this was the first rule to be broken when a group of students approached him about his favourite topic: Were the Caribs and Arawaks the first to arrive on the island? Were the Caribs really cannibals? Who really killed off the first peoples? How did the indentured labourers arrive in the country? Was the Fatel Razack really a Muslim ship?

Now there were specific answers for high school students, the ones that they ought to put on their exam papers, but then there were those unmasked theories in his head. The Saladoids were among the first, he told them. They came to Trinidad around 300 BC. But when Columbus came there were mainly Arawaks. And no, the Caribs were not cannibals. That was just a myth to encourage Spanish brutality towards the Amerindians; there were no documented cases of people eating people; no archeological proof. When slavery was abolished and the Europeans needed to develop the land, they brought in the indentured labourers on the Fatel Razack; they came from diverse regions, some Muslims, some Hindus, but all poor, and all hoping to make a better life. And some did, indeed.

Behrooz wasn't known to tolerate equivocation, speculation and unpredictability in his day to day life. Thus, when he'd arrived home with the bunch of students, Sara was taken aback. So, look who is going back on his promise, she said. Just happened, he told her.

Behrooz would bring out his white board and show the kids what Sir Walter Raleigh had not relayed, that the Saladoids and others like them could not be pigeonholed to fit the descriptions of Caribs and Arawaks, and that there were a great many tribes with their own culture and history, wiped out by Spanish colonisers. In fact, he even made a game of it, with one student acting out how the Amerindians felt when Columbus arrived. He would quote his favourite and most apt poem: '…And he, in fear, this naked man alone/His fallen hands forgetting all their shells/His lips gone pale, knelt low behind a stone/And stared, and saw, and did not understand/Columbus's doom-burdened caravels/Slant to the shore, and all their seaman land.'

Then it all stopped. 'The boys aren't coming this weekend?' said Sara.

'No, was thinking we could spend quiet time alone,' he said.

'We spend time. It's good having them here. You're making a difference with them.'

But the boys did not return that week or the week after, till it had been months since they had come.

'We'll see,' he'd said. 'My spare time is for the family.'

Indeed, he and Sara made Nisa their priority.

They'd rejoiced in her first crawl and step, as her legs grew stronger, and watched her grow into an energetic bundle.

The onus then fell on Sara to ensure that she excelled at school, attended her Maktub classes, and made good friends, whom Sara would often invite home for birthday parties, milestones or on school holidays.

So when Nisa passed her Common Entrance exam for a prestigious school, her parents were of course jubilant, and invited all her friends, their parents, and the entire street to celebrate. Nisa herself had long decided to allow her parents to fuss over her; she figured that they needed to, after the tragedy that befell them with her older brother. She loved them too much to deny them the pleasure of that endless fussing coupled with goodnight kisses.

She had a particular attachment to her father; somehow she had the feeling that he loved her more. Absurd though it was. She knew how much her mother loved her, but her bond with Behrooz was decidedly different. He was the first she'd tell if she got a good grade, or won a prize, or was rebuked, or got licks. He praised her, but not as excessively as her mother did; he scolded her, but not as determinedly. Sara had greater expectations of her, and was easier to disappoint, even with the most trivial of matters.

On rare occasions, when Nisa was particularly upset with her mother, she'd make a point of showing her preference—something Behrooz disliked. Don't make your mother feel left out, he'd tell her. But what they both came to realise was that Sara never noticed the subtlety of her daughter's message. This, Nisa was grateful for.

Behrooz was the first to admit that Nisa was unlike her parents in many ways. She was not as practical or sensible. In fact, Behrooz often wondered how he and Sara could have borne her. She lived in her head, always in a daydream, always restless, and never seemed to know what was going on around her. This nature made her parents question how she'd manage through school; but she managed, and did well.

Her primary school teachers were initially concerned that she was attention-deficit, a theory later belied by her excellent grasp on the topics taught. But it was in fact this very nature that brought her at odds with her mother, who, unlike Behrooz, saw something disturbingly wrong in it. And it was this very friction, buried amongst everyday civility, that Behrooz sought to negate. Thus, he was guarded in the affection shown to both wife and daughter, which he believed should be meted out evenly, albeit differently. He found himself in a tangle should one be upset with the other, and saw it as his personal duty to unravel any bad feeling.

But, contentions often come to the fore, and this case was no different.

It all began with Princess, the loveliest German Shepherd on the street. Her fur was gold with that iridescent quality, and shone white in the sunlight; she would often hoist herself onto her hind legs and stand tall and menacing when strangers approached; but once she became familiar with someone, she was the gentlest creature. Behrooz had found her abandoned on the winding hillside that led to their home, and couldn't help but love her. He'd brought her home for Nisa; he thought her the perfect companion for his daughter.

Though Nisa never had much to give in the way of affection for dogs, she did enjoy a rough and tumble with the pup, falling straight out of the garage hammock onto her buttocks; and so the games went until both she and Princess were all grown-up. By then, they were inseparable. Nisa even engaged her mother in negotiations to let the dog sleep with her, a request which Sara never gave in to. Instead, the creature was given her own little quarters in the family's garage, and slept in the hammock.

On one Friday afternoon, Nisa's Maktub class had finished a little earlier than planned, which meant that she had time to spare before her mother could pick her up; she'd gone into Miss Grace's garden to while away the time, and sat on an old rusted iron swing that squeaked as it rocked. That's when they came at her. Two honey bees. They stung her several times on her face. Her mother arrived soon afterwards, but by the time they got home the swelling had increased beyond what was usual for a bee sting.

Her parents raced her to the hospital, where they found out that Nisa was not only allergic to bee stings, but also would develop allergies to other insects in the future, including ants and mosquitoes.

They'd left home in such a rush that day, that the garage gate was left open. 'Princess is on the street,' Nisa had cautioned.

'We can't turn around,' said Sara. 'Drive.'

When they returned home, Princess was nowhere to be found. Nisa, who had apparently forgotten that she was only an hour ago puffed like a balloon, was terribly grieved. She was looking forward to Princess licking the redness off her face and soothing her bruises while she complained about her ill luck.

In that state of mind, she had no qualms blaming her loss on her mother. 'You forgot,' she said. 'You're always the one to close the gate and you didn't. You said to leave her there. Said don't turn around.'

'It's my fault,' Sara said to Behrooz.

'That's ridiculous. You were worried about Nisa. There's no blame in that.'

Behrooz was not sure whether Princess's disappearance or the spat between mother and daughter upset him more, but he spent the rest of the night circling the hill looking for the dog, peering into every fence, staring suspiciously at people he didn't know, and praying every step of the way that the dog would turn up, somehow, somewhere. Every rustle and movement in the shadows gave him hope. But alas, it was midnight, and there was no sign of Princess.

He inquired of the two teens sitting at the street corner whether they had seen the dog. He showed them photos of her with Nisa which he kept in his wallet. She might be further up the hill, he was told. They were referring to a shady area about a mile away. But don't go there; it not worth it. Some real thugs living up there.

Behrooz did go. He found a compound fenced off with galvanised sheets; the corner peepholes provided a glimpse at the tiny structure inside; on the outside were piles of grey stone, for construction perhaps; the place smelt like burnt refuse.

An unofficial watchman was out front. The man wore a white turban wrapped around his head, in an ironically royal fashion, complemented with a gleaming gold tooth protruding from the front of his mouth.

'I'm looking for my dog,' said Behrooz. He showed the photo to the guard. 'She's missing.'

'Ain't no dog here,' said the guard.

Behrooz tried peering into the fenced area once more.

'You deaf? I say there ain't no dog.'

'I heard you.'

'Kailash, come out here,' said the man. 'We have a troublemaker.'

Behrooz had not noticed anyone behind the fence; but the

fence wall opened, and the man called Kailash appeared. He, too, was a contradiction—his midnight black muscles rippled with a six-pack, and around his waist a spotless white dhoti. His torso shone as if he'd just returned from a beauty treatment, except for the fresh blood leaking from his right nostril. Behrooz did not have time to contemplate why he was bleeding.

'What you want?' said Kailash.

Again, Behrooz showed the photograph. 'Looking for her.'

'Man. I have she. But you ain't getting she back.'

'She's here?'

'Yes, she here. And I have a few pitbulls in the back too,' said Kailash.

'I will call the police if you don't show me what's behind there.'

'Man, police doh bother we.' Kailash picked up a boulder from the rubbish heap. 'You go before I hadda pelt stone.'

'Look man, you have any children? She is my daughter's dog, and I can't go home without her.'

The man's nostrils flared wide and round as his buttocks. 'What reach here ain't leaving here. You get me?'

Behrooz preferred not to be rattled; he had a family to protect and knew well the reputation of gangsters. Expletives were thrown and vapourised as he headed to the car. Had they stolen the dog? He was never certain. The only certainty was that he returned home defeated.

'If I didn't get stung, none of it would have happened,' said Nisa.

'I'll get you a new Shepherd,' said Behrooz.

'No, I don't want another.'

'Fish won't run away. How about a goldfish?'

'Not even a goldfish.'

Later that night Behrooz pressed his chilly toes into his wife's warm calves under the blankets. 'I did search everywhere,' he told her. 'Except that place way up on the hill.' He had decided not to relate that incident.

Sara made no effort to snuggle into him.

He buried his face into her hair. 'She does not hold this against you, you know?'

'Whatever,' said Sara. 'It's just a dog. The girl will grow up and get over it.' She hoped to annoy her husband, to earn his wrath. For years he had been the good Samaritan, beyond reproach, doing everything and anything to earn her pleasure. Didn't he ever get tired, angry, upset?

'Goodnight, sweetheart.' Behrooz kissed her mouth and turned on his side.

'So aren't you going to tell me off?' said Sara.

'Should I?'

'I mean, I just said something so insensitive, and you haven't said a thing.'

'We've both had a long day.'

'No lecture on how important it is for kids to feel safe and not abandoned, like you were? Even if by their pet? When Asim was alive, I would not have been able to attempt to say something like I just did without you coming down on me.'

Since they'd moved to Mountain View, she and Behrooz had meshed into a perfect, serene existence that precluded conflict, arguments, confrontation; a situation as ideal as the tranquil nature around them, with the ease and happiness of family life.

She could not find the words to say to her husband how much his civility hurt her. Though he loved her endlessly, boundlessly, and did everything to protect her, what she found lacking, and terribly so, was the necessary conflict that arose from and drove passion. Yes, she thrived on order, comfort and stability—but Behrooz was suffocatingly stable, unmovable, and unshakable even. Did he actually live, breathe, feel? Why, then, did he play the saint?

30

Rest

Saba never yearned for The Yard whilst abroad, until she realised that her husband of five years was actively courting another woman on the Internet. She'd dismissed the discovery at first, thinking that he'd inevitably get over his inherent childishness and work towards their marriage and making a family. That is, until the day he brought her home: his second wife.

She'd assumed that meeting a spouse in London would make all the difference. She had met Henk in their last year of college; they dated for nine months, and eloped. She'd telephoned her mother with the news, and the woman both congratulated her and told her off at the same time. Didn't she want an actual wedding? Didn't she want her family to witness their union? Didn't she plan on having a reception at home? Later, both Zia and Mona called, from London and Canada respectively, sad that they weren't invited. Saba explained that the wedding was impromptu. Then, she received congratulatory calls from her sister and aunties in The Yard who asked when she was retuning home with her new husband. She thanked them, promising to visit them all soon. But truthfully, Saba wasn't interested in returning to The Yard for any reason.

She was acutely aware of how things had panned out for those who resided there, and was happy to be rid of their circumstance: Zaki married a girl he barely knew, then had a baby with her; Alia's husband cheated the family out of property and never returned; Riyad paid ten years of community service when his father forced him to admit to setting her childhood house on fire, an act of aggression which almost killed her sister.

Saba was so removed from the drama, and hardly sympathetic towards the people involved, that it was an ironic surprise when she found herself embroiled in a double-duty drama of her own. For months she felt as though she were in her own soap opera, created and directed by herself. Like Zia's husband, Ron, hers had decided to convert to Islam. She condoned this decision on account of how adamant her father was in Zia's case, and thought it living up to his unsaid expectations.

She'd married right, indeed. And up to the four-year mark, could not have been more content. Henk, who had chosen Sayeed as his Muslim name after conversion, was funny, attentive, smart and cultured. He took her to places she'd never been, from Paris to Italy and Greece. Then one day, upon glancing at his computer screen as they were both getting some work done—she, writing an article for a London magazine on expatriate living, and he, creating software for the engineering company he worked for—she'd spotted an image of a woman in hijab with whom he was conversing. She asked who the woman was and he dismissed her with a shrug.

She later discovered that Henk had his own master plan. He didn't convert to make their lives more compatible. It turned out that he'd always had his heart set upon having four wives. When confronted about his plotting he confessed that he wanted to build four homes for each one and rotate his nights among them. This, he never bothered to mention before marriage.

Thus, when she received Maya's phone call, and learnt of Mother Dianne's passing, returning home seemed the only sensible option. She packed her life into two larges suitcases and left. She needed The Yard, and didn't see herself returning to London. More so, she deeply regretted not visiting her mother for so long, and realised she really missed her sisters.

*

Mother Dianne passed away peacefully in her sleep. She had grown fatigued in later years, but had not suffered. There were no signs of pain or immobility. The doctors deduced that she'd died from heart failure. Though, some on the street heard rumours that her own daughter had stifled her in bed, and some even said that they heard her cry out.

'I heard a muffled scream while I was praying,' said Arif. He was certain that in the dead of night even the most inaudible sounds could travel long distances. 'I know the exact hour she passed. I'm sure of it.'

Maya didn't care what was said. She contrived to plan her mother's funeral exactly as the woman envisioned; Mother Dianne had a sixth sense about her passing, and confided certain preferences to her daughter.

'You must have orchids,' she'd said. 'You know how I love them.'

'Don't talk like that, Mother,' Maya said. 'The doctors didn't find anything wrong with you.'

'I'm just saying,' she'd said. 'You never know what might happen.'

'And nothing too fancy,' she'd continued. 'A simple coffin. And just a short talk by the Imam; just short and sweet.'

Thus, the orchids were ordered, the coffin mandated and the Imam scheduled.

Next, Maya dialled her sisters.

Zia did not say much on the phone initially, but she called back almost instantly to confirm that she was booking a flight for home. She was heartbroken that she had not seen her mother before she died and worried about Maya having to handle everything on her own. Though, to Maya, she sounded uncannily cheerful, as if something happy had just occurred, giving her the ideal excuse to visit. Then, Maya recalled that cheerfulness was Zia's way, even in calamity, even in death; and once more, wished she was more like her sister.

The twins were also due to arrive home, just in time for the funeral. Maya deduced that Saba was happy to return; though, Mona was placed in an unfortunate predicament where she was not allowed time off from her medical internship, but decided that there was no way she was going to miss her mother's funeral. Thus, it came to pass that all four sisters were reunited to deal with grief.

*

Maya did not leave the verandah; not even for Mother Dianne. She witnessed everything from above, ignoring the sympathetic glances thrown her way. She watched as people she did not know lined up to view the body. She never did understand the purpose of viewing a body. Was that really the last memory you wanted of a person?

She saw her sisters place orchids in the coffin before it was hoisted way. A few old women threw rice on the hearse as it retreated.

'Women aren't allowed in the cemetery,' Edward had reminded the sisters earlier.

'It's our mother!' Maya had said.

'Trust me,' said Edward. 'The burial is not something you'd want to remember.'

Maya watched as her sisters served water and orange juice in tiny plastic cups to all remaining guests, whilst comforting some of the elders among them who seemed to be more struck with grief than they were. The girls rejoined her on the verandah, once the crowd had formed into smaller conversational groups, and everyone had gotten a chance to share their sympathies.

'Why didn't you come down?' said Zia.

'I don't interact well,' said Maya.

'Never did,' said Zia.

The men returned exactly forty minutes from whence they departed. Edward sought out the sisters to assure them that their mother was buried in the lot right next to their father's, and that he'd marked the spot, so that they could visit whenever they liked; never mind that it was frowned upon. With that assurance, all four women turned in, and shut The Yard out.

*

There was, in fact, a whole new generation in The Yard. A new breed of strange and energetic children scampering around. Maya saw them frequently but wasn't bothered with figuring out who belonged to whom, though, one could easily guess from looks and mannerisms. She'd heard names being shouted helter-skelter; but to match names with faces was too much effort.

Zia quizzed her on the goings-on, as they sat, looking out the bay window. She told her sister what she knew:

Aunt Lulu had not been heard from since she left; Uncle Khidr was in good health and still resided at home with his two daughters and Fauzia's husband, Edward; and Aunt Hala's house was never sold and remained hauntingly empty.

She knew all this, and so little, because Edward was her only welcomed visitor.

'Fauzia is pregnant,' he'd told her, a few days prior. 'We're having another baby.'

'Congratulations.' She'd tried to remember what the first baby looked like.

'You can't jail yourself here,' he said.

'You visit, that's all I need.'

'Feels like I'm visiting a prisoner. There are others who'd like to see you, you know?'

Edward always referred to Aunt Hala as 'others' in this bizarre way, as if saying her name would make clear the hidden request. 'It's not like I don't want to see her. I appreciate that she comes by.'

'You crawl under your bed and hide.'

'I don't!'

'Okay, you lock the door and pretend you're not here. Same difference. And how stupid do you think we are anyway? You never leave here. I won't even bother to find out who's running the shop. What I do know is that the driver has a full-time job running errands for you! If Mother Dianne only knew...'

'How was she in the last days?' Zia interrupted her thoughts.

'Brave,' said Maya. 'Always brave.'

'Did you spend much time with her?'

'Yeah, I was always here.'

The next day both Mona and Zia said goodbye. Mona was negotiating with her boss to hold on to her internship and spent many hours of her short visit on her mobile, while Zia needed to get back to her family. I'll be back soon, Zia said. She'd said the same thing the last time she had returned for a funeral.

*

Maya's art class often brought a sense of dismay in The Yard. Her students were different from the kids there; they looked upon her amiably, not like a foreign recluse. She was a mentor to most and enjoyed that right. She recalled lucidly the compost heap of paintings on the night of the fire, and how the flames spread around them and onto the sofa, and made it her business to continue the work that inspired such malice, though quite aware that art was only a symbol of all that was wrong in the world, by righteous law.

She'd started weekend classes roughly a year after the fire. Edward had helped her circulate some fliers to the students attending the nearby high schools, offering the classes at affordable prices. Luckily, two parents made contact and she enrolled her first three kids. Now, she had about thirty students on Saturdays and Sundays, coming from all over the island. She still managed the upholstery business from a distance. Luckily, the manager, Kayo, treated the business like his own, and proved himself capable. She met with him every other week at her home so she could keep abreast. Otherwise, he only bothered her when necessary.

It was the last class of the season and the children were excited to submit their final masterpieces. Deena, in particular, was nervous about her drawing. She took Maya's tutoring seriously and didn't want to disappoint her dearest teacher.

'Miss, tell me truthfully; do you like it?' She had drawn a picture of Maya facing away from The Yard, towards a calm ocean.

Maya knelt to the child's eye level. 'Can I keep this one?'

Deena nodded.

Maya smiled. 'Okay, then.'

'Bye, Miss.'

It was usual for Maya to stand guard as the children made their way to waiting cars; the other kids in The Yard seemed afraid of them. They were terrified in fact, that ghost-like Aunt Maya would inhabit one of the little ones and find her way upon them. No doubt some of their parents regaled them with woeful tales of their deranged aunt.

However, it proved unfortunate that Maya did not adopt her usual police stance that day.

Little Deena, making her way downstairs, found herself flanked by two bullies at the landing. Maya identified them as Riyad's sons, perhaps from her own prejudice, as she couldn't be certain.

The plumper of the two commanded, 'What have we here?' He pinned the girl against the wall.

'Stop it!' said Maya. She made her way downstairs and pried the visibly shaken girl into her arms.

The gifted painting wafted to the floor. 'It's okay, sweetie.'

The plump boy grabbed the picture, and smirked. 'Beady little girl hugging our ghost aunt. Sweet! Strange but sweet.'

'Give that picture back,' said Deena.

'This? I'll rip it up and throw it in the drain.'

'Give it back,' said Maya.

'Come get it, ghost woman.' He waved the picture back and forth.

'Do as I say,' said Maya. 'Or I'll ram my fingernails into your head!'

The boy intuited that Maya was intent on making good on that promise. He immediately threw the picture at Deena's feet, but a sudden breeze wafted it into the ravine. Deena ran towards the wall and watched it float away.

'What on earth is going on here?' said Uncle Ansar. The last thing he wanted was for his family to have another altercation with Maya.

'We will not tolerate this, you hear?' he said. His grandsons were visibly afraid of him.

Maya gave her uncle a menacing look and walked away.

'Go inside!' Uncle Ansar commanded, and his two grandsons ran towards their house.

*

'Look at the way they taunted that little girl,' Maya said to Edward later that day. 'It's passing from one generation to the next, and it's never going to stop.'

'They're not evil. They just think differently.' He'd seemed convinced of his viewpoint.

'What about Jules? You can't invite her here, can you?' Maya accused. 'Now that she's married a woman. They'll rip her to shreds for her lifestyle.'

'I speak with my sister. She understands.'

'She understands!' Maya mocked.

Edward struggled with an explanation. 'Some in The Yard may not tolerate Jules' choices. But humans have been known to adopt even more sinister ideologies. It's our condition. Everyone here has their opinions on things. We're just in such close proximity to each other that we feel it more intensely.'

'Don't visit me again,' said Maya. Edward had been kind to her. But he could tolerate the hatred and malevolence all around them. She couldn't.

'Are you kidding?' Edward threw his hands in the air. 'Seriously, is there any human being you can get along with?'

'Tit for tat,' she said.

'I've never harmed you, Maya.'

'No, but you're free in The Yard. You, the source of trouble that could have cost me my life. And you accept it, all of it.'

Edward never returned, nor was he ever expected.

Maya's complete break from her dearest friend took a toll on her body in the following days, leaving her with an exceedingly high temperature, and a throbbing headache coupled with exhaustion.

This presented the perfect opportunity for her most adamant visitor to find her way in.

At first, Maya resisted care, but once provided, she welcomed a soft blanket, a hot bowl of soup and a wet rag on her forehead.

Aunt Hala's white hijab flounced angelically about her, and Maya looked upon the woman as an angel. When she felt strong enough to take care of herself, she thanked her aunt, and asked if she could be left alone. She sensed the woman's disappointment, but her heart was too lumpy to oblige generosity.

'Forgive them,' Aunt Hala said. 'Forgive it, or you will never survive.'

'Get out,' said Maya.

'At least your little sister is here to deal with you,' said Aunt Hala. 'I'm glad of it.'

Maya too was pleased that Saba was there. The girl came to her with cheerful news. She'd gotten a new job, and would be staying in The Yard for a while longer. Maya congratulated her sister, surprised that her usual fear about others invading her refuge did not manifest. This tiny feeling was creeping up upon her; almost like her own time in The Yard was drawing to a close. Like her time was up.

31

The Break

*B*ehrooz was dressed for work by 6 a.m., though he didn't have to leave before seven. The hour in between was normally slotted for tea and reading the morning paper, with the morning news on one of three local stations playing softly in the background.

'Lipton or Red Rose?' said Sara.

He was already at the kitchen table. 'Lipton, of course.'

'The usual, then?'

'Yes,' he said.

Sara set out the beverage. 'Did you bring in the paper?'

'Nope.'

That was the indicator that something was amiss. 'So, Nisa told you, then?'

'Yes, more news than I could handle this morning.'

Sara looked sceptical. 'I'd hardly call it news.'

'Oh?'

'You knew this was happening.' Nisa had already been accepted at Mona campus, Jamaica.

'I meant that no one asked me anything,' he said. 'She comes to me for everything and now all of a sudden I'm the one in the dark.'

'She knows how you feel.' Sara sat across from him. 'She couldn't exactly say, "Oh, Dad, I'm going to college in another country." She was afraid of telling you…didn't want to upset you.'

'You know what, I'm sure this tea is cold already.' He shoved the cup aside. 'I hate cold tea.'

'You know, I was always the over-protective one,' said Sara. 'Now, look at you.'

'Where did she disappear to, anyway?'

'Right here, Daddy.' Nisa entered the kitchen wearing a pair of white linen pants and short tee, with a multicolored sequinned bag across her torso. 'I'll see you in five,' she said, as she clicked off her phone.

'Is this what kids are wearing these days?' said Behrooz. 'Where are you off to?'

Nisa sat purposefully next to her father and tucked a strand of hair behind his ear. 'Meeting some friends who are enrolling in the same programme,' she explained, 'we're going to the bank to organise some currency, and then book our tickets, so we'd be on the same flight.'

'I see.' Behrooz gulped the cold tea anyway.

'I'm not leaving you, Daddy,' said Nisa. 'It's three years, just three years, then I'll be back.' She kissed her father on his cheek. 'Jamaica is not even that far away.'

'Is this because Princess ran away? 'Cause if you want, I could go beat up those gangsters on the hill.'

'I appreciate that, Daddy. But no thanks.' Nisa closed the velcro opening of her cloth bag, and walked to the doorway. 'See you both later?'

Sara nodded.

'I was thinking we could throw her a party,' she said, after her daughter left. 'You know, a going away party with some of her friends. Like the ones we had for her when she was little. I'm sure they'd want to say goodbye.'

'No party,' said Behrooz. 'She can go. But no party.'

*

Behrooz returned from work that day at 3:30 p.m. exactly. He took the garden hose and washed off the sand from his car. There was a construction site near where he parked at work so his car was always sullied when he arrived home and it was his everyday endeavour to make it clean again.

He was acutely aware, with every movement, that his daughter would be leaving home the next day, but it seemed silly and fussy that that knowledge should interrupt his routine from which he'd sought much comfort over the years.

Nisa was not at home that afternoon. Then again, her schedule was never predictable. No doubt she was out somewhere shopping, or celebrating with friends. He could not stop her. It was wrong of him to feel like he wanted to, to feel like she belonged there with him, always. It was more than wrong. It was so wrong that he could not put the wrongness into words.

One thing Behrooz knew was that he could trust his daughter. He didn't have to worry about alcohol on her breath, or fast driving, or boys with tattoos. Nisa was well adjusted, smart, and always listened to her father. She was his baby girl. After all, she did have a pajama pant with 'baby' printed on one butt cheek, and 'girl' on the other.

It was 10:35 p.m. when he heard the creak of the front door. Nisa found him lying in bed feigning sleep.

'Somehow I knew you'd be here,' she said. She crawled in and curled up at his side. 'This reminds me of old times. Snuggling here.'

Behrooz turned on his back. 'It's past curfew.'

'Can't ground me on my last night,' she teased.

'I guess not.'

'Daddy?' Nisa sighed. 'Sometimes I feel like you and Mummy keep things from me.'

'What things?'

'I'm not sure, really…'

'Well, we do,' he said. 'Parents don't always tell their children everything.'

'Where were we before we came here?'

'We've told you. I lost my memory. I only remember from when I met your mother.'

'And you were always sketchy on those details.'

'There were some good people who took me in, and sent me to school, where I met your mother. Then we left to come live here.'

'All my friends have families, with aunts and uncles and cousins and grandparents…'

'You have your grandmother.'

'And I love Granny. But don't you wonder, whether we have family out there?

'I can't recover my memory. And no one has ever said they're related to me. Ever.'

'I know,' she said. 'But sometimes I feel strange. Like I don't know you. And I want to know everything about you.'

'You know me, sweetie. You, of all people, know me.'

'I want you to be happy.'

'And I want you to be happy.'

The next evening Behrooz and Sara dropped their daughter off at the airport, and watched as she walked past the security guards into the duty-free terminal, where she stopped to wave once more. She then ascended the staircase to the second security checkpoint where they could no longer see her.

'This is it,' said Sara. 'Three years for ourselves. How about a getaway? We haven't vacationed in years. A European tour maybe?'

Behrooz put his arm around his wife. 'Who needs a vacation? I've got all I need right here.'

*

When Behrooz pulled into the driveway later that night, he spotted an all too familiar figure sitting on the stoop of their doorway. He and Sara stepped gingerly out of the car, and his heart palpitated as he came face to face with his old adversary.

'Behrooz. Sara. I greet you with salaams,' said Uncle Ansar.

A bewildered Sara invited their unexpected guest into their home. 'Nisa is not here,' she volunteered. 'We've just dropped her off at the airport.'

'I see. I'm sorry to come at such an inconvenient time.'

Uncle Ansar glanced at the framed family photos in the foyer. There were three photos of Nisa as a baby standing with her parents. No one from The Yard was pictured.

'May I speak with Behrooz?' he said. 'It's about a simple matter, really.'

He turned to Behrooz, 'I won't take much of your time.'

'Sure,' Sara hesitated. She could not imagine that Uncle Ansar would have anything simple to say. Behrooz nodded at her as she exited.

Both men sat on single armchairs facing each other. Neither afraid to look the other in the eye.

'We're very surprised to see you,' said Behrooz. 'You, of all people.'

'I must confess,' said Uncle Ansar, 'I had no choice but to come.'

'I must tell you. I don't want any news of The Yard.'

'I bring no news.'

'All right. So why are you here?'

'Aunt Maab and I are going on a pilgrimage.'

Behrooz grimaced at the name. He recalled instantly the way Aunt Maab had meddled in his affairs.

'The Muslim pilgrimage of Hajj,' Uncle Ansar continued. 'One of the stipulations before we leave is that we must ask of those whom we've wronged...'

'Their forgiveness?' said Behrooz. He knew the custom.

Behrooz gazed upon the man to ascertain his sincerity, but realised that genuineness, whether real or imagined, didn't mandate forgiveness; in this case, forgiving would be a release of burden for the forgiver.

'It's forgiven. You can go to Hajj in peace, knowing that.'

'Aunt Maab asks pardon as well. She feels she may have wronged both you and Sara.'

'My wife is a very forgiving person. So I'm certain you can consider yourselves pardoned for any harm done upon her or myself.'

'I'm glad of it. Grateful even.'

'Glad I can help,' said Behrooz, standing. He was eager for the man to leave.

'That's not all.' Uncle Ansar patted the now vacant chair next to him. 'Please, sit.'

Behrooz reluctantly obliged.

'The pilgrimage isn't the only reason I've come. It's Father Khalid.'

Behrooz raised his eyebrows. He felt caught between the love of the only father he'd known and a desire to relinquish the family he'd left behind.

'Since he passed,' Uncle Ansar continued, 'I've had this feeling that hasn't left me. I felt that he would have wanted me to come see you. To make sure all was well.'

Behrooz was incredulous. 'After eighteen years, you've come? To make sure all was well?'

'I don't blame you for doubting my intentions. My wife has warned me to ask forgiveness and leave. She thinks you'd loathe to see me.'

'Loyalty to Father? That's why you're here.'

'Loyalty. And more.'

'Well. You've come. You've seen.' Behrooz motioned around the room. 'And all is well.'

'You still call him Father?'

'I don't call him.'

'Aren't you going to ask about her?'

Behrooz paused. 'No.'

'Or Mother?'

'No.'

'Okay. I see you're in denial hiding out here.'

'The people I love are here.'

'The people you love are also there.'

'Don't you think you've caused enough trouble for us?'

'Yes. I often wonder…' Uncle Ansar touched his forefinger to his chin. 'If it weren't for me, would Maya have left that day? Left so she wouldn't have to face those she found hard to face? Would you have married Sara? And eventually have to leave The Yard?' His face grew somber. 'Would my sister-in-law, who my brother loved more than all of us and his whole self combined, would she have had to suffer? For so long I have been faced with these demons.'

'Do you really feel that you've single-handedly orchestrated all those events?'

'I'd like to negate responsibility,' Uncle Ansar admitted. 'But I think these things may not have occurred without my influence, and that is a heavy burden to carry as one approaches old age.'

Uncle Ansar straightened in his seat, determined to say more. 'My sons have followed along in my footsteps. Years ago, not too long after you left The Yard, my elder son set Maya's paintings on fire; there were paintings of you. The fire spread from the living room to the bedrooms. Maya was found inside and hospitalised for weeks afterwards. When she came home, she didn't want to see anyone.' He returned Behrooz's stare. 'She's barely left the house since.'

'The pain you've caused,' said Behrooz, 'cannot be undone.' He bolted from the chair and exited to the kitchen. He sat on a bar stool near the doorway for some minutes. Images were simultaneously constructed and smashed in all around him.

The concrete Maya standing in the verandah, hair about her face, crumbled brick by brick, replaced by another image of a scarred woman, trapped in her own home. Always trapped. He turned around and smashed his fist into the wall.

'Go see her,' said Sara.

Behrooz was startled. He hadn't seen her standing by the sink. 'No,' he said. 'We've come this far.'

Sara lowered her head. 'I see.'

*

Three uneventful weeks passed after the dreadful visit. Monday through Friday, Behrooz rose at the scheduled hour, got dressed, had his morning tea, and read the paper. Then went to work, came home, washed his car, helped Sara prepare dinner, after which he pursued new interests, outdoors.

He'd gotten into the habit of sitting by the street corner with two teenagers who lived on their street. He found being outdoors gave him time to meditate. One of the teens, Jamal, seemed to know a lot on the topic. 'The human mind is unfocused,' he's said. 'The trick is to get focused. Visualise one spot and keep looking at it.' But Behrooz found that for him the task was mission impossible.

'Confront the thing that troubles you,' said Jamal. 'Clear your mind…'

Maya. His brick of a heart would not let him confront that.

He decided to give up meditation.

The following day, he returned to the street corner. 'Didn't think I'd see you after last time,' said Jamal.

'The boy here for a drink.' The other teen grabbed a beer from its crate.

Behrooz declined. 'If I start that, I won't stop.'

'You coming and going for weeks now,' said Jamal. ' Trouble with the mistress?'

'Not exactly.'

'With the horner woman then?' said Jamal.

'Ey! I didn't know you had it in yuh!' said the other teen.

'No horner woman,' Behrooz assured.

'Then what?' asked Jamal.

'It's like I have two minds fighting a war for supremacy,' said Behrooz.

'You too bright for me, pappy,' said Jamal. 'Oh God. Is this good over evil? You going an kill someone?'

'I think I may already have.'

The teens looked at each other. 'We should dial the cops.' Jamal was half-joking.

'No. Not in that way. I mean…never mind.'

'It don't matter which way,' said Jamal. 'The universe don't care if it's physical.'

When Behrooz returned home, Sara seemed to be asleep. He crawled into bed, kissed her cheek, and turned his back towards her as he snuggled in. His body always felt strangely comforted against hers.

'I waited up for you,' she said.

'Sorry.' He was surprised that she was still awake. 'Was just hanging with the boys outside…'

'Any luck with the meditation?'

Behrooz sighed. 'No. I kinda gave up on it…"

'Okay. Can we talk?'

'About?'

'About why you can't meditate. And why you needed to meditate in the first place.'

'My friend is a guru, came back from India.'

'Your friend is a teenager.'

'He knows stuff.'

'This is about Maya. What did you expect had become of her?'

'Not that.'

'Did you think she'd moved on?'

'I…ah…don't want to talk about it.'

Sara was quiet for a few seconds before she replied. 'We have been not talking about it for eighteen years. Because you won't talk to me.'

The Yard

'Sara…haven't I been good to you?'
'Yes, you've been good to us.'

*

Behrooz awoke alone the following morning. He found that Sara was gardening. Odd, he thought. Sara never gardened. He felt badly about the conversation they'd had the night before and wanted to make it up to her.

He went into the backyard, spying the strange roots, and revelling in the fresh air. Despite his love of archaeology, he was convinced that he could not tell chive apart from celery. 'What are you planting?'

'Herbs. Thought we could use some fever grass.'

'Can I help?' He stooped and kissed her on the cheek.

Sara's hands seemed knowledgeable in what they were doing. 'I've got it.'

'I was thinking,' said Behrooz, 'that we should do this European tour after all. It's going to cost us a bundle but it would be worth it.'

Sara's smile widened, 'Really?'

'Sure.' This was the perfect getaway that they both needed.

'That's great, honey,' she said. 'What made you change your mind?'

'Well, I do have everything I need here, but once we're going together, I can have everything I need there too.'

'I'm glad you decided,' said Sara. 'Why don't you go to the hardware store and get me some tools? I need a new hand shovel and watering can. When you get back we can talk about it some more.'

'Sure.'

Behrooz returned home twenty minutes later, hardware supplies in tow, to find two familiar suitcases in the doorway.

He walked into the backyard. 'What's the suitcases about?'

'We're packed.'

'For the tour?' He laughed. 'Honey I meant…'

'No. You're going on your own.'

Behrooz dropped his purchases on the grassy patch at his feet. 'You're throwing me out?'

'You can look at it that way.'

'What's going on, Sara?'

'I am your wife.'

'I know that already. That does not explain why my clothes are packed and waiting on the stoop!'

Sara stood and mindlessly wiped her hands on her denim jeans. 'You made a promise to me many moons ago, and you intend to see it through. But that's not good enough for me any more.'

'Is this about last night? I'm sorry…I will come straight home from now on.'

'It's much more than last night. The way I see it…we have fulfilled our obligation to each other.'

'How so? You said till death do us part.'

'I've let you abandon your family for me. Allowed you to convince me that it was better for us, when all the while, I knew the truth. That if you were to see them, to love them, your life would fall apart. And do you ask yourself why? It's because you love them. You love her.'

'Sara, I stay away for us. See, this is exactly what I've been trying to avoid. It took one visit from one of them to hurt you.'

'I'm not giving you a choice. You're afraid. You don't want to put everything on the line to be hurt or abandoned again. But you cannot hide out here anymore.'

'I cannot start over.'

'You won't have to,' Sara's voice was tender. 'She's just as you left her. Waiting for you all this time.' She wrung her hands. 'I told her years ago that I could make you into something different, and that was my first mistake.'

'Hearing about what's happened to her…'

Sara shook her head. 'It's hurting you?'

Behrooz was silent.

'You need to go.'

Sara continued planting her trough, and when she heard the roll of the suitcases, slam of the trunk and start of the engine, she buried her face in her hands; her body quivered, and tears streamed hopelessly into a bed of celery. 'He's dead.'

Behrooz appeared in the doorway again. 'I know what you're doing, Sara. Thank you. But I won't leave you in pain.'

'Then you must go,' she said. ''Cause there's no greater pain to endure than the pain of someone you love.'

32

Scar

*M*aya felt that The Yard was ready to embrace her once more; or rather that she was ready to embrace it. She was no longer perturbed by the bird's nest on the eaves, the blackbirds that pecked at her shutters, and the crickets that crescendoed at night. She had the overwhelming sense that this entity, and all it contained, was done with her, in some way. And with that feeling came an unsettling kind of peace.

A specific incident had much to do with it.

Two days prior, when illness was still upon her, she'd settled into a strong daytime sleep. She dreamt of a field ablaze in yellows, oranges and golds, instead of the ravaging reds. In this dream she lay next a to a milk bed, basking beneath the golden shade of trees, all of which floated upon a pillowy cloud. She looked down ever so often to see blue sky beneath. She reposed here for some leisurely hours, until rudely interrupted by an unwelcome, clanking sound. She awoke with her hands over her ears.

'Aunt Maya!'

Maya was startled, and even more so when she realised that the clanking sound was real. Little Amar, Zaki's son, had apparently taken up a pastime of throwing pebbles at her window. She got up, pulled down one end of the wooden shutter, and peeked outside with a barely opened eye. A pebble flew at that eye.

'Aunt Maya, come out, I have something to show you.'

Maya refused to be drawn out. The child quickly gave up—he was no doubt familiar with his aunt's anti-social behaviour, and did not take it personally. Though Maya soon found out what all the fuss was about.

Later that day, after she'd made herself a cup of coffee and settled back on the sofa, she saw that beneath the doorway, little Amar had slid a lost present, retrieved. In those seconds of discovery she forgot to breathe and afterwards made a conscious effort to do so. Her fingers gingerly traced the picture of her, standing on the verandah, looking past The Yard, towards a serene ocean.

Her eyes teared up as she thought of Deena, and the perceptive student that she was; she pondered the kind boy who'd thought to return this keepsake. She never thanked him. Though, against all odds, she found herself transported to that place, where animosity was put to rest.

*

Maya found herself more frequently upon the verandah, paintbrush in hand. Only, she did not paint people. She painted the world. The trees as she saw them, tall and creaking, their fingers splayed beyond the roof; the blackbirds guarding their young atop the electricity wires; bleached-white houses lined up against blanket clouds and hovering sky. She saw it all anew.

One clear-skied afternoon, Saba made two cups of tea and joined her outside. Maya took a break from her work-in-progress and they sat facing the roadway. 'Why don't you paint a picture of me?'

'Because you,' Maya teased, 'I could never capture beautifully enough.' She meant it. She admired the twins' chiselled features and lovely cheekbones; and more so, her sisters' warm dispositions.

'Funny,' said Saba.

'You know better than that. I don't joke.'

'When Mona and I were little girls, we were so jealous of you. You had the prettiest hair. We used to love when you made up our faces like yours, and fixed our hair. Made us feel like princesses.'

'And look at us now,' said Maya. 'Who's the beauty, and who's the old maid?'

'You're not an old maid.'

'Nah. Just a little scarred for life.' Maya rolled up the sleeve of her shirt, revealing a dark patch on her arm, the size of a prune; a constant reminder of the malice that found her.

Saba placed her hand over her mouth in shock. 'Maya...this

doesn't make you less lovely.' She gingerly touched the area. 'Will it fade?'

Maya shrugged. 'It doesn't matter. I've resigned to spinsterhood.'

'I believe there's hope for you, Maya.' Saba's face turned serious. 'But I can't say the same for me. I have to divorce him. Henk has left me no choice.'

Maya took her sister's hand. 'There's hope for you. You have the impossible thrust upon you, but you'll grow courage you never thought you had.'

'Can I ask you something?' said Saba.

Maya nodded.

Saba looked serious. 'How do you forgive those who've betrayed you? Move on from the hurt they caused? Does forgiving mean you've given them a pass?'

'Forgiveness is tricky.'

'Right…what if you can't forgive?' said Saba.

'I've often felt like I can't,' said Maya.

'But if you don't…'

'You're trapped,' they said in unison.

Maya hugged her sister. 'Forgive him, sweetie…for your own release. He's chosen his own path and he'll have to learn his own lessons, maybe the hard way. Life won't give him a pass he doesn't deserve. And forgiving him doesn't mean you have to live with him.'

'I just don't know how he could be so cruel.'

'Maybe when you let it go…you'll understand better, gain more insight from the whole thing.'

'Who knew you'd turn out so wise?'

'Too many visits from Aunt Hala, I guess. The woman has an irritating way of getting through.'

'I'm glad.' Saba's eyes widened in surprise. 'Because you're going to need some of that wisdom.'

'What do you mean?' Before the question was asked, Maya discerned a familiar figure in the gateway. Her heart quickened. *It's not him.* Yet, she knew that she'd recognise that stride anywhere. 'He hasn't come all this time, not even for mother's funeral. Why has he come now?'

Her sister looked sheepish. 'Uncle Ansar said he didn't know about Mother.'

'How does Uncle Ansar know that?' said Maya. 'Wait! You knew he was coming?'

Saba lowered her gaze. 'No…but I know Uncle Ansar visited him; it was the gossip in The Yard.'

Maya glared. 'You all kept this from me? What else didn't you tell me?'

'Nothing.' Saba explained, 'We were afraid to mention it…of how you'd react. I didn't want to dredge up the past.'

Maya wrung her hands in disbelief, until they burned red. She marched down the stairs and into the courtyard to greet Behrooz. 'You just show up here?' He was at her side.

A crowd formed into a wide semicircle around them. Maya was certain everyone in The Yard was there; faces in her peripheral vision registered disbelief, confusion, amusement. She knew they were waiting to see their visitor—more so, waiting to see the outcome of his visit. She saw Uncle Ansar push his way to the head of the throng, keeping the others at bay. Her paternal aunts and Edward stood together. Aunt Hala had her arms wrapped around little Amar.

Maya felt fear constrict her chest. Had Behrooz found out about Mother Dianne and come to give his condolences? For sure it was that. She was prepared to be civil, formal even. She would receive any greeting, be accommodating to any news, act the arbiter were there any dispute, or compromise should there be a list of demands, for surely someone was in violation of the rule not to seek him out.

'I wanted to surprise you.' Behrooz's lips curved into a smile.

Surprise her? Did he think this was a casual visit? Didn't he have a message? Wasn't he upset about something? 'What makes you think I want to see you, after so long?' Did he really expect her to lay down the welcome mat?

'You have to.' There was something pitying in his eyes. 'Because no matter how grown-up I pretend to be, I'm still that lonely, frightened boy who came here many years ago, seeking your approval.'

Maya's heart softened. Standing before her was the boy who had been hers above all others, who required her affection, her admiration; the boy she had let down and who let her down. He had become the man she loved.

'So, why do you smell so bad?' There were giggles from the crowd.

'I've just walked a mile.' Behrooz felt childlike again. 'Can't you cut me some slack?'

'You need a bath.' More giggles all around.

'Are you going to lend me your shorts again?' said Behrooz. 'Because I don't wear girly shorts anymore.'

'I didn't loan them willingly. Zia took them from the drawer. Imagine my horror when I saw you in them.'

'I look cuter now though, right?'

'I'm not.' Maya gestured to her exposed arm. 'Damaged goods.'

'You think your scar will throw me off?' Behrooz's levity had dissipated.

He took her arm and pulled her towards the orchard wall away from prying eyes. It was time to have the conversation he'd avoided for so long.

Maya pulled from his grasp. 'What are you doing?'

Behrooz pretended not to hear her. He lifted her onto the wall and crashed his lips against hers. Maya returned his kiss, remembering his mouth, tracing her fingers along his jaw. She pulled away, scared and suspicious.

'What is this?' she breathed. She glanced around feeling grateful their audience didn't follow them into the greenery. 'Where are Sara and Nisa? Why are you here?'

Behrooz sat close to her. 'Sara is at home and doesn't want anything to do with me. She sent me here. Nisa has left for college.'

Maya felt like she was in one of those dreams where nothing made sense. 'Sara left you?' She fired questions at him. 'Why? Is that why you're here?'

'My wife knows me too well. Apparently, I can fulfill my obligations to the end and forget my soul. She wouldn't let me.' His voice was tender. 'I belong here, Maya. Not in this place, but with you.'

Maya was flummoxed. Behrooz had come. He wanted to be with her. But did they still belong?

'I've loved two women,' he said. 'One was my wife and the

mother of my children. She was strong and true and kind. The best kind of woman a man could ask for.'

Why was he telling her this?

'And the other woman I've loved...I love her wildly, beyond reason, without explanation. The kind of love that puts down roots, and brings you back to your core.'

Maya closed her eyes briefly. Her body shook slightly as she registered his words. 'Will you be happy with me forever? Wouldn't you think about her? Worry about her too?'

'Naturally, my heart is torn in two different directions. But only one path leads me home.'

Maya felt hope swell throughout her body. She wasn't sure what Uncle Ansar told Behrooz about her circumstances, but she needed him to know she was all right. 'I know Uncle Ansar told you about Mother's passing. And it's more than likely he told you about the fire too? But I want you to know that I have made my peace with it all.' She wasn't abandoned or pitiable. She smiled as she remembered her art classes. 'It hasn't been perfect, but I'm okay.'

Behrooz wrapped his arm around her. 'I'm glad.' His thoughts seemed far away. 'When I think of how I've hurt our family over and over again, making trouble for Father Khalid and Mother Dianne, doing as everyone predicted when Father brought me here...' His expression was tense. 'I was what I feared.'

'They've never regretted you,' said Maya. 'Mother Dianne had your number. I don't know how she got it, but you were always in her thoughts and she knew how much you loved her.' Maya's voice was low. 'Plus, I'm the one who started the trouble when I left.'

'We were just kids. Dealing with emotions, expectations, and prejudices that were beyond us. We were both terrified back then. But time has shown we're a train wreck apart.' His eyes lingered on hers. 'It's necessary for me to spend the rest of my days with you.'

'You know how you score points with me?' Maya smiled. 'You must be up for a dare.'

He was a sucker to accede to her request. 'You plan to topple my world again?'

'Leave this place with me?'

The two returned to the courtyard hand in hand, their audience awaiting them. No one said anything. Rather, they all seemed to understand how it would end. Little Amar wrapped his arms around his aunt's jean-clad leg. 'I love you, Aunt Maya.'

'I love you too,' said Maya. She knew that she'd be leaving The Yard; and that the boy at her knees, though she never knew him, would be just fine without her. She knew that all those she'd leave behind would be.

The Yard, their childhood playground, and its forces from within and without, had brought Behrooz and her together, had made them companions, then lovers, had ripped them apart, and pieced them together again. There was such a design, such an intention about it, that as they both walked away, they knew they'd been swallowed up and spit out, and set right together again. They also knew that they would not return.

Maya stopped at the gate, to wave at Saba, who was still standing in the verandah. Their home was all hers now. She could not help but smile at Aunt Hala and Edward. Among them were those who cared deeply for her, who saw her through the darkest times; then there were those who showed indifference and sometimes malice. Forgive, Aunt Hala had said. And so it was that she did.

She saw smiling faces, some amused, and others perplexed, but none, she saw, begrudged her this. And lastly, she saw him, Father Khalid, smiling at her from the open verandah.

Acknowledgements

Thanks to those who made it happen:

Speaking Tiger—for enabling me to publish this debut novel

Renuka Chatterjee—for believing in this unusual tale and providing gentle guidance and encouragement throughout the editing process

Roslyn Carrington—for your encouragement at the beginning

Barbara Scott and Tanushree Luthra—for giving me the confidence to send this work out to editors

Amshard and Donald—you're never forgotten

Naim Khan, Sarah Husain, Saleem Husain, Isa Mohammed, Karen Adam and Zarene Baksh—for listening to me ramble and putting up with my madness

The Eniath family—for your inspiration

Peter Jarrette—for being in my corner

Daren Johnson and Antony Scully—for your support in creating the cover

Naf-a-Laf and T-Rex—for your warm hugs and unconditional love